CW00530147

The Repulse Chronicles
Book Two

Invasion

by
Chris James

www.chrisjamesauthor.com

Also by Chris James

Science fiction novels:
Repulse: Europe at War 2062–2064
Time Is the Only God
Dystopia Descending
The Repulse Chronicles, Book One: Onslaught
The Repulse Chronicles, Book Three: The Battle for Europe

Available as Kindle e-books and paperbacks from Amazon

ISBN: 9798654540812

Chapter 1

04.02 Sunday 19 February 2062

Corporal Rory Moore listened as the Spanish *Cabo* instructed: "Attention, all units. Numerous enemy ACAs are approaching. Advise the civilians to take any available cover and then return to base immediately. Confirm, please?"

The English Corporal tensed in growing apprehension. An operator on the other side of the small, mobile command post reported: "Lead ACAs will engage in three minutes. Altitudes are ranging from fifty metres to sixty thousand metres." Rory admired the operator's impassive professionalism, as though this were merely another exercise. She leaned back and dabbed at panels above her station, saying: "Temperature fourteen, winds southwest at two, one-tenth cloud cover."

The *Cabo* addressed her: "Fine night for an invasion. But I don't see any estimates on landing zones."

She replied without looking at him: "Our super AI is assigning this attack a fluctuating probability of an invasion starting—"

"Yes, between ninety-one and ninety-seven percent—"

"One step at a time," the female operator cautioned. "This could just be another softening-up raid like the attacks on Rome and Athens last weekend. If an actual invasion begins, the SkyWatchers will be the first to see."

Rory's attention came back to the *Cabo*'s screens, which described the thousands of Caliphate autonomous combat aircraft hurtling in to attack them. His beloved Pip was out there, part of a larger, multinational patrol. He should have been with her and the rest of his regiment. But he'd been ordered on temporary secondment to the mobile command post thanks to NATO's peacetime habit of integration. And now, because of it, as the attack began he could do nothing to help Pip.

The *Cabo* muttered acknowledgements of responses as they came in, from squad leaders and corporals and captains reporting their return to their autonomous air transports for the journeys back to X Division's main regional base at Cordoba. They mentioned distressed civilians asking if the soldiers would protect them. Rory wondered how the troops could reply. An entirely new kind of warfare was about to begin, and the troops could only tell the people to get to cover.

"Many of the civilians are heading southeast into the valleys," the *Cabo* noted.

Rory said: "Probably as good as anywhere, maybe even better than being in a built-up area."

"There are many caves and disused mines in the area."

Rory wished he could leave the command post, but he would have to wait for the commanding officer, a stern and focused Spanish Lieutenant Colonel, to give permission.

From a third station behind them, a masculine voice announced in accented English: "RIMs launched, converging in eighty seconds. Four waves of PeaceMakers following at ten-second intervals."

2

The Lieutenant Colonel ordered: "Tell the Battlefield Support Pulsars to light up."

"Yes, Sir."

The female operator said: "The waves of enemy ACAs are approaching almost flat, with only mild undulations. Their tactic appears to be a head-on attack."

Rory glanced over his shoulder at the central holographic display and saw a range of coloured lines splay out, representing the opposing forces' armaments as they converged. The image looked familiar because it suggested yet another exercise, a charade that everyone involved pretended to take seriously, even though none of them would be obliged to suffer the slightest discomfort, let alone pain. A shiver ran up his spine and over his shoulder blades when he realised he stood in what had to be one of the enemy's primary targets. The shudder passed and he steeled himself for whatever might happen, training and regimental pride supressing mere mortal fear.

"Lead elements engaging now," the female operator reported.

Rory watched the central display in breathless fascination as the lines of light met: those representing the NATO ACAs disappeared; those representing the Caliphate machines continued on.

The voice of the Spanish Army's super AI announced something, and Rory caught the words, "*minutos*" and "*segundos*".

The Lieutenant Colonel's thick, black eyebrows came together in a frown and he muttered: "How nice."

Rory glanced above the central display to see a countdown resolve over the battlespace, reading four minutes and twenty seconds. He looked down at the *Cabo*, indicated the countdown, and asked: "Is that what I think it is?"

The *Cabo* gave him a mirthless smile, nodded, and said: "Yes, that is how long until enemy forces destroy this command post."

"Sir," the female operator called, "the Super AI is recalculating the threat constantly—"

"Prepare to evacuate," the Lieutenant Colonel announced.

Above the holographic display, Rory saw the predicted destruction of the command post drop from four minutes and ten seconds to one minute and five seconds.

The *Cabo* abruptly announced: "SkyWatchers reporting new contacts, coming in behind the Caliphate ACAs—and these are huge."

The Lieutenant Colonel turned to the female operator and asked: "What are they?"

"We've never seen them before." She shook her head and frowned. "The super AI is giving a ninety-eight percent probability that they are troop transports. Sir, all RIMs have been destroyed for zero enemy losses. The PeaceMakers are outnumbered twenty to one, and—"

"Very well everyone, let us evacuate now. Your Squitches will guide you to the transports to get you back to Cordoba. Good luck."

Rory hurried out of the command post, unwilling to wait while the Spanish followed standard NATO procedure and instigated self-destruct protocols for equipment that would in any case be destroyed in seconds. He emerged into the mild night air that carried the chill rolling off the recent snow on the nearby Sierra Nevada Mountains. His mouth fell open at the violence in the sky above him. Distant explosions and the sounds of grinding, screeching metal came to his ears. He stared, fascinated, at the orange balls of flame which erupted all around him, and a part of his mind marvelled at the staggering difference between real warfare and mere exercises.

4

He reactivated his Squitch. At once, it lit up with numerous threats close by and urged him to find cover. The lens in his eye overlaid in his vision the multiple dangers and their distances, and lit the surrounding terrain in subdued brown and green hues, thermal imaging and night vision fluctuating as required between the darkness and bright explosions. The Squitch instructed: "Danger. Seek cover now."

"Bollocks," Rory muttered, and hurried to the other side of the small command post to retrieve his personal weapons. He ordered the Squitch: "Locate Private Philippa Clarke, Private Ian Pratt, Private Colin Wimble—"

The Squitch broke in: "Your unit is in transit returning to Regimental HQ in Grenada. You should seek cover now."

Rory paused to allow the armoury lock to scan his hand. He queried: "The CO mentioned Cordoba. I thought we were going there?"

"Your seconded regiment remains at Grenada."

After a mechanical whirring, a hard metal panel slid open and his PKU–48 smart assault rifle emerged from the recess. He grasped his Pickup and then snatched the six magazines of ammunition resting on a recessed shelf behind it. He snapped one magazine into the Pickup and stuffed the rest into pockets on his tunic. He pulled out the Stiletto Z–50 single-shot smart missile and slung the metre-long tube over his shoulder, and then turned and hurried away from the command post.

His Squitch told him that twenty-eight Caliphate Blackswans had approached to within a kilometre of his position, and the command post was certain to be attacked in seconds. Rory leapt down a stony, muddy incline among scattered scrub. Details of the ground in front of him resolved too slowly for his speed. "Enhance map!" he demanded, and the details of the terrain in Rory's vision gained definition just in time for him to avoid a two-metre drop over a nest of rocks immediately in front of him. He sprang to his right, stumbled and skidded down a gentler incline of loose stones in dry dirt, kicking up dust before coming to a stop.

He looked back at the ridge above him and the silhouette of the mobile command post disappeared in a cloud of smoke and a deep thud under the impact of a Spider, the Caliphate's autonomous cylindrical bomb with eight articulated appendages. There came a screeching of metal and a whoosh of flames erupted into the night sky. A tremor ran through the ground around him and a few small stones rolled on, as though they too could sense the danger from above and wanted to get away to safety. Two more dull thuds followed. He waited to see if anyone from the command post followed him, but a sense of mild panic caused him to doubt the wisdom of remaining immobile.

Rory turned and continued jumping and running along the flatter terrain. His Squitch spoke: "Multiple Spiders are in close range and seeking targets. You should take cover now."

"Show me... some cover... and I'll take it," Rory spat between gulping in breaths of air.

"No cover is available in the immediate vicinity. Please head north for one-point—"

"So stop telling me to take it, for fuck's sake—"

"Excessive profanity may be reported to your commanding officer."

"Where is the nearest NATO transport that can take me back to HQ?"

"Insufficient data."

"So rescan, now."

Somewhere behind him, there came a piercing human shriek that terminated in the distant thud of another explosion, and his mind recalled the reports of the previous Caliphate attacks against civilians, especially the notorious image of a woman and her young child on a bridge in Istanbul, enveloped in a Spider's dark embrace an instant before it exploded.

The Squitch's tone suddenly hardened: "Danger: Caliphate Spider approaching rapidly from the south. You are its target. Distance nine hundred metres, closing in a straight line. Take defensive action immediately."

"Shit," Rory swore. He unslung his Stiletto and slid the catch on the side of the tube to 'active' as recollections of briefings about these machines flashed through his mind. The main conclusion had been to hope that a NATO ACA would be on hand to help. Despite being on secondment in a part of Europe that had been expected to be on or near the frontline, Rory hadn't really believed he'd see combat so abruptly.

The Squitch said: "Distance seven hundred metres and closing."

He hefted the metal tube onto his right shoulder and stabilised his stance, ready to fight without realising he was. The weapon linked automatically to his Squitch, and via the lens in his eye, Rory saw the aptly named Spider charging towards him with terrifying dexterity. Its eight 'legs' threw up clouds of dust that looked like green mist in his magnified night vision. He fought to control his breathing: the Spider would injure him if it detonated within fifty metres, and kill him if it detonated within thirty.

He steadied his grip and pressed the trigger. With a searing hiss, the missile streaked from the weapon and raced the six hundred metres to its target, exploding in a bright orange pop when it hit the Spider. Before the missile had gone halfway, Rory threw the Stiletto away and swung his Pickup off his left shoulder. He raised the weapon as the explosion from the Stiletto dissipated.

His Squitch announced: "Distance four hundred metres and closing."

He squeezed the trigger and bullets fired, reassuring him. Repeated green flashes from the Spider confirmed the hits. In seconds, he'd emptied the magazine. He ejected it, letting it fall into the dust at his feet, and then grabbed and snapped the next magazine into place.

"Distance two hundred metres and closing."

He resumed firing. The green flashes when the bullets hit it ceased, and Rory realised the Spider's shielding had gone. Six shots later, it blew up sixty-three metres from him. The change in air pressure threw him on his back and left him partially stunned. He heard a shower of dirt and stones rain down in front of him, and wondered how badly he might've been injured had he destroyed the Spider just a few seconds later.

"Any further targets?" he asked, staring up at the black sky and realising that if the answer were affirmative, he would not be able to defeat them.

"Enemy forces have saturated the battlespace. However, you are not currently targeted."

"Yet," Rory added as he pulled himself to his feet. "Summarise that engagement, please." He staggered away, grasping his Pickup and stumbling on over rocks and through dusty scrub, forcing his legs to carry him onwards and away from the area. In the distance and from every direction, lights streaked through the sky, ordnance detonated, human voices shrieked faintly. His breathing became shallow and accelerated. His shoulders and arms began to shake. He jerked his head back and forth, unsure of from where the next danger might approach.

Instead of giving him the facts of the engagement, the Squitch said: "Please note that you are starting to hyperventilate. Bring your breathing under control."

The strength in his legs deserted him. He collapsed to his knees and swore aloud. He repeated the curse half a dozen times, and this time, the Squitch didn't attempt to censure his profanity. War was not supposed to be like this anymore. The new doctrine insisted that war meant the ACAs duking it out. Modern warfare meant the complete removal of flesh-and-blood soldiers from the battlespace. He should not have had to fight an enemy ACA on his own. How much firepower had he needed to take that Spider out? The Stiletto and over seventy smart bullets? That was outrageous. He could shoot down four PeaceMakers with that amount of ammo. Panicked confusion swirled in his head at how any device so small could be defended by such formidable shielding. He clenched and relaxed his fists several times to dispel the shock and anxiety.

He heaved in deeper breaths and understood he needed to concentrate if he were to survive this engagement. "How many more Spiders are there in this vicinity?"

"Three minutes ago, there were approximately four thousand."

"Shit."

"Over half of these appeared to be forming a stationary, defensive perimeter around a predefined area."

"Where?"

"Two-point-five kilometres to the south over a broadly level area of several hundred hectares."

Rory glanced in that direction, but low hills obscured his view. A dull, red glow lit the undulating ridges. "Why?"

"Probably to establish and defend a secure zone."

"What for?"

"The highest probability is a landing area for invading forces."

Rory's breathing slowed. "Where are the NATO transports?"

"Increased enemy jamming is preventing effective communications. However, a number have been destroyed and there is a high probability that many more failed to escape the battlespace."

"Please try to contact the other members of my squad."

"Comms are not possible at this time."

"NATO defences?"

"Non-operational at this time."

"So where do I go now?"

"Insufficient data. According to the most recent data, you should seek cover and wait until friendly forces retake the battle sp—"

"That's not going to happen. Which way is Grenada, the Armilla base?"

"Eleven-point-six kilometres northwest," the Squitch replied, and directional data appeared in Rory's field of view. It continued: "However, you are certain to meet enemy forces. You should seek cover and wait for friendly—"

"Shut up. So, how, exactly, does a Spider target a person?"

"Attack patterns to date suggest numerous methods, including thermal imaging and electronic emissions."

A plan began to form in Rory's mind. He said: "In other words, they can see my body heat and detect your contact with the network... So if I switch you off, I'll halve my chances of getting killed, yes?"

"Deactivating your Battlefield Management Support System is not recommended—"

"And then, if I put on my BHC sleeve, I'll be in a pretty good state to evac the battlespace, wouldn't I?"

"Your BHC sleeve is designed primarily for static camouflage."

Rory cursed inside when the Squitch reminded him. He hadn't put on a BHC sleeve since his basic training, and recalled that he'd barely been able to move in it. However, as he stood and began jogging over the dry rocks and scrub, panic rose like bile and clawed at the back of his throat. In the sky above him raged a battle controlled by super artificial intelligences that considered options and made decisions thousands of times more quickly than his own brain could. He stopped himself from glancing upwards, lest panic cause him to freeze. He knew that his active Squitch—scanning all kinds of frequencies to find out what was happening, to 'help' him—acted like a beacon to the hostiles all around him, while his exposed body-heat announced his presence on the night-time terrain to those machines as though it were broad daylight.

He reached an incline, slung his Pickup over his shoulder, and climbed. The violence in the sky lessened. Minutes passed; his panic rose again. How many of the enemy's ACAs were needed to defend a landing zone? How many would be free to pick off NATO stragglers at their leisure? He stopped, breathing heavily from the exertion. "Right, that's enough," he said. "What are the possibilities that the enemy can detect me in other ways, for example by the metallic composition of my Pickup?"

"Insufficient data."

"So conject—you're supposed to be smarter than me."

"It is possible the enemy has built-in redundancy and seeks targets using numerous indicators. However, it is reasonable to believe that the enemy is assured a limited number of established methods that provide certainty of detecting NATO forces."

"Sweet Christ Jesus, I'd be lost without you, wouldn't I? Now, shut up and shut down."

"Deactivating your Battlefield Management Support System is not recommended in your current environment."

"Even if you might get me killed?"

"You will have no notifications of approaching threats and no way to navig—"

"Okay, have it your own way," Rory replied. He reached an outcrop of rock under which he could conceal himself. He opened a flap over a small pocket on his right thigh. He pulled out a thin, circular device the size of a large coin. He placed his right thumb in the central depression to confirm his identity, and holding the central part firmly, with his left thumb and forefinger he twisted the outer rim one-hundred-and-eighty degrees, deactivating the Squitch. He put the device back in its pocket and made sure the flap was secure.

He muttered aloud: "Right, time to disappear." He set his Pickup against the surface of the rocky outcrop and unwrapped the BHC sleeve from its thin pouch in his trousers on the back of his right calf. Memories of his basic training came back to him, and he tried to recall the sleeve's tolerances. He sighed and gave up. He spread the sleeve on the ground, placed his booted feet on the bottom of the gossamer-thin material, and rolled it up the length of his body. At the waist, he located the two openings for his arms. A memory from years earlier surfaced: at the urging of the training sergeant, he and several other rookies had opened a BHC sleeve and tried to rip it apart. Despite it having the texture and weight of tissue paper, it resisted all of their combined strength to damage it. A half-smile crossed his face when he recalled how they'd tried every possible way to rip it, and had given up in sweaty exhaustion after half an hour of relentless effort.

Rory pulled the hood over his head and wrapped the gauze face covering across his mouth and nose. He sat on a large, comfortable clump of soft grass, leaned back against the rock, and questioned his memory again. The BHC sleeve would prevent his body heat being vulnerable to enemy detection but would keep him at his normal temperature for, what was it? Forty-eight hours? Seventy-two? He couldn't remember. But now, for the first time since the battle began in the mobile command post a little over half an hour earlier, he could pause and assess the situation. He had no food, but that did not trouble him: he could go without it for ten or more days and his greatest discomfort would be headaches and tiredness for the first few days, nothing else. Water, however, was a different matter. He had two, half-litre NATO canteens tucked away in his tunic, but—

An abrupt change in the air pressure around him interrupted his thoughts. An insubstantial yet unmistakable trembling vibrated through the rocks and ground. Above him, thousands of new lights streaked into view. He caught his breath when a pinprick shot down almost directly at him, stopping at what he judged to be a couple of hundred metres' distance. Something smaller flew away from it. The Spider swooped towards Rory, and for a moment, he thought it would kill him. But it flew over his outcrop and swung back into view in a graceful arc which he realised was an optimum search pattern.

Suddenly, dull shots popped off distantly, and Rory stared at the green flashes as the shells hit the Spider's shielding. The Spider immediately dived at the source of the attack; the firing continued. Its eight appendages snapped out from the surface of the flying bomb, and Rory thought he heard a truncated scream before the explosion when the Spider detonated. Orange light flashed over the uneven terrain, and Rory could not think of a worse final image before dying than to see that terrifying machine racing in for the kill.

He had little time to reflect on this morbid consideration. From behind him, the Caliphate's Blackswans escorted a fleet of the largest aircraft Rory had ever seen. He shook his head in wonder, wishing his Squitch were active and sending what he saw back to HQ, and knowing at the same time that he'd be dead in an instant if that were the case. Flashing red lights betrayed the outlines, and he realised that

13

each one must be able to carry at least a thousand troops. He counted ten of the behemoths as they cruised with ominous potency towards the area that his Squitch had earlier identified as a landing zone. Each transport trailed an expansive cloud of Blackswans, flying geometric patterns around their charges to monitor the maximum amount of land and sky for the least energy expended, and doubtlessly ready to dispatch a Spider to deal at once with even the minutest threat.

The Caliphate's air transports disappeared over the far ridge, and Rory wondered what he should do next. He did not doubt that the barracks at Grenada had been destroyed, for the basic military strategy of such an invasion would insist on advance forces—in this case, the Blackswans—eliminating all organised resistance. As he himself was part of a defensive force which, he had to assume, had been wiped out, he questioned where he should go now, given that he had no food and only such water as he might eke out for forty-eight hours.

He recalled conversations and meetings since his regiment's arrival in Spain the previous Monday, and made his decision. He sat still in the darkness and slowed his breathing. He said a quiet goodbye to his beloved Pip and contemplated not only his own bleak future, but also that of Europe's. A small part of him revelled to be alive at such a time in history, to witness the destruction of Europe. At once, a pragmatic voice questioned exactly how long he would live to see the conclusion of that destruction.

Chapter 2

04.14 Sunday 19 February 2062

P rivate Philippa 'Pip' Clarke pressed a metal tube close to the girl's ankle and reassured her: "Only a few more moments."

The girl smiled back while her parents stood over them with concerned faces.

Standing over her, Crimble urged: "Come on, Pip. The transport is not going to wait much longer—"

"I know," she replied, glancing up at him. "I can hear my bloody Squitch as well as you can hear yours. But I'm waiting till the sprain is fixed properly. She's got to be able to walk if she's to stand a chance."

In her ear, her Squitch repeated: "You must go to the transport now."

The girl's olive-skinned father stuttered in heavily accented English: "We thank you. But if you must to go, then go. Please."

Pip replied in succinct determination: "Just another minute. Her ankle will be fine." She glanced at the traipsing lines of people of all ages as they filed across the flat rock plateau which led into a valley at the northern tip of the Sierra Nevada Mountains.

A new voice spoke in Pip's ear: "Squad Delta Four-Two, advise the civilians to take cover. We've got a ton of incoming; the screens just lit up."

Crimble spoke: "Pratty, are you on the transport?"

Pratty's laconic tone replied: "Yup, engines powering up now. Captain says we're going back, not waiting for any more slackers like you. So I reckon you two are going to be on an AWOL charge before dawn."

The device Pip held against the girl's ankle beeped twice, and Pip put it away in her tunic. She helped the girl to stand and said: "You're all right now. Please go and find somewhere to shelter, okay?" The girl's glistening eyes showed more gratitude than comprehension. The parents repeated their thanks. Pip turned to Crimble and the pair walked away from the civilians.

"Pickup?" Pip asked.

He handed the rifle to her. "We're going to be right in the shit if they put us on an AWOL charge," he noted, running his thumb under his moustache.

Pip shouldered her weapon and replied: "Not sure it's going to be so important if Operation Certain Death has actually kicked off." She pointed upwards: "Look."

Wave after wave of missiles streaked through the sky above them. Pip and Crimble turned with everyone else to witness the clash of military hardware overhead. White and orange flashed off the people and rocks and trees in sudden bursts of light. Vast, angry explosions split the air. Children cried, women screamed, men shouted, and all ran for lower ground in the valley, some discarding their belongings as they did so. Pip unslung her Pickup, unsure what contribution she could make.

She felt Crimble grab her shoulder and he shouted above the din: "If our defences aren't enough, we're going to need better gear."

She nodded and shouted back to him: "Let's get back to the landing zone in case the transport sets down again." She tapped her ear and yelled: "Pratty? Where are you?"

Pratty's agitated voice answered: "In the shit. We're screaming at the AI to get us on the ground, but it's flying around in bloody circles."

Pip ran, sensing Crimble at her side. "Overlay!" she cried, and her Squitch added digital references in the lens in her eye that included details of the terrain around her as well as the location of the transport above them.

Pratty spoke to her, his voice carrying the faintest trace of desperation, "The stats here are starting to look a bit tedious. Seems the PeaceMakers have done all of their missiles and the BSLs are out of line of sight."

"If the super AI won't land the transport, why doesn't the captain override?"

"Christ, I don't know," Pratty exclaimed. "I think the super AI and the captain are expecting our defences to get the upper hand, but it's not happening—"

"We're almost at your position," Pip broke in. "If we get overwhelmed, we are going to need more firepower than Pickups."

"Well, it's not decided yet—"

Pip's Squitch reported: "A Caliphate Spider has targeted NATO autonomous aircraft ESP378–002, you should seek cover—"

Thirty metres above Pip, the descending transport containing Pratty and over fifty other NATO troops shattered under the impact of the Spider like an egg hit by a bullet. The ball of orange flame curled in on itself and the broken pieces of the transport tumbled out of it. Dismay swept over Pip. She took a step forward to sprint for the wreckage when Crimble grabbed her arm and stopped her. "What?" she demanded.

"They're already gone, pal. You won't help them," he said.

Pip couldn't believe Crimble had misunderstood her. She repeated: "We need better gear, and it's on that transport." She snatched her arm away, turned, and ran.

In her ear, her Squitch advised: "Danger, you are approaching an unsafe location. You should seek cover and wait for assistance."

She ignored the Squitch, realising that if it hadn't been for that young girl's sprained ankle, she and Crimble would also be dead now. She slowed as she advanced on the burning debris falling from the sky. A gust of wind blew glowing embers into her face and she winced at the pain when a hot piece of wreckage touched her skin for an instant. She paused while the last of the remains hit the ground. Pip knew there could be no survivors. In the unlikely event the Spider blast hadn't killed all of the occupants, the fall to earth certainly would have.

She reached the edge of the debris field. The Squitch repeated its warning, but Pip replied: "I need gear. Where is the armaments locker?"

"Armaments stored aboard autonomous aircraft ESP378-002 have been subject to pressure and heat levels—"

"Overlay, now!" Pip demanded, but in her vision, nothing changed. "I said 'overlay, now'," she repeated with venom in her voice.

The Squitch replied: "Increased enemy jamming is preventing effective communications. However, you are currently in danger from your immediate surroundings and enemy ACA activity. You should seek cover and await—"

"Shut up," Pip said, stepping gingerly around the wreckage and bodies.

She heard Crimble's voice in her ear: "Pip? Pip? They're flooding the battlespace and jamming comms. We need to get away from here before they start targeting individuals."

"Okay, okay," she replied. On the verge of giving up and unable to do more than skirt around the outside of the debris field due to the heat, she suddenly saw half a dozen metal tubes lying in the dirt. She tightened the strap of her Pickup to hold it close to her back, and then scooped up an armful of the Stilettoes. A glance at the glowing sky and southerly mountain ridge reoriented her after her search among the wreckage, and she hurried away.

"Pip, Pip!" Crimble's voice rose above the crackling flames, the screams and moans of civilians, and the whooshes of ACAs splitting the night air above them.

She ran towards his voice, noticing the chaos of fleeing civilians as they moved to cover, holding lights to guide their owners down into the valley.

She reached him and asked: "How can they jam our Squitch?"

Crimble's stubby arms took and cradled half of Pip's single-shot missile launchers. He said: "Dunno, but if the saturation gets any worse, we could be have real problems."

"Okay, let's get to lower ground."

"Okay."

They followed the remaining civilians off the plateau and down a narrow path. Pip tapped Crimble on the shoulder and said: "Let's go through the forest."

He gave her a half-smile and said: "Quicker?"

"Safer for the civilians if we get targeted."

Crimble's moustache slumped as his smile vanished. He said: "Don't be too positive, will you?"

"Come on, Crimble. We're trained for this shit; they're not. And they're losing their homes."

They moved off the path and away from the frightened and disorientated civilians. As they trekked, Pip realised that Rory must be dead along with Pratty, as the mobile command post to which he'd been seconded would surely have been a primary target. They came to a narrow, shallow mountain stream and the bubbling water made a vast contrast to the night's violence.

Pip took out her canteen, drank, and topped it up from the stream, glancing at Crimble as he did the same.

Crimble's faced lowered. He asked: "What happens when they send Spiders after us?"

Pip smothered her own uncertainty and replied: "We've got the gear," indicating the half a dozen Stilettoes.

"How many of them will that lot be able to take out?"

The Squitch interrupted in Pip's ear, and the reaction on Crimble's face told her that it had in his ear as well: "Latest battle analyses indicate that only comparable autonomous combat—"

"Where are the closest NATO ACAs?" Pip asked.

"Insufficient data. According to the most recent data, you should find cover and wait until friendly forces retake the battlespace."

"If this is the invasion," Crimble asked, "how long do *you* think we might need to wait for that to happen?"

"The current tactical situation is not favourable to a swift resolution."

Crimble looked at Pip and said: "Diplomatic little shit, eh?"

She shook her head and replied: "No, we need to know what we can do next. We need to help those civilians. We also need to work out how we can avoid those bloody Spid—" she stopped when the view in her lens changed abruptly.

Crimble swore as the Squitch announced: "Two Spiders approaching from the northeast. You are their targets.

Distance one thousand metres, approaching in a straight line over rugged terrain. Take defensive action immediately."

Pip reached down for a Stiletto while loosening the Pickup on her back. She grabbed and activated the nearest single-shot portable missile launcher while keeping one eye on the digital representation of the oncoming Spiders when the Squitch said: "Two more Spiders approaching from the southwest. You are their targets. Distance nine hundred metres, approaching in a straight line over rugged terrain. Take defensive action immediately."

"Shit," Pip swore. "You take those two; I'll deal with the first pair. Mind the back-blast from the Stilettoes."

"Back-blast is going to be the least of our problems. Look at the speed these bastards are coming in at," Crimble noted.

Pip grunted her agreement, hefted the Stiletto onto her shoulder, and took aim.

Chapter 3

04.43 Sunday 19 February 2062

Trainee nurse Serena Rizzi gripped her brother Max and shouted over the relentless din of chaos: "You have to get out of Rome."

"No," he yelled back, "I must go back and take our mother to safety."

"Look at it," she answered, waving one arm at the dark red and orange flames flashing and passing inside palls of billowing black smoke. Explosions rang out a symphony ranging from the deep rush of collapsing masonry to the sharp reports of splitting metal.

"We must stop them," Max cried. "This is not fair!"

Serena's heart cracked a little more at her younger brother's plaintive grievance. Her fingers dug further into his bony shoulders and she said: "It does not matter what is 'fair'. Mother can hardly walk. You cannot—"

"But someone must help her—"

"No one can help. If you try, you will become another victim—" She pulled him out of the way as a wailing ambulance raced along the street, swerving to avoid debris and bystanders. Injustice burned inside Serena, but she knew she had to reach the hospital and help them there. "Come with me, you will be able to do some good," she urged.

"No," he shouted, shrugging her hands from his shoulders and backing off. "That would be only fighting the symptoms, not the cause. But first I will get our mother out from the building and to safety. Goodbye, dear sister."

She watched him turn around and run towards the apartment block whose residents included their elderly mother. Earlier, she'd told him and their mother that the hospital needed her, and insisted he take mother to the building's basement as management had been reinforcing it since the first attack on Rome the previous week. But instead, Max had panicked and chased after her, accosting her in the street amid the increasing violence.

Now, with foreboding she watched him hurry to the small apartment block which sat in a nest of such blocks close to the Viale Marconi main arterial route. Then, she sensed rather than saw a line of small black dots descend out of the mass of flying devices above them, down into the neighbourhood, among the apartment blocks. Serena stared transfixed as puffs of smoke blew out from the corners of each building. The three or four floors of each unit concertinaed down in the manner of a demolition rather than destruction.

Among the numerous people on the street, she saw her younger brother recoil and stagger back as smoke and dust engulfed him for a moment. A strong breeze passed over her and she felt that it carried her mother's spirit. The smoke billowed upwards in the fiery gloaming and her soul reeled at the relentlessness of the attack. Serena realised that tonight meant something greater than the attack a week earlier. Now, the aggression appeared more methodical, better planned, and she wondered if anyone in Rome would be left to see the dawn.

Max covered the last few metres to her and shrieked: "Did you see that? Did you see what they did? They just killed—murdered—our mother! Did you see?"

Serena felt her lower jaw tremble and her eyes well, but she readied herself and said: "We must help defend the city. Come with me to the hospital, now."

Tears ran down her brother's smoke-blackened cheeks and he shook his head in rejection. "No," he said between breaths. "Last night, Lorenzo told me he had found a flaw in their software. He thinks he can stop their machines. I will go and help him."

Serena's shoulders fell. She'd heard Max talk about Lorenzo before. "Do you know where he is?"

"Yes, I think so, but I can't reach him now. Nothing works."

She said: "Please come with me, Max."

Her brother shook his head again, turned and left to find his own way through the chaos. Serena headed for the hospital, only half-expecting it to be standing when she arrived. The two-kilometre walk became a worsening struggle against the hellish turmoil. She imagined all of the dead and injured in the buildings as the Caliphate's ACAs streaked from the sky to inflict such precise demolition, but she knew the hospital was the only place she might be able to help.

She increased her pace to a fast jog and felt a surge of gratitude for the Caliphate's attack the previous week, for not only had she survived through a miracle, but the GenoFluid pack had completely repaired her smashed legs, and as she ran she felt new strength in her stride. A sudden and loud collision in the air above her made her veer off the pathway and towards a building from which bright flames lit the surroundings. She looked up and gasped when flashes as bright as lightning burst overhead in quick succession. No thunder accompanied them, only a sound of blunt metal shearing, like a fork dragged across a china plate.

The flaming remains of machines crashed to the ground around her; heavy, deadening impacts that thudded into the pavement and tarmac and made the ground tremble. She remained immobile in the open as these pieces of metal rained down. Presently, the deluge eased and a voice in her head told her she'd been lucky again not to be hit. At once, she knew luck had nothing to do with it: she had been spared for a higher purpose, only she did not yet know exactly what her true role might be.

She continued, now obliged to navigate a waking nightmare of heat and fire, of burning debris and distant screams and shrieks that might have been caused by metal or injured people. The air reeked of pungent smoke and burning plastic and metal.

She passed one fallen ACA and stopped on hearing a strange clicking sound coming from within it. She stared in curiosity and recognised the mangled form of one of the Caliphate's ACAs, the one she had read about, which held fifty of the autonomous mobile bombs which everyone called *ragni*. The device looked like a vast ball of metal twice her height, despite a portion of it buried in the ground. Parts of it burned and hissed, while the clicking sound grew more frantic, as though some aspect of its super-artificial intelligence wanted to broadcast that it protested the damage it had suffered. Serena wondered when her curiosity should become concern, but the clicking sound had a hypnotic quality. The jointed, metallic leg of a Spider shot out from the wreck, gripped, and then tapped urgently on the tarmac, like a trapped animal trying to free itself. This strange noise brought Serena back to her senses and she fled.

Two minutes later, she arrived at the south wing of the hospital. Exterior lights floodlit a scene of hundreds of victims from both genders and all age groups. She hurried through row after uneven row of haggard survivors. A harassed-looking young doctor in a blood-stained white jacket told her to go to the main reception. As she made her way past more injured people, she wondered if there could be enough GenoFluid packs in all of Italy to treat everyone. But at the back of her mind, a more pressing concern arose: why had the hospital not been destroyed?

She reached the crowded reception area, steering past an old man sweeping glass from smashed windows. She found herself in front of a soldier, focused hazel eyes staring at her from under heavy, black eyebrows.

"What?" he demanded.

"I'm a nurse, I've come to help," she said, deciding to omit the 'trainee' part of her job title.

He nodded to the rear and said: "There might be some GenoFluid packs left in the storerooms, but you will be lucky to get there and back."

"Why?"

"We are due to evacuate soon."

"What?" Serena said, aghast. "Who's in charge?" she asked, looking around the area but only seeing bloodied casualties and military personnel.

"The Major, but he's coordinating our defences."

Serena voiced her concerns: "Why has this hospital not been hit? There seem to be more than enough of their flying bombs."

"They probably plan to use it when they inva—" he broke off and Serena saw his eye twitch. He said: "That's it, time to move. All troops, close in on the enemy transport's approach." He glanced down at Serena and said: "There are evac craft in the grounds at the rear. If you want to survive beyond this night, you had better get on one."

"But what about all of the injured?" she asked him as he left her.

"If they cannot get to a transport, there is nothing to be done," he answered as he left her.

Serena stared at the soldier's back as he jogged through the entrance, and she realised that nothing would persuade her to get on any kind of transport, not with the sky full of those evil machines.

Distant cries of "Evacuate!" pierced the sounds of battle. Serena looked around her, nonplussed at the prospect of so many casualties being left to the mercy of the Caliphate, while a more detached part of her mind noted the increased activity and running soldiers.

A sudden increase in light and noise outside the building caught her attention. With equal measures of caution and curiosity, she moved to the damaged entrance and crouched down on broken glass. Either side of her lay inert bodies on stretchers, partially covered by GenoFluid packs whose displays blinked red in warning of their patient's impending expiration. Torn between events outside and the victims around her, before Serena could investigate the nearest case to see how she might help, urgent shouting and a sense of panic came from outside the hospital. She looked up and the source of the brighter light revealed itself as a vast aircraft, larger than anything she'd ever seen. White lights shot beams out to illuminate the darkness at all angles as it hovered above the broad, debris-strewn street. Its short, stubby wings seemed to taunt the laws of aerodynamics and Serena struggled to see how the huge transport could remain airborne.

She gasped as a handful of missiles streaked out from the darkened surroundings and exploded against the transport's shielding, which gave off a transparent green flash. The huge aircraft itself did not move. Then, in counterattack more punishing explosions erupted on the ground, hurting her ears and shaking the building. Serena realised that the soldier she'd spoken to a moment earlier was probably dead. She gripped the remnants of the doorframe and sobbed. All around her, GenoFluid packs beeped in urgency as patients died from their injuries.

The vast Caliphate air transport came down to land with a menacing grace that stopped the breath in Serena's throat. Common sense insisted she would shortly be a victim and she felt oddly comforted that she would be reunited with her mother so soon. But then her memory reminded her that she'd been spared the previous week for a more important purpose, not merely to die now, at the hands of whatever creatures would shortly emerge from the aircraft.

Stumbling over bodies, her shoes crunching on broken glass, she backed away from the hospital entrance, no longer noticing the dead and dying around her, seized by a new terror. Slits of darkness appeared on the outside of the enemy air transport as doors retracted, and the first Caliphate warriors to set foot in Rome leapt out.

Chapter 4

Major Kate Fus stared in dismay at the screens in front of her as they detailed the enemy forces' relentless advance. She insisted: "Bolek, for the sake of the Lord tell me you are instructing those units to fall back asap."

"Yes," the Polish Army's super AI replied in a tone of mild indifference.

"Good. Well, no urgency, then," Kate responded with irony, her amber eyes tracking the data on the displays in front of her. "Zoom in on the eastern flank. Enlarge Troop Foxtrot's location. Report."

One of the images in front of her grew to show digital representations of a section of the troops under her command as their transports retreated in the face of the Caliphate's onslaught. The super AI said: "Enemy ACAs are approaching more quickly than the NATO transports can retreat. The probability of Troop Foxtrot successfully escaping enemy forces continues to fall."

"But if they can make it to Haskovo, will the BSLs there not slow the enemy down?"

"The Bulgarian supply base at Haskovo is equipped with two Battlefield Support Pulsars which, at current estimates, will be obliged to defend the base against three-to-four-hundred Blackswan ACAs."

Kate frowned and said: "You could have simply given me the probability."

"The base's complete destruction is a certainty."

"And how long will it take enemy forces to get here?" she asked, aware that the mobile command vehicle in which she sat currently rested in the foothills around Bulgaria's second city, Plovdiv, less than sixty kilometres to the northwest of Haskovo.

"You will need to commence retreating in approximately twelve minutes."

"There is nothing approximate about the number twelve; that is in fact quite precise."

The super AI did not respond to her pedantic observation. Kate scanned the displays and felt the panic claw at the back of her throat again. She still could not make sense of the storm that had erupted. Her decision ten years ago to choose a career in the Polish Army had a certain inevitability, coming as she did from a martial family. Her father had glowed with pride when she was commissioned as an officer in the summer of 2053. Kate had expected little more than the usual NATO war games and gradual promotion as the old soldiers at the top retired. All levels of every European country's army regarded a real shooting war as highly unlikely. For years, NATO's simulations revolved around Russia wanting to reclaim its lost Soviet Empire, or a rehash of the Arctic drama in the late 2040s, when Russia, China and NATO had come close to open conflict when the natural resources under the rapidly thawing icecap became easily accessible.

In any case, if a war did break out, everyone expected it to be fought between the machines. Now, Kate's mind had to accept that a new, unsuspected enemy had erupted on Europe's southern borders and proceeded to trample over what little defence NATO could offer.

An unexpected shift in the image in front of her brought her back to the moment. She queried: "Why is that transport slowing down?"

The super AI appeared to ignore her question and said: "Troop Foxtrot is continuing to be outrun—"

"No," she broke in, "Troop Sierra. One of the transports is slowing." She heard the faint trace of panic in her voice.

"The transport reports that it has to take evasive action due to falling debris from ACA combat above it."

"The enemy is literally on top of them."

Kate ran her index finger along the lip above her cleft palate, a habit she'd had in stressful situations since childhood. Her sense of impotence grew. Like so many other officers in the NATO armies, she was a commander who did not command in any meaningful sense of the word. Most people outside the military did not fully comprehend the extent to which the super AI took almost all of the tactical decisions. The armed forces of most European nations still adhered to traditions that, in some countries, were centuries old. But in truth, for a mid-level commander such as her, there remained little to do apart from watch events unfold.

A new male voice crackled into the mobile command vehicle and demanded: "All units on the approach to Plovdiv prepare to retreat. Confirm."

Kate jolted; again, this order did not require human intervention. Nevertheless, she answered: "Sector zero-three, confirmed."

She caught her breath when a blip representing one of the Troop Foxtrot transports flashed and disappeared. "What was that?" she asked.

"NATO autonomous aircraft HU329–006 has been destroyed by enemy fire."

"What?" Kate said in astonishment. "Why? Why did you let that happen?"

"Enemy forces are overwhelming the battlespace. Priority is to minimise casualties with the available defensive resources."

"What?"

"Ensuring the safety of those closest to reaching safety is the priority given the current battle situation."

"But—but," Kate stammered, appalled that the super AI was now deciding who among the troops under her command should live and die. "We need reinforcements," she managed to mutter. She recalled distant memories of seminars on the ethics of hypothetical military situations that might require such decisions, but she never thought they would actually happen, let alone immediately at the beginning of a conflict.

The super AI announced: "The minimal reinforcements available are too far from the battlespace to affect the outcome, and will in any case be reassigned in less than three minutes, when a sufficient number of NATO troops will have been killed to make such reassignment tactically prudent. In addition, it is certain that the SkyWatcher battle management satellites will be destroyed in less than two minutes. When that happens, there is further certainty that enemy jamming will render continued retreat the only tactical option."

Kate tried to recall any training or simulation or war-game that had covered a scenario where NATO forces were so completely outnumbered and outgunned, and could not. She shook her head in dismay, heaved a deep breath, and stabbed a comms panel below the screens. She tried to sound as authoritative as she could when she spoke: "Attention, all troops. You are free to disable the super AI and take control of your transports."

There came an immediate rebuke: "What the hell do you think you're doing, Major?"

Kate's focus increased. However much turmoil she felt inside, she would be damned if her commanding officer would sense it. She answered: "General Pakla, our defences are insufficient and reinforcements too limited. I am already losing troops—"

"You and every other front in this damned invasion."

"I do not believe we should rely on the super AI after everything it missed in the last two weeks—"

"That's not your decision, Major."

"Those Hungarian soldiers on their transports are dying, Sir, and I believe they are better suited to decide how they should die more than the super AI."

"Our super AI is operating to maximise efficiency and minimise casualties. Your insubordination is noted, Major."

"Understood, Sir," she replied without enthusiasm.

"Good. Pakla out."

Three seconds later, the super AI announced an incoming secure communication and Kate smiled in relief. General Pakla's voice again filled the mobile command vehicle, quieter and with a caring lover's softness. He said: "Events are too chaotic to talk now, but you did the right thing, which is why I did not countermand your order."

"Will that not cause you problems later?"

"In a few days, missing-presumed-dead troops will be the least of our problems. This is not merely another exercise."

"I know."

"Get out of there as soon as you can, please. We will be together again in a few days, I promise."

The connection ended and Kate murmured: "Bolek, delete all records of that conversation and retreat. Notify local commanders that the line should fall back."

The Polish Army's super AI acknowledged: "Confirmed. General Pakla's post has ordered the front to retreat now."

"Windows please, Bolek, the usual configuration," Kate said and then sighed. The data on screens around the sides of the mobile command vehicle vanished to reveal clear windows offering views of southern-European pine forest and winter-bare birches. Kate lolled her head back in the main command chair. Through the window in the roof above her, she saw the sky shining a bright, cold blue with the promise of spring.

"Please secure yourself, Major, as we are approaching uneven terrain," the super AI suggested.

Kate immediately reached for the chair's thick black straps and buckled herself in, recalling that for Bolek, 'uneven terrain' covered everything from slight inclines to sudden near-vertical drops that could test the strongest of stomachs. The vehicle rocked and bounced between trees while its sole occupant kept looking at the sky above her. "What is the situation in Plovdiv?" Kat asked.

"Substantial numbers of refugees are fleeing the city and there are reports of localised civil disturbances."

"Most of those people are going to die, are they not?"

The super AI's tone did not change: "Total projected casualties vary too broadly to have any meaningful value at this stage."

"Oh," Kate said with irony, "even the super AI doesn't know how bad it is going to be."

"The situation is too fluid at this stage. Variables include how many and in what formations the enemy deployments att—"

"And in what we can do to counteract them?"

"Nothing, to any significant degree."

"What? What on earth are you talking about?"

The super AI replied: "Continually updated forecasts suggest that if the New Persian Caliphate continues to attack NATO with the current level of firepower, their invasion will be complete and Europe overrun in—"

Kate's brow furrowed at the super AI stopping in mid-sentence. The mobile command vehicle jolted and slewed before righting itself on flatter terrain, and when Kate had managed to steady herself in her seat, she barked: "Go on, in how long? When?"

"Access to that information has been restricted."

Kate knew better than to argue. She asked: "How long until we reach the air transport facility? And do not say 'approximately' if you intend to give me a precise figure."

"Five minutes and… thirty-seven seconds."

"That's better." With her index finger, she traced a line above the lip of her cleft palate again as she attempted once more to grasp the magnitude of what was happening around her, minute by minute, hour by hour. A part of her mind observed in detached fascination as the very essence of history itself seemed to be shifting and sliding like some vast rocky mountain that had begun to collapse because one tiny grain of sand too many had slid from underneath it.

She considered where it might all end more than how it had started. The whole world had treated the Caliphate with suspicion for as long as she could remember. But ever since her childhood, the received wisdom insisted that the Caliphate was simply too backward and too consumed with its own internal strife to pose any threat to the rest of the world. Her teachers at school, the media in her home country of Poland, and everyone else it seemed to her, considered the sealed-off Caliphate the least of the world's problems. Worsening climate change occupied most of the global armed forces, who could support a country's regular emergency services in evacuation and rescue duties. In the last few years, China growled more like a lion than a dragon once it had become by far the largest economy on Earth, and Russia engaged in its usual subterfuge without understanding that Europe had for decades known the measure of its ham-fisted duplicity. At the same time, knowledgeable Americans lamented the erosion of their once-insurmountable empire with a regret singularly lacking in the British a century earlier.

However, quite suddenly and from out of nowhere, that backward Arab conglomerate which was thought to be fighting medieval levels of poverty and corruption, into which anyone could enter but from which no one could leave, exploded onto the international stage, destroying the accepted world order in mere days.

Kate tilted her head forward to see pines and birches flash past outside as the mobile command vehicle sped along a well-established but dusty forest track. She turned to the remaining screens to follow the battle and sighed when she saw the increasing list of casualties. Hungarian, Czech and Polish troop transports had fled to the ground if they'd lasted long enough. Many had been destroyed. The displays looked like some appalling video game, but the graphics represented actual deaths and injuries to real people. Her spirit sank.

In a few days, she would be with the General, the only man who understood her, the only man who'd looked at her as a woman and not as some kind of strange freak for not having her cleft palate corrected. She exhaled and told herself that yes, the General, *her* General, would know what would happen next.

Chapter 5

06.31 Sunday 19 February 2062

General Sir Terry Tidbury fought an onslaught of inward alarm as he stood in front of the screens in the new War Rooms in Whitehall and observed the unfolding disaster. With his extensive military experience, he knew how to retain a calm exterior, but the effect of his entire career having passed in peacetime—only to face this most brutal war at the end—hit to the centre of his being. Now, in real time, NATO forces were enduring losses never before seen in the organisation's one hundred-and-thirteen year history.

Each second brought new reports, new indications, new super-AI assessments of how long his forces, and by extension Europe, could expect to survive, as well as new reports of casualties, updated estimates of the numbers of the Caliphate's victims, and the projected spread of the invading warriors.

In a thumbnail in the top left-hand corner of the main screen, the African-American face of Supreme Allied Commander Europe, General Joseph E. Jones, peered in fascinated concentration, which, Terry assumed, matched a similar look on his own face.

From one of the monitoring stations, a young man announced: "Organised resistance in Spain has collapsed. Remaining NATO forces now outnumbered over two hundred to one."

Terry turned to the central holographic display console, which displayed a digital representation of the battle taking place over Grenada in Spain. Blotches of light representing his troops and his arms winked out of existence. The image shrank to bring the whole of southern Spain into view. Illuminated markers with time stamps showed how the Caliphate's ACAs had made landfall on a one-hundred-kilometre front from Cartagena to Alicante. Once over Spanish territory, this spearhead had split north and south, and Grenada was the southernmost Caliphate landing point. Terry shook his head at the question-mark icons that denoted suspected landing points for Caliphate invasion forces.

"Any new data on the invading forces?" he asked the room.

"No, Sir," came the immediate response.

Terry turned back to the screens around the perimeter of the room, and kept his breathing even. In the zone designated 'Central', the city of Rome was suffering another intense assault, but the country around it had been caught in a pincer as enemy forces destroyed all in their path on two fronts, fifty kilometres apart. The local people had barely begun to recover from the punishment attack a week earlier, and now they were obliged to suffer even greater destruction.

Athens endured a similar misfortune: mere days after vast swaths of the ancient city had been levelled—including the Acropolis—Caliphate ACAs now swarmed over the remnants, pulverising what little resistance Greek and allied forces could offer, and then embarking on the systemic annihilation of the remaining civilian population. Further east, reports detailed Caliphate forces pouring into Europe through Istanbul and surging up through Bulgaria, wreaking a similar havoc.

From the screen, Jones growled: "Secure channel. General?"

Terry glanced at his adjutant, Simms, and said: "I'll be in my office." The General left the station and entered his private office next to the main entrance to the War Rooms. He closed the door and called: "Squonk? Link to SACEUR, evaluate potential for compromise."

Terry paced around the small, windowless room as the British Army's super AI answered: "Less than three-thousandths of one percent."

"Proceed."

Jones's face resolved on the largest wall in the room in two dimensions, Terry eschewing the holographic option which he could have over his desk. "What's the matter, General?" Terry asked, struggling to keep the frustration from his voice.

"How would you assess morale over there, General?"

The American's question nonplussed the Englishman for a moment, but he answered: "Holding up. Obviously the situation on the continent is looking less than ideal—"

"You realise we're gonna be fortunate if we last more than a few weeks?"

"The rearmament progra—"

"Eighty sites scattered over northern Europe? The enemy will pulverise them before a single PeaceMaker rolls off the line."

"Perhaps not if we can delay his advance with reinforcements from your forces?"

Jones's eyes narrowed: "Unlikely, because we have to do the job with the resources we currently have avail—" He broke off and peered at something Terry couldn't see.

Abruptly, he ordered: "Pass it around," and turned his gaze back to Terry. "Looks like we finally got some intel."

Terry instructed: "On the desk, Squonk," and spun round from the wall to see a holographic image resolve of some kind of aircraft. The image flickered and flashed with indistinctness, and Terry realised he watched a running loop of a few seconds' movement that repeated. The aircraft had a thick, tubular fuselage with a flattened underside. The wings seemed stunted, although Terry was no expert on aeronautics. The aircraft had no visible means of propulsion.

From behind him, SACEUR's voice growled: "Ample Annie is getting it all figured out."

Terry muttered: "Just how big is that thing?"

Squonk's asexual voice announced: "Received data confirms a wingspan of two hundred metres with a total lift capacity of—"

"Christ," Terry said. "How many troops can it carry?"

Squonk replied: "Initial estimates range from one to two thousand, depending on the extent of support equipment."

"How on earth is it powered?"

"Insufficient data, however a preliminary analysis points to an above-average probability of increased development of the units that power the enemy's ACA flee—"

"Don't be ridiculous," Terry broke in, his distrust of super AI flaring again. "The units which power ACAs absolutely cannot be made large enough to lift such vast craft. That kind of tech must be years if not decades away…" His words trailed off and he spun back to face General Jones on the wall-screen.

The American let out a sigh and said: "I'm no engineer either, General, but if the enemy's tech really is so far ahead of ours, then our chances of holding their attack up, never mind reversing it, are shrinking real quick."

Terry tapped the desk with a finger and said: "We need answers. We need to develop countermeasures," but even as he spoke the words, he understood the flaw in his reasoning.

General Jones said: "We ain't gonna have the time, General. Seems to me we've been outmanoeuvred by a goddamn dictatorship."

"There has to be an alternative," Terry said with scant notion what that option might be.

"Militarily there's only one, and you know what that is, General."

Terry folded his arms and stared back at the American. He said: "Now hang on a minute. Surrender? Already? The invasion has only just begun—"

"And it's a whole new ball game. We're completely outmatched and outgunned, and our damn computers are gonna reach the same conclusion real soon. And when they do, our political masters might decide it's the only way to go."

Terry shook his head and insisted: "That's never going to happen, Sir. The enemy's behaviour to date totally precludes that course of action."

"So what do you suggest, General?"

"We have to give our people some kind of hope, however vanishing."

"Hope in a hopeless situation?"

Terry nodded, understanding that the only option available to NATO was a fight to the bitter end, which might arrive much sooner than even the most pessimistic forecasts suggested.

Chapter 6

Crispin Webb, Principal Private Secretary to English Prime Minister Dahra Napier, stared at the back of his boss's head and wondered what must be going on in there. He himself had run out of superlatives in the last week: the most unimaginable, the worst, the most nightmarish. The sense of inescapable finality caused the mood in Ten Downing Street to fluctuate wildly from the height of stoic resilience to the depths of resigned pessimism. On this night, which had seen the promised invasion begin, he had not slept, mainly thanks to a not-entirely-legal supply of reengineered GenoFluid bots suspended in a pill. His boss had retired but returned less than two hours later to monitor the data coming from the War Rooms a couple of streets away.

Now, she stared through the windows into the dark night outside. He followed her gaze and considered that at nearly seven in the morning, the blackness remained impenetrable. She spoke, her voice hoarse from exhaustion: "We have to wrest back some modicum of control."

Crispin had to smother a guffaw. There could be little doubt who had control. He said: "The only thing we can do is try to exert more diplomatic pressure, boss."

She didn't reply, but her shoulders rose and fell as her breathing deepened. He considered again if he were about to have to deliver the same speech he'd given her more than once over the last few days.

She turned around and hissed: "The rest of the world must come to our aid. Pressure must be brought to bear on that damnable Caliph."

"We're doing all we can in that direc—"

"Well, it's hardly enough, is it?"

Crispin took a deep breath. He said: "Diplomacy takes second place behind trade, boss. Old allies further afield of course condemn the Caliphate's aggression, but as long as China refuses to rein the Caliph in, none of them is going to risk upsetting their most important trading partner. Too much of their economies depend on having Beijing on-side."

"But this is Europe, the cultural centre of the world. The rest of the world cannot simply sit back and watch us be put to the sword."

"Yes, I think they can. And I also think the Chinese might have something to say about where the cultural centre of the world is." Crispin hesitated when he saw how his words affected Napier, and a distant memory surfaced, a piece of advice from his predecessor given to him a few days before Crispin had followed Napier into Ten Downing Street eight years earlier. The chief aide to the outgoing PM had told him always to remember that English politicians carried substantial baggage with them: the Empire, the Victorians, and an inability to accept that the old power had been lost forever. It didn't matter how clear-sighted they might be before their election, once they set foot inside the Palace of Westminster and were immersed in the iconology of Great Britain's past glories, all but the most pragmatic succumbed. And the effect became even more pronounced when they discovered the further trappings of power: stately homes like Chequers, Chevening and Dorneywood. He warned Crispin that centuries of martial success and international deference clouded their acceptance of England's vastly weakened place in the world. Like a Greek who complained bitterly that more people should remember his country invented democracy, or a Roman who daydreamed of her ancestors' overwhelming dominance, so too the English could not quite untether themselves from the knowledge that fewer than two centuries before, theirs had been the most advanced and powerful country on Earth.

Crispin repeated what he felt sure he'd already told the Prime Minister more than once over the last week: "Boss, it's been a while since we could make foreigners do what we wanted them to do—"

"Don't patronise me. I know that," she shot back. "Come along, I want to go to the War Rooms and see for myself just how bad things are." She strode to the door and exited. Crispin hurried after her and followed her down the stairs from the third-floor apartment. With every tread and riser, they passed portraits of previous incumbents, descending as though through a time machine, going into the past, each preceding prime minister having wielded more power and authority than his or her predecessor. Napier continued: "The fact that England is not the world power it used to be is not lost on me, I can assure you. But what the Persian Caliphate is doing today cannot go unchallenged. Yes, I am perfectly aware—as you've mentioned more than once lately—about how little weight England carries in global affairs, but that is not the point."

They hurried past Churchill, MacDonald and Asquith, each of whom stared out unmoved by their descendants' approaching destruction. Crispin held his council, wondering whether Napier had accepted the objective truth of their situation.

She continued: "Untold millions are going to die if this madman is allowed to invade and occupy Europe. If we're talking about trade, how many Chinese businesses will suffer? How many Chinese and other ex-patriots reside in Europe, in harm's way?"

"Beijing might not see it as sufficient reason," Crispin countered, as with twitches of his eye muscles he called up the relevant data in his lens. "Trade between China and Europe accounts for less than one percent of China's total volume of global trade."

"But they control him," she complained. "He will do what the Chinese tell him to do."

"That was the assumption, until last week," Crispin said. "Now it seems he wants to show the world his independence. We know the Chinese government is consternated at his actions, and like the rest of the world, is still coming to terms with his wholesale destruction of Israel—"

"Apart from those anti-Semites who think it wasn't a bad thing," Napier interrupted in a cynical tone. "Remind me, which one of the South American countries said the Caliph should be applauded for 'resolving the Jewish issue once and for all'?"

"Venezuela."

"And only the UN censured them."

They arrived at the ground floor lift that would take them into the depths underneath Whitehall and finally on to the War Rooms.

Crispin steeled himself and said: "Boss, when we get down there, you're going to see a pretty bleak situation. And it might be one that could be turned against us in unexpected ways."

Napier's finger stopped in mid-air as she went to dab the pad that would call the lift, and her eyes narrowed. "What do you mean?" she asked.

Crispin lowered his voice: "He hasn't yet, but we can be certain the Caliph will demand our surrender, especially when it becomes clear NATO is incapable of mounting any kind of remotely effective defence—"

"He can demand it all he wants—"

"All of our super AIs forecast mere weeks before effective NATO military resistance is destroyed. When the Caliph demands our surrender, we will have no choice but to comply."

"I rather think—"

Crispin held a hand up to silence her in an unfamiliar reversal of authority. He said: "If we do not surrender, and if the bloodshed were to continue needlessly, then despite the Caliphate—"

"You can't be suggesting we simply yield to their barbarism?" she broke in, a look of horror on her lined face.

"Despite the Caliphate having been the aggressor, the rest of the world may take the view that the governments of Europe are the more foolhardy, and we could end up squandering what little sympathy we currently enjoy." Crispin finished by playing to his boss's ego. He whispered: "And history might well view our 'determination to resist' as truculence, and our 'resilience' as murderous arrogance that led to the unnecessary deaths of millions."

Chapter 7

15.56 Monday 20 February 2062

The Englishman walked along the concourse of one of Beijing's largest shopping malls. He did not notice how the elegant, curved design of the roof splayed the bright sunlight so it dappled the fronds of the cypresses and firs that sat in pods dotted in front of the shops. He ignored the dead-eyed stares from the local people. The Englishman strode head and shoulders above everyone else, and in better days he used to joke that he walked at the same speed at which most normal people jogged. The Chinese habit of staring at foreigners had never bothered him to any significant degree, but he admitted to himself that his day was going badly, so his reciprocal glances would not be friendly.

This Monday offered little to comfort him. He should've been at a famous restaurant in a northern district of the vast city, keeping up his cover as a seller of the finest English wines, using his pigeon-Chinese to try and flog the Home Counties' cats' piss, but he'd been obliged to feign illness. For what was happening on this bright afternoon should not be happening. He blinked as tears welled in his eyes. He refused to believe the data his lens ran up in his vision. Frustrated beyond measure, he cursed the super AI, cursed the vanadium dioxide in the hardware which must surely be malfunctioning and conducting heat after all, and cursed the numbers scrolling up in his vision, which wobbled and shimmered as his tear ducts reacted to the emotions inside him, emotions which he fought to control even as he knew he no longer wanted to control them.

He stopped walking outside a shop that sold erotic underwear and choked back a distraught sob of despair. His lens listed the five largest stock markets in the world by capitalisation: 1, Shanghai; 2, Shenzhen; 3, Mumbai; 4, Tokyo; 5, Buenos Aires. Despite the sudden explosion of violence from the Caliphate against Europe, these indices were barely experiencing a tremor, much less suffering the shockwaves he'd expected to pummel all of them. The destruction the Caliphate was currently inflicting on his home continent should not be passing unnoticed by all of the most important global financial markets. They should be crashing, preferably, or at least shedding value in response to the chaos and uncertainty. But the fluctuations his lens reported denoted the same variations as could be expected on any average trading day. This meant that the rest of the world did not care about Europe, as though it were some third-world backwater whose battering by a more powerful entity could be overlooked in favour of doing business as usual.

His spirits lifted abruptly when Shanghai dipped and lost almost a quarter of a percent, mainly in tech stocks. He checked to see the other Chinese indices follow suit, caught his breath, and muttered, "Finally," to himself. He resumed walking, oblivious to the more intense stares from the people around him: "Come on, you bastards. Crash, you pieces of shit…"

The leading markets dropped further, red becoming the dominant colour on the graphs in his vision. A 'Breaking News' icon flashed in the lower righthand corner. He ignored it until a voice in his head suggested that the market falls might be related to this new occurrence—events in Europe had been unfolding for several hours, but the stocks had only just began to drop. With a twitch of an eye muscle, he read about an explosion at a dysprosium processing facility close to Chengjiang, south of the city of Kunming. Initial reports insisted hundreds must have been killed.

"No, no, no," the Englishman repeated to himself in despair, the fist of realisation crushing the opening bud of hope. Until today, the Englishman had never really believed the Caliphate's invasion would be allowed to progress. Although his lover, Marshall Zhou, had warned that an invasion was inevitable, the Englishman knew that his own upbringing had polluted and distorted his view: the Englishman still believed his country and the rest of Europe meant something in the world, that it had not yet been eclipsed by the economies of Asia-Pacific and South America and Africa. The pain he felt, he now realised, constituted the final disabusement of this illusion.

He reached a key junction in the mall at which five concourses converged in a cavernous atrium that yawned five floors above and three floors below him. He looked around him, but this part of the mall echoed in emptiness. He regulated his breathing as he prepared his report for London and gathered his thoughts. After further twitches of his eye muscles to encrypt his message, he began: "The Englishman reporting from Beijing. Time of report: 16.01, Monday 20 February 2062. Report begins…"

He paused, his easy erudition abruptly deserting him. In despondency, his glance took in the vast construction around him, concrete and steel and consumerism that would not feel the merest breeze from the storm raging seven thousand kilometres to the west. He swallowed his emotions and said: "It currently appears that the world's most powerful economies are not moved by events in Europe. Z. accurately stated when the invasion would commence, and now claims it shall not be stopped or reversed. The invasion will consume Europe and the rest of the world will not lift a finger to save it. Europe is fucked."

Chapter 8

Geoffrey Kenneth Morrow looked out of the rain-spattered window of his dilapidated south London apartment, heaved a sigh of frustration, and said: "I can't write anything worthwhile here. This is pointless."

"So?" said a female voice behind him.

He turned and looked at the woman, a familiar frown on her usually smooth forehead. He shrugged. "I have to go," he said, and held his breath in anticipation of her reaction.

She nodded in apparent reluctance and replied: "I know."

He breathed a sigh of relief, crossed the small living room, grasped her shoulders, and said with passion: "This is the greatest single event of our lifetimes, Lisa."

"I know," she repeated with a forlorn listlessness. "And from what I've read, we're all going to be dead within six weeks."

"Don't believe everything you read in the papers," he said with a knowing wink.

Lisa shook her head and said: "Only you journalists talk like that."

Geoff wanted to tell her so much. But his instinct cautioned him that if he went on another assignment, she might not be here when he got back, especially if the rumoured Caliphate jamming was as complete as he'd heard and they wouldn't be able to stay in contact.

Geoff allowed Lisa to take his right hand and place it on the slight bump protruding above her waistline. She whispered: "That's you in there, Geoff. Your child."

"Our child."

"Why won't you protect us?"

"The Caliphate's machines are hundreds of miles away on the other side of the continent. Do you have any idea just how big the European mainland is?"

"Why can't you protect us?" she asked.

"You don't need me to 'protect' you, Lisa. The British Isles are at almost zero risk. The Channel has saved us so many times in the past and will do so again. Besides, there are your parents and my par—"

"But you own this flat. We've no debt on it. We don't need the money you get from that bloody media outlet."

"Lisa, that 'bloody media outlet' is one of the most prestigious brands on the market. If they use my stuff, if I get a byline on a piece—even only a lousy contribution—it helps me build my own brand." He sensed he might have said the wrong thing. Again.

There came a pause and Lisa's face hardened. Her hazel eyes shone like circles of varnished teak as they reflected the weak light. She shook her head and whispered: "Can't you see? Are you—?"

"Lisa, please, don't—" he stopped when she put her index finger on his lips to shush him.

She whispered: "Just one question, Geoff. Just a single observation."

Geoff gave a slight nod.

"What use is your fucking 'brand' going to be when the British Isles are, like Europe, reduced to a massive, smoking ruin?"

Geoff turned away, saying: "It won't come to that."

"How do you know? All of the media is reporting that their ACAs are virtually unstoppable."

"That's what the media does, Lisa: sensationalism. It's their job."

"You'd think they'd hardly need to bother after what's happened in the last couple of weeks."

An incoming communication icon flashed in a small part of Geoff's vision. It was the call he had been waiting for, from one of the most important editors in London. He saw Lisa recognise the familiar change in his demeanour and heard her exhale. With a twitch of an eye muscle, he opened the link. "Hi, Alan, thanks for returning my call. Finally," he said, struggling to keep the sarcasm out of his voice.

"Yeah, whatever. I'm busy, Geoff. World War Three has well and truly kicked off, so what does a hack like you think he can do for me?"

"How many stringers have you got on the continent?"

"Don't be a prick," Alan spat. "I've got more content than I can use, and I don't need any bloody stringers. And you know what? I also don't have the time to talk bollocks with you, so—"

"Wait," Geoff shouted before Alan terminated the connection.

"What for?"

Geoff saw a look of disgust form on Lisa's face so he turned away from her, not wanting to think about what would happen at the end of this call. He spoke with urgency: "Alan, you're going to need old-fashioned reporters out there, on the ground, especially when the Caliphate's jamming kicks in."

"No, this content will keep on com—"

"It won't. You'll need bodies on the ground, if we overlook the double meaning—"

"Yeah, nice one—"

"Look, all autonomous travel is on lockdown, right? No one, absolutely no one, can go anywhere without official approval, yes?"

"That's a great story on its own: the authorities have shut down everyone's self-driving cars because fucking GCHQ has overridden the local police forces and taken control—"

"Yeah, I know," Geoff said as he felt his heartrate increase to a canter now he'd got Alan listening. He went on: "We've all heard about those poor sods dying because of missed hospital appointments, but that's not the top story now."

"And?"

"You can sort it. You've got the clout. Send me over, Alan. I'll get you the best content, even maybe from behind the lines—"

"Don't be stup—"

"I'm serious, Alan. Your outlet can get me onto the continent and across it. For sure, I could never do this now, as a private citizen. I'd be lucky to get as far as Kent."

"And to do that you'd have to walk."

"But you can get the clearances."

"It's not as easy as you think, Geoff."

"Don't give me that."

"Seriously. We're in a state of emergency. Nothing is going nowhere without full justification."

Geoff paused and wondered how honest Alan's defence could be. He said: "It's up to you, Alan. You must have loads of guys like me begging you to get them across the

Channel and close to the action. I mean, with the odds so heavily stacked against NATO."

Alan replied: "All right. Sign this contract."

Geoff opened the icon that arrived in his lens. "Okay," he said, "give me a minute to look at it."

"Hurry up," Alan answered.

"I can't find the clause on life insurance."

"That's because there isn't one."

"Come off it, Alan. It's a fucking war zone over there. You can't—"

"Yes, I can. I am not sending you into a war zone. I only want you to report on how those countries are coping with the approaching disaster, that's all. This is our standard emergency T&C. If you want life insurance, buy it yourself."

"You're a charmer," Geoff said as he approved his digital signature on the contract. With a blink of his eye, he sent the contract back.

Alan said: "Right, you're on the firm. Our super AI will schedule your transport. Go to Paris first, then head south towards Spain. That's the closest front to the UK, so I want regular progress reports. It will probably take some time to organise your transport approvals, so you won't hear anything for two to three minutes."

"Understood."

"And I want quality. You file any old shit or plagiarise a Euro outlet and the contract terminates."

"You don't say," Geoff replied with irony, and terminated the call. Then, he muttered: "Sanctimonious little prick," before he caught Lisa's icy stare.

"You're a bastard, Geoff Morrow," she said with open bitterness.

"I told you this is the most important single event of our—"

"You don't even care about us, do you?"

"Of course I do," Geoff said, a little too automatically, he realised. His mind whirred as he began deciding what he could and could not pack in his rucksack. A part of his brain made a note to contact his parents and ask them to look after Lisa while he was away. His parents had always helped him but now their aid took on a new importance.

"I do wish you did care," Lisa was saying. "Any last wishes you'd like me to pass on to your child? Any nuggets of your journalistic wisdom you would like me to convey to your son or daughter when he or she asks me what his or her Daddy was really like?"

Geoff approached Lisa and replied: "If it comes to that—and I don't think for a moment that it will—then I trust you to tell him or her for me, Lisa."

He saw Lisa bite her lip and tears well in her hazel eyes, causing them to shimmer, just as the authorisations allowing him to travel to the European mainland arrived.

Chapter 9

Private Philippa 'Pip' Clarke scanned the mountain ridges for any movement and exhaled, relief calming her nerves now darkness covered the terrain. She glanced back into the cave behind her and heard a gargled snore from Crimble.

Opposite the rocky overhang under which she crouched, across a broad valley, the mountain ridge became better defined, a shadowed grey above which the winter sky glowed an ugly, angry red. She rubbed the fresh bruising on her thigh and shin, recalling the engagement with the Spiders that had caused it as well as Crimble's broken arm. A sigh escaped her lips and she doubted for the hundredth time if ditching the bulk of their equipment had been the right decision. Her memory replayed the details of the firefight, how she and Crimble had ripped off the components of the Battlefield Management Support System, how they'd fled the immediate area, and how swiftly the next Spider had come down on their abandoned gear and destroyed it. Crimble had tried to suggest that deactivation might have been enough, but the violence and urgency of the battle saw both of them rip the modules and elements off their heads and out of their uniforms before retreating as fast as they were able. On the surface, of course it had been the right thing to do, but now they were isolated, faring little better than the civilians they were supposed to be defending.

Hours of searching for a suitable temporary refuge had ended in this dank cave. Pip hadn't realised how much the journey must have drained Crimble. With his broken arm trussed up in a splint composed of the flattest piece of wood Pip could find on the forest floor and torn strips of his tunic, he'd appeared to manage. But on reaching the cave, he crawled to the damp, craggy rear, pulled his legs up into a foetal position, and fell asleep almost at once.

Again, Pip scanned the distant, layered ridgelines of the Sierra Nevada Mountains and thought she saw the figures of refugees shuffling far away in the deepening gloaming. Pinpricks of light crisscrossed the orange sky and the distant mechanical noise made the Caliphate's machines sound like especially vicious mosquitoes. Confusion burned inside her, questions and potential answers flying back and forth in her mind like the enemy ACAs over their position. She shivered as a breeze of cooler air entered the cave and wondered how many ways the Spiders detected and selected targets.

"They must prioritise them," she mused aloud. "Military hardware first, personnel second, then... civilians?" She recalled the briefings they'd had before their deployment and replayed scenes of Caliphate brutality captured in Israel, Turkey and the European capitals. Her thoughts drifted to Pratty and Rory and all of her comrades who had died, to the certain decimation of her regiment, and then to the current situation and her own likely fate. Contradictory feelings jostled for supremacy inside her: on one hand, her eighteen months in the British Army had instilled an almost-complete reliance on the Squitch Battlefield Management Support System. Suddenly cut off from all of that support created a certain terror. On the other hand, this new freedom also fired her curiosity and caused the skin on the back of her neck to tingle, which balanced with the other, raw sensation she ascribed to survivor's guilt. A cynical voice in her head urged her to enjoy the reprieve while she could, for her odds of survival now had to be minimal.

They had a martial obligation to attempt to return to their unit, but Pip did not need her Squitch to tell her how impossible that would be. She favoured staying with the local civilians, perhaps trading survival tips for assistance. They'd probably be able to identify places offering the best cover. But in the longer term, in particular if they could not find a replicator, the problem of food would soon become acute. On the other hand—

Her thoughts stopped when, to the northwest and between thirty and forty degrees above the highest ridgeline, a group of pinprick lights suddenly broke out of the crisscross patterns she'd hitherto followed with her eyes. In seconds and without making a sound, at least fifty dull orange glows swept towards the closest ridgeline, descending in a graceful geometric pattern that reminded Pip of a theatrical light show her parents had taken her to see when she was a child. These lights erupted in puffs of explosions at various points along the ridgeline. A moment later, the dull thuds reached her ears.

Pip opened her mouth to ask the Squitch what had happened before recalling that now the Squitch wasn't there. She knew she'd just witnessed the battle-space saturation the briefings had talked about. With all military opposition neutralised, the enemy could begin wiping out the civilian population at its leisure. An arrow of guilt stabbed deep inside her spirit because she was part of the force responsible for protecting those civilians, and now they had no defence. She shuffled backwards into the cave, the rock surface damp and cool to her touch. Distant human shrieks drifted on the still night air and a rock fall whooshed down from somewhere far away, the stones sounding like a wave of water that stopped abruptly.

Her hand traced around to the body-heat concealment—or BHC—sleeve, packed in a pocket on the right calf of her trousers. Her index finger pushed the zip down to open the pouch. She tried to believe that the Caliphate ACAs had detected the civilians trying to use tech that the enemy had jammed. From a deep, fearful part of her mind, a voice doubted her conclusion, and suggested another answer: enemy ACAs also used old-fashioned thermal imaging to detect their targets.

Pip suddenly felt naked and vulnerable; just as she had when she'd ripped off her Battlefield Management Support System. She disliked disrobing under threat. She edged back further into the cave, aware that a passing ACA might detect a flash of her body heat. There would be little room for heroics: without her Squitch, a Spider could descend, attack and blow them to pieces before they were even aware of its approach.

"Crimble," she hissed.

"What?" he mumbled in an exhausted voice.

"We need to get our BHC sleeves on."

"Why? No, I'm knackered. Let me sleep."

She glanced through the entrance and half expected a Spider to come clattering through. Her muscles tensed as she told herself to get a grip. She zipped the pouch containing the BHC sleeve back up, common sense insisting they could not be detected inside this cave unless a Caliphate ACA flew right up to the entrance. However, going outside—for example to find water and food—now presented an entirely new level of risk.

She repeated to herself that those civilians had been detected by their tech: they tried to contact loved ones, the Caliphate detected the signals and attacked. But then, the enemy must have made huge territorial gains in the last two days, tens of thousands of square miles, and its ACAs had to have some kind of limits, either in number or range. A new consideration came to her: such gains must spread the enemy's resources. Rather than having to be fearful of attack from a Spider at any moment, perhaps there might be a way to estimate the risk more accurately? Pip glanced back over her shoulder at the injured Crimble, and in her mind the outline of a plan began to form.

Chapter 10

Turkish engineering student Berat Kartal stared in disbelief at the ragged people slouched by the side of the barn, part of a makeshift refugee camp. Unshaven men languished and their dishevelled women appeared gaunt. Young children languished in the women's arms and on their laps, while unkempt youths glanced at their parents for reassurance, or perhaps in a longing for food. This far south, the winter sun still burned with a heat that made frightened people sweat.

A flabby, belligerent Greek waved a stubby finger at a younger, dark-skinned man, who looked to be Turkish, and declared in halting English: "You do not know what you are saying. Of course our devices will come back—the government cannot let those *κακό* do what they like."

The younger man shrugged and answered in flawless English: "And you do know what you're saying? It's over. They've invaded and we're in more trouble than you realise."

A bearded man flanked by two teenagers shouted: "We should get to the coast and get a boat to Italy. It is only a few hours that w—"

"That is shit," shouted the Greek in increased dismissiveness. "We should do what our government told us. We do not need to run away—"

"You are a crazy old man," the bearded man responded with a contemptuous wave of his hand. "Come on," he said to the two teens. "Get your mother and aunt. We will continue." The two boys obeyed.

The obese Greek held his tongue, and Berat sensed that the man had decided to avoid inflaming the confrontation further. The younger man with the flawless English spoke to the Greek: "Our governments are finished. It's no use waiting for them to do something."

The Greek sniffed and said: "You are wrong. They know we are alone." He shrugged, which made the flesh on his arms wobble, and added: "Without data, we know nothing. We cannot be expected to cope in such situation."

The young man shook his head and replied: "Then shouldn't we assume the worst? Why do you think there is anyone left who might help us?"

The Greek nodded at his interlocutor and answered in a sarcastic tone: "Ah, so you are one of those young people who will always think that they know better, yes?"

"My age has nothing—"

"So I agree with you. Of course our very well defended governments are completely destroyed after only a few hours. You must certainly know that there is no hope left for any of us—"

"I spoke to some of your countrymen not one hour ago, and they insisted that they found a number of uniforms—police and fire-fighter—suggesting that the members of those services have decided to dress as civilians."

"Not true, not true!" the Greek man insisted after an offended gasp.

Berat's gaze drifted to the rest of the camp as the conversation droned back and forth between the two men. Hundreds of refugees lay resting or milled about the stream that wended and bubbled along at the lowest point in the valley. On either side of the unofficial camp, hills of green forest rose up to terminate in slate-grey rocky outcrops.

He shook his head at the incongruity of the scene about him. Whenever in his life he'd been in a large group of people, there had been a reason: his university campus; the electric atmosphere of a football match; the joyous noise of a music concert. Now, the individuals constituting this group all suffered, whether from thirst, hunger, injury, a lack of regular medicine, or simple fear. They languished, sullen and scared of what the future held. Berat's memory recalled his incredible journey so far: the first realisation that the Caliphate must have attacked when key components in his personal tech were burned out in the middle of the night; the desperate flight through his own country, struggling to keep ahead of the erupting storm; the boat from Turkey to Greece, full of refugees and the stench of claustrophobic fear; then the terrifying attack on Athens.

Without thinking, Berat patted the part of his rucksack that held his leather-bound paper journal. Of course it was still there, and he made a mental note to find a quiet place and describe this day's events before the light faded in a few hours. His determination to record as much as possible represented the core of his indignation and fury at what was happening to his country and Europe. With the Caliphate having disabled all modern technology, and apparently able to destroy anything its madman leader wished, Berat feared a complete rewriting of history. If the Caliphate overran and dominated Europe— which appeared to his engineer's brain to be a certainty—then he had to do something, however ultimately futile it might transpire to be, to satisfy his urge for defiance.

Berat's looked up the blue sky and his mind moved on to more immediate and practical issues. He estimated he was one day's good walking from the border with Albania. Like the bearded man and his family, many of the refugees had decided to head for the coast, close to the island of Corfu, and to attempt to get a boat to Italy and, they assumed, safety. However, Berat found it inconceivable that the Caliphate had only invaded on a single front—from out of Turkey—and believed they must also have opened fronts in Italy and probably other locations as well. The single fact of the lack of any international assistance for Greece's plight seemed to be more than sufficient confirmation that the countries closest to them must be enduring similar attacks.

The people around him, cut off suddenly from their technological crutches, did not appear to grasp the true extent of the disaster. To Berat's logical mind, one action allowed the supposition of other actions, then the construction of a web of reactions and the probability of them having occurred. He would have preferred to have had access to accurate data in real time, but he did not see its abrupt cessation as a sufficient reason for any kind of panic.

His stomach yawned, a vast bubbling contraction that caused him substantial discomfort and brought his mind back to his current situation. Again without thinking, he took out his bottle and poured some water down his throat, using liquid in place of food to try to fool his body into believing it was nourishment. Instead of refreshing him, he felt another stab of pain as his empty stomach contracted more strongly in protest at the absence of anything substantial. Over the last twenty-four hours, this discomfort had increased to actual pain, and he realised he needed to find some kind of sustenance.

He left the other refugees and headed north towards the Albanian border. His experience in Athens had taught him that crowds were best avoided in the event the Caliphate's machines fell on them without warning. As he followed a well-trodden trekking path into a sparse forest of young oaks and spruces, he tried to control the memories of pain and suffering he'd seen on the faces of the other refugees.

A shuffling noise caught his attention, and an old, thin man emerged ahead of him from the trees and shrubs. Berat assumed the man must have gone there to relieve himself.

The man called out: "Why are you going that way, little boy?"

Berat stopped and turned back. "Because I want to stay ahead of the invading forces?" he offered, unmoved by the look of contempt on his questioner's weathered face.

The old man gave a mirthless smile that revealed brown, rotted teeth and retorted: "And how will you do that, eh? Nothing works anymore. You cannot know even the time of day, except by guessing by the position of the sun. How can you find your way? How will you know anything, little boy?"

Berat couldn't decide how to reply. The man's odour rankled worse than most of the refugees, but his blank, simplistic conclusion left Berat nonplussed. The young engineering student shook his head and answered: "It is not possible to cope without our devices?"

The man scoffed and replied: "Look at them," he said, waving a withered hand at the makeshift refugee camp. "Lost, fat, struggling even to get the water from the stream, never mind food. What makes you think you can, eh?"

Berat decided to move on. He said: "I don't think the coast is the correct place to go," turned away and trudged on.

From behind him, he heard the old man call out: "What is better, little boy? The fear of uncertainty, or the certainty of knowing that we will die?" but the young Turkish engineering student ignored the question.

Chapter 11

07.34 Wednesday 22 February 2062

Fifteen-year-old Penka Genkova ran as fast as she could, her trainers crunching on the gravel pathways that separated the animal enclosures in Sofia zoo. She knew how to avoid the keepers, who were in any case few at this hour; she knew where to find her beloved Sasho, the one creature who never questioned her, who never demanded anything of her. A sudden crosswind blew strands of brown hair across her face and she sucked a few into her mouth as she gasped in the next breath. She pulled the hairs away and tried to tuck them behind her ear as she skirted an ornate water fountain which sat, dry and neglected, with only a few of the previous year's autumnal leaves in its basin.

The pain from yet another tumour burned inside her head, but she put that down to the abrupt stress of the invasion everyone had been talking about. She'd left her alcoholic mother in their dank, rundown flat in the notorious *Mladost 3* district and caught one of the early trams into the city centre. Instead of going to the hospital for her treatment, she'd come to the zoo. If what everyone said was true, then

Penka could forget about her treatment. At least that's what Penka's mother seemed to think, when she'd shouted at Penka through another drunken haze the previous night. Penka shook her head to dispel the unpleasant images. She wished she could help her mother, but it seemed her mother did not want to be helped.

She slowed to a jog as familiar pain began in her knees and hips, deep inside the ample flesh on her limbs. The chill morning air stung the split lower lip her mother had given her the previous evening. There was much Penka did not fully understand, foremost why her mother drank so much *rakia* when all it did was cause upset and anger.

Last week her physics teacher, who used to be kind to her, thrust his hand between her legs and told her she needed to 'give something back' for all the help he had given her. She'd quickly pushed him away and humoured him with a joke and a half-promise on which she intended to renege, just like she'd heard the other girls in her class do with their boyfriends. No boy her own age had ever shown an interest in Penka because her illness made it difficult for her to control her weight. It didn't matter: Penka had developed a resilience. She read romantic stories—just to know, she always told herself, to have an inkling of what other people enjoyed but which, like so many other things, had been denied· to her. These stories allowed her an escape with none of the real-world complications that she'd heard the other girls complain about.

She also could not work out why fate had decreed her to be one of the first to develop one of the new 'super cancers' which fought back against the all-conquering Geno-Fluid nanobots. As the increasing pain made her slow to a fast walk, recent memories surfaced in her mind's eye, of doctors and consultants shaking their heads at the rarity of her case, of their surprised and shocked looks that cells could still mutate so radically, even when surrounded by nanobots that were supposed to manage the sites. Penka's young body had become a microscopic battleground as micro-tumours grew in every limb and organ inside her. The nanobots chased them down only for more to spring up in different areas of her body. Specialists from around the world suggested that responsibility rested with a leak of a secret, synthetic biological weapon years previously, which had finally found its way into the food chain. She recalled one doctor, with very dark skin and an intense stare, who looked at her keenly and said that cancer had been 'eradicated' but now it had returned, a new and voracious strain in Penka and a few others like her around the world. But none of the experts could really answer why. The doctors helped her, they said her chances were good. She was young and strong. Then this morning, at last, Penka knew the nanobots—and therefore she—would lose. The invasion would destroy the hospital and the doctors.

Finally, she reached the primate enclosure as her ears noted new and strange sounds in the distance. A chill breeze blew her hair out from her head. She wished again that the lens in her eye worked and fought down her earlier confusion and panic when it had abruptly gone dark late last night. Of all the things that had happened to Penka in her young life, being cut off from society so suddenly had frightened her almost as much as the super-cancer.

She pushed the door in the high wooden structure that swept around in a horseshoe surrounded by a small lake and climbing frames for the gorillas and chimps to play on. Penka entered the house and hurried along the deserted corridor. She stopped and caught her breath. She rested her hand on a stripped-oak upright support and felt a trembling vibrate through the wooden post. Distant thuds punctured the air. She listened and concentrated to try and separate the sounds of the city from the noises the animals in the enclosure made.

She stopped when she saw Sasho a few metres from the glass. She ran to him.

Sasho sat close to a rope swing opposite the glass. Penka's smile faded when she saw his melancholy expression. She could sense at once that he was worried about her. She reached the glass that separated them and placed her hand on it, fingers spread out.

His simian brow furrowed and then he rolled his eyes as if to say, "What a mess, huh?"

Penka smiled and nodded her agreement.

Shasho shrugged and loped over to her. He put his right hand on the glass opposite hers, fingers also splayed, as he always did. Only the glass separated their touch.

Penka's breathing shallowed and accelerated as she struggled to find the words. Part of her brain noted that Sasho could not hear her words nor would he understand them if he could, but she spoke them anyway: "I'm sorry, I'm so sorry. They're coming. Bad people..." she reconsidered for a second, tutted, and amended: "Even worse people."

Sasho shrugged again and pursed his lips. He shook his head, heaved a sigh, and looked down at the floor of the chimpanzees' enclosure. To Penka, this meant: "Yeah, they're all horrible, but you've still got me."

"I know, I know," Penka said, slipping seamlessly into the same conversation she had with Sasho every time she came to be with him. Part of her mind had decided to block out the obvious, the inevitable, even as her ears registered the growing cacophony of deep thumps which could only denote explosions.

She tried to explain to the only creature that cared about her: "But you know, my dearest Sasho, they don't know what they're doing. They think they are being kind to you and your family. They try to make you happy, they try to show they care—" she stopped as a thud from outside seemed to rock the entire zoo. A loud rain of heavy things thumped onto the outside of the roof.

Sasho suddenly began shrieking, a piercing tonal bark that Penka had never heard him make before. Other members of the troupe behaved in a similar manner. Sasho left the glass and swung up on the ropes and dead tree limbs of the enclosure. Penka shivered at the sudden change in demeanour; now the family of chimps howled and flew about their mock jungle environment in fear-driven fury.

An abrupt shudder shook the ground around her, like a small earthquake, and she lost her balance. Dazed, she looked at the fresh graze on her hand as crimson blood oozed through scuffed skin. Pain invaded her senses. Sounds seemed to be very distant. Her young spirit questioned again why she had to feel the pain, why she had to suffer. She felt so tired of having to bear pain.

The door at the entrance to the enclosure collapsed with a tearing, wooden shriek. Penka hoped it was help, that someone, somewhere would care about the animals, if not her; that someone would do something. She looked towards the entrance and saw a large ball of silver metal partially embedded in the ground there. Articulated arms snapped out from the surface, and the last thing Penka saw was the Spider as it clattered towards her to take her in its deadly embrace.

Chapter 12

C rispin Webb watched the man with the cropped hair and rectangular glasses shake his head as he repeated: "Quantum encryption simply cannot be broken or otherwise circumvented, that's the whole point of it. How many times must I repeat myself?"

The Prime Minister, Dahra Napier, pinched the bridge of her nose and replied: "Doctor Canham, while we appreciate your explanations and your time in coming to speak with us today, we can't impress on you the seriousness of the situation facing us. Some kind of shortcut to help us reach our objective would be greatly appreciated by our defence forces."

The uneasiness on Doctor Canham's face amused Webb as he wondered what fiendish genetic problem the man must have to be obliged to wear glasses. In better days, Napier's aide mused, it used to be an enormous pleasure to watch the way people reacted if they couldn't give the boss what she wanted, especially when they had been summoned to a COBRA meeting. Enjoying the discomfort of others had been a pleasurable benefit of having power, but now an even

79

greater power from outside cast its shadow over all of them, and this tempered Webb's satisfaction.

"With the greatest respect, Prime Minister," Doctor Canham said, sounding sycophantic, "one would have to go back to a time before quantum computing—over thirty years—in which citizens' private data could simply be scooped up by, for example, GCHQ, and processed in bulk to identify certain trends in the general population. Those 'Wild West' days of no privacy and subverting democracy have long been over."

The Home Secretary, Aiden Hicks, said in a nasal tone: "But are you absolutely sure there is not a way super artificial intelligence can be repurposed to overcome this encryption?"

Doctor Canham's face seemed to be a mask of strained patience. He said: "As I explained at the outset, not without the data subject's permission—"

"In which case we'd hardly need super AI anyway," Napier broke in.

The doctor continued: "I'm no lawyer, but any attempt to breach citizens' privacy in such a way—"

The Foreign Secretary, Charles Blackwood, said: "They won't be worried about their privacy if they're dead." Webb noted Napier's sigh.

Aiden Hicks's double chin wobbled as he turned his head back and forth to look at everyone around the table. He said: "It looks like we have to accept the need to conduct a general appeal."

"My god," Blackwood complained, "when was the last time an English government conducted any kind of public information campaign?"

The answer immediately flashed up in Crispin's vision, so he said: "That was in March 2048, when Wood's government appealed for volunteers to assist with tidal—"

Napier silenced him with a raised hand and said: "Yes, thank you, Crispin, but I rather think the Foreign Secretary's question was rhetorical."

Hicks spoke: "Besides, this is hardly an appeal for assistance. What we need now is as many young people as we can muster who are willing and able to join the Armed F—"

"Er, if I might make a suggestion, Prime Minister?" Doctor Canham broke in, with more than a little courage, Webb thought.

She nodded her assent.

The doctor continued: "I believe it might be worth utilising the local civil defence groups that are already quite well established."

Heads around the table looked in surprise at the dowdy, middle-aged civil servant who'd been summoned to brief the COBRA meeting on the potential by-passing of quantum encryption and the on-going recruitment drives for the Armed Forces.

Doctor Canham went on: "With all due respect, Prime Minister, and—er, the rest of you—I believe many people already comprehend what is happening on the continent, and are, shall we say, quite ahead of His Majesty's Government in this respect." Doctor Canham paused as if unsure of whether he had overstepped his remit.

Napier glanced at Webb and gave her aide a half-smile. She said to the doctor: "Please, go on."

"I think that instead of trying to find a shortcut of doubtful legality to reach people, which would run the risk of offending and alienating quite a number of the general population, it would be more productive to be open, to run a public appeal for volunteers. The advantage would be two-fold. First, you would create a sense of us all being in this together, rather than those in power resorting to some kind of subterfuge. And secondly, this would cause those who want to help to do so, possibly with more willingness. Whether you use subterfuge or not, it will not make a difference to those citizens who will refuse to help due to ill-health, indifference or age."

Webb watched his boss push her chair back a little and cross her right leg over her left. A priority communication arrived in his lens that told him Sir Terry Tidbury was ready to give COBRA the latest update on the progress of the invasion. Webb said: "Okay, thank you, doctor." He stood up and indicated the door. Doctor Canham also rose.

"Yes, thank you," Napier added. "That was very informative."

The doctor pushed his glasses up his nose and picked up a small briefcase.

Webb opened the door to the COBRA conference room and let Doctor Canham go first. "We need you to wait outside for a few minutes for security reasons. We will call you back in shortly."

The doctor nodded his understanding.

Webb followed the doctor through the door and called out to the woman waiting at the reception desk in the open space: "Monica, would you organise some refreshments for the doctor?"

Napier's PA acknowledged Webb's request with a nod and Webb returned to the conference room. Some of the attendees muttered to each other but stopped when the door clicked shut.

Napier said: "That was a good idea. While certainly not one of the original intentions of their formation, the civil defence organisations could also be used to coordinate a recruitment drive to the Armed Forces. Very well, we'll design and commence a more... traditional appeal." She looked at Webb and instructed: "Link to the War Rooms now, please."

"Of course, Prime Minister," he answered. He tapped a screen in the worn oak table in front of him and paused, waiting for a response. When it came, Webb tapped again and the bald, round head of General Sir Terry Tidbury filled the south wall.

The commander of the British Armed Forces said: "Good morning. I hope you're not projecting me at full size on that wall there. That would be disturbingly close."

Faces broke into half-smiles as Webb reduced the size of the General and his surroundings to dimensions that matched more closely those of the physically present attendees.

Napier said: "Let's begin with the latest news from the fronts. General?"

Terry's face remained passive and his voice flat, as though he were relating a weather report. "Day four of the invasion is seeing the enemy advance broadly as our computers have forecast. He is making rapid gains on all four fronts. If I may, PM?"

Napier answered: "Of course."

A thumbnail emerged from the bottom of the screen, smothering Terry's head and expanding to cover all of the south wall. A map of Europe faced Webb and the others in the conference room, and various areas enlarged and retracted as Terry spoke: "In Spain, the enemy's Warrior Group West has two spearheads advancing from the south and west, gaining an average of fifty kilometres a day. We are getting reports here of very aggressive tactics towards the civilian population on the spearheads' flanks, which go some way beyond the militarily required minimum to ensure no interference from NATO forces.

"Further east, Italy has now been cut in two. The southern half of the country is isolated, and due to the impenetrability of the enemy's jamming, we have no information on what is happening there. Over in Greece, the situation is little better. Advance units of Warrior Group East are making rapid progress, so much so that NATO forces there are taking casualties because they can't pull back fast enough. It goes without saying that our troops are being obliged to allow tens of thousands of refugees to fall into Caliphate hands.

"Finally, the Istanbul front is advancing up through Bulgaria and we have lost contact with Sofia. The computers forecast that the two eastern fronts will be the first to link up, which we anticipate in the first few days of March. So far, the enemy has only deployed its primary, bomb-armed ACA, the Blackswan. Its secondary ACA, the laser-equipped Lapwing, has yet to make an appearance over the European battlefields."

Webb saw Napier look at the others around the conference table and her face seemed as ashen as theirs did. A pink-faced young male assistant to the Chancellor made an audible gulp.

With a note of despondency, Home Secretary Aiden Hicks repeated Terry's observation: "So the invasion is indeed progressing exactly as our computers said it would."

Napier asked: "Are there any options to delay the enemy's advance, no matter how improbable?"

Webb felt a flash of cynicism mixed with respect at the bravery the boss always seemed to deploy when in front of her subordinates, constantly looking for positives.

The map of Europe withdrew to reveal Terry's bald head. He said: "SACEUR in Brussels is coordinating research into alternatives, however remote they might be. But the enemy is sweeping over the continent in an invasion that, so far, has been perfectly executed. And frankly speaking, our forces are no match for him."

"But won't they be obliged even to pause for at least a while? Overextended supply chains and all that?" Blackwood asked, aghast.

Terry replied: "We do not anticipate that, no. We need to bear in mind that this is the first major war that has been fought with super artificial-intelligence and other modern technology. We must assume the enemy, like us, has replicators for food and water for his armies. Up to now, we believe that, also like us, they cannot replicate certain munitions, but given their advantage in firepower, that might not matter in any case."

Napier spoke: "General, thank you for this update. Before you joined us, we had been debating the best recruitment strategy to encourage people to join the Armed Forces in England and, we hope, the other Home Countries. Would you like to have some input on that?"

Webb bit his lip. A voice inside his head asked what the fucking point of that was, and part of him hoped the head of the British Army would say exactly that.

Terry's brow furrowed in consideration and he replied: "I suppose there might be a scenario in the future when more troops could help to delay the inevitable, but in the current circumstances, I would suggest it is highly unlikely any number of new troops—barely trained, inexperienced in battle—could seriously hinder the invasion of the British Isles in a few weeks' time."

Napier said to Terry's image: "But it might be a good idea to get people busy, keep them occupied, yes?"

Terry head tilted in consideration. He answered: "That would be more of a political decision, PM."

"Quite," she said. Then to Webb: "Crispin, show Doctor Canham back in, would you?"

"Of course," Webb replied, getting up.

Napier looked at the image and said: "Sir Terry, we have an expert with us who has prepared a report. I have invited him here to deliver the summary in person. I think you might like to hear what he has to say."

"Very well, PM," Terry replied.

Webb showed Doctor Canham back into the room. The slight, bespectacled form shuffled to the seat he'd vacated only a few minutes before.

Napier spoke: "Welcome back, Doctor Canham. Please give us a summary of the assessment you and your department have carried out regarding expanding our Armed Forces."

Canham said: "All data I will use is the most current available. As of today, England has a little under sixteen million, seven hundred thousand people of military age—in the eighteen-to-forty-nine age group. As our remit was to assume the introduction of conscription—"

Foreign Secretary Blackwood broke in and spluttered: "PM, are you serious? If we take such a radical step—"

"Charles, it's quite all right," Home Secretary Hicks said, raising a placating hand. "The PM and I discussed this purely as a hypothetical scenario and only to be implemented if the volunteer campaign does not yield sufficient numbers."

Charles Blackwood let out an offended huff.

"Let's just get on with it, shall we?" Napier said.

The doctor cleared his throat and resumed: "Data analysis by super artificial intelligence has confirmed our suspicions regarding levels of obesity in the general population." He gave the room a long look before continuing: "One of this government's key pledges since the last general election has been to lower levels of obesity in all age groups."

Webb had a morbid feeling as the new double meaning of the phrase 'the last general election' came to him. New data announced itself in the lower right of his vision, and as a distraction he began reading secure updates on the Caliphate's advance.

With one ear, Webb listened to Canham continue: "Success can be described as patchy at best. Diet and lifestyle choices, in addition to societal peer pressure, have prevented substantive measures from having the anticipated impact…"

Reports from the four fronts scrolled up Webb's vision and he marvelled at the destruction being wrought in southern Europe. A sudden change in the atmosphere in the room dragged Webb's attention back to his immediate surroundings.

Foreign Secretary Charles Blackwood's round head whipped back and forth, looking as though it might topple off his slender neck. He said: "That's ridiculous. One in three? One-third of the entire able-bodied population of the Home Countries? There must be some mistake."

The bespectacled civil servant remained unfazed, saying: "Not at all. It is, in fact, quite an interesting irony."

"What do you mean?" Napier asked.

The doctor explained: "At the outbreak of the First World War a hundred and fifty years ago, the British Army had a similar rejection rate—thirty-two percent—that we can expect to see today. Then, the cause was poverty-driven malnutrition and its effects, whereas now it is due to poverty-driven obesity and its effects."

Hicks looked at Napier in disquiet and asked: "Where's Joanne? Shouldn't she be here to explain this?"

Webb answered: "She's on maternity leave, scheduled to give birth in a few days."

"How ironic," Blackwood muttered, "a Health Secretary absent for health reasons."

Home Secretary Hicks spoke again, his nasal accent starting to grate on Webb's nerves: "It hardly matters. I agree with the PM: let's give people something to do, something to focus on." Pudgy hands reached for the carafe of water in front of him. He filled the glass next to it and said: "In any case, we still won the First World War."

On the screen, Terry frowned and announced: "PM, three of the five Spanish transports have just touched down at Brize Norton."

"The other two?" Napier asked without confidence.

"Contact was lost shortly after take-off. It's unlikely they're still in the air."

"Thank you, Terry."

Hicks looked at Napier and asked: "Our people or Spanish VIPs?"

Webb thought he heard his boss's voice crack a little when she replied: "No, Spanish. Wives and children of Spanish government members, among others. Sir Terry, any news of the evacuations from the other countries under attack?"

Terry shook his head.

"Thank you. Very well, let's end there for today."

Webb stood up at once, as it pressured the others to do so, thereby helping to end the meeting as expeditiously as possible.

Most of the attendees also rose, but Hicks remained seated and said: "Excuse me, PM, but can't we find some time to review tidal defences?"

Webb flashed the man a stern look, but the Home Secretary offered a disinterested sneer in response.

Napier replied: "Not today, Aiden, there really is too much—"

"With respect, PM," Hicks broke in, "more than a hundred people drowned last night around the coast of England, more than three—"

"Yes, and the Minister for Coastal Defence briefed me earlier this morning, so there's no need for your concern, Aiden," Napier insisted. She turned and left the COBRA meeting room, and Webb followed her, making a mental note to recommence digging into some suspect business deals in which Hicks had been involved when on the back benches, just in case the boss needed some ammunition with which to replace him in the near future.

Chapter 13

20.59 Wednesday 22 February 2062

Maria Phillips gritted her teeth and looked down at the pack of cards as she shuffled them, over and over; cut, shuffle, over and over.

"Come on, dear," she heard her mother say.

Maria said: "First jack deals," and started flipping a card over in front of each player around the table: her mother Jane, her oldest brother Martin, and their father Anthony. The seventh card was a jack, landing at her father's bony hands. "Your deal, dad," she said, scooping up the cards and handing the pack to him.

"Right-ho," her father answered, giving the pack another shuffle and dealing.

Maria saw the look on Martin's face opposite her. He raised an eyebrow in inquiry; she gently shook her head. She glanced down and drew the scoring grid on the paper in front of her: the first four columns for each player's bid, the second four for their scores. "Okay. Forecast whist, hearts are trumps. My first call and lead."

Maria's father finished dealing and set the remaining cards to one side. As the four players picked up their hands, Maria heard Martin give a cough and her heart began beating harder in her chest. To delay the inevitable, she announced: "I think I can win three of these," and wrote the digit down in the 'forecast' column on the pad.

Without being asked, her mother said: "Put me down for one please, dear."

Keeping her eyes on the pad and pen in front of her, she asked: "Martin?"

Her brother cleared his throat and said: "Listen, guys. Me and my little sis have got something to tell you."

"Not yet," Maria cautioned.

"It's okay, Maz," Martin answered.

Maria flashed Martin a reproachful look. They'd agreed earlier that they would wait a few hands before giving their parents the news. At the same time, Maria knew her brother and understood how he hated waiting where difficult or problematic situations were concerned; he preferred to get things out of the way.

She saw that both parents had stopped looking at their cards and now stared at Martin. Her father's brow creased and he said: "Yeah? What is it?"

Martin drew in a breath and said: "Maria and I have decided to join up."

"What?" their father exclaimed.

"The army is going to need—"

"You must be out of your minds," their father broke in. "What on earth do you think you're going to be able to do? Apart from get yourselves killed?"

"Dad," Martin began, "the government put out an appeal this afternoon. Napier explained—"

"Her? You shouldn't listen to that lot. They're shysters, cheats, career politicos who absolutely do not give a single sh—"

"Anthony, let the boy speak," their mother urged.

"Dad," Martin said, "you were okay with this last week. You accepted it then. What's changed?"

"They've let the war start and we're losing, that's what's changed," he spat. "Last week, it was preventable. It could've been stopped. It should've been stopped. Now, people are dying, lots of them. And it's Napier's and Coll's fault. Whatever they bleat on about in public, they could've made China stop those crazies. The fact that they haven't implicates them."

Maria saw anger flash across her brother's face. He said: "Dad, don't you think it's about time we let go of that partisan bullshit? I say we've got to go beyond what we've been used to, you know?"

Anthony said: "You start down that road if you want to, but don't expect my support. You don't know where this is all going to lead—"

"We're facing the destruction of Europe," Martin said, shaking his head in defiance, but Maria noticed a tremor in his jaw.

Their father's voice rose in anger: "I'll tell you where it's going to lead, shall I?" A tense silence descended before her father spat out two words: "Cannon fodder."

Their mother put her cards on the table and said: "Darling, I don't think it's right to draw historical paral—"

Anthony stopped her with a raised hand. "Yes, yes it is right. And it is even more relevant today." Maria and Martin shifted under his piercing gaze as his head turned back and forth. He told them: "There's a book I've got upstairs, I read it again at the weekend. It was written nearly a hundred and fifty years ago, in the 1920s."

"Oh, bang up to date then," Martin muttered, and Maria wondered how much time her brother would give their father.

"Yeah. A load of interviews with young couples, people not much older than you, young lad. And you know what? They decided not to have kids. And you know why?"

No one spoke.

"Because they knew there'd be another war, and they weren't prepared to have kids that the military would use as cannon fodder. Think about that. They decided not to have children so as not to see what they'd love and nurture blown to bits for nothing. And they were right, too."

"That's hardly a valid comparison, Dad," Martin said, his voice thick with sarcasm.

"Yes, it is. You spoilt brats don't realise how lucky you've been, how lucky we've all been, in truth."

Maria said: "I think we're a bit old to be called sp—"

But her father spoke over her: "The same goes for my generation, and several generations before that…" he voice trailed off. Maria saw melancholy glisten in her father's eyes. He lamented: "We took peace for granted. They took peace for granted."

Martin said: "Dad, I get how you feel, I do, but we've got to adjust to the new reality. We just can't do nothing."

Maria's mother added: "I've told you before, darling: we do not write our children's scripts. Their lives are their own, not ours. All we can do is nurture them and help them where possible."

Anthony sat back in his chair and sighed. To Maria, he appeared to have aged five years in the last five minutes. He picked up his cards and stared at them. Maria did the same, noting her mother and brother also picking theirs up. Her father's voice sounded lower when he spoke, still staring at his cards: "We should enjoy it, then. In a few weeks we'll all likely be dead."

"No, we won't," their mother replied.

"How many tricks do you want, Martin?" Anthony asked.

"Yeah, I'll have three."

Maria noted the number down and said: "You can't call zero, dad."

"Two," he replied.

Martin said: "Dad, it's the machines that will do the fighting, not people. I'm reading the news—I've got three feeds running in my lens right now—and all over the place NATO pulls the troops back when our own ACAs are done for."

Maria laid the strongest card in the pack, the ace of hearts, and said nothing. Her mother tutted and laid the three. Her brother shook his head and laid the seven.

Her father said: "Nice one, love," and laid the eight.

Maria collected the first trick and then laid the queen of hearts, which elicited scoffs from around the table.

"The point is," their father said, "that NATO can only pull back so far before some kind of stand has to be made. What's happening to all the civilians left behind then, eh?"

Martin's thick eyebrows came together and he said: "Well, er, those who can't escape—"

"Right," her father broke in. "The invasion's started. There's this great big wave of shit heading up from the Med towards us…"

Maria stopped listening as her father ranted on, glancing instead at her mother. Jane's shoulders slumped in their familiar way when she sat at the dining table, listening to Anthony. Maria saw the grey roots of her mother's hair and how the skin on her neck had gathered in narrow folds. Maria understood and admired her mother's strength; strength that only a woman and a mother could marshal. Men could always be angry, even violent; they never seemed to have to think about the consequences of their actions. Like an avalanche or rockfall, men clattered their way through life, upsetting and destroying order and bringing chaos, only for the women who could muster the energy to care for them to clean up their mess—

The door to the dining room crashed open to reveal her older brother, Mark. His tall, slender frame heaved in breath after shallow breath. A stench invaded the room, like a cesspit.

With a nonchalance that Maria knew masked a deep resentment, the oldest sibling Martin laid his cards on the table, turned in his chair, and said to the middle child: "Hello, brother. It smells like the piss and shit sacks in your total immersion suit need emptying. Do you still have sufficient muscle mass to manage that?"

"Fuck you, brother," came the sneering response.

Martin began to get up, but Maria's father grabbed Martin's arm. Anthony hissed: "No, I won't have that. Not in the family." Anthony left his seat and limped over to Mark, and Maria wondered how much her father's bad knee must have been paining him. He spoke to Mark: "That was the last time you speak to anyone in the family like that, fella."

"He started it."

"I don't care who started it. You're still kids, all three of you," their father shouted. He pointed a finger at Mark: "You, in your twenties and still playing stupid kids' games, while those two think they're going to join up and do god-knows-what in the army, when they look like they're only just out of nappies."

Maria cringed when she heard her father reveal what she and Martin had decided to do, and she saw Mark's jaw fall open. Mark looked from their father to Martin and then to

Maria. "Seriously?" He said. "You're going to join up? Really?"

Martin stood up, his slim body partially turning out of the seat to face Mark. He said with menace: "Do not mock us, brother, for doing something in this reality which you only pretend to do in your fake realities."

Mark took a step back and Maria saw everyone glance nervously at each other. Mark's shoulders slumped and in a calmer voice he said: "Mock you? Why would I do that?"

"Watch it, lad," their father cautioned, limping back a step.

Mark glanced from his father to his siblings at the table. He said in a neutral tone: "In there," he said, thumbing back to the room from which he'd emerged, "I can die a hundred times a day, but I'm still all right. Out here, you can only die once, and then you're dead forever. So, who do you think I reckon has the right idea about all of this Caliphate bullshit?"

Anger burned inside Maria. Before anyone else could speak, she stood up and her chair fell backwards, making a loud scraping noise as it hit wooden slats on the patio window behind her. She hissed: "How dare you come in here and spoil our game of Forecast Whist?"

Mark put his hands out in mock offence and said: "Hey, little sis—"

"Don't patronise me, Mark."

Mark shook his head, saying: "I only came out here for a clean up and something to eat. You people really are totally—"

"Tell us, Mark," Maria asked with as much venom in her voice as she could muster, "what will you do when the Caliphate come knocking on our door? When the power is cut and you and your juvenile friends are forced out of those immature games that no stupid little boy over the age of nine should be allowed to play? What then, Mark, when one of

97

those crawling Caliphate bombs comes to wrap itself around you before blowing you into a million little pieces?"

Mark's chest heaved as he breathed. He sneered and said: "Because it is not only about stupid games, little sister. There are networks in there, networks very alive to the threat all of you out here face. And you better believe me—and I mean all of you—when I tell you that what we're doing will lead to changes here, in the real world."

"Care to explain?" Maria asked in open cynicism.

Mark shrugged and answered: "I can't. It's secret."

Maria decided she'd had enough. She said: "Bullshit. Go back to your games, little boy."

Chapter 14

Trainee nurse Serena Rizzi had lost any concept of the 'worst day of her life'. Back then—*then*—the normal times so brutally terminated twelve days ago with the first attack on Rome, the 'worst day of her life' would constitute losing a patient unnecessarily, perhaps a GenoFluid pack malfunction or a cloned organ replacement gone unexpectedly wrong. But such losses used to be very rare. She would discuss these cases with her fellow nurses and the doctors, and there was always an element of novelty in each one, as if the act of dying itself had become a noteworthy event that affected only centenarians struggling with too many repeatedly cloned organs and those who suffered the most outrageous bad luck.

However, in the last few days Serena had witnessed more death than she thought she would in her entire career. And on this chill Thursday morning, as she peeked with terrified curiosity over the sill of the smashed window, she realised she was about to witness more death. Twenty metres below her in what used to be a school athletics area, she guesstimated two hundred men had been herded into sports courts surrounded by chain-link fencing three metres high. The dull grey cloud meant that she could barely see the faces of individuals, but they seemed to be men of all ages: gangly youths, defiant men in their thirties and forties, and older ones bent over with age. They stood still and silent in immobile groups with only occasional glances among each other.

Around the perimeter stood Caliphate warriors armed with long-barrelled guns. Flowing head-coverings came down over baggy tunics with legs covered in a type of desert-camouflage material. Masks covered their eyes, noses and mouths. Thirty or more of them stood immobile outside the chain-link perimeter. Spats of cold rain began hitting the ground, the men, the warriors, and Serena's window sill.

From outside her field of view came the sound of whining, a coarse grating of metal on concrete that must have been made by some kind of vehicle. Despite her fear, she pushed her head forward and craned it to the right to see a large, tracked vehicle—certainly not anything recognisably Western—trundle along the street. It appeared to be driverless, with a bulbous front giving way to a rear of high, straight lines that looked as though it could be carrying some kind of cargo. Parked vehicles at the roadside disappeared under its tracks with sounds of grinding metal and the tinkling of broken glass. For an instant, Serena wondered why the super AI that controlled the private vehicles did not intervene, before remembering it could not and never would again. The Caliphate vehicle turned to the right, its tracks churning the kerb stones as its five-metre length moved closer to the chain-link fencing that held the local men.

The cold, damp air thickened with a sense of foreboding. The vehicle stopped adjacent to one side of the chain-link fencing. In the middle of the rear section, two white, featureless panels slid open to reveal a convex, opaque shape that appeared to be made of glass, like a huge camera lens. The captors moved away from the vehicle, all the time pointing their guns at the men trapped on the sports court. Abruptly, a spark of panic must have flared. A young, athletic man shrieked, threw himself at the fence and climbed. At once, a Caliphate warrior aimed his rifle and fired. The athletic man's left arm flew away from his body, taking a chunk of torso with it. Both body and limb fell to the ground, landing with wet slaps that Serena heard over the rain.

She gasped, momentarily forgetting the extreme danger she herself was in. She looked down on the scene with growing despair as the violence caused panic to spread. First, the captive men moved *en masse* away from where the victim fell. Then, the guard who had fired shouted something in a language Serena did not understand, and his compatriots laughed with sufficient vigour that she could be certain from her vantage point that they were indeed laughing.

She felt tears well in her eyes as all of the guards opened fire. Panic swept through the enclosure as the trapped men ran this way and that, not knowing how they could avoid the random slaughter. Most of them lay flat. After around twenty shots, one particular Caliphate warrior shouted something and the others stopped firing. The Caliphate warriors moved further back from all sides of the chain-link fence.

Serena noticed an odd, distant clicking sound, rapid like a cricket chirruping to a mechanical time signature. The fence closest to the vehicle melted. The trapped men who still stood turned as one to move away, and then each of them collapsed and burned. The myriad colours of the clothes—denim, T-shirts, shirts, jackets—uniformly blackened. Occasionally, Serena saw a flash of orange flame among the hissing steam and smoke that poured off the bodies, but the only sounds that reached her ears were truncated shrieks and moans. A few outliers in the group leapt for the fences at either side, but barely pulled themselves up to the top before their clothes and hair erupted in flame.

When the men must have all been killed, Serena expected the machine to stop. But to her surprise it kept on clicking. The rain continued to drizzle, and steam wafted up from the pyre. Minutes passed. The burned bodies liquefied, congealed, merged, and the singular black mass in the centre shrank, the sharp edges of bones protruding. Black lumps around the peripheries—that a few minutes earlier had been men—also reduced down as time passed. The Caliphate warriors moved off, probably to loot, Serena conjectured.

Still staring in fascination, she backed away from the smashed window. Her calves, knees and thighs ached and broken glass crunched under her feet as she staggered back into the abandoned apartment she'd taken refuge in the previous evening. Her stomach ached but she couldn't decide if the cause was hunger or dread. Her right hand stroked her thigh and felt again the long kitchen knife she had tied under her skirt with a strip of material torn from some linen she'd found in a cupboard.

She did not know where to go next; she did not understand why she had been spared at the hospital. *Then*, she had been sure; *then*, she had known—even felt—that God had protected her because he had further use for her on Earth, but since *then*, doubts had sprouted like autumn mushrooms in the darker parts of her soul.

Broken glass crunched under her feet once more as she returned to the window and looked down at the pyre. In fifteen minutes, two hundred men had been reduced to a boiling black slurry that might be carted away in the back of a pickup truck. Serena felt a wrenching inside her spirit, as though God now guided her head and eyesight, as if he said to her: "Child, your journey now, for me, will be filled with pain and suffering, but this is the role I have ascribed to you. You must witness—"

Serena's communion with the Father snapped when she heard footsteps outside the apartment door. A glance through the window showed that most of the warriors had disappeared. Her mind cut through her sudden panic and ordered her to the bathroom, the location furthest from the front door. Glass crunched underfoot but the movement of her limbs helped her to focus. In the bathroom, with her back pressed against the wall between the shower and bath, she angled her head so that the large mirror on the opposite wall allowed her to see through the doorway, into the spacious hall. She fought to control her breathing as her chest heaved in and out. She had to decide what course to take. Did she want to die here, now?

The loud, deliberate footsteps advanced into the apartment at a leisurely pace. Serena's hand felt again for the large kitchen knife that made sweat collect where it rested next to the skin of her thigh. She saw a small movement reflected in the mirror, and then with a sudden, deafening explosion and crash, the mirror shattered into a thousand pieces. The whole room shook, and Serena gasped in shock and pain. Dust billowed out from the impact. She looked down and saw fresh, discoloured liquid on her legs. She slid down the wall and coughed.

Footsteps crunched into the bathroom and Serena lifted her head to see a Caliphate warrior pointing a rifle at her. He made a series of urgent sounds. Serena thought he would kill her. She began to reach for the knife, but he stepped forward, lifted the rifle out of the way, and punched her on the side of her face. With more guttural utterances, the warrior grabbed Serena's hair and, with great strength, dragged her from the bathroom.

Chapter 15

18.16 Thursday 23 February 2062

Corporal Rory Moore let the water soak into his gums for a moment before gulping it down. He felt his body come back to life as the liquid chilled the back of his throat and made his headache return. He recalled his training and knew he had to fight the urge to gorge himself, so after enough gulps to satisfy his initial thirst, he paused, heaving in breath after breath and listening to the soft rush of the waterfall on the other side of the small lake.

"Bastards," he hissed. "Fucking bloody bastards." Speaking the words caused his lips to split again and sting. The urge to keep drinking until his stomach burst gnawed at him. He swore aloud again and then forced himself up from the edge of the lake to sit back against a hard, cold granite rock. He looked at the smears of dirt on his BHC sleeve and a part of him still marvelled at how it could remain intact after four days of crawling and hiding and witnessing a slaughter of civilians that he never imagined could happen.

With refreshment came the shaking. He tensed every muscle in his body to stop it, and a moment later the shaking morphed into shivering before finally abating. The cavity below his chest shrank back so that his stomach muscles seemed to clench around his spine. He reflected sardonically that he'd never been in such great shape. Partly healed cuts on his hands wept pus which, he considered, would have smelled worse if he'd had food in his body.

Rory knew that these were the least of his problems. He could not estimate the number of civilians killed by Caliphate ACAs. At first, he'd tried to note and remember the details of the raids: the number of ACAs, location, speed, distance, direction and estimate of potential casualties because, although he doubted the intel would be of any use if and when he returned to his unit, it helped him find some kind of order. But the random, indiscriminate nature of the attacks soon defeated him. He'd been shadowing some of the hundreds of civilians who had fled into the Sierra Nevada Mountains when the invasion began and their towns had been devastated. He assumed they would be the experts in keeping out of sight. Instead, he'd witnessed how the enemy's relentless assaults slowly whittled their number.

As the cold from the rock seemed to seep into his bone marrow, the image of the boy in the cave came back to him. He'd died in agony, the only conscious survivor of a Spider attack some time previously. Morbid curiosity had driven Rory close to the cave entrance; the boy's pathetic mewling had pulled him inside, into a shelter turned into an abattoir. He died with terrified, pleading eyes.

Rory slapped his hand on the wet stones at the edge of the lake and swore again. He could manage the guilt; he knew he had to if he were to last any length of time. Besides, the fact that he could remain almost invisible inside his BHC sleeve was merely an accident of circumstance. But the overwhelming sense of fatalism became increasingly difficult to control. It felt to him that the entire population of Europe had mere weeks before the endless swarms of these ACAs dispatched them by blast or flame.

He leaned back down to the lake's edge and sucked more water into his empty stomach. He tried to return to his priorities. Greatest urgency was security of shelter; he needed to find a building or village with a deep cellar or other underground facility that could be barricaded or otherwise defended. Four days without food did not trouble him; he'd decided the weight loss would do him good and for the first ten days he needn't worry. His only concern would be that any replicators were certain to be smashed or otherwise broken, and as it was February, he didn't expect there to be a great deal of fresh produce.

From history lessons at school, he recalled stories of stored foods, preserved in metal containers that allegedly used to last for years, but the only types that had survived to the present day were fruit preserves and some tinned meats. Even the thought of such food made his stomach ache in painful yearning.

He pulled himself up onto all fours and then used the cold, damp granite rock to get to his feet. As usual, he waited a few seconds for the light nausea to pass before he dared to take a step forward. The gloaming increased as night came on and he wondered if the growing shadows would play the same tricks on him as the previous evenings, by making small crevices in rock surfaces appear as secluded as caves. He took an unsteady step towards a shadow which he hoped would offer a passably dry cave for the night. The water had refreshed him, but the hunger stole his strength like a thief. Nevertheless, fortune favoured him on this evening as the first crevice he entered swallowed him whole. Inside, he found an angled bed of slate formed millennia ago which, when he covered himself in his BHC sleeve, offered a surprising level of comfort. As soon as he lay down, exhaustion swept over him.

Cuts and bruises became tolerable if acceptance of the discomfort they caused allowed him to rest.

Chapter 16

Two hundred and fifty metres southeast of the cave in which Corporal Rory Moore slept, and approximately eighty metres lower among the rocks and forest, Private Philippa 'Pip' Clarke stared out at the sky as the first stars appeared, sharp and bright, and she wished herself away to whatever planets orbited those suns.

Crimble's voice croaked out from behind her, in the darkness of the cave. "How's it looking tonight?"

"Getting better every night, mate," she replied.

Crimble groaned and said: "Tell me again how that's possible."

"Simple," Pip began, noting the brief yellow streak of a falling star. "Assuming the enemy is advancing unopposed, then they are gaining tens of thousands of square miles of territory every day."

"So?"

"So, unless they've got unlimited supplies of ACAs, those that they have got, have got to cover more and more territory."

109

"Meaning your Operation Certain Death has lost some of its certainty, yeah?"

Pip smiled to herself and replied: "Yup, we could replace 'Certain' with 'Highly Likely'. And with each day the bastard Caliphate moves further into Europe, the better our odds become."

"Odds of what, pal? We're behind the lines, in the middle of fucking nowhere."

"There's always a way out. Well, that's what I ended up telling my last boyfriend, anyway."

Pip heard a shuffle as Crimble shifted his position. He said: "Pal, we've got no guns, no tech, and our unit has been destroyed. We're only still alive thanks to dumb luck. I seriously admire your positivity, but we are as essentially screwed as the civilians."

"How's the arm, mate?"

"That's the other thing. It's starting to whiff a bit, you know? Do you know what can happen to broken bones that don't get treated with a GenoFluid pack within a few hours?"

"Not sure. How bad does it smell?"

"Not good."

She recalled what she knew about wounds that became infected. She said: "We should get you to a hospital."

"Yeah, piece of piss, that, especially in these circumstances," Crimble muttered.

Pip retreated into the cave. She reached him, wished again they had at least kept a torch, remembered that would've meant keeping the tech attached to it, and thus they'd certainly be dead now, sighed, and said: "How much is it hurting, really?"

"I try not to think about it, to be honest."

Her vision improved a fraction in the darkness, aided by the weak light outside reflecting off the wet surfaces in the cave. She could make out Crimble unwrapping his infected right arm. "Christ," she said when the smell reached her.

"Yeah, I said it wasn't good," Crimble replied.

"We've got to get moving—"

"No, I'm knackered and this arm's itching like a bitch with a dose of the clap. Let me sleep."

"Sorry, mate. Not tonight."

"What are you doing?" Crimble asked in response to Pip putting her arms around his shoulders.

"We've got to move. Now. Cover that stinking mess up, will you?"

"Jesus," he said, pulling the material back over the bloated, gangrenous arm. Then he swore aloud again.

"It's so painful?"

"Yeah, slightest touch. It's bollocks, frankly speaking."

"Shit," Pip said, wondering how quickly it would worsen. She recalled reading somewhere that septicaemia could kill within days or even hours, depending on a number of variables.

Crimble said: "I've got an idea. Just let me rest, okay?"

"I have a better idea."

"Oh yeah?"

"But it means you moving."

"Then I'm against it."

"The coast is less than thirty clicks southeast. If we could find some way to make contact—"

"Are you serious?" Crimble asked, incredulous. "I can hardly bloody walk, pal."

"You remember the briefing, the day before all this shit kicked off? If the enemy really doesn't have a navy, maybe we could contact a sub. For sure, Brass will be looking to get stragglers like us out."

She heard Crimble sigh and lean back against the cold rock. "I can't believe you think—"

111

"It's your arm that's buggered, mate, not your legs. Come on."

"Just one little thing?"

"What?"

Crimble hissed: "We're behind the fucking lines in hostile territory and could get blown to bits at literally any fucking second without any warning because we don't have any fucking tech. Are you sure you're still right in the head?"

"Look, you're not well, mate, so I'll make allowances for the outburst, this one time. But I've been noting the times of their attacks. They're following a logical pacification pattern, not an emotional, random one."

"So you think you know—"

"Not think. I do know, and we can predict, roughly, when their ACAs will make a pass."

"Nah, that's way too—"

"And what's better is that as they gain more territory, their super AI is going to direct their forces to pacify the newly conquered areas, with less attention given to places a long way back from the front which have fewer people." Pip could see only the outlines of Crimble's features as he appeared to consider her words.

He said: "I still don't think I'm in any shape to cover that kind of distance over this terrain."

"Bollocks," Pip fired back. "We'll take it one step at a time, mate. As long as we can get our BHC sleeves on at the right times, we can make it. The sun's not long gone down, so were good for at least four hours."

"Yeah, but with nothing in our lenses and other tech, how the hell are we going to find a way?"

Pip tutted and said: "Er, we could navigate by the stars at night, if we can see them, and by the sun during the day."

"You know how to do that?" Crimble asked, clearly impressed.

112

Pip paused for effect before answering in a tone thick with sarcasm: "No, I haven't got a clue. That's why I suggested it, dummy. Come on, I'll give you a hand to pack your BHC sleeve and then we're on the move."

A part of Pip knew she behaved with an element of selfishness, but she had to move somewhere, anywhere. The stench from Crimble's festering right arm matched the foulness of her mood. She'd lost Pratty, lost Rory, and now, if she didn't do something, she'd also lose Crimble.

Chapter 17

00.05 Friday 24 February 2062

Max Rizzi glanced from the screen to his best friend Lorenzo and back again, and urged him: "Stop it; I do not think we can destroy these *bastardi* so easily." He saw the beads of sweat on Lorenzo's olive-skinned forehead gather until a droplet ran down his friend's straight nose to drip onto the screen that Lorenzo kept tapping in urgency.

Lorenzo wiped the salt water from the screen with his thumb as his light, effeminate voice complained: "I have to let it recalculate the shortest-form disrupt—"

"Do not do this. It will not work. And then their machines will know that we tried and where we are and one will fly here and kill us," Max said, wiping sweat from his own forehead with a forearm and wishing he could escape the confines of this claustrophobic basement.

Lorenzo looked up: "You are far too negative, my friend," he said with a petulant flick of his head. "We are in the middle of a medium-sized city, south of the greatest of all cities in history. The tower block above us has already been hit more than once—"

"Because they can probably already detect what we are doing down here."

"Their microwaves have burned through civilian comms."

"Which must make us even more visible," Max exclaimed. He wished his hands would stop trembling. The assuredness he'd experienced when he left his sister Serena had now deserted him. He felt certain Lorenzo's actions would only bring calamity down upon them.

Lorenzo said: "I told you: we can thank my brother for that. He only showed me what he had hidden in our apartment just before he left. I did not know before then."

"Do you know where he went?"

Lorenzo scoffed and replied: "The last thing he said to me was that he had been ordered to barracks in the north of Rome, but that was Sunday before the attack, and in the last five days, I have heard nothing. I believe he is dead. Probably killed days ago."

"I think you are right. I believe the same about my sister, Serena. She must also be dead," Max replied, the image of their mother's apartment block being destroyed in front of their eyes still fresh in his memory.

"Over half of the people of Rome are dead, and its buildings destroyed. That is why we must stop them."

"But, friend, do you not think the enemy is unreachable, even with military-standard comms? And which other super AI do you expect to sneak it in with?"

Lorenzo didn't reply. He looked up at Max, moved further along the workbench and took a disposable cup from a dispenser. He filled it from the water replicator, a small, squat device with a thin, bent metal pipe protruding out of it.

Max demanded: "And there's another thing: the Caliphate's systems are completely unknown to us. How can we create something to defeat it? Well?"

Lorenzo's angular face turned askance. He nodded back to the screen and said: "It's a completely independent super AI in there. Wolfram Omega."

Max felt yet another stab of disbelief, on a night that had delivered a year's worth of stress in just a few hours. He stammered: "But, that—that is illegal… Where did you get it?"

Lorenzo gave another laconic shrug and said: "My brother didn't tell me, but I knew he had contacts which, if the military authorities had known, would very likely have seen him court marshalled."

"Really?" Max said in a tone thick with sarcasm. "If our country was not being blown to pieces around us, I might ask where he or anyone else could have got the money to pay for it. Honestly, friend, all the years we have known each other, I was aware of your past, but never thought—"

"When your paternal grandfather was as notorious as mine, the effects can ripple down for decades."

Max shook his head in bewilderment and said: "With a Wolfram Omega, it really is possible we could do something. But I still think their super AI will have anticipated this. And we are probably just one of hundreds, maybe even thousands of people who are trying to do something simi—"

Lorenzo cut Max off with a raised hand and a tut, followed by: "No, they are not."

"How do you know?"

"One: all civilian comms have been burned out by the Caliphate's microwave bursts. Without access to military hardware, people cannot possibly know even what is happening, let alone do anything about it. Two: all military hardware is currently subject to NATO's super AI. Three: Wolfram Omega is the ultimate in quantum software."

Lorenzo paused and a mirthless smile creased his face. He said: "We are going to stop this war now, tonight, here."

Max felt his chest heave in and out with each breath. He gasped: "This is incredibly dangerous."

Lorenzo drank the water and threw the paper cup into a compost bin on the wall of the stifling basement. He returned to the screen laying on the bench, saying: "It could be. But once we let this little viper go, we shall run out of this building as fast as we can." He looked at Max: "You have discarded all of your tech, yes? You are sure you have not forgotten anything?"

Max replied: "I am sure, friend."

"So we only need to wait for our Wolfram Omega to create its little snake."

"What will it do? Send their ACAs into constant diagnostic mode?"

Max wilted under Lorenzo's look of feline contempt. He replied: "Hardly. This is not some kind of game, Max. And even putting their ACAs to sleep would not give us any significant advantage."

"Why not?"

"Because our ACAs and lasers are too weak to destroy them."

"So what will the Wolfram Omega do?"

"Set them against each other, to attack one another."

Air whistled between Max's teeth. "If that works, it will truly be a miracle."

Lorenzo peered at the screen and tapped it. Without looking up, he said: "And why would it not work? Wolfram Omega acts like the most voracious cancer, only rewriting instead of consuming. That's why they are illegal."

Confusion rose again inside Max. He said: "But it is only illegal for civilians. Our governments have it. NATO has it. Surely, if it would work, they would have used it by now, yes?"

Lorenzo's head snapped up. "We cannot be sure why—"

"Or even if they already have tried it and it failed," Max interjected.

"But I estimate that the super artificial intelligence considered it, calculated the probability of success as too low, and discarded the option, potentially without even troubling to inform the humans."

"But I thought that did not happen any longer?"

Lorenzo shrugged again and said: "Among this chaos, who knows? I think that perhaps all of those politicians, who have failed us so badly, have failed us in many more ways about which we do not know. Think, Max. How did they not see this eruption coming? Do you believe them when they say that the Caliphate was too secret, too hidden, and that they honestly knew nothing?"

Max didn't hesitate: "No, of course not. They must have known something was going to happen, but I think that they could not stop it. I think they tried, but they failed. So, instead of admitting their failure, they decided to pretend that they had known nothing all along."

"And now look. It is a travesty," Lorenzo whined, his effeminate lilt for the first time grating on Max's nerves. He went on: "And the most we can hope for is that those who led us into this disaster will have to pay in the same coin."

Max nodded to the bench and asked: "Is it ready yet?"

"No, their interference is impressive. It is taking the Wolfram Omega some time to navigate the jamming."

"But it only needs the tiniest fraction of space. It is not as though we want to send an actual communication."

"Indeed. But it will become locked in a hyper-encryption battle to evade being defeated... There. It is complete. We have an estimated seventy-five percent validity for up to three minutes."

"Only seventy-five? That will not be enough. Do not attempt it," Max urged as Lorenzo lifted his right index finger and it hovered above the screen.

"I do wish you would have a little more faith. This is too small to be found. Like a virus, it will sneak in and poison their systems. It will stop this madness in less than a hundred seconds."

Max padded over to the door. His senses tingled with dangerous excitement. He asked himself silently if such a well organised attacked by an overwhelmingly powerful foe could harbour any such weaknesses which his friend thought the Wolfram Omega could exploit.

Lorenzo turned and smiled. He said: "Although I do agree with you that now is the time to leave this building."

With his hand already pulling the door open, Max said: "So, you are not entirely sure then?"

Lorenzo replied: "I am seventy-five percent sure."

"Do not do it, friend."

"Our leaders have failed. NATO fails us with each passing moment as more lives are lost. We must try."

Max caught his breath as Lorenzo's finger stabbed at the screen on the bench.

"There you are, you filthy *bastardi*," Lorenzo hissed. He stepped back from the bench, his face creased in grim satisfaction. "Now we will see how those—" Lorenzo stopped abruptly when a spark crackled out from the screen.

Max felt a strange, new pain in his head. He gasped and opened the door as an incredible searing sensation burned on the inside of his skull. On the bench, the screen fizzed with a burning electronic hiss and Max heard Lorenzo exclaim, "No, that cannot—" before Lorenzo shrieked in sudden agony.

Max forced his legs through the doorway and out of the basement. He turned back and as the door closed behind him, he saw Lorenzo collapse in apparent agony, his form silhouetted by a bright, white-hot glare from the exploding screen. The door banged shut and Max fell down onto the hard, cold concrete steps which led up to the exit. The phenomenal pain that ran around the inside of his skull abated. Then, the lights went out and he could see nothing in the darkness, the outline of the bright conflagration jumping on his retina. He put his hands to his ears and felt them covered in a warm, sticky wet liquid. He turned over and smelled the dank, muddy moisture of the thousands of footsteps that had trodden on the staircase.

Max crawled up the stairs. Behind him, Lorenzo's shrieks weakened to a pathetic whimper before stopping. But something was wrong. Although the pain in his head had lessened, after a few seconds he couldn't find the next step up on the staircase. He waved his arm out in front of him, the blindness caused by the power outage creating a growing panic. Suddenly and for no apparent reason, his jaw smashed into the concrete and his absolute confusion was complete. He reasoned that he should keep still and wait until his eyes adjusted to the darkness. Exhaustion swept over him and part of his mind reeled in amazement as it seemed he could no longer be certain which way was up. Through his confusion, he could make out distant click-clack sounds of metal on metal as Caliphate Spiders quickly positioned themselves at the weakest parts of the tower block to ensure its complete demolition when they detonated.

Chapter 18

Major Kate Fus prayed with an intensity lacking since her first communion some twenty years earlier. The mid-range autonomous air transport she was strapped into careered all over the sky, the super AI apparently determined to test the aircraft's structural tolerances to their limits.

Her stomach heaved but she'd eaten little in the intensity of the retreat over the previous few days. The lens in her eye relayed a simplified version of the super AI's navigation as it directed the craft through the air in a ceaseless effort to evade the enemy. Digital representations made the battlespace appear as a kind of vast Christmas tree. At the top were the low-orbit battle management satellites, protected by the heaviest shielding against attack from missiles and lasers. Underneath them, fleets of high-altitude ACAs climbed and dived and pitched and rolled and yawed as their controlling artificial intelligences sought to gain the slimmest tactical advantage. Lower still, at altitudes with which humans could more easily cope, the transports of numerous NATO units fled headlong from the approaching Caliphate machines. She counted more than twenty mid-range transports full of troops, each of which flew seemingly impossible courses of outrageous aeronautical extremes, but all of which fled headlong from the enemy.

The odour of freshly extruded bile came to Kate's senses and made her own stomach clench until she thought it might tear. She minimised the view from her lens and opened her eyes. The twenty or so other evacuees strapped in along the length of the fuselage opposite her lolled and grimaced in their seats, and she wondered if she looked as bad as they did. She closed her eyes again and manipulated the data in her lens to bring the immediate battlespace into focus. It revealed a much tighter chase than she'd been involved in the last few days, at least since the hasty withdrawal from Plovdiv in Bulgaria.

She swore silently at the maddening view in her eye as two lead enemy ACAs closed in on her transport. With twitches of her eye muscles, she tried to contact General Pakla, just to hear his voice a final time, but the comms request was declined. She zoomed the view further to see two Blackswans diving in a pincer movement towards them. She yelled above the tearing sounds of air rushing past outside: "Bolek, please tell me you have got this under control."

The super AI's voice responded in its familiar tone of unimpressed indifference: "All steps are being taken to ensure the minimum casualties within the battlespace."

Kate stole a glance at the others, all of whom appeared to be suffering too much discomfort to be fully aware of the growing danger. She shouted: "What is the probability of this transport being shot down?"

"The figure is fluctuating. Please specify a timeframe."

"Before it is able to fucking land," Kate spat, the cumulative effect of the noise, stench and relentless aerial acrobatics testing her patience.

"Unnecessary profanity may be reported to a superior officer—"

"I have the rank of major and this is a life-threatening situation, so shut the fuck up about profanity and answer the question."

"Insufficient data. Reinforcements have been assigned but may be subject to rerouting if new threats materialise, or the existing threats are reassessed and priorities change."

"Next time, just say: 'I don't know'."

"You will need to specify the exact parameters—"

"Not now," Kate yelled as the transport went into a near vertical dive. She squeezed her eyes and tensed every muscle in her body. The image in the lens twisted and upended as the transport accelerated towards the ground, some two thousand metres below them. Kate gasped when she saw the two foremost Caliphate Blackswans release their Spiders in geometric surges that inappropriately reminded her of a penile ejaculation. From the opposite side of the image, a swarm of hundreds of dots rushed in and collided with the Spiders, and she realised these were Equaliser bomblets launched by NATO PeaceMaker ACAs. She wondered why the super AI did not fire the missiles in the transport's fuselage. From what she had seen and what had been reported, she doubted Equalisers alone would be sufficient.

Her eyes opened to see the faces opposite her clenched in the same grimaces. The view through the transport's windows offered only grey, impenetrable cloud, giving no indication of the fury raging outside in the battlespace at the centre of which were the fleeing NATO transports.

The lens zoomed the digital representation of the confrontation closer as more Equalisers collided with the approaching Spiders. The enemy's flying super-AI bombs seemed to absorb an impossible number of Equaliser hits. Some of them peeled off towards the PeaceMakers above them. Kate knew the statistics: all available data from the first five days of the invasion suggested the Caliphate's armaments enjoyed substantial superiority over anything NATO could field.

The altimeter in the bottom-left of her view dropped through four hundred metres and her stomach and sinews squealed in protest as the transport came out of the dive and levelled out. Kate groaned aloud and tried to ignore the growing sense of foreboding, manifested in the sheer pain of tendons and muscles trying to cope with such punishing G-forces. Considering all of the data the lens furnished in her vision, she saw the chances of them escaping this confrontation wither. Then, one of the larger icons in the representation of the battle vanished.

"What was that, Bolek?" she asked.

"NATO autonomous aircraft POL509-101 has been destroyed."

"Reason?"

"Enemy saturation of the battlespace."

Another NATO transport fell out of the sky. And then another. The view in her lens shimmered, crackled and disappeared, replaced with a refined white noise.

"What's going on?" she asked, although she knew.

"The enemy is projecting electronic interference into the battlespace."

"Can't you do something?"

"Countermeasures have been activated."

Kate felt the transport lose more height. Through the windows, the tops of bare trees and evergreen firs streaked past. The graphic in her lens returned suddenly. She saw that NATO SkyWatchers in combination with missile-armed

Blackswans and ground-based lasers were being coordinated, but still the number of Spiders reduced with painful slowness.

"How many Spiders are still pursuing us? What about enemy reinforcements?"

"We appear to have reached the forward edge of the enemy's likely range based on its tactics to date. The probability is increasing that the enemy will reassign its assets remaining in the battlespace. This should allow a window for further withdrawal and evacuation."

"How long do you estimate the window to last? And don't say 'approximately' and then give me a precise figure."

"From nine to thirteen minutes."

"Estimate to where the enemy will reassign its remaining assets."

The Polish Army's super AI replied: "Highest probably is reassignment for civilian pacification."

"Can we prevent that?"

"To attempt to do so would involve reassigning insufficient reserves and carry the probability of almost-certain failure, leading to the loss of all assets involved."

"Next time, just say: 'No'." Misery engulfed Kate's spirit. Memories of lines of thousands of refugees traipsing away from the direction of danger, hoping to be saved, only for the enemy to overtake them and snare them into a fate which Kate tried not to imagine.

"Landing in thirty seconds."

"What?" Kate opened her eyes to see the other evacuees rubbing their necks and stretching as much as they could in the confines of the straps that held them in their seats.

In the seat next to her, an unshaven Romanian captain stretched his arms and concluded: "We must have reached Serbia."

Kate craned her head and saw bare trees and yellow grass outside. The transport bumped down on to the ground and halted. At once, the fuselage echoed with the sounds of clasps clicking open to free the occupants. Kate undid hers as well, and for the first time since the flight began, she ran a finger over the lip of her cleft palate. Her muscles expanded or contracted in relief, depending on what the journey had done to them.

The Romanian captain noted: "We should alight at once so the transports can go back to evacuate more troops."

"But why have we stopped here, at a staging post?" Kate asked, not caring what the Romanian thought of a Polish major asking for such an explanation from a captain.

"Major," the man began in deference, apparently only now realising the rank of his travelling companion, "we will continue retreating in land-based transport because—"

"Because all the air transports are needed elsewhere," she finished for him.

"Or are destroyed," he answered pointedly.

Kate wondered what had happened to him recently to make him say such a thing, but at once discarded the thought. She called out to the other evacuees: "Collect your weapons before disembarking. We are still at risk."

Kate took her place as an orderly queue formed at the rear of the transport and the mixed bag of NATO troops retrieved their Pickups from the armoury. "Bolek," she asked in a quieter voice, "list any current threats at this position."

"Current data suggests negligible threats."

"Where are the land transports?"

"Less than two kilometres to the northwest and closing. Recommend you switch over to your Battlefield Management Support System as you will shortly be in a potential combat situation."

"Okay," Kate answered, momentarily confused because she felt sure she'd asked Bolek to switch to the Squitch automatically without prompting her in such situations. She leaned out of the queue to get people's attention. "Okay, everyone," she urged, "this transport is needed back where we came from. Hurry it up, please. And activate your Squitches if you have not already done so."

A surge of movement greeted her request and she allowed herself the luxury of a smile. At least discipline remained intact so far.

She unclipped her helmet from her belt, put it on her head, and closed the strap under her chin. The Squitch, with a voice similar to Bolek's, spoke in her ear. "Warning. Potential threat detected."

"Specify." She reached the automated armoury. Her PKU–48 smart assault rifle slid out of a hatch and she grabbed it with both hands, turned left, and trotted down the exit stairs among the others, noting the drop in air temperature on leaving the aircraft but enjoying the wave of relief to get her feet finally on solid ground. A soft breeze tugged at her tied brown hair and the scent of leaf mulch reminded her of a world beyond all of this drama and chaos.

Her relief was short-lived, as the Squitch informed her: "Six Spiders from the aerial engagement remain unaccounted for. Increased elec—"

"Are you all getting this?" Kate shouted to the other troops as two other transport alighted on the scrubland at one-hundred-metre intervals. An assortment of confirmations came to her ears before she instructed: "Code twenty-two in this vicinity."

The Squitch answered: "Confirmed and initiated. However, thus far—"

"Where are all the other transports?"

"Destroyed."

Kate swore under breath and then asked: "What about survivors, the injured?"

"There is a near-certain probability that any survivors will have been killed."

Kate stopped walking and surveyed the terrain. Sixty or seventy troops from a mishmash of the unit and corps of half a dozen armed forces, all armed, proceeded on foot from the three surviving autonomous air transports to the western edge of the large, open area. Several NATO personnel carriers rumbled into the area, emerging in a line from a forest track. Kate saw they were the older model Autonomous Land Transports on which she used to train years before. "Are there any medics on those," she asked the Squitch.

"Negative, however they are fully equipped with—" the super AI stopped in mid-sentence.

"What?" Kate demanded testily.

"Danger," it responded. "Six Caliphate Spiders approaching from the west. You are their targets. One thousand metres and closing abreast in a straight line. Take defensive action immediately."

Kate activated her Pickup and inserted a magazine into the rifle. She briefly wondered if the Squitch had made a mistake, for when the super AI said 'You are their targets', it had used the Polish singular pronoun, meaning Kate personally, rather than the plural pronoun meaning all of the sixty or seventy troops in the area.

Out of the corner of her eye, she saw the other NATO soldiers also take defensive measures. Many shuffled closer to the transports from which they had only recently alighted, guns raised. Kate decided that given the volume of explosives hurtling towards them, gaining cover offered little tactical advantage.

The Squitch updated: "Eight hundred metres and closing."

With gentle mechanical whines, panels on the fuselages of the autonomous air transports and on the roofs of the

130

Autonomous Land Transports retracted and banks of missiles rose up. Kate breathed easily, ready as though this were simply another NATO training exercise.

"Six hundred metres and closing."

Kate thought she could hear a clicking or clacking sound. The Squitch overlaid estimated positions of the Spiders as they approached. "Where the hell did they come from?" she asked.

"Assets remaining from the attack on the air transports. Reassigned for a harassment attack. Four hundred metres and closing."

Hisses ripped the air as the missiles launched from the transports and sped over the ground towards the treeline at the eastern end of the clearing. Kate followed the vapour trails as they flew over the scrub and low dunes of beige dirt. When they reached the treeline, a series of orange and black balls of flame erupted, interspersed with green flashes. Deep pops followed on the air.

With a glance around her, Kate breathed in relief to see a number of troops with Stilettoes poised on their shoulders. She looked ahead and six separate clouds of dust rapidly approached their positions, with around thirty metres between them.

"Two hundred metres and closing."

More hisses split the air as the single-shot missiles left their launchers. Other troops opened fire, their rifles making loud cracking sounds. Kate's breathing remained even. She fired. The NATO ordnance hit the Spiders but did not slow their approach. Green hues kept flashing on the enemy devices as the ordnance hit them, and disbelief surged inside Kate that anything could withstand such concentrated firepower. The magazine emptied. As she had done ten thousand times before, she dropped the empty and slotted a new one in less than two seconds. In the heat of this battle, two seconds felt like minutes.

The middle pair of the six Spiders appeared to be hurtling straight towards her, and as she kept firing her Pickup, she realised the shells from other guns around her were being directed towards the pair of Spiders coming at her. In dread she realised that these Spiders had indeed targeted her personally. In response, the NATO super AI redirected the shells fired by the other troops closest to her, so that they also hit the two Spiders immediately in front of her.

Kate barely had time to understand this when NATO fire finally overwhelmed the two Spiders and they disintegrated. She felt a vast, powerful, unseen hand pick her up and toss her over as though she were a doll. Her Pickup left her hands. She rolled in the dirt a few times, and the sensation of dry, tasteless granules being forced into her mouth and nostrils almost made her choke.

At once, she pulled herself onto her hands and knees, desperately wanting to spit and cough the dirt from her mouth. But before she could, the noise of shots and shouts coalesced in urgency before being swamped by more explosions. The change in air pressure forced Kate back into the dirt and she shouted when something heavy hit the back of her right thigh. More debris thumped into the dirt around her and she tensed, ready to be hit again.

The sounds of crackling flames mingled with shouts, cries and moans. Pain surged up Kate's right leg. She tried to rise but the effort was too great. "Report," she ordered.

"Enemy ACAs neutralised," came the Squitch's succinct answer.

Anger rose to meet the physical pain inside Kate. She spat: "Bolek? How could those machines hide? From the aerial battle to when they attacked us on the ground, why didn't you know they were there?"

The Polish Army's super AI, with a voice only a little lower in pitch than the Squitch's, answered: "Initial research suggests that the burst of electromagnetic interference had sufficient duration to allow the enemy's assets to travel to an unanticipated location and reduce their ambient power levels to avoid detection."

"And then attack us when we thought we were in the clear... In other words, they hid from you, and you fell for it, right?"

"The most probable forecasts were made with the available data at the time. There is little to be—"

A figure running at her caught Kate's attention.

"Major? Major? Are you all right? Can you stand?"

Kate craned her head up to see a young corporal silhouetted against the cloudy sky. She considered his question but her right leg felt like a slab of dead meat, and her left stung badly when she tried to move it. She said: "Something is wrong with my legs."

She saw the young man peer over her and the look on his face changed from fearful curiosity to revulsion. "Er," he stammered. "I need to get a GenoFluid pack on to your legs, asap. Don't move, okay? I mean, er, don't move, please, Major."

Kate managed a weak smile and said: "Go and get the pack. I'll wait here."

The young corporal jogged off and a breeze blew dust from his steps back into Kate's face. She worked up saliva in her mouth that turned the dirt into mud and spat some out.

"Bolek, you made a mistake."

"With respect, Major Fus, accepted military doctrine was adhered to, and despite the low probability of the harassment attack, casualties are within what is considered to be the acceptable range."

Exhaustion swept over Kate. She wanted to know how many casualties. She wanted to force the super AI to admit it had made a mistake. She wanted to compose her assessment of the engagement for other commanders in other theatres to read and use to anticipate enemy actions. But suddenly she had to rest. She lay her head back in the dirt and told herself that a few moments would not make a great deal of difference in the context of the entire invasion.

She came to abruptly, as though waking from a nightmare, somnolent neurons meandering their way to pathways in her higher brain functions. Her head no longer rested in dirt. She felt the movement of the ALT as its suspension system absorbed the worst of the terrain's imperfections. She judged the vehicle to be travelling at speed. She still lay on her front, the left side of her face resting on a cold, black, soft material that carried a partially sterile aroma. With a blink of her eye muscles, the lens came to life and informed her that she was in an ALT heading towards Sarajevo and that she should not move due to the GenoFluid currently effecting repairs to her shattered legs. The lens listed a history of communications and other events. She scanned down noting attempted contacts from friends and colleagues.

She whispered, unsure of who or how many other people might be within hearing range: "Bolek, how bad?"

"Your right leg was almost severed; your left leg crushed. The GenoFluid pack has notified that repairs will take twenty-four hours."

"Okay. Tell the pack to send some bots to my bladder, will you? I'm bursting for a pee."

"Done."

"Now place a secure communications link to General Pakla, please."

"Secure comms are unavailable at this time."

Kate sighed and said: "Then standard will do. I would like to report to my superior officer."

She heard a slight hiss; the ALT crossed more rugged terrain which made her head bump into the padded surface on which she lay, and a new voice spoke: "Major Fus? Are you all right?"

"General Pakla. Thank you for accepting my communication. I would like to report on the harassment attack via secure comms, but the super AI says they are not available."

"Wait, please."

Kate heard another hiss and a sharp click. General Pakla spoke: "You are now on my private channel, Major. However, given the current situation, we should take care in case the enemy is eavesdropping."

A smile creased Kate's deformed mouth. His reference to 'the enemy' meant all those who should not know about their affair. She said: "Understood, Sir. I believe we urgently need to review tactical protocols. The super AI did not give sufficient credence to the probability of a harassment attack by the enemy with its assets that remained in the battlespace."

"I agree," the General—*her* General—replied. "I have set up a tiered diagnostic regime for the army's super AI which will take a couple of hours."

"Thank you, Sir."

The General's business-like voice softened a fraction as he asked: "The medical records say you'll need the GenoFluid pack for twenty-four hours. How do you feel?"

Kate had not asked that question of herself, so she answered with her first thought: "I am very grateful I was fortunate enough to survive."

"It was not down to luck, Major."

"No?"

"You were the senior officer present, so the super AI accorded you the highest priority from among all of the troops there."

She sensed the General wanted to say more, but she replied: "So the artificial intelligence decided that I should live while others should die, yes?" And the recollection came to her that when the attack had begun, her Squitch had indeed used the singular pronoun when it had said, 'You are their target'.

The General's voice softened further: "It was not so far removed from what we have all debated in ethics' seminars and in numerous wargaming exercises, Major."

"Except this time it was real, and real people died so that I, as the senior ranking officer, would live."

There followed a pause, and Kate imagined what the General would say if they could have been certain of the security of their communications channel. Instead, he said: "Major, let me know if you require counselling or any other support services. I wish you a speedy recovery and look forward to a full debrief when you return to Sarajevo."

The communication ended and Kate sighed. The motion of the ALT had settled into a more predictable undulation from side to side, and occasionally up and down, and this made her feel sleepy. Alternatively, she reasoned, it could be the management nanobots inside her body deciding their subordinate tissue repair bots might perform more effectively if their host were asleep. In any case, the pressure on her bladder had eased, which helped her relax.

With a twitch of an eye muscle, various analyses of the aerial battle in which the twenty transports were lost and the subsequent harassment attack on the ground presented themselves for her consideration. Her spirit seemed to divide in two. Part of her viewed this tiny fragment of the unfolding European disaster with pragmatism. On numerous occasions,

NATO training exercises had suggested the potential of losing substantial numbers of troops, although nothing like on the current scale.

Another part of her mind absorbed the full impact of the General's words. One report revealed that from the eighty-seven individual evacuees on the three surviving transports, thirty-one had been killed in the Spider attack on the ground. She replayed sections of visual and audio recordings from various participants' Squitches. With her eyelids growing heavier, she noted the names, ranks and armies of those who had been obliged—unknown to them—to forego their lives to preserve hers.

As sleep finally overcame Major Kate Fus, her eyes moistened and she felt a deep emptiness inside her spirit. Abruptly, a lifetime of training had ended. Years of pretending to be a NATO soldier without ever truly expecting to have to engage in a real conflict had been concluded by time, by history, by inevitability.

Chapter 19

Prime Minister Napier's haggard face stared out of the screen and her tired voice rasped: "Operation Defensive Arc is not going very well."

David Perkins, the Head of MI5, thought that a vast understatement, but waited for the Prime Minister to get to the point.

"Can you tell me what is going on behind the scenes?" she asked.

Perkins, who had fought to garner more funds for most of his time as the head of England's only secret service, once again overpowered the urge to educate his boss in certain fundamental truths. He said: "PM, the service is working to correlate data from numerous sources, but we do not have sufficient resources to establish facts through our own efforts. We rely on our allies." He shrugged as he stated what was, to him, blindingly obvious.

"We need to increase diplomatic pressure on Beijing," Napier said.

Perkins smothered a guffaw and answered smoothly: "I believe we have made the Chinese government fully aware that we expect them to rein the Caliphate in, but—"

"It's getting a little late for that, Mr Perkins. I want the Chinese to pay. I want us to do something that will hurt them. We're seeing thousands of people dying in Europe by the hour, and if they won't stop it, then they need to know they are not going to get off scot-free."

Perkins stopped breathing in disbelief. He asked himself what on earth this woman thought a little island country could 'do' to the most powerful country in the world to make it 'pay' for not preventing a war which, Perkins believed, it had not been entirely instrumental in starting. Perkins peered into his boss's face as the screen in his desk presented it, noting the red eyes that appeared to burn with frustration. Fine, he told himself, she's had another bad night, disaster piling on disaster, but she still could not accept the limitations of the enfeebled country she ruled.

He said: "I am due to receive a report from one of our key operatives in Beijing, PM, and will be happy to update you as soon as you're available…" then, his mischievous side got the better of him, and he asked: "Er, how do you think we might make the Chinese pay?"

Napier glanced at something or someone outside the camera's field of view, as though seeking confirmation. She said: "For now this is top secret, but the government will seize all Chinese-owned assets in England. That might make them think. They have invested countless sums over the last few decades, and as things stand, the Caliphate will destroy them in a few weeks—as they're already doing to Chinese interests in southern Europe. Perhaps Beijing will reconsider bringing the Third Caliph to heel."

Perkins stammered: "Er, right. A potentially useful strategy," while inside he screamed in frustration at such a facile plan. However, he replied: "Currently, we have no hard evidence that the Caliphate is in fact answerable to the Chinese, despite what the press is saying."

Napier shook her head and said: "You know how it works, Mr Perkins: the act of the press saying it's true almost makes it fact in the minds of a large section of the population. Whether true or not, many people believe that China made the New Persian Caliphate. Therefore, those people believe that China exercises control over it, and can as a result stop this war before it gets any worse."

"But PM, the Chinese president and a number of his high-level ministers are on record distancing themselves from the Third Caliph's aggression. All covert data we have points to Beijing having put significant pressure on the Third Caliph since the attacks on the navies and Israel, but to no effect."

"Mr Perkins, please use our more unorthodox channels to convey to the Chinese leadership that their response to this crisis is simply not good enough."

Perkins felt himself shrug again as he replied: "That's what we've been doing since the seventh of February, PM."

Napier hissed: "Well, try making a bit more effort, before we're all dead in a few weeks, understood?"

Perkins nodded and said: "Of course." The screen went blank. He exhaled loudly and in his mind, he bemoaned his department's impotency. He stood and padded across his spacious office, the huge, deep-pile rug on the wooden floor deadening his steps. On the wall hung a portrait of the old GCHQ at Cheltenham, a vast circular building from a time when the former United Kingdom had still wielded some measure of power in the world. He scoffed aloud when he recalled that it had been sold in the vast asset-strip of 2050, when the English government had needed to raise funds to purchase equipment to fight the rising sea levels. He strained his memory to recall what the building was used for now—a distribution centre for a Chinese logistics company? Today, the term 'GCHQ' referred to the now-defunct MI6 headquarters at Vauxhall as the bulk of MI5's operations were run from that dilapidated building.

A small notification in his lens flashed in the bottom-right of his view. "Finally," he muttered aloud. "Computer?" he called, eschewing the popular habit of giving the assisting machines silly pet names.

"Yes, Mr Perkins?"

"Confirm contact and secure, please."

"Affirmative and secured," came the instant reply.

"Play on general audio." He did the top button of his suit jacket up and folded his arms. He stared at the mud-brown River Thames as it flowed towards London Bridge. Above it, the leaden February sky promised only more rain.

The voice of the Englishman in Beijing seemed to speak from each corner in Perkins' office. The spy's normally confident tone sounded more subdued than usual: "The Englishman reporting from Beijing. Time of report: 14.23, Friday 24 February 2062. This has been a bloody trying week with precious little progress. Actually, make that no progress at all. Our diplomatic mission is in despair. Everyone, from the ambassador down, frets and worries about the destruction happening in Europe. Worse, there really does seem to be little any of them can do. One of the staffers in the embassy related a meeting in which the ambassador suggested that perhaps if they sent the Chinese politburo replications of every invention Great Britain had produced in the preceding four hundred years, it might help those stuffy old men to reconsider their inertia. The staffer described the atmosphere in the meeting as 'beyond pathetic', like the Greeks whining they should be spared because they invented democracy.

"The Chinese, as is their wont, are more concerned with the potential embarrassment—or loss of 'face'—that the

Third Caliph's adventures might cause them in the eyes of their partners in countries in South America and Africa. According to my military contact, Chinese embassies in the affected European capitals are trying extremely hard to get their nationals out ahead of the invading forces, and despite the speed at which European countries are collapsing, he seemed to think the invaders have been instructed to allow safe passage to fleeing Chinese craft. My contact also implied some of the wealthier and better-connected Europeans were escaping to China on these transports, but whether they will be permitted to stay in the Middle Kingdom remains an open question."

Perkins wondered if the spy would say anything remotely useful or relevant to England's predicament.

"Finally, I cannot overemphasise how little impact the Caliphate's invasion of Europe is actually having inside the vastness of China. Minor disasters like super-AI traffic malfunctions and mid-level corruption scandals garner far more cross-media attention than international events in relatively obscure parts of the world. Even on the international stage, the invasion falls behind tensions with India. Part of this can be ascribed, as I've mentioned, to the idea of the loss of Chinese face, so the government prefers the official media to downplay what is happening.

"However, in my opinion, much of the reason for the lack of concern is simply that the Chinese population does not see the Caliphate's invasion as a priority. Indeed, last night I attended a soirée at the new Brazilian embassy, which must be the most well-appointed foreign embassy in all of Beijing. In their vast ballroom, I found myself chatting with a mixed bunch in a smallish group, and a young Chinese man lamented what was happening. Then, like so many before him, he wondered aloud how the people of such a small island like England could have come to rule a quarter of the globe, and how sad it was that they were now so impotent. I wanted to glass the slit-eyed bastard right across his wide, round, and very arrogant face, but I didn't. Message ends."

A wry smile creased Perkins' face. He said: "Computer, let me know when the PM has a break in her schedule."

The computer answered: "Requests are currently being deferred to her chief aide."

"Oh god," Perkins muttered, "spare me pretty-boy Webb. It's not important. It can wait."

Chapter 20

Asudden dread deep inside Corporal Rory Moore's spirit warned him that danger approached. He made his best effort to push the fatigue back but what little energy remained began to desert him. He heard steps inside the dank and cold cave, slow and delicate and cautious. He regarded this development positively, for if it were the enemy, he would be dead by now. He heard distant whispers but could not understand them. The footsteps stopped.

Adrenalin poured into his bloodstream once again and gave him the strength to lift his head and see darkened figures in the cave. But the adrenalin could not fully mask the pain of moving from the cold rock. The figures in the cave entrance receded and he felt relieved, but he could not think why he should. He let his head relax back against the rock. Dryness in the back of his throat made him cough suddenly. The cough became a choke and he felt his whole chest ache, protesting the lack of food, the dampness, and the chill. The choke passed but the pain remained to recede at its leisure, as if it wanted Rory to know that it owned him now, and would take its time as it wished.

At the entrance, he saw that the figures had returned. Masculine outlines approached him. One asked him something in Spanish that Rory didn't understand.

"NATO," he hissed, shocked at how difficult it had become to push air through his throat with sufficient power to form a sound.

There followed an exchange between up to four men; Rory couldn't be sure how many people were in the group. One murmur sounded conciliatory, the next dismissive, the following aggressive. Suddenly, he heard a sharp scrape, like a blade being pulled from a scabbard, and one of them became angry. He spoke a volley of hard, aggressive sounds. This outburst was followed by a sequence of calmer utterances, and Rory began to wonder how much danger he was in.

As dawn's light increased outside the cave, details inside became clearer, and Rory began to make out faces and heads and stomachs that sagged over tattered jeans. He counted five figures, all male, but their statures suggested varying ages. One took a few steps to him and asked: "You not speak Spanish, no?"

Rory shook his head and said: "No, sorry."

"This man here," the individual said, pointing to one of the figures further back. "He want to kill you. All his family dead because NATO no good."

This seemed unreasonable to Rory, and abruptly he felt the full hostility that his lack of the language had thus far only suggested. He croaked, "I am sorry," but stopped because the fear and effort of speaking combined to silence him.

Rory's interlocutor turned back to his colleagues and there followed more dialogue, much of it sounding placatory to Rory's ears. A part of Rory's mind wondered why they should blame him personally for the military of which he was a part having insufficient resources to defend these civilians. Did they think this was a picnic for the soldiers?

The man leaned back in and Rory smelled stale sweat and urine. When he spoke, his voice carried an undercurrent of threat: "If you will walk, you can come with us. We will take you to food and shelter. If you not walk, you stay here."

With a supreme effort, Rory forced himself off the rock. At once, a wave of dizziness swept over him and he gripped the rock and paused. When it passed, he pulled himself upright. None of the other men made any effort to assist him.

He threw them a weak smile and rasped: "I'll walk, guys. It'll be fun."

Chapter 21

11.19 Friday 24 February 2062

With a sense of melancholy that made each step twice as heavy as it should have been, Private Philippa 'Pip' Clarke trudged up the path that would take her over the low mountain and onto the next village. Crimble's deep moans still rung in her ears, and she doubted she would see him alive again.

The doctor—or at least the haggard, unwashed young woman who'd claimed to be a doctor—only gave Crimble a fifty-fifty chance of surviving the amputation. The weight of melancholy built up until it morphed into dismay. The relentless stress of covering distance over mountainous terrain when a Caliphate ACA could appear out of nowhere and kill her in a moment, ground her spirit down. She hated herself for leaving him, but they both knew she had no choice. One of them had to try. And anyway, even if he survived the amputation, he wouldn't be able to travel for several days at least. The lengths of time injuries required to heal when GenoFluid packs were unavailable frightened Pip.

The distance from the first village she'd almost dragged Crimble to, Capilieria, and the coast where they might contact a submarine for extraction, was a mere twenty-five kilometres in a straight line. This would be a day's pleasant jog in full kit and full health. Now, exhausted, under immense pressure, and enfeebled through a lack of nourishment, the distance seemed to present a near-insurmountable challenge.

Pip cursed the rocks and stones that littered the track she climbed, and kicked the occasional one out of the way to relieve the frustration. The sun beat down hot and bright, and it struck Pip how rapidly events had unfolded: less than three short weeks ago, the New Persian Caliphate had exploded— both figuratively and literally—onto the global stage, annihilating American and British naval formations and then burning Israel to a crisp. Now their ACAs and armies swarmed over southern Europe, killing and destroying at will. She reflected that NATO might have already collapsed under this onslaught.

Pip crested the hill and looked south at the distant blue haze of the Mediterranean as it shimmered where it met the lighter blue sky. She spun left, right, and all around in a half-hearted attempt to scan the sky for any tell-tale black dots in the distance, among the flecks of high cloud, that might be roaming Caliphate machines. For the umpteenth time, she told herself that if she ever were to see such a thing, she'd only have enough time to say her prayers. Once again, she repeated to herself that the absence of tech on her body meant invisibility. In the dank warrens of caves inside the mountainsides around Capilieria and the two closest villages, Pip found out that the local population had realised, with a speed that only instant death for failure could engender, that any tech at all would bring the Caliphate machines to rain down destruction.

She took a step forward and began a long, shallow descent along a path that she saw disappeared into a forest of evergreens. The monotony of descending calmed her mind and gave her a certain clarity after the violence of the preceding days. When she judged the sun's position had moved sufficiently across the blue sky, she found a rocky overhang under which she could shelter. She collected some broken branches, pines, dead leaves and other handfuls of forest debris to make a less-uncomfortable place to rest. She extracted her BHC sleeve from its pouch and wrapped herself up. Once settled, she could see only a small part of the afternoon sky. She wanted to watch for enemy ACAs but she began to doze.

Pip woke with a start and realised at once that a couple of hours at least must have passed. By her own calculations, she now had between three and four hours before nightfall which should be safe, providing the Caliphate adhered to its current search routines. As she peeled off the BHC sleeve, she reassured herself that the Iberian peninsula was vast indeed, and the enemy only had so many machines in theatre, most of which were hopefully engaged supporting their advance. With her BHC sleeve stowed in the pouch behind her calf, Pip pushed on towards the coast.

Chapter 22

14.16 Friday 24 February 2062

Rory licked the bowl of tomato soup clean. The older man who'd first spoken to him in the cave, called Pablo, had told him its Spanish name, but Rory couldn't recall and now did not care. At last, with proper food in his stomach, his exhaustion lifted with his mood. He glanced around the darkened area, part of a disused mine a long way from the entrance. Tar torches lit the walls like some medieval castle and made the still air smell of burning liquorice. The dirt floor had a layer of straw to deaden sound, and Rory was one of thirty or more people sitting at tables scattered around the area. On the far side, he saw teenage boys hauling buckets of water in and placing one under each torch, lest a drop of burning pitch escaped its holder and set the straw aflame.

Rory felt a firm hand on his shoulder and heard: "How was the *gazpacho*? Good?" Pablo sat down on the bench next to Rory.

The Englishman answered: "The best thing I have ever eaten."

"Good."

Rory looked into Pablo's craggy face topped with a sprinkle of white hair and said: "Thank you."

The old man shrugged and said: "We have enough food for now. And it is not your fault it all go so bad."

"What about the guy with the machete?" Rory asked. "Does he agree with you now?"

"Bruno?" Pablo queried with a scowl. "Do not be worry about him. He say he knew all time about Caliphate and war." Pablo shook his head as though in confusion, then shrugged again and concluded: "But he also suffer, like we all suffer. Friends gone, family gone. Very bad."

The soup that had so refreshed Rory now sat heavy in his stomach. These ordinary people, only different from him because they spoke another tongue, were enduring a new reality that would in all probability dominate the whole of Europe in a matter of weeks. He looked past the wrinkles into Pablo's eyes and saw a flash of pain there that he felt inside his own body, the pain of lost certainty, of lost futures for all of them.

"Gah," Pablo said, breaking eye contact. "Come with me. I must show you something." The old man leaned on the table to stand up and walked heavily towards one of the four tunnels that led out of the main area.

Rory followed, catching up with Pablo in a couple of strides. Pablo did not speak as they passed other smaller areas hewn from the rock. Rory was at a loss to think what could have been mined here, perhaps tin or some other metal, but did not want to ask his companion, who stared at the ground and appeared lost in thought.

Suddenly, a shriek rang out from an area off the main tunnel up ahead of them. Pablo sighed and said: "This is bad. The injured suffer too much. Worst."

"Can't you get any supplies, even anaesthetics?"

"Where from? Villages all destroyed. Hospitals, people destroyed. Any tech and you are dead in one minute."

Rory didn't know what to say.

They walked on in silence and then Pablo steered them right into a small, apparently closed area, lit by more of the same torches. Rory counted half a dozen people lying flat on their backs on the straw-covered floor.

Pablo motioned to a woman who approached them. He stuck a thumb out at Rory and told her: "Here is NATO soldier."

The woman appraised Rory, tutted and tilted her head so that her straight, brown hair came out from behind her ear. She tucked it back again and said in accented English: "We are having two, over there and there. Perhaps you are knowing them?"

Rory stepped over to the first figure. The gaunt, pasty-white face seemed familiar, but the thin moustache confirmed the patient's identity. "Crimble," Rory said in shock.

The woman said: "You know who he is, yes?"

Rory spoke through his shock, leaning in to take a closer look at his erstwhile comrade. The straw crackled gently under his boots. "There's no doubt," he said. "That is Private Colin Wimble, Royal Engineers, one of my squad. But I still don't believe it's really him. It can't be."

"Why, what happen?" the woman asked.

"They—the rest of my squad—were on a transport taking them back to barracks. It must have been shot down. All of the transports must have been destroyed. No way could any of them surv—shit, what's that?" Rory said suddenly on realising that there was no limb below the bandage on Crimble's right upper arm.

"Gangrene," the woman said with a shrug.

Rory looked at her and asked: "Will he live?"

155

"I do not, I cannot, know. I never deal with such problems before. Maybe fifty-fifty. I do not know."

Pablo said: "There was woman came in with him, young like him—"

"Pip?" Rory exclaimed, his heart suddenly racing. "What did she look like?" he asked, wanting to be certain.

The woman shrugged and said: "Not too tall. Short black hair. Round face."

"Where is she?" Rory asked.

Pablo and the woman looked at each other in some confusion. The woman said: "She left. Few hours ago."

Rory brought his feelings into check. Every moment he had spent lying in that cave, he'd felt certain his beloved Pip must have perished. "Where was she going?"

"To the sea," Pablo answered. "She not want to stay here. She see him in bad way," he said, glancing down at Crimble. "She decide better to go."

"Christ," Rory breathed. "She thinks she's going to get out on a sub."

"What?" Pablo asked.

Rory shook his head, looked at Pablo, and said: "But she hasn't thought it through. Without tech, she's got no chance."

The woman said: "She seemed determined."

"I don't doubt that," Rory said with a short laugh. "I need to get to her. Do you know which way she went?"

Pablo looked askance at Rory and said: "There are many, many paths through the mountains to the sea. I not see her go."

The woman said: "I did. She say she go straight, that is all I hear. From this valley, there is one long path. It go to top of mountain. From then, there are three main paths, but one have more paths which go off to other places."

"But what about the risk? Just one enemy ACA is all it would take."

"She say she… work out pattern. For some time is okay to move. Then not move and hide."

"Thank you," Rory said. "Thank you so much." He grabbed Pablo's hand and shook it.

The old man insisted: "You need rest. Two bowls of *gazpacho* not enough for such trip,"

"If you could let me have one more bowl before I go, I will be fine."

Pablo shrugged and Rory followed him back into the tunnel, turning to thank the woman doctor again. However, the initial euphoria had already begun to wear off as the logical part of his mind pointed out that even if the balance of probabilities went in his favour, he'd need luck to find Pip. He strained to recall briefings from before the invasion began: their unit's area of operations, local forces, the area around the garrison. Then he remembered one piece of information that could help, which might pull the odds more in his favour. His sense of elation returned: Pip was alive, and he would see her again.

Chapter 23

Hunger gnawed inside Pip as she climbed the steep rise, and she wondered if Crimble were still alive, lying where she'd left him on that smelly straw, with that smelly doctor who spoke such poor English, and they'd amputated his arm and if he would survive with only backward tech centuries out of date. She recalled her last conversation with Pratty, as he laconically related what was happening on the transport before a Spider destroyed it and him.

Pip's journey from the caves had been tough but not the most demanding trek she'd ever done in the British Army. Streams flowing out from the mountains had provided her with plenty of water, but as she neared the coast a complication had arisen: without tech, she had no way of making contact with friendly forces to arrange her retrieval. She thought back to the refuge she had shared with Crimble after the firefight, when she'd first had the idea of escaping the Caliphate's deadly embrace. It seemed incredible to her now that she hadn't realised this simple problem.

In addition, the final mountain range before the coast was extremely steep, and she'd thought it might be better to go around rather than over. But she'd elected to go over, and now, with at least four hours before Caliphate forces should make a pass in the area, at last she crested the final ridge with aching limbs. A thousand or so metres beneath her, the blue Mediterranean lay flat and calm and inviting. All along the coast for as far as she could see, palls of smoke marked the pyres of what had been towns and seaside resorts.

Three hours later, Pip walked through the remains of residential areas whose names she did not know. Despite the fatigue her hunger and exhaustion caused, she hurried past blasted and blackened buildings, past destroyed super-AI controlled vehicles that were still hot to the touch.

It was the child's body that finally made Pip break down and cry. No more than a hundred metres from the stony beach, at a point where she could hear the whoosh of waves and where the scent of seaweed finally began to dent the relentless stench of burned material, there lay a child's form, disfigured and charred, its legs still astride a tricycle. From the absence of a clear and obvious cause, Pip deduced that a blast from the nearest building had knocked the child over, whereupon some kind of explosion overtook him or her and created the tableau she observed, probably the only human being who would ever witness this lone child's death.

She forced her legs forward and beyond the destruction, down onto the stony beach. Waves lapped and the water made a shimmering sound as each wave washed back through the stones. She looked up to check the position of the sun and realised that she would soon have to take cover. Suddenly, she saw a black dot in the blue sky and stopped breathing in dread. She blinked hard a few times in the vain hope that it might be an optical illusion caused by a fleck of dirt on one of her corneas.

Pip stood frozen in fear for some seconds. Part of her mind tried to persuade her that any danger must be too remote to be an immediate threat. Another part of her feared that even the slightest movement would be seen. Time passed. Her heart rate accelerated. She could not see if the black dot in the sky drew nearer or remained at the same distance or moved further away from her. She reflected that by the time she would be able to work out what the black dot was doing, it would be too late. She wished the Squitch were in her ear to tell her what the hell was happening. She wished she had her Pickup, half a dozen mags stuffed into her tunic, and a couple of Stilettos.

Pip finally concluded that the black dot was coming straight towards her and she fought to control the rising panic. She sprinted for the nearest cover, a blast-damaged row of villas across a road on which charred autonomous vehicles still gave off wisps of smoke. She leapt over a row of low bushes and into the nearest garden. She entered the villa through the shattered front door and took refuge in the damaged living room on her right. She opened the pouch containing her BHC sleeve on the right calf of her trousers and began yet again the painstaking process of opening it out and rolling the gossamer-thin material up her body. She'd long since decided that it had a major design flaw as it should have two legs so the wearer could move.

"Peacetime design," she muttered out loud. "Only ever bloody tested in bloody exercises." She considered that someone, somewhere had likely suggested a design modification, and Brass probably deemed it too expensive, so the troops were stuck with a sleeve for hiding in but not for moving in. Seconds later, only her face remained partly exposed. She'd worked out that the best way to move on open ground in the sleeve was to pull herself along on her backside, but now, in a rubble-strewn urban setting, she could use her

161

surroundings to move. She pulled herself along by using the window sill. She desperately wanted to get out of this building because if the Caliphate ACA had seen her, she could not afford to be in the same location if it attacked.

From outside, the relative peace of the sighing of waves on the beach was broken by an airborne hiss which grew louder and then terminated in a stony crash.

"Fuck it," Pip swore. With extreme caution, she pulled herself to the doorway of the living room and looked down the damaged corridor and out through the smashed front door. For a moment, nothing happened and she thought she might have imagined the noise. Then, twenty-five metres away on the beach, stones leapt into the air as eight metallic legs snapped open. A Caliphate Spider rose up and strode straight towards the unarmed and defenceless Royal Engineer.

Chapter 24

Fewer than two thousand metres to the northwest of Pip's confrontation, an exhausted Rory Moore snuggled inside a depression at the base of a sprawling yew tree in front of the last ridge he had to cross to reach the coast. His BHC sleeve kept him warm as well as concealed, and as much as he wanted to hurry on and continue his journey to find Pip, he found the required guesswork of estimating when Caliphate ACAs might pass overhead unnerving in the extreme.

He pushed himself further into the morass of half-exposed roots and tried not to think about the ants and termites and other pests that dwelled there. "No," he whispered aloud, "that's just dirt shifting underneath you because you're moving. It is absolutely not anything alive."

Apart from the stress of guesstimating when the enemy's machines might patrol this area, none of those to whom he spoke in the caves appeared to appreciate that the Caliphate might—indeed probably would—vary these times. In fact, military tactics insisted that the enemy should make sorties as random as possible to prevent to the greatest degree precisely what he and Pip were now doing. Another part of his mind countered that suggestion with the consideration that the enemy might not be troubling themselves any longer with civilians trapped in occupied territory. Perhaps, he reasoned, now the Caliphate had instilled the fear of instant death in the general population, its governing super AI will have concluded that further harassment raids were not required?

Almost at once, Rory was disabused of this possibility when the sounds of explosions came to his ears, a series of distant crumpling thumps, like a mechanical digger dropping a large bucketful of earth. After a few moments, lazy smudges of smoke wafted high enough above the trees for him to see the gentle breeze push them further inland.

Rory allowed a further ten minutes before finally deciding the threat had passed for another few hours. He extracted his arms from the BHC sleeve, rolled it down his body, and folded it up so it fitted inside the pouch on his right calf. He brushed imaginary woodlice and centipedes from his uniform, glanced a last time at the yew's tangled roots, and resumed climbing. An overgrown path took him eastwards and avoided the highest part of the ridge. Twenty minutes later, he emerged to face the blue expanse of the sea, and dismay flooded his spirit. All along the coast, he saw only destruction: blasted and blackened buildings and vehicles that smouldered still, and he wondered if any of the explosions he'd heard had happened here.

With a heavy heart at the realisation that Pip could be anywhere along this stretch of coastline and a unnerving foreboding at what awaited him, Rory advanced down from the ridge determined to find answers to the questions that burned inside him.

Chapter 25

P ip's blood froze. She kept her body as still as possible. In the distance, her ears registered the shuddering tremors of distant explosions. But inside her, an overwhelming anger burned because she was about to die wearing a ridiculous BHC sleeve. She couldn't walk in it and she couldn't take it off. She watched the Spider as it approached the damaged villa in which she sheltered. A curious irony struck her: this lethal device was constructed of, and contained, the most advanced tech which, conversely, made it appear as though it were biological, a creature of the Earth that had evolved over millions of years. The fluidity of motion in its eight, triple-jointed legs amazed and appalled her in equal measures.

The Spider reached the road and stopped. Pip wondered what it was waiting for. She had not moved any great distance since the Blackswan must have seen her from kilometres away in the sky and sent the Spider to deal with her. Could the BHC sleeve blind this advanced autonomous bomb so completely? Pip considered that it must be able to detect the heat from her partly exposed face, and would hopefully ascribe it to the presence of a small creature like a bird or rodent, but not in general something worth detonating itself to destroy.

The Spider sat unmoving in the road. The centre of the metal body faced the shattered entrance to the villa. Pip swallowed and wondered what would happen next. Time passed. She noted the matt finish on the body and wondered from which metal it was constructed. She waited for it to move. It did not. She felt the pressure of the standoff increase. She began to fear making the slightest movement. She took the shallowest breaths possible. Her eyes began to well with tears as she fought the urge to blink. Finally, she knew she had to move. Either the Spider could see her or it couldn't. If it could, it should attack. And if it did, that would be that.

Pip pulled on the doorframe to slide her legs back into the living room. Masonry crunched and crumbled under her bound feet as she moved. The Spider took no action. She put her head into the living room and exhaled loudly, blinking and stretching her jaw. She mouthed a curse but made sure not to emit any actual sound. With agonising slowness, she used broken furniture to drag herself far enough into the debris-strewn room to see the Spider through the broken window, still immobile in the road.

She asked herself how long it had been there—five minutes? Ten minutes? Time meant something different now. She decided to let it be. She would make herself comfortable and wait. Sooner or later—

The sudden crack of a gunshot outside the villa shattered her thoughts. She turned and looked through the window. Another shot rang out and the Spider's shielding gave off a green flash. Clicking sounds came from it as it turned. In an instant, it accelerated off along the road and out of Pip's view. A rapid volley of loud shots rang out.

She bashed loose shards of glass clear from the bottom of the window frame, and leveraging with her arms, she jumped through the window and fell on the grass outside. Her knees knocked together painfully on impact due to the constriction of the BHC sleeve, and at that moment she elected to take it off, whatever the risk. The thought of dying with it on terrified her even more than the increased risk of being visible and unarmed. She shimmied it off her body. Instead of packing it away in its pouch, she tied it around her waist.

The pace of events accelerated. Ahead of her along the road, the Spider blew up, but the cause looked to have been opposing fire rather than the machine's own decision. A black pall of smoke curled in on itself and rose up. From further away, there came another explosion. Suddenly, a military figure appeared through the smoke billowing from the destroyed Spider. He moved with the purposeful gait of a soldier who'd just survived combat.

"Hey!" Pip yelled as she broke into a trot.

The figure saw her and raised his gun.

"NATO," she shouted.

"*Detener!*" he yelled back.

Pip slowed to a walk and looked at the soldier. Suspicious black eyes stared out from a dark, dirty face that looked at her from down the barrel of a Pickup.

"English?" he asked as she came to within a few metres of him.

"British Army, Royal Engineers."

He lowered his weapon and said: "I did not expect there to be any other NATO troops left alive here."

"Never mind," Pip replied feeling the urgency increase with each passing second. "You have to get rid of your gear, now."

167

"What?"

"You've got minutes, that is all. More Spiders will come, many more… Just where have you been the last week?" she asked in response to the look of confusion on his face.

"Behind the lines, special ops. We were hiding until dawn. But we hit them, just a few clicks over there. Now, we are being evacuated in ten minutes," he said.

"Shit," Pip breathed. She didn't quite believe her eyes as three more Spanish special ops troops ran towards them.

She asked: "Do you know what is about to happen now you've engaged the Spiders?" She began to back away, realising she needed to get back into her BHC sleeve and take cover. Whatever arms these troops had, they were in enemy-controlled territory now, without friendly ACA support. She pleaded with them: "Please, ditch your weapons, comms, ditch your Battlefield Management Support Systems, all of your tech."

The three other men reached their commanding officer and threw her curious looks. Then they each turned to scan the sky at a different point of the compass.

"No way," the commanding officer said to her. "We just knocked out one of their manned posts. Killed at least twenty of them. Now, we do not wait. We get out. We fight again."

Pip shook her head and pushed aside the doubt that this squad could have done what the commanding officer claimed and escaped this far. She said in exasperation: "No, you will not get out and fight again. Now you've engaged the enemy, more will follow, and they will keep coming until they kill you. Is that clear?"

The commanding officer and the three troops on sentry duty all glanced at her with expressions she knew well: contempt. Their faces gave off faint smiles, as if the little woman did not know what she was talking about. Pip smothered her anger and said: "Don't believe me? What about their jamming? Have you got comms?"

The commanding officer's face became more thoughtful. He said: "Our super AI has not worked correctly for days. It said comms were jammed but we think it might be an error or a malfunction."

Then it was Pip's turn to look confused. She asked: "So how did you arrange the sub to retrieve you?"

The commanding officer shrugged and said: "We are following a pre-war schedule. The sub—a Royal Navy one, by the way—comes in and goes out at prearranged times. If we can get out there, it will pick us up."

Pip shook her head, the urgency clawing at her. "Okay," she said, backing away further. "Your super AI is not wrong. The enemy is in total control of this battlespace. Please listen to me. You need to ditch all of your tech and get your BHC sleeves on."

"Incoming!" shouted one of the others. All four of the troops turned to face the direction of the threat and each spread to put distance between them.

With dread, Pip looked into the sky to see another black dot. She shouted: "Guys, for the last time, ditch your tech and get your BHC sleeves on if you want to survive." Without waiting for a response, she turned and ran, one hand gathering her BHC sleeve as it flapped out from her waist. Her mind ran with her body: how many Spiders would come this time? How much ammunition did that squad have? Where could that submarine be, and how could she get to it?

When she had gone fifty or so metres, she turned to see the special-ops squad make their pointless and futile stand. Her heart hammered in her chest from fear and she panted from the exertion of running. Without taking her eyes off the scene on the road, she unfurled the BHC sleeve, ready to pull it over herself and disappear.

She ducked into the garden of a villa and tried to see what happened while organising her BHC sleeve. The enemy would only need to assign one Blackswan, as each Blackswan carried fifty Spiders. She'd taken part in enough NATO exercises to know that such irregular threats as those special-ops troops now presented to the invader had to be eliminated absolutely. Her memory replayed fragments of the pre-war briefings they'd had, and she could recall agreeing with her squad that the special-ops guys were the most doomed, certainly more doomed than the regular troops.

She rolled the BHC sleeve up her body and felt her eyes well in sudden regret. The special-ops troops must think getting out to the sub would only require the shooting down of a limited number of Spiders. She looked again at the bright blue sky and cursed the unfairness of it all. She missed the Squitch telling her how many of the enemy were approaching and from what directions and at what speeds. Squinting against the brightness above her, she thought she saw the black dot multiply; but, as earlier, she could not be sure that impurities on her corona were the cause.

An urgent shout came to her ears. Now the BHC sleeve restricted her movements again, she struggled to lean forward on the low wall and peer through the trunks of the palm trees. The Spanish squad had split into two pairs. One pair had taken up firing positions in the road, Pickups pointing skywards, while the other pair had selected one of the large rowing boats that lay abandoned on the stony beach and were dragging it to the water's edge.

On another shout, the pair in the road opened fire. Dozens of shots cracked out in almost-continuous fire. Pip strained her head to see an explosion burst a hundred or so metres in the air, and she let out a whispered, "Wow," as the fire pair turned and ran for the boat, ejecting the empty magazines and inserting new ones as they went.

Another shout went up: "Incoming, east!" The pair who had been dragging the boat unslung their Pickups and fired into the sky. The pair running from the road both slammed into the boat shoulders first. This shifted it enough that it scraped across the stones and the bow entered the water.

For a brief moment, Pip began to wonder if they would be able to escape, but a rare breeze lifted the fronds of a palm tree to reveal part of the sky with black dots coming down in a line. Pip gasped in dismay. The troops opened up with the same rapid rate of fire that, after just a couple of seconds, ended in another deadening explosion above them. That pair then also discarded the empty magazines and reloaded.

The squad shouted to each other again but the crash of waves kept their words from Pip. The rowing boat slid further into the slight swell and the bow began rising and falling. Two of the squad jumped into it, steadied themselves, and raised their Pickups and pointed them eastwards. The other pair paused, and then one turned and faced north, while the other turned to the west. All four of the troops opened fire simultaneously.

Although Pip could not see the whole scene, the soldiers' defensive reaction carried a sense of desperate inevitability. On a martial level, Pip admired the four men for their prowess, but on a human level, her spirit buckled under the strain of watching them die. For several seconds, all four fired as continuously as their Pickups allowed. Pip marvelled at their professionalism: at least three were always firing, with only one of them reloading at a time. Spiders came at them from the east, north and west, but of course the enemy's super AI used standard military tactics to outflank its enemy. It sent Spiders flying in a straight line to come down on top of them, and then landed more on either side on the beach, allowing those to clatter their way to the target, as the troops concentrated their attention skyward. From the blue expanse

171

above them came the sounds of explosion after explosion as the four special-ops troops worked together seamlessly doing what they had trained to do.

The Spider that finally defeated them clattered along the beach not thirty metres from where Pip huddled against the wall of the villa. It raced past her and on towards its target. Despite the squad firing at their maximum ability, the Spider strode up to them, and although one trooper saw the danger and reacted, it detonated. In an instant, the special-ops troops, the rowing boat, and several tons of stones were picked up and thrown skywards in an explosion that Pip felt vibrate through her whole body. She stopped breathing. A wave of debris rained down around her. A sharp piece of stone hit her exposed face hard, and she sobbed in reaction. She felt her skin split and warm liquid run down her cheek and collect in the ridge where the edge of the BHC sleeve pressed against her face, before she sensed the blood trickle over.

She looked at the beach, at the destroyed boats, at the remains of the special-ops squad, and wondered how on Earth these awful machines could ever be defeated. Pip felt an abyss of helplessness, of a crushing certainty that Europe, with all of its culture and history and its learning from which the whole world could have benefited, would soon join those empires that history had all but forgotten. A century and a half of liberal progress would now end in a vicious, overwhelming assault to which NATO had no answer.

Other Spiders crashed into the beach and the road, and a few fell into the surf with a splash. Pip watched them as their legs opened and they clicked and clacked around the crater in the beach. With each wave, more and more water sloshed into the ditch, which in turned caused stones of all sizes and colours to slide down the sides. One Spider walked further away from the site of the explosion, in Pip's direction. Her mouth dried and her heart rate picked up again. The Spider stopped close to a piece of debris. The two foremost legs turned upwards and acted like arms as they lifted part of the torso of a soldier and appeared to examine it. Pip peered more keenly but she could not see any other markings on the machine.

It dropped the body part and repeated the process a number of times: selecting a piece of debris, picking it up, analysing it, and discarding it when finished. It clicked and clacked around the debris field while its compatriots moved further along the beach and onto the road. Pip stared in fascination: she'd never considered that the Spiders would do such a thing. They certainly had not during the earlier attacks; but then, she reasoned, then the enemy hadn't been in control of the territory.

Abruptly, the investigatory Spider made a rapid series of clicks and took off, rising straight up into the sky at high speed. The others did the same an instant later, and Pip shielded her eyes to watch them leave, noting how the eight legs withdrew to merge with each Spider's body. In a few seconds, the black dots receded almost out of sight. Pip sagged back against the low garden wall, shattered. Her body and spirit cried out for rest. She laid down on the soft, yielding dirt of a flowerbed and told herself she could have just a micro-sleep—

"Pip? Pip?"

She only felt her head nod and blink, and suddenly the daylight had all but gone and a new yet familiar face was looking at her. She thought she dreamed, but her senses rushed back to her and she knew reality had returned. "Corp.?" she asked.

"Yeah," Rory said. "Have you any idea how long you've been AWOL?" he asked with a smile.

"You're not gonna put me on a charge, are you?" she replied.

"That depends. What happened to your face?"

She touched her cheek below her left eye and felt swelling there encrusted in dried blood. "Lucky break. There are four squirrels on the beach who got pulverised. You should've been here."

"I wish I had been."

She pushed herself up to a sitting position and said: "They must've shot down ten Spiders. Really bloody impressive, Corp."

"They didn't know they should ditch their tech?"

She shook her head and answered: "I tried to tell them but they wouldn't listen. Said they'd taken out actual ragheads inland and now they had a sub about to retrieve them." Pip saw the look of suspicion on Rory's face and was glad he appeared to feel the same, for if the special-ops squad had attacked part of the enemy's invasion force, it was inconceivable that they could have survived long enough to reach the coast.

Rory said: "How could they contact the sub with enemy jamming blocking comms?"

"Prearranged. The sub comes in and goes back out at set times."

"Jesus, we've got a way out of here."

"Just what I thought," Pip said with a flicker of a smile.

Rory put his arms around her with a level of intense concern Pip mistakenly ascribed to the stress of the situation. He said: "Come on, let's get you inside. Tomorrow we catch the sub and get out of here."

Chapter 26

The closer journalist Geoffrey Kenneth Morrow got to the danger area, the stronger his sense of foreboding became. The monorail train sped south-westwards through the stunning French countryside towards Spain, and he had the whole carriage to himself. For the train's return journey, they'd be cramming evacuees on the roof.

He liked to think he had been no slouch as a journalist; yes, everyone read roundups and even in-depth stories written by super AI, but human journalists still existed to add more life and flavour to reportage, to give those shocking stories a sharper edge when they broke. Super AI could aggregate, extrapolate and then write copy in any one of a thousand styles, but enough people still wanted to read copy written by human hand, and even forgave the occasional typo or rare factual inaccuracy. This happened in cycles every few years: the fashion went towards the latest generation of artificial-intelligence constructs, invariably leading to headlines predicting the end of human involvement in newsgathering and reportage, until something went wrong and popular opinion swung back in favour of real people, and the headlines asked how artificial intelligence could ever have gained such dominance.

Geoff's most frequent editor had a favourite Orwell quote, framed and hanging behind the wall: "Journalism is printing something that someone, somewhere, does not want printed. All else is public relations." Few people actually printed anything anymore, but the essence remained sound. On the other hand, Orwell's famous quote had never meant as little as it did now. Never in Geoff's memory had any international news event been so black and white. His hack-sense screamed that there must be a conspiracy, there had to be more to it. The reason the Third Caliph had given for the unprovoked assault did not convince a great many of the people of Europe.

The media in the Home Countries and the other European countries bristled with accusation, theory, conjecture. Fingers pointed at Russia, at China, and even at the USA on the preposterous grounds that the removal of European markets would finally allow the American economy to begin to recover from the worst crash in its history twenty-four years earlier. However, once Geoff scratched the surface, none of the theories held much water, unless quite the most unlikely and outrageous diplomatic truces had been made. No, the causes of this shocking destruction might not be fully known for years or even decades—

A flashing icon in the lower left of his vision broke into his thoughts. He said: "Lisa?"

His partner's voice came back tersely: "Where are you, Geoff?"

"What? Can't you see?" he said, wondering what might have happened to stop her knowing exactly where he was.

"No, or I wouldn't have to ask, would I? The government has brought in more data restrictions under emergency powers. So, where are you?"

"About fifty kilometres from Toulouse, I think," he answered, part of his mind suddenly running with the idea of the invasion just being a front for the current English government to carry out a massive power grab. The idea fizzled under the weight of its outstanding improbability in less than a tenth of a second. A reminder popped up from somewhere in his memory that his partner was pregnant with their child, so he asked: "How are you? How are you feeling?"

"Yes, fine," Lisa answered in her unhappy voice.

"Have my parents visited?"

"Yes, they've been. It was nice to see them."

"They can't wait to be grandparents, can they?"

Silence.

"Lisa?"

"Yes?"

"It's going to be okay, don't worry."

"I do worry, Geoff. What if it's like Nairobi last year?"

"No way, not a chance—"

"You nearly died."

For the hundredth time, regret surged inside Geoff that he'd told her about Nairobi. "But this is nothing like that," he said.

"Really? You got yourself lost in a city of twenty million where law and order had completely broken down—"

"It was a hot story, Lisa. Chinese, Russian and African mafia going at it like hammer and tongs. Kenyan officials taking bribes from all of them. The government was falling apart—"

"Geoff… Please come back. It's not safe there."

Geoff clamped his jaw shut to stop the sigh being audible to her. The monorail train whooshed into a tunnel and

Geoff saw his head reflected back at him in the black window glass. The tight curls sat unruly on his head and he recalled that he'd meant to get a dry cut before he left. A second later, the train exited the tunnel back into bright sunlight and his view of the countryside returned as the train rose higher than the embankments on either side. Patches of evacuees moving on foot came into view on a road that ran parallel with the monorail.

"Geoff? Geoff? Are you still there?"

"Yes, Lisa. Try not to worry, will you? I'm not going to go anywhere near the frontline. Everything's going to be fine and I'll be back in no time."

"Oh, that's a great help. Thanks," Lisa said and ended the connection. Geoff sighed aloud in relief. He knew his platitudes sounded hopelessly insincere but could not think what else to say. He often wished Lisa would just understand and support him a little more. He'd never made any secret of his career and she'd gone into their relationship with her eyes open. Geoff thought it wasn't reasonable to expect him to change just because they were going to start a family.

The data feed in his lens announced the train's imminent arrival at its destination. The names of the city's tourist attractions flashed up for his consideration but he blinked them away, not interested in Toulouse itself, only in how he might find a connection south, closer to the action. Geoff felt the deceleration as he continued to stare at the snaking lines of evacuees that had continued uninterrupted since the end of the call with Lisa. Questions formed in his mind: why are they traipsing along on foot like that? Do they already know they won't get official transport to take them north? As his suspicious journalist's mind constantly queried, his lens flashed up a sudden diversion. The train was not following the monorail to the city centre as it normally would, but now turned to the east, heading into the outskirts. For several minutes, he passed urban streets.

New data and instructions flashed up in Geoff's view. The super AI controlling transport in this part of France had abruptly reassigned this train as a medical evacuation transport. A slight movement as it adjusted its heading made Geoff put out his arm to steady himself. He watched with growing curiosity as his transport moved towards a different terminus. Hordes of people watched in the distance as the train veered to another platform. The crowd stared but did not move.

Geoff grabbed his rucksack and moved to the nearest door. The monorail stopped. The door opened and he stepped out onto the bright concrete, noting the handful of others who also exited. Barriers guided all of them to the exit. Geoff barely noticed the growing commotion because his lens told him he would have to travel across the city almost to the airport to get a connection south on a provincial line. He watched the display in his lens as it established for him the least-troublesome way to cross the city to his new destination. He did not feel like walking but the lens told him he had no choice.

A growing commotion pulled him back to his surroundings. A cacophony of shouts went up distantly. Geoff had never learned French or any other foreign language because his lens would flash up working translations if he needed them, but in crowded situations like this he had to keep that feature deactivated otherwise his vision would be overwhelmed with too many fragments of text—

Abruptly, an unseen force pushed Geoff down onto his right side with crushing power. For an instant, he felt as though he were on a ride at an amusement park, but the burning heat from his cheek as the force pushed him across the polished concrete began to hurt at once. A deep boom shuddered through the air. He stopped sliding when the pressure vanished as suddenly as it had arrived. He noted human screams in the distance, shocked and scared and urgent. He lifted his head and a vicious pain stung all around his face and crawled over his scalp, as though he'd woken up with the worst hangover imaginable. His lens offered to transmit a live feed to his editor Alan in London, to which Geoff acquiesced with a painful blink.

The screams grew louder, and as a result, Geoff deduced that he could not have been very close to the centre of the explosion. He heaved himself onto his hands and knees, noting how much effort that required, and then a voice in his head pointed out that Alan would not appreciate images of the concrete floor at the current time.

With the side of his head feeling as though it were on fire, he pulled himself upright and saw black, smoke-filled chaos in the terminal.

"What the fuck just happened there, Geoff?" Alan's voice broke in. "Can you hear me?"

"Yeah, yeah," Geoff mumbled. "Looks like a bomb."

"Why? Who by? What for?"

"Give me a minute," Geoff croaked, swaying on his feet.

"Take your time," Alan said. "The pictures are great. Just try to get a little closer when you can."

"Okay," Geoff said, wishing there was a wall nearby against which he could steady himself. People ran to the left and right in front of him, panic on their faces. Geoff fell down into a sitting position and noticed the blood on the floor that must have come from him. He swore aloud and galvanised himself, standing up again so Alan would get better pictures. The smoke rose towards the high ceiling and the scared and wounded people became visible.

"That's great, Geoff," Alan said. "We're running your feed out on numerous platforms."

"I want a percentage," Geoff said.

"Check your contract, you'll get a bonus."

"Jesus, you're so generous."

"Still better than market average... Pan left, what's that commotion?"

"Not sure," Geoff answered, unwilling to speculate. The sense of chaos and the fear of newly hurt victims remained raw. He said what he saw: "There appear to be individuals doing something to the front of the train."

"Hijack?" Alan asked in incredulity.

"Impossible," Geoff replied at once. "Encrypted management is insurmountable. It must be something else." He ducked when a volley of shots rang out. "Christ," he said.

"Get out of there if you feel threatened," Alan said.

Geoff smiled at the qualification despite the pain he felt from his face. He observed: "How long before the 'breaking news' novelty wears off and the top stories go back to the invasion fronts?"

"Already happening," Alan replied at once. "We're getting a general release from the French Interior Ministry of an attempted takeover—"

"Hijack? Seriously?"

"Yes. Looks like coercion—"

"Yeah, I'm getting the details in my feed now," Geoff said, feeling a brief return to times past, when a breaking story broke and then advanced in a logical manner until its conclusion. Local super-AI civil pacification units had resolved the misguided adventure likely undertaken by citizens who were already on society's margins.

"Initial estimates say fifteen dead, forty injured. I like it, Geoff: you've still got your talent of being in the right place at the right time."

"No shit," Geoff answered as the numbness in his head spread. "I feel like shit, now, you know?"

181

"Maybe, but those were some great pictures."

"So I can go somewhere quiet and write up a one-thousand word opinion piece now, yeah?"

Alan laughed and said: "Nice one, Geoff, good joke. No, right, there's a medi-point close to your location. I'll try to get you VIP'd from here so you don't have to wait. Get your arse to your next transport. I've got a good feeling about you now, Geoff."

Geoff replied: "I'll try to live long enough not to disappoint you." He walked away from the terminus. Outside, the piercing yellow streetlights of Toulouse stung his eyes. He recoiled in pain when he foolishly touched the side of his damaged head. He wished Lisa had been right and this was only going to be as bad as Nairobi, instead of being far worse.

Chapter 27

21.58 Saturday 25 February 2062

Serena Rizzi looked into the young girl's pale blue eyes and tried to reassure her: "They will not harm us further."

"But, but how do you know?" the girl whined, her terrified face conveying a horror Serena also felt.

Serena considered before answering, glancing at the far wall of the prison cell. The single white light in the ceiling made the cell look sterile, although she felt completely violated. She had to balance honesty with helping the girl cope with the trauma. "Because," she began, "we are more valuable to them in… a better condition."

"So we still look pretty when they violate us again?"

"What is your name?"

"Liliana."

"What did he tell you?"

"I don't know. I couldn't understand him. He was just an animal—" she broke off and sobbed.

Serena stroked Liliana's soft, matted hair and whispered: "Please try not to make a noise."

The young girl didn't respond so Serena simply held her as they sat on the single bench in the cell, which was the only surface for sitting and sleeping on. A deadening clunk sounded outside in the corridor and the light went out. Serena felt Liliana's slight body tense so she shushed her and said: "Do not worry. It is ten o'clock so they have switched the lights off and now we should sleep."

"I am scared."

"So am I."

"What will happen to us?"

"I do not know," Serena answered, recalling the violence she had already witnessed as well as endured. "We have to stay strong, that is all I can tell at this moment."

Liliana whispered: "I am ashamed because I am bleeding."

"Is it the normal time of the month for you or is it because of what he did to you?"

"I do not know, to be honest. I am sorry."

"It is normal for us to bleed when we are in such danger."

"But I am frightened they will want to violate us again and be angry if we are bleeding."

As vague details of the ceiling above them began to form in the darkness, exhaustion swept over Serena. She wanted to reassure Liliana as much as possible but also needed to rest. The stress of the last two days and her own experience had also left Serena bleeding. Images flashed through her tired mind of the warrior who had claimed her in the apartment, of how he had found the kitchen knife strapped to her thigh and debated, she felt certain, whether to slit her throat with it after he'd raped her.

She whispered: "We should rest. We should preserve our strength. We cannot know what we will face, child, but we can be sure we will need strength." Serena used the word 'child' but suspected that Liliana was only a few years younger than her. Serena gently pushed so they both lay down on the unyielding bench.

"I am afraid I will have nightmares," Liliana said.

"So am I," Serena replied, unable to keep her eyes open any longer. She said: "So we will be here for each other if we have a bad dream. Agreed?" but fell asleep before she heard Liliana's positive reply.

Serena slept through Liliana's fitful rest. She felt her compatriot's shifts and moves as distant events, relevant but temporarily disconnected. At a deeper level, Serena's body decided when it had rested sufficiently and then increased its level of awareness. Serena's spirit rose to a semi-waking state where she could accept the injustice and funnel the anger so she might use it to work for her, not against her.

At six o'clock the next morning, the overhead light clunked back on again, searing like a spotlight into the two women. Liliana woke up and both women stood and stretched, Serena insisting that they had to be ready as soon as possible. She noted how the rest had seemed to refresh Liliana, who still looked worried but who agreed with Serena more readily.

The sound of heavy footsteps thumped along the corridor outside. Serena held Liliana, who whispered a prayer for both of them. Serena sensed the stress increase as the doors to other cells were opened and spoken orders mingled with fearful moans and heavy steps.

With a dull, electronic beep, the heavy metal door swung open. In the doorway stood a tall, thick-set man and a dark, thin, robed man. The smaller one indicated that the women should leave the cell. In accented English he ordered: "Out. Go upstairs to outside space," and moved on. The tall man sneered at them.

The women left the cell and joined the others shuffling along the corridor. Serena led Liliana in the queue of women. They went up some stairs and then left along another corridor. They queued for a few minutes. Serena looked ahead to see, at the exit, three guards processing each woman. One man placed a device on each woman's right upper arm, held it there for a second, and then muttered something official. Next to him, another guard said in English: "You are now the property of the merciful Third Caliph."

Serena also kept her head lowered to avoid making eye contact with the guards. She felt a cold sting on her arm and heard the incomprehensible words, and then the English words, and reflected that they meant nothing to her. She glanced behind her to see Liliana follow with a terrified expression on her face.

Ten minutes later, Serena and Liliana stood next to each other in a line of a hundred or so women, which constituted the front row of five such lines. They had emerged from an expansive police station in a large town which Serena did not recognise. They faced a vast open space that Serena assumed must have been the original town square. Black smoke wafted from office and residential blocks in the distance. She breathed the cool, early-spring air and looked at the grey sky above. The first spats of rain hit her head.

When they had been standing there for some minutes, the rain seeping into torn and dirty clothes, a small group of robed men appeared and began walking past the front row. Serena kept her head down but could sense the menace in them.

Suddenly, a voice spoke inside her. She could hear the words as though she were thinking them herself. She looked at the group of men to see one of them speaking. The voice inside her head said: "Listen, all of you. You should count yourselves extremely fortunate."

With horror, Serena realised that the man speaking from the small group in front of them could project his voice directly into her head. If the implant they had all received allowed their captors to do that, what else might they be able to do? Whimpers and sobs from around her told her that all of the women suffered this same, new violation.

The man continued: "You are infidels. You should die. But, in his mercy, the Third Caliph has decreed that some of you may live to serve him and his empire. You have been chosen because—"

The voice stopped when a cry went up from somewhere behind Serena. A young woman rushed out screaming defiance at their captors. Serena thought the girl had a kind face and a few weeks ago was probably a teacher or a care worker or a—

The young woman abruptly stared back at the rest of the women, almost into Serena's eyes, it seemed, put her arms out either side, stopped breathing, and flopped onto the ground.

Serena froze, wondering if the young woman was actually dead. Nothing happened. She glanced at the man who had spoken, who gave his audience a satisfied half-smile. Two armed guards trudged into view. They each picked up one of the young woman's arm and dragged her body away.

Again, the voice spoke inside Serena's head: "You each have an implant that any Caliphate citizen can use to kill you at will."

A few gasps and sobs came from around her, but Serena regarded this announcement as merely another test on the road to the task she had been set. Conversely, with each setback, with every new violation and affrontery, Serena felt strengthened, emboldened to continue on this path, *her* path.

The man continued: "Do any more of you have anything to say?"

Silence unsurprisingly greeted his rhetorical question.

He went on: "You may now bid farewell to your former home. You will be taken into the Caliphate, there to serve Caliphate citizens. And I warn you: you must obey your new masters. Any failure to do what is required of you will result in your immediate death."

From the sky above them, a vast Caliphate transport ship descended with a hissing buzz that belied its massive size and weight. As soon as it touched the ground, slits opened in the body, revealing darkness inside.

The man said: "The first row shall proceed in an orderly fashion from the right, and enter the transport."

To Serena, this aircraft appeared to be the same design as the first one she'd seen land in Rome on the previous Saturday night at the hospital; six days past, which now felt like six decades ago.

The line moved off. Serena glanced at Liliana and a touch of hands reassured Serena that her compatriot could cope for now. She followed the women in front of her and mounted the steps into the transport. She fought the urge to glance behind her and look at her home country for what she knew would be the last time. Serena stepped into the transport knowing that her journey was only now beginning.

Chapter 28

14.23 Sunday 26 February 2062

Corporal Rory Moore sipped from the mug of hot, sweet brown tea he held in both hands, savouring every drop of the malty flavour. In the seat next to him sat Pip, blowing gently across the surface of her tea to cool it.

The door to the meeting room slid open and a tall, diffident woman stepped over the flange, ducking a little so her Royal Navy cap did not snag on the doorway. She walked up to the table and introduced herself: "Chief Petty Officer Pettifer," and then added: "Julia Pettifer," and Rory realised he must have failed to keep a straight face at the alliteration of her rank and surname. She continued: "Welcome aboard HMS *Spiteful*. Now, I know you've been asked a few questions already, but I'd like to clarify some things if that's okay?"

Rory nodded and heard Pip answer: "If you keep giving us unlimited tea like this, you can ask as many questions as you like."

Pettifer smiled and said: "Good, no problem. Right, Private Clarke, first question: Are you sure the special-ops soldiers you encountered were Spanish?"

"Yes," Pip answered at once. "The insignias on their uniforms definitely included the Spanish flag, but as I told the debrief officer, I didn't get close enough to them to see any more details, and at no time did they mention or offer to tell me their regiment."

"Right, okay," Pettifer said, looking down at a handheld screen. "Corporal Moore, you said that when you arrived on the beach, the engagement was over and there was nothing substantial left of the special-ops' unit, yes?"

Rory began to wonder when the Chief Petty Officer would get to the difficult questions she must have come to ask. He and Pip had been debriefed immediately after their medical when the submarine had picked them up. In the intervening hours, *Spiteful* must have been in touch with London, and someone there wanted more answers. He said pointedly: "Yes, when I finally caught up with Pip—er, Private Clarke—the engagement had been over for at least two hours. I know this because, as I mentioned during the first debrief, I heard the engagement taking place and took cover outside the town."

"So we only have the Private's word for what happened on the beach?"

Rory shrugged and said: "Why wouldn't that be enough?"

"Because both of you discarded your Battlefield Management Support systems," Pettifer said, all of her initial friendliness vanishing.

"Yeah," Rory answered, trying to contain growing frustration, "because if we hadn't, we'd be just as dead as all of the other NATO troops in Spain." He saw Pettifer glance down so he said: "Pity you subs couldn't have given us some support instead of hiding under the sea out here, eh?"

"Steady on, Corp.," he heard Pip mutter.

Pettifer's face hardened. She said: "London wants to know exactly how two lower ranks such as the pair of you managed to be the only NATO troops to escape from behind enemy lines. Especially when we consider the number of extremely well-armed NATO special-ops inserted with the sole objective of causing disruption behind the lines, none of whom have shown up for extraction by us or any of the other submarines off the Spanish coast."

Rory said: "I don't believe for a minute that we were the only ones to work out what you had to do to survive." Anger and irritation fused inside Rory before burning out to leave only exhaustion in their wake. Now they had secured safety, he struggled to comprehend why anyone should doubt answers that he regarded simply as common sense. The claustrophobia caused by the small, sterile meeting room made his head hurt. Too many recent memories played on a loop in his mind. He knew, as he suspected did Pip, that this was survivor's guilt, but identifying a problem was only one step to resolving it, not the whole journey.

"Okay," Pettifer said, "let's go back a little further—"

Pip broke in: "Must we? Do you really need to ask these questions now?"

Rory glanced at her and silently thanked her.

Pettifer pulled down the cuffs of her pressed white blouse and answered: "London needs all the information we can gather. The invasion is going very badly for us, all of us. So far, you are the only two individuals to have seen combat with enemy forces and lived to tell the tale. Your superiors— and mine, by the way—have considered the responses you gave during your initial debrief after you came on board, now they'd like you to answer these questions, if you feel up to it, of course—"

Pettifer broke off when Rory scoffed.

She continued: "However, your CO understands the urgency of the situation and has approved this Q&A."

Rory said: "I just don't know what more we can add."

"Okay," Pettifer began, "when did you, Corporal Moore, first realise you would stand a better chance of survival without the use of your Battlefield Management Support System?"

Rory looked at the Petty Officer and asked: "Look, are you sure you don't have records of my last conversation with the Squitch?"

Pettifer shook her head and said: "Enemy jamming disrupted too many relays from the in-space SkyWatch—"

"How?" Rory asked in exasperation. "We're supposed to have the best tech. What the hell did the enemy hit us with?"

"You're not the only one asking those questions, Corporal. That's why I and the people in London just want to go over what happened to the pair of you again. Now—"

"It really was a very simple, logical choice. The first Spider I destroyed required one Stiletto and over twenty, I think it must have been at least thirty, smart bullets to destroy. The Squitch told me the battlespace was saturated with enemy targets and no NATO presence left. It actually kept telling me to take cover—"

"Yes, but when did you decide to deactivate and discard it?"

"I'm not sure exactly. Transports were being shot down, other troops were getting hit, but the enemy had deployed none of its own troops, as far as I was aware. So, obviously, they were hitting us only with super AI, and that had to identify and locate us somehow." He frowned and asked: "Isn't this all really bloody obvious?"

"And you stand by your conviction that the BHC sleeve kept the Spiders from seeing you?"

"Absolutely," Rory answered, hoping the interrogation would end soon.

Pip said: "We have to get rid of that hideous design flaw. We have to put legs in them so we can move about in them more freely. That restricted movement was nearly the end of me."

Pettifer's face tipped down and she murmured her understanding.

Rory drained his mug of tea and asked: "Is there anything else? Because I don't know about the Private here, but I could really do with some rest."

"Yes," Pettifer said with no trace of sympathy. "Regarding the local population, how would you describe their morale?"

Rory closed his eyes and let out an expansive sigh, but he heard Pip put her mug of tea down on the table and say: "The people we met were scared but stoic. They worked out, sooner than us I think, that using any kind of tech is only going to bring a Spider down on their heads. The mountain villages we passed through were already abandoned and for the most part destroyed, and the survivors had taken shelter in old, disused mines. I want to stress again that despite their own disasters, they still took an injured comrade of ours in and operated on him."

"Operated?" Pettifer queried in shock.

"No GenoFluid packs."

"That is tough," she said in a level tone. "Were there any reports of the enemy capturing local civilians?"

"Not that we heard," Pip answered.

Rory said: "Seemed to me they're going for straightforward annihilation."

"Finally, did you witness or see anything to indicate that the enemy preferred some targets over others? Anything that suggested something outside normal military tactics?"

Rory shook his head and glanced at Pip to see her do the same.

"Very well," Pettifer said. "Thank you both for your time. I'll have a rating show you to your quarters."

"Thanks," Rory said in a tone which he hoped sounded neutral.

The door to the meeting room opened, and Pettifer stopped as she stepped through it. She turned back to them and said: "Listen, I don't want to think about what the pair of you have been through, but it's really bad for us up there, and London and NATO need every scrap of information they can get. Anything could be important and the enemy is starving us of intel."

Rory said: "Just one thing: when do we go back to Blighty?"

The Chief Petty Officer shook her head and answered: "Not for a while. We're stationed here to retrieve special-ops troops who haven't turned up yet, and the way this war's going, in a few weeks there may not be a Blighty to go back to."

The door slid closed after her and Rory said: "Shit, Pip. And I was thinking of asking them if they could lend us a few people to try and get Crimble out."

"Don't think they'd do that no matter how well or badly the war was going, Corp. If survivors can get out to the sub, they'll get picked up, like us. But if not, they're stuck."

"Do you think he survived the amputation?" Rory asked.

"No idea, but I hope so."

"Me too."

"Well, we're stuck on this giant metal coffin now, for God knows how long," Pip said with an impish grin.

"Better get some rest then," Rory said, thanking whatever gods existed again for sparing both of them.

Chapter 29

06.47 Monday 27 February 2062

"Thank you, Maureen," Terry Tidbury said to his wife as she placed a plate with two poached eggs on toast in front of him. He sat, lost in thought at the unremitting bad news. Operation Defensive Arc had fallen apart in the first twenty-four hours and now defence consisted only of NATO forces retreating at the slowest possible rate on all of the four fronts, each of which the enemy harried relentlessly.

He looked at the yolks on the plate in front of him as they wobbled in the whites. He took his knife and slit one so the liquid flowed out like yellow blood. The yolk sack collapsed and the liquid ran around the plate and soaked into the toast like blood soaks into clothes. He had never before realised the viscous similarity between runny egg yolk and blood.

He heard Maureen say: "Time's getting on, Terry dear. Don't eat if you're not hungry."

Still staring at the eggs on his plate, Terry replied: "Oh, I am hungry. You're right, thank you." He cut into the toast and ate.

Maureen sat down opposite him at the breakfast bar in the spacious kitchen and placed two mugs of steaming tea between them. He saw her look at him and sensed how she hid her concern.

"Things are bound to improve when we get more information," he offered, wanting to reassure the love of his life.

She half-smiled and said: "Do you know how many times you have said to me we should always remember that we make our decisions based on the information we have to hand when we must make them? And that if it turns out we didn't make the right decision only after new information comes to light, we have nothing to reproach ourselves for?"

Terry smiled and said: "Yes, but I'm not convinced that mantra can be applied to the current situation." He put another large piece of egg and toast into his mouth and chewed, savouring the flavour.

"Why shouldn't it be?" Maureen said, cutting into her own poached eggs and toast. "You have done what you could with the information you had available."

Terry shook his head and said: "Too many choices, Maureen. It hasn't been—and still isn't—simply a question of not enough information, although we're going to need a lot more if we're ever to make any progress. It's about the options we had, and about the options for the future—"

A soft chime from the screen in the wall next to the cooker interrupted him. The house's super AI said: "Terry, your vehicle is relaying a message from the Ministry of Defence that has requested your presence on-site as soon as possible. Your vehicle notes more traffic than usual on the motorways into central London. As this may increase your journey time by up to four minutes, your vehicle requests that you take this into account. Thank you."

Maureen let out a laugh and said: "Polite little bugger, isn't it?"

Terry said with a smile: "Such a long-winded way of telling me to get a bloody move on." He put the last of the egg and toast in his mouth, swallowed, and gulped down some tea.

Five minutes later, Terry sat in the back of his Toyota Rive-All as it autonomously navigated the local residential streets. At the junction with the first main road, the vehicle paused for a few seconds before nipping into a gap among the continuous flow of traffic as the super AI governing the majority of England's roads assumed control.

Terry took out his slate and spun it open to review the overnight situation reports when the vehicle interrupted him: "Sir Terry, Squonk is relaying a request from SHAPE. Would you prefer I send it to your slate or the screen?"

"On the screen for a change," Terry answered, looking to his left and taking in the grey dawn outside, droplets of rain running horizontally along the side windows due to the vehicle's speed.

General Joseph E. Jones's saturnine face appeared on the screen in front of Terry's seat. Terry had never seen his African American chief appear so serious yet miserable. Jones said: "Good morning, General. Thanks for taking this call on your way into the office."

Terry found that he appreciated the General's good manners more as the military situation worsened. Although an American, there was something British in Jones's demeanour which engendered in Terry a sense of trust in his superior's judgement. Terry said: "No problem, General. Is it something urgent, specific, or to do with current deployments?"

Jones sighed and said: "I think we're in for another problematic Chiefs of Staff meeting this morning. Our resources continue to dwindle, General, and it makes the choices tougher... In addition, we have confirmation of what we suspected in theatre a few days ago."

Terry tried not to look as disheartened as he felt. "The Lapwing?"

The Supreme Commander of Allied Forces in Europe nodded and said: "Yes, the subjugated populations are now subjected to the same laser-equipped ACA the enemy used in Israel."

"I think we should assume it's been deployed in all theatres, not only West."

"I guess we could've expected it, but I was kinda hoping for later rather than sooner. Anyway, I expect the news to cause a few ripples politically so I wanted to give you a heads-up."

"Have you decided whether to inform the other European generals?"

Jones's answer surprised Terry. He asked: "Would you?"

Terry responded at once: "Yes, Sir. Despite the current situation, I believe they have similar problems that I have regarding my political masters, so it would be fair to let them know that once the news breaks, we can expect increased political tension."

Jones nodded and said: "Good."

"Have the naming committee got back to us with the designation for the enemy's main troop transport craft?"

"Not yet, but given the size of the damn thing I think we should just call it the 'Big Bastard'," Jones replied with a mirthless chuckle.

"I see the overnights mention reports from the subs. I thought the enemy's jamming would've prevented that."

Jones shook his head and said: "We got those reports thanks only to the vagaries of atmospheric fluctuations, General."

"I was hoping they might have extracted some special-ops troops rather than just a pair of ordinary Royal Engineers by now. We could do with the intel."

"Have you read what the two troops who did get out had to report?"

"Not yet."

"You might wanna, it's still useful, although the local civilians left there won't have much of a chance if they've got Lapwings in addition to Blackswans hunting them. Another thing we need to discuss at the meeting, cos it's also gonna cause political issues, are all the ships heading for Spain and Portugal to take refugees off."

Terry said: "Is that going to have such an impact on ops?"

"Uh-huh. We got private individuals trying to take pleasure boats out into the Bay of Biscay like it's another goddamn Dunkirk. Coastguards can barely cope, especially in this weather, and are pleading for us to mount recovery ops."

Terry shook his head and said: "As if we didn't have enough to deal with."

"General, we can't let what's going on around the periphery distract us from the key issues."

"Agreed," Terry said with a shrug.

"Nothing's gonna change till we get answers to two questions: one, what is the answer to the power of the shielding on their ACAs, and two: how do we cut through the enemy's jamming and re-establish comms? Till then, we're just managing a fire in a whorehouse. See you at the meeting, General."

The screen went blank and Terry glanced out of the left-side window. The rain had stopped and the clouds parted to reveal the red and orange hues of a colourful dawn. As the vehicle sped to his central London destination, he tried to enjoy the view because he felt certain such luxury would not last much longer.

Chapter 30

13.21 Monday 27 February 2062

Professor Duncan Seekings muttered to himself as he strode towards the Dog & Partridge public house in Salisbury town centre. Today was the first day he hadn't gone to his laboratory and office at Porton Down military research establishment in over two weeks, on the insistence of one of the chief executives who'd visited him the previous day and dropped large, unmissable hints that he should take a day off.

"What was her name?" he spoke aloud. "Joanne? Jennifer? Juniper? Doesn't matter. Best interests at heart, I expect. Just wanting to help, indeed. Get some fresh air, yes. In the pub. Great idea."

He walked across the parking area and pushed open the small door to the public bar, ducking so as not to hit his head on the lintel. He tutted at being obliged to continue to keep his head down to avoid the original Elizabethan oak beams in the low ceiling.

At the bar, he addressed the young man who greeted him: "Good afternoon. I have a table booked upstairs in the name of Seekings."

"Yes, sir, just a moment." The young man's eye flickered and he said: "Right-ho, table number three. Something to drink, sir?"

"Yes, thank you. A light and bitter and a pint of Guinness, please."

The young man reached under the counter and retrieved a set of snooker balls in a tray. He said: "If you'd like to go up, I'll bring your drinks."

"Thank you," Duncan said, taking the tray of balls. He kept his head down until he went through the door at the back of the bar. This led to a more modern annex at the back of the Dog & Partridge, built as recently as the Victorian era. He went up the staircase and into the snooker room. He was pleased to see that all of the four snooker tables were free, and that the barman had already switched on the light above table three.

"Jolly good," he muttered, putting the tray on the table and picking each ball out of it. He set the balls up and then selected a cue from the dozen that stood in a rack by the wall. He looked down its length to ascertain if it was straight, and then tutted and put it back. On the fourth attempt, he muttered: "I suppose it will have to do."

The door opened and a short, stocky man entered carrying a narrow, long case. "Good afternoon, Professor," he called in a cheerful tone.

"One-thirty. You are exactly on time as usual, Graham," Duncan said, standing his cue by the wall and shaking Graham's hand.

"I can't believe they let you out of the place," Graham said, putting the case on the side of the snooker table. "What's this? A day off for good behaviour?" The case clipped open under his thumbs and he took out two halves of a snooker cue, which he screwed together.

Duncan picked up his half-pint of bitter and the bottle of light ale, and poured the latter into the former. He said: "I think the situation is getting too hectic—dare I say, even a little too stressful—for those youngsters."

Graham stood his cue by the wall and picked up his pint of Guinness. "Cheers," he said.

"Cheers," Duncan echoed. He watched his oldest friend look up at him and said: "Actually, I am glad to get away to somewhere outside, even if it is for just a few hours."

"You'll be going straight back after this?"

"Oh, yes. It's all getting rather boring."

"But the last time we spoke, you said you'd worked out what that bloody Caliphate had been up to. Shall I break?"

Duncan nodded. "Go ahead," he said.

Graham picked his cue up and placed the white ball between the yellow and green balls. His jeans and shirt stretched as he leaned forward and broke the frame off. The fifteen reds in the pack at the other end of the table split open and the white ball rolled back up to the baulk area, close to where it had begun its journey.

Duncan said: "Good break, you've left me nothing to go at, as usual." He walked around the table, choosing which red to aim for. He said: "Yes, we know roughly how the Caliphate has created its weapons, but the problem is that we will probably need years to develop better weapons."

"Yes," Graham said. "And our damnable computers are flapping almost as much as the politicians."

Duncan leaned down at the table and played his shot: the cue ball glanced a red which rolled into a cushion before hitting another red, while the white ball kissed the blue and stopped in the middle of the table. "Damn," he said at the result of his effort.

"Hmm, thanks," Graham said, before getting down and smartly knocking a red into one of the middle pockets. "One," he announced.

Duncan said: "The key problem, as far as my people see things, is replication. Its uses are still very limited in military affairs. Of course, our super AI can design improved weapons relatively quickly, but new ACAs would still have to be manufactured in physical production plants. Only a few components would be able to be replicated. Perhaps we need some ideas?"

"My team assumes," Graham said, lining up a shot on the blue, "the Caliphate, having stolen a march on us, has the advantage and could theoretically keep ahead of us." He played the shot and the blue ball wobbled in the jaws of the pocket before falling. "Six," he announced, retrieving the blue and replacing it on its spot.

"You can miss now, if you feel like it," Duncan said testily. "Their advantage is one thing, but nowhere near the most important."

"Oh? Are you in the same boat as me?" Graham said, lining up the next red.

"Yes, I do think so, don't you? We must find ways to minimise or neutralise their blasted advantages now, not in twelve or eighteen or twenty-four months."

"We've already found a couple," Graham said, before knocking another red into a corner pocket. "Seven," he said with a smile.

"Have you been practising without telling me, old chap?"

Duncan's friend looked taken aback as he said: "As if I'd do such a thing. Offensive you should even suggest it, sir." He smirked and lined up a shot on the brown ball.

Duncan rolled his eyes and said: "Spare me your mock offence. I know it's a bit tedious, but I do think those in power expect us to come up with some answers very, very smartly."

"At my place, we were quite impressed with the captain of the *Hyperion*. Did you see what he did before his ship sunk?" He played the shot and the brown ball hit the near jaw of a middle pocket and ran into some reds. "Damn. Well, seven's a fair start I suppose." Graham stood upright, went to the wall and moved a gold-coloured metal indicator on an antique scoring board.

Duncan scoffed: "That will be the highest break of the frame." He leaned his long, thin arms over the table to try a red to a corner pocket. "No, I saw a brief summary of the engagement but events have been moving rather quickly." He hit the red and it disappeared in the pocket. "One," he announced.

"Good shot," Graham said. "He and his ships varied the coherence length on the shots from their Sea Striker laser canons. It's a feature the Yanks' Mark Three Pulsars don't have. It let those Royal Navy lads shoot down twice the number of enemy ACAs the Yanks did."

Duncan lined up a shot on the black, but no longer looked along the cue. His friend's observation caused a spark to flash in his mind's eye. He hit the shot, and to his complete shock, the black ball hit the back of the pocket with a loud thud. "Oh, that's eight," Duncan said, seeing his own surprise reflected on his friend's face. He retrieved the black from the pocket and put it back on its spot, asking Graham: "But that would only work until the enemy ACA registered the variation, and then adjusted its own shielding frequency to match, thus negating the advantage, wouldn't it?"

"The engagement in the Med only had a few moments to run, so it didn't matter greatly on the night. But since then, the lasers we're using to fight the enemy have shown that the variations are not sufficient."

"And?" Duncan asked, lining up his next red ball.

"And what?" Graham asked before taking a pull from his glass.

"What's the current situation regarding this advantage?"

"It's been forwarded for consideration in the next generation of weapons."

Duncan played the shot, missed the red, stood up, and said in exasperation: "But unless we do something now, there isn't going to be a next generation of weapons, for Pete's sake."

Graham put his glass down on the small table by the wall and went to the table. "That's why I wanted to meet you like this, in private. Come on, Professor, things haven't only been a tad hectic the last few days, they've been positively manic—"

"I don't think we should over-dramatize things too much, old chap, but I do take your point."

Graham leaned over the table to take his next shot and said: "The super AI is spitting out all kinds of suggestions, projections, simulations. Our political masters are overloaded with this; the military are struggling to manage what is becoming a total rout." A red disappeared into a middle pocket. "Good ideas, things that might actually help NATO troops in the field, can slip past everyone without being noticed."

Duncan had already called up the relevant data in his lens. He said: "But the battlefield pulsars out there now are all based on the Yank design."

"Yes, the modification was made but ended when the enemy's super AI noted and adjusted the frequency of its ACAs' shielding to negate our advantage." Graham took on an ambitious pink to a centre pocket and missed. "Just the one," he announced. He said: "I wanted to be sure you were aware of the whole story, Professor."

"Hmm," Duncan said, staring at the snooker table but not seeing anything, his mind buzzing with thoughts. He said to Graham, without looking at him: "You know, I have been wrapped up in two very important aspects at my place: the fusion reaction behind the enemy's propulsion systems and their remarkable jamming systems."

"Got anywhere with them?" Graham asked before sipping his drink. "I was quite surprised at that Reyer fellow working out the large-scale fusion issue like that."

"Oh, me too. Some of his research is very good." Duncan had a half-hearted attempt at a red but missed. He stood, looked at his friend, and said: "Yes, I am playing around with a couple of ideas regarding the enemy's jamming. Personally, I regard their behaviour on that score as deeply unsporting; we should do something to stop them getting away with it as soon as possible."

"So how about a trade?"

"What did you have in mind?"

Graham leaned over the table and his short, thick arms stretched as he aimed his cue. He sighed, gave up, and reached for the rest that hung under the end of the table. He said: "What about randomising coherence-length variation on each Pulsar shot?"

Duncan took a pull of his light and bitter and stared at his friend. He knew something had been bothering him since Graham had brought the subject up. He said: "Of course, randomisation will prevent the enemy from making adjustments to the frequency of its ACAs' shielding, but, wait, will there be enough—"

"Yes, there will," Graham interrupted. "I ran a secret simulation and I am certain it will work."

"So why don't you put it forward yourself? Why are you telling me?"

Graham played his shot with the rest and potted a red neatly into a corner pocket. He said: "One... Because it's a little outside my field, Professor. If I put it to my committee, they would be equally as likely to berate me for wasting my and their time when I and my team are supposed to be finding an answer to the enemy's jamming... Black."

"Oh, I've looked at that. The answer is somewhere in the super-high frequencies, in highly concentrated beams. They could 'burn' through the jamming, creating directional corridors to allow comms."

Graham missed the black and stared at Duncan, mouth agape. "What did you say?"

Duncan said: "Hmm, yes. If there is enough wavelength... and an inducer that randomised... Yes, I do believe that would work." He glanced at his friend to see Graham's eye twitching and asked: "Well? I must admit, it is only a theory I came up with at one of those interminable meetings we seem to be obliged to attend almost every day now."

"You must admit, Professor, there is quite a lot to have to keep up with. Your shot."

Duncan shook his head and muttered: "But where are the snags?" He lined up a red, played the shot, and missed.

"Must there always be snags?" Graham asked with a sigh, picking up his cue.

Duncan walked back from the snooker table and said: "Of course. How many times do I have to tell you—"

"It was already too many at least ten years ago, probably longer."

"The snags must always be found before one makes oneself look an arse in public."

"You're right there," Graham said, impressively potting a long red.

Duncan saw this and said: "Damn and blast you, sir. You have been practising without telling me, haven't you?"

Graham smiled and replied: "The way this war's going, I thought I might as well enjoy it while I can. I can't imagine a world without snooker."

Duncan scoffed and said: "Wouldn't be a world worth living in, that much is certain."

Chapter 31

Crispin Webb hurried along the ground-floor corridor in the Houses of Parliament, not seeing the other members, the interns or the assistants who stared at him. Webb no longer cared what those in lower positions thought of his behaviour; the pressure on his boss had to be handled, and that was his job. In his lens, he followed numerous media feeds, his combative anger looking for a target. A more sober voice pointed out that perhaps he should not have taken that last pill with the reengineered GenoFluid bots.

He called one of Napier's other assistants and barked: "Monica?"

"Yes," came a distant, feeble response.

Webb asked: "Are you still asleep?"

"What? No, of course not. Too many late nights and early mornings, that's all."

"I don't care. Check the media now. A few outlets are carrying reports that Philip is under pressure to resign. Refute, now."

"Okay."

With twitches of his eye muscles, he called his least-favourite editor. "Morning, *Mister* MacSawley," he said.

"Anyone ever told you when a joke stops being funny?"

Webb let out a chuckle and said: "What is this shit your outlet is disseminating about people drowning in the Bay of Biscay, and the government 'doesn't care enough to rescue them'?"

Webb felt pleased when he heard defensiveness in MacSawley's voice. "What has that got to do with the all-pulling-together bullshit we agreed to three weeks ago? This is a genuine human interest st—"

"Bollocks, mate."

"Fuck you, Cris. We've got ordinary civilians taking their boats out to sea trying to pick up refugees off the coasts and not all of them are coming back. And the English coastguard, underfunded by successive governments for decades, doesn't have the gear. That falls way outside the scope of the agreement."

"No, Andy. It's war-related and that means you should run it by me first, got it?"

"No fucking way," MacSawley spat.

Webb slowed his pace as the voice in the back of his head urged caution. MacSawley was editor of *The Mail*, the most powerful media outlet in England and all of the Home Countries.

The editor, now sounding far angrier than defensive, hissed: "Don't you start acting like you're some kind of censor, Cris. That's not what 'all pulling together' means, you little shit. My readers want to know what's going on, got that? These people with their boats are bloody heroes, making a fuck-sight more effort than either of us, safely tucked away in our London cocoon."

"Don't accuse me of censorship," Webb argued back, his own fury starting to crackle and burn at MacSawley's repeated shortening of his first name, which he loathed. "I'm talking about working together so we don't accidently panic the entire populations of the Home Countries. One wrong headline from you, and—"

"What 'wrong headline' are you talking about? Did you even read the story?"

"I don't have to; I know—"

"I suppose you don't know about the recruitment drive we're doing for the British Army, either? Have you seen even one of the features we've run this week?"

"That's not the same thing, not at—"

"Listen, twat, you do your job and let me do mine. We know what your boss needs. And with all the shit going down right now, you and me are wasting what little time we've got left arguing the fucking toss over the cubed root of fuck-all."

MacSawley terminated the call and Webb swore aloud, eliciting a frown of disapproval from a woman passing him. He arrived at his first destination and resisted the urge to walk through the door without knocking. Instead, he gave the deep brown oak panelling a few heavy raps with his knuckles. A second later, there came a cough from the other side of the door, and that was good enough for Webb. He entered.

Behind the desk on the far side of the room, Defence Secretary Philip Gough heaved a sigh when his eyes met Webb's. He said: "I thought it was a little early in the day for the PM to unleash her number one jackal?"

Webb ignored the taunt and strode up to Gough's desk. He said: "Who's been leaking that you're under pressure to resign?"

Gough laughed, which surprised Webb. The Defence Secretary stroked his trimmed beard and said: "Who cares?"

"What? Listen, the PM is very keen to keep a united front. No resignations, no firings. So why are there reports this morning that you 'might be asked to resign'?"

Gough sat in his plush chair with a look of bewilderment on his narrow, angular face. He held his arms open said: "Why are you asking me? Perhaps someone misheard something. Perhaps some over-eager hack wanted to freshen up some tedious AI-written copy? How the hell am I supposed to know?"

Webb stared at Gough's eyes and his instinct told him nothing suspicious was going on. Gough might hate him—his boss didn't pay him to be popular—but nothing in the Defence Secretary's demeanour suggested subterfuge. He said: "So take my visit as a friendly reminder from the PM that no one's resigning." Webb turned to go.

"Wait a moment," Gough said.

Webb stopped and turned back. "What?"

"Do old habits really die that hard, Mr Webb?"

"Old habits?"

"Yes. You storm into my office—and, by the way, next time you had better wait for my clear invitation before entering—and start implying that I, or someone in my department, has leaked something patently untrue, as though we're living through a normal Parliamentary session of the old fun and games. Have you seen the overnight situation reports from the four fronts?"

"Er, no, I haven't had time," Webb replied, feeling nonplussed for the second time in a few minutes.

"Estimates range between ten and thirty thousand casualties, just while you and I were sleeping peacefully in our beds last night."

"Yes, well, we're all at some risk I sup—"

"But that's just it. You, me, the PM, the people on these islands, we can all sit back and relax while those

Europeans get slaughtered like cattle, and no one saw it coming. I suppose I should congratulate the PM for reining the media in to some degree. When all this kicked off, they were baying for political blood, preferably mine. And I would've given it to them, too, if it had made a jot of difference. But it wouldn't have then and it won't now. The media can see it. The country can see it. But you can't. You need to adjust to the new reality."

"Is that it?" Webb sneered.

"Yes. Now get out of my office and only come back when you have something important to say, jackal."

Webb slammed the door when he left Gough's office and strode on to his next destination, deeper in the warren of the Palace of Westminster. He made another call and said: "Monica, update now."

He heard Monica say in his ear: "Yeah, refuting, can't find a source."

"Keep an eye on any other bullshit that starts gaining traction."

"Will do."

Webb noticed broken filaments high above in the gothic stone architecture and recalled a recent report about how the Palace of Westminster was once again beginning to sink into the Thames, despite the billions spent a mere thirty years earlier to shore it up.

Webb considered Gough's words and wondered just how much truth they contained. The voice in his head noted his own cynicism: who cares if the Palace of Westminster slides into the Thames now, when in mere weeks it would likely be blasted to rubble anyway? But nevertheless, here he was running around trying to micromanage media opinion as though the only important forthcoming political event was a general election. He concluded the effect of the pill must be wearing off.

He arrived at another vast and imposing panelled door and knocked. He waited for a distinct, "Come," before entering.

Webb entered to see the Leader of His Majesty's Opposition, David Bentley, turn from a tall bookcase and walk towards him. Despite being the political enemy, Webb admired Bentley's style; always well turned out, Bentley still put credence on the old-fashioned view that presentation counted, even if he were a known alcoholic.

Bentley looked askance at Webb and asked: "Is everything all right with the PM?"

"Yes, she's fine," Webb lied. "She asked if you wouldn't mind explaining your concerns to me and I will relay them to her. The PM hopes you'll understand the pressure she finds herself under these days."

Bentley shrugged and said: "If you like, although it is not so very important, I suppose. Have you had breakfast?"

"Er, well..." Webb stammered, nonplussed for the third time in almost as many minutes.

Bentley clapped his hands and said: "Good. Come along, then. We can talk over coffee and eggs benedict." The Leader of the Opposition opened the door and went through. Webb followed. They walked along the high gothic passageway with the winter sun flashing off the surface of the Thames outside. Bentley said: "It's an issue I've mentioned to Dahra before, but I really think she should put some of the shadow cabinet in positions of government if we want to avoid the need for an official coalition."

"The PM gave you seventeen committee positions last week, half of which you've still to nominate."

"On the understanding that we would consider and get back to—"

Webb glanced and saw Bentley's eye twitch.

Bentley said: "Not now, Martin, I'm with the PM's PPS... Listen, Mr Webb, a number of Right Honourable Members are beginning to express, shall we say, certain reservations regarding the immediate future."

Webb wondered if his interlocutor was trying to be funny, but said nothing.

"They see little sense wasting time—as they see it—in the House. They have families, children, they want to spend some quality ti—"

"Yes," Webb interrupted, "we in government are also aware of that, but the business of government will go on."

"Until the bitter end?"

"I expect so," Webb replied, feeling a sudden hotness in his chest that spread up to his face.

"My point is," Bentley said, "that I'd be grateful if Dahra could consider filling any sudden vacancies with some of the very talented individuals we have on the Opposition benches..."

They reached one of the entrances to the vast Members' Dining Room. Bentley put out an arm to signal Webb to go first.

Webb saw this but could not react. The voice inside Webb's head tutted as the hot flush climbed like a massive, angry, burning centipede over and around his shoulders. He briefly registered a look of abrupt concern on Bentley's face and wondered why it should be directed at him. He fell back into the panelled door, which also surprised him. He tried to straighten up but the door upended itself and Webb found himself staring at eye level with the red carpet on the floor. In the corner of his vision, a notification flashed in his lens that he required medical attention. "No shit," he murmured before the heat and sudden exhaustion swept him into unconsciousness.

Chapter 32

Maria Phillips hollowed out the canvas holdall with her hand to be able to pack as many things as she could. The British Army's guidelines for new recruits stated the maximum size of the bag they should bring and gave a helpful list of things it did not provide so the recruits could prioritise for themselves.

Her older brother Martin appeared in the doorway and said: "Step on it, Maz, there's been a change of schedule."

She looked up and said: "What?"

He tutted and said: "You don't have your lens in, again?"

"No," she said with a frown. "I don't like being constantly distracted."

"It does have a 'sleep' feature, you know."

"Whatever. What's going on?"

"Our transport times have changed. We need to be at the station in half an hour."

Maria's shoulders sagged, "I thought we'd have more time."

"We did. Now it's gone."

"Piccolo," Maria called, addressing their home's super AI, "why do we have to get to the station sooner?"

A high-pitched robotic voice answered: "Your transport's original time has been brought forward due to changes concerning British Army logistics. Would you like me to detail them?"

"No, thanks," she mumbled, packing clothes and a toiletry bag. "Any delays getting to the station?"

"No."

"And where is my brother, Mark?"

"Currently in an artificial submersive gaming environment."

"For how long?"

"Question unclear: please specify past or future meaning."

Maria did the zips up on both sides of the holdall, sighed, and said in a sarcastic tone: "How much time has elapsed since my brother, Mark, entered the artificial submersive gaming environment?"

"Five days and twenty hours."

"Do you think he'll come up for air anytime soon?" she asked, hefting the bag and putting the strap on her shoulder.

"The highest probability is that he will emerge for food sometime during the next three to six hours."

Maria took a long look at her room. She saw the pictures on the walls, the four trophies she'd won for playing the piano years ago as a child, the pretty blue model tree on the shelf from which hung her earrings. Then she recalled why she was leaving: to join the British Army and begin her basic training.

"Maz," Martin called from the downstairs hall.

She turned and left, almost skipping down the stairs with a sudden enthusiasm to discover the future that awaited her. At the bottom, her parents wore positive expressions but Maria made sure not to look too closely lest she see deeper truths which might make parting more difficult than it had to be.

"Right the pair of you," her father said, clapping his hands, "remember to take care of yourselves, got that?"

"Got that, Dad," Martin said.

Maria's throat abruptly constricted, but she managed to look at her mother and utter: "Sorry to leave you with Mark."

Her mother shrugged and said: "Doesn't matter. He's hardly ever here, anyway." Mother and daughter embraced and Maria heard, "Look after your brother if you can."

Maria thought better of reminding her mother that she and Martin had been ascribed to different regiments and would be split up after the first week. She embraced her father and then she and her brother walked out of the front garden, followed by their parents.

Martin said: "If things get really bad, me and Maz will find a way to get back here, don't worry."

The reassurance sounded false to Maria. She looked up at Billy, the faded wooden rabbit that sat on the chimneystack. The bright early spring sunlight highlighted how worn he had become. She had an odd sense of premonition but put it down to the stress of the situation and the excitement of a future unknown. Her enthusiasm deflated to a subtle foreboding.

Chapter 33

Geoffrey Kenneth Morrow had never been so scared in his life. The crowd of refugees had turned into a mob at the impact of the first explosion, and he struggled to stay on his feet in the mayhem. The monorail station he'd been approaching was surrounded by thousands of refugees desperate for transport north to escape the approaching Caliphate forces.

Fury raged inside him: he'd been interviewing a photogenic young Spanish teen who'd lost the rest of her family when the monorail from Madrid had arrived in Zaragoza, Spain's fifth largest city and a major hub for the evacuation of civilians northwards to the border with France, a little over a hundred kilometres away. The pleas from poor Jimena, with her scared face, tear-streaked cheeks and pretty bun on her head was viewing gold, and just what Alan in London would love—as soon as Geoff could find somewhere with comms so he could transmit. She spoke in simple, halting English that exposed the depth of her fears even more heart-wrenchingly, with the light glittering off a delicate silver brooch she wore on her jacket. But he'd barely got thirty seconds with her before the Spiders began attacking the city.

When he'd arrived, he'd made sure to stay on the north bank of Ebro River even though he could've got local city transport heading south over it, and now congratulated himself on his foresight. Southwards, Zaragoza's architectural treasures were silhouetted against palls of black smoke from which orange flames flashed and passed. Tremors from collapsing buildings vibrated through the ground all around him and the dust they threw up added to the mayhem. Explosion followed explosion, and the sky was littered with contrails as the ACA battle raged above them. If he'd gone south of the river, he'd already be dead now.

He glanced at the innumerable figures who rushed every which way around him, desperately trying to relocate Jimena—she could not have gone far. But such was the volume and the speed of the people, he could glimpse an individual for no more than an instant. His morbid curiosity had been satisfied to the point of satiation with gruesome images of dead and injured civilians scattered on the local streets.

He heard yet another explosion distantly and a further volley of shouts and screams went up. Geoff wished the people would stop shouting and screaming. A gout of flame erupted from a building to the northeast and Geoff convinced himself that the monorail station around which a crowd of thousands buffeted had to be on the enemy's target list. He understood the need to get away but wanted to find Jimena first.

He gave up. He silently wished Jimena good luck, turned, and began forcing his way against the general flow of people hurrying to the station. A large, unseeing male barged into Geoff and knocked him down. Geoff rose at once as renewed panic lent him the extra energy and dexterity to get up from the ground. He felt pangs of guilt as he tried and often failed to avoid treading on those who had already fallen. Mostly these were elderly people who, Geoff reasoned, didn't really have a chance of getting out anyway, but occasionally he had to step over a small child rolled into a ball.

The ground heaved under his feet and he fell again, this time on his side. Less than a hundred metres in front of him, the roof of what looked to be a large warehouse or distribution building peeled open as though a giant hand pushed it up from the inside. It fell back with a loud crash and the ground juddered. In reaction, he forced himself back up onto his feet and fled south towards the river. The people thinned out and it became easier to avoid collisions. He glanced skywards and muttered: "Where are you, you bastards?" in frustration.

He arrived at a wrought-iron barrier and leapt over it to land on a path that ran alongside the river. Palls of black smoke drifted past in the gentle breeze. A sudden rush of falling masonry caught his attention and the spire of an ancient church collapsed.

As the minutes passed, Geoff sensed a pattern in the destruction. He noted that certain buildings were destroyed, while the Caliphate's ACAs ignored the general population. The aerial dogfights in the bright blue sky above lessened and then seemed to stop altogether. Geoff kept twitching the lens in his eye to see if it could link to anything and establish comms, but from what he'd read, only military-grade comms would work now.

After more than an hour of cautiously stalking along the path by the river, taking cover by the wall on his left a number of times, the frequency of explosions seemed to lessen. The breeze picked up and pushed the voluminous smoke out of the city and over the countryside. Fires crackled and the materials within them hissed and snapped as they burned. He felt an overwhelming sense of shock and recalled a misadventure in his youth, when he'd got into a fight and a much heavier man had beaten him almost to a pulp. Through his pain, he'd lain on the ground waiting for his punisher to do more damage. But instead, the man walked away with an air of victorious supremacy. Now, that feeling from so many years ago came back to Geoff. Like him, Zaragoza had been beaten to within an inch of its life by a much more powerful antagonist. But instead of finishing it off, the bully had turned his back as if to say: "There, that'll do for now."

People began to walk upright again amid the carnage and chaos. The journalist inside Geoff insisted that he observe and note; his lens recorded everything his eye saw, but the lack of comms in his location meant it could be some time before anyone viewed these images, and probably a very long time before Geoff himself could write up his own copy.

Survivors called out words that Geoff assumed were the names of lost loved ones. He headed back towards the monorail station wondering where the emergency vehicles could be; he heard not a single siren among the crackling flames, moans of the injured, and calls from the survivors. Then he chided himself when he realised that those vehicles would have been quite high on the Caliphate's target list and had certainly gone.

"Jesus," he mumbled to himself, "what if this shit happens to London?"

As the afternoon wore on, survivors with missing loved ones congregated around the most severely damaged locations and started their own rescue work. After touring the area, stupefied at the extent of the destruction and how a modern European city could be reduced almost to rubble in moments, Geoff began to appreciate the subtlety behind the Caliphate's tactics. For decades, international attention had focused on powerful nuclear weapons; a single munition that could level vast areas at a stroke. But, Geoff reasoned, the Third Caliph

226

needed to keep global public opinion on his side. So, as with the navies in the Mediterranean, as with Israel, and as with Turkey, he hit his targets with munitions which he could spin as somehow merciful in their limited destructive capabilities.

As Geoff stood staring at the devastation all around him, he understood a key aspect of the Caliphate's invasion strategy. Given all the chaos he could see, Zaragoza might as well have been hit by a nuclear weapon; the only thing lacking was the radiation, which in any case the Caliphate did not want if it were to overrun and dominate Europe.

"¡Eh, tú!" a voice shouted.

Geoff looked over at three men lifting and throwing chunks of rubble. "English!" he yelled back.

The man who'd shouted stuck out a stubby arm at the rubble and asked: "Help?"

With no official rescue services around, he decided to assist them. In addition, he saw that his wandering had brought him back to the monorail station at which he'd first arrived in the city. One man tried to talk to him in Spanish, but with no comms the translation feature in his lens would not work.

Geoff found the work relieved him somehow after the remarkable stress of the day. The sky reddened as the sun touched the horizon. They pulled the first body out; an old man covered in blood whose limbs must have been broken in many places. Geoff grabbed an arm of the corpse and when he pulled he felt the lifeless limb come out of the shoulder socket inside the victim's clothes.

The dusk deepened. The three men conversed and Geoff assumed they talked about when to stop and where to spend the night. Still, two hours after the attack ended, there was no sign of any civic or military support. He wondered why the authorities hadn't made any effort. Moreover, now his own safety had been secured, at least for the time being, a sense of self-preservation reasserted itself. A voice in his head urged him to find a way out of Zaragoza, for this attack had to be the prelude to the invading forces' arrival, and he really didn't want to be here when they did arrive. He stopped lifting and throwing chunks of rubble and looked at the ruined monorail station. He asked himself how he could or would get out if all transportation in the city had been destroyed.

A grunt from one of the others drew his attention to the next body in the debris. Squinting in the fading light, Geoff crouched down, threw away some smaller pieces of concrete, and put his arms around the female's narrow shoulders and pulled. When she came up, he saw that half of her face had gone, making her unrecognisable. But when the others helped him turn the small body over, Jimena's delicate silver brooch caught a ray of light and glinted out from her dried blood.

Chapter 34

The English Prime Minister, Dahra Napier, tucked her hair behind an ear and exhaled, feeling in the best frame of mind she'd been in for some days. Sitting behind the desk in her office at Ten Downing Street, she looked at the men opposite her and wondered with a little mischievousness if they considered her methods a little too unorthodox. She smiled at Monica as her aide filled her glass.

She stood, walked around the desk and leaned back on it, taking a sip of wine. She said: "Good evening, gentlemen. I appreciate this meeting is a little unusual, but given the speed of events, I do feel we can drop certain protocols. I think an informal appraisal of what we currently know will, if nothing else, give a more... human view of the issues. Cheers."

Terry Tidbury tilted his scotch and ice towards Napier and returned the toast. Defence Minister Philip Gough sipped his cognac and the mercurial Head of MI5, David Perkins, nodded and drank from a glass of orange juice. From further back, standing by a large, antique sideboard, the portly Home Secretary, Aiden Hicks, and Foreign Secretary Charles

Blackwood both stared at Napier as they each lifted and sipped from a glass of red wine.

Napier said: "I would like to start with some good news. At least we should still regard it as good news: Joanne gave birth this morning to a baby boy, and mother and child are both doing well." Faces smiled and murmurs of congratulation floated around the room, but Napier sensed politeness to be the real reason rather than any serious interest that their colleague, the present Secretary for Health, had been safely delivered of a child. Napier went on: "I'm sure you all join me in wishing her and her new family all the best, despite the rather trying circumstances in which the young man has arrived."

"Hear, hear," Hicks said a little too enthusiastically, and Napier wondered if he thought he was in the House.

She took a breath to continue but the door opened and Crispin Webb hurried into the room. "Sorry, I'm late," he said in an apologetic tone.

"How are you?" Blackwood enquired, his bald head leaning back.

"Yes, fine, thank you. Still ticking," Webb replied, tapping his chest with a flat hand.

Napier asked: "Are you sure you shouldn't rest a little longer?"

"No, no need, really. A few hours with a GenoFluid pack and a decent night's sleep is more than enough, thank you."

Napier didn't know whether to believe that he had indeed recovered from the heart attack he'd had in the House of Commons two days earlier, but she did know that she needed his help and felt glad to see him back. "Very well. Monica, get Crispin a drink, would you?"

"Just a glass of water, thanks," Webb said to the aide as she rose to fulfil Napier's request.

The Prime Minister said to the room: "The Leader of the Opposition was quite shocked when my PPS collapsed like that. Said he thought it might have been a ruse of some kind, although I can't think for a moment what. Anyway, I want to start with Charles and David. As of this evening, what is the latest on our and our European friends' diplomatic efforts?"

Blackwood shook his head and said: "We'd need a microscope to measure the progress. In particular, like almost all wars in the last two hundred years, now the shooting has started, the general consensus in Beijing is that it can no longer be stopped purely by diplomatic efforts."

"But what about the cost to Chinese investors?" Napier asked. "They've sunk trillions in Europe and the Home Countries. Isn't there any pressure at all on the Politburo from those interests?"

Blackwood glanced at Perkins and answered: "If there is, we don't know about it. I had the Treasury make some calculations and the worrying thing for us is how diffused Chinese investments are." Blackwood sipped his wine and went on: "For example, most of the big Chinese conglomerates have less than two percent of their total investments in European countries. In addition, one vital consideration our embassy in Beijing has identified is that the Chinese government has agreed to underwrite a special compensation package which will pay out funds to companies that can prove losses due to Caliphate action."

Napier was appalled: "My god, are we, as a country, really such small fry now?"

Blackwood shrugged and said: "PM, I'm no bean-counter, but the numbers aren't difficult to grasp. On devolution, the United Kingdom's economy was the seventh largest in the world. Now, if we combine the current strengths of the Home Countries' economies, jointly we would be the thirty-seventh largest economy in the world. So, to answer your question, from the perspective of what is by far and away the largest economy in the world, we are indeed small fry."

Napier felt devasted. The health benefits she'd enjoyed from having two days taking a backseat, 'recharging her batteries' as her husband had quaintly put it, threatened to be undone sooner than she thought possible. She saw Blackwood's blue eyes piercing into her own, the intensity of their glare heightened by the black of his thick eyebrows, and wondered what he must be thinking. No matter. She went on: "So, if we have no leverage economically to force the Chinese to bring the Third Caliph to heel—"

"Er, sorry to interrupt, PM," Blackwood said, "but I am not convinced the Chinese do have quite the power over the Third Caliph we ascribe to them."

Mild frustration flashed inside Napier, but she let it pass. "Meaning?" she asked in a neutral tone.

Blackwood answered: "We tend to take the historical approach. Yes, the Caliphate's existence was mainly a result of Chinese efforts, and the rest of the world has relied, and even taken for granted, Chinese assurances that the sealed political entity it created maintained peaceful intentions. But the Chinese response since this absolute chaos began does beg the question: did they even know about it?"

Napier conceded: "Fair comment, I suppose, although since the war started, Chinese support has seemed the only route to stopping it… What about behind the scenes, David?"

Perkins spoke at once: "There's never a shortage of gossip leaking out of the sieve that is the Chinese civil service, but all of it is the kind of tittle-tattle that amuses the average Chinese citizen. This week, as an example, a recording leaked of a regional head in the Agricultural Ministry having intimate relations with a certain type of wildfowl. Cheap entertainment for what we used to call the chattering classes, but not a great deal of use otherwise."

"And our best contact?" Napier asked.

"Still active, but they consistently report a lack of material interest among either the general population or the Chinese government itself."

The Home Secretary said to Perkins: "But surely, the Chinese government must be feeling some pressure, mustn't it? All right, England and even all of the Home Countries might not pack much of a punch anymore, but we're talking about every European country here, and the United States in addition. Don't all of them combined count for something?"

Blackwood answered: "You are correct regarding the European countries, Aiden, but don't forget that while the US supports us, it is not subject to attack. Even if we take the Euro countries in sum, their economies are dwarfed by those in Asia, Africa and South America. What is happening here now is like some lower-tier news story where people tut and say that something should be done while not knowing—and, if we're brutally honest, not really caring—how it is done or who does it."

Napier felt the mood in the room darken with fatalism. She let her gaze drift and caught Hicks's eye. He seemed to take this a cue to speak.

"One positive," he began in his nasal voice, "is that I have been in touch with my counterpart in the Coll administration, and he told me that emergency evacuation plans are almost in place for the Royal Family and the entire government."

Napier's eyebrows rose and she noted similar reactions from the others.

Hicks appeared to see this and stammered, "Well, that is, er, at least something… isn't it?"

Blackwood scoffed and said: "You evacuate if you want to, dear man."

Before Hicks could protest, Napier held a hand up and said: "We'll see what happens when push comes to shove. In the meantime, I hope you conveyed our gratitude for their consideration, Aiden."

"Of course, PM, goes without saying," Hicks blustered, chins wobbling.

"Good." Napier replied. She glanced around at her colleagues and then spoke to Monica: "Would you refill, please?"

"Of course," Monica said.

Napier went on: "So, on the military side, I believe some progress has been made, is that right, Terry?"

"Yes, PM," Terry replied, the overhead light reflected on his bald head as he nodded.

Napier knew that out of all of them, Terry least appreciated such an unorthodox briefing, but she'd convinced him earlier that the measure was not so very drastic.

Terry went on: "If some of this is a little technical for any of you, let me know. Firstly, our people have built on the laser coherence-length issue. You should all have been briefed how the Royal Navy fleet in the Mediterranean lasted some time longer than their US Navy counterparts when the captain of the *Hyperion* varied the coherence length on each laser shot."

"Yes," defence Minister Gough broke in, holding his glass out to Monica for a top-up, "and I still don't understand why we put an R-Notice on it. Thank you, Monica." He sipped his cognac and added: "I think we missed a huge PR coup with that."

Napier saw Terry frown as the General answered, with a faint trace of derision: "Because it was a tactically sensitive development about which we did not want—"

"But as soon as we employed the tactic on land the enemy knew about it, so I don't see what the—"

Napier broke in: "Phillip, there's no need to discuss past decisions now. Please let Sir Terry continue."

Gough shrugged and stuck his face back in his snifter.

Terry continued: "Our people at Porton Down have come up with a device to alter the coherence length on each and every shot. Unlike the confrontation with the navies, this randomisation will have much greater coherence range, and only a new generation of weapons will be able to defeat it. An inducer has been designed and is going through a range of tests now. If everything goes well, it should be fitted to all Pulsar lasers within a few days."

"Can you say how much this will increase each laser's effectiveness," Blackwood asked with keen interest.

"Twenty to thirty percent. Until it's used in battle, we can't be certain, obviously."

"And the Caliphate's ACAs will not be able to counteract it?" Blackwood asked.

"No, they will not. The inducer is not the kind of development that will change the course of the war, but it will help."

"Some good news from the army, finally," Hicks muttered.

Napier threw him a reproachful look.

Terry spoke: "In addition, our scientists at Aldermaston have come up with a potential answer to the enemy's jamming capabilities. Currently, the enemy can shut down all civilian comms and render military comms problematic in all areas where it successfully projects its force. Last week, the USAF mounted a low-orbit attack on the enemy's satellite nest from which this jamming emanates. The attack failed completely. In response, Aldermaston has identified a potential way to burn through the interference to allow our forces to communicate. Again, on its own it will do little to change the course of the war, but it is another positive development."

Napier glanced around the room and sensed expectancy that Terry had more to offer. She said: "Thank you, Terry." With those words, she saw the others' faces drop. "Would you mind showing us the current state of the four fronts?"

Terry nodded and said: "Squonk?" calling on the British Army's super AI.

There was no response. Napier apologised and nodded to Webb, whose eye twitched.

Webb said to Terry: "You're good now."

"Squonk?" Terry repeated.

"Yes, Sir Terry," the gender-neutral voice responded, audible to the whole room.

"Please show today's situation report at my location."

"Your location shows you are in the company of persons not authorised to view NATO situation reports."

"Override that restriction. Authorisation Tidbury, Sir Terry, General. Confirm."

"Confirmed."

The side wall lit up with a map of southern Europe. Napier watched the members of her cabinet and Perkins adjust their positions to view the image more comfortably.

Squonk said: "Sir Terry, do you wish to describe the situation or would you prefer narration?"

"Narration," Terry said. "Only keep it brief; I'll stop you if I have any questions. Begin with the Western Theatre."

The map on the wall zoomed into the Iberian Peninsula, with Madrid at the centre. Squonk spoke: "As at nineteen hundred hours today, advance enemy units were reported on the outskirts of Malaga and fifty kilometres from Cordoba. In the last six hours, force-projection attacks have taken place in Seville, which has suffered an estimated sixty percent destruction of its metropolitan area. To the north, reports place advance enemy units one-hundred-and-twenty kilometres south of Madrid. Force projection attacks have taken place in Zamora, Soria, Zaragoza and Barcelona."

On the map, a pool of red appeared and spread up to the mentioned places to show the territory the Caliphate was known to have captured, and then continued in a lighter shade to show the further areas at immediate risk. To Napier, it looked like a pool of blood spreading irresistibly over the land. She wondered if the artificial intelligence had chosen the colour intentionally.

Squonk went on: "All NATO units maintain a full fighting retreat." Blue circles and squares appeared on the map with the designations of corps and regiments. "The forecast remains unchanged: total defeat is so highly probable it should be considered a certainty."

Napier heard muted gasps and muttered curses around the room, which afforded her a modicum of grim satisfaction.

The map withdrew to show more of Europe, then moved left and zoomed in on Italy. Squonk said: "In the Central Theatre, enemy advance units have been reported seventy kilometres south of Florence. In the last six hours, force-projection attacks have taken place in Pisa, Bologna and Ravenna. It is worth noting that this is the fourth consecutive day of force-projection attacks on Bologna, and eighty-five percent of its metropolitan area is now destroyed. In addition, all comms with the country south of the Rome-Pescara line have been lost and that landmass is now cut off."

"Christ Jesus," Napier heard one of the men mutter. She sipped her wine.

Similar blue circles and squares appeared dotted around northern Italy. Squonk said: "All NATO units maintain a full fighting retreat. The forecast remains unchanged: total defeat is so highly probable it should be considered a certainty."

The view withdrew once again and shifted left. By now, Napier felt sure, everyone knew what was coming. Squonk repeated its mantra, first for the Eastern Theatre where the Balkan countries suffered, and then the Turkish Front, where enemy forces were laying waste to Romania. Finally, on her instruction, Squonk told them the estimated numbers of killed and wounded since the invasion had begun. The numbers were already in the hundreds of thousands killed and millions wounded, and were certain to continue to rise.

When the British Army's super AI had finished, Charles Blackwood mused aloud: "So, it is true."

"What is?" Napier asked.

"Oh, about Italy," he answered, accepting a refill of red wine from Monica. "Obviously, I am in almost constant touch with our European colleagues, but I have to admit I did not quite believe their insistence that the southern half of the country had been turned into one vast concentration camp."

"And not only," Gough said over the rim of his cognac. "With Blackswans and Lapwings free to roam and kill at will, it will be a massacre there."

"Much the same as the rest of Europe," Hicks noted sardonically.

"PM," Blackwood said, "in my position as Foreign Secretary, sooner or later I am going to have to respond to Italian demands for assistance for the southern half of the country."

Napier looked at Terry and asked: "Is there anything we could do?"

"Highly unlikely, PM," Terry replied with a shake of his head, and Napier caught the look on his face which meant he thought that was a vast understatement.

"For now, stall them, tell them we're looking into it."

Blackwood said: "Very well, but the subject will be on the agenda of the next NATO country-heads meeting, PM."

Napier nodded. She glanced around the room and asked: "Any questions?"

"Just one," Defence Minister Gough said. "What about the overall predictions? If we include these new 'developments' that Sir Terry told us about, do they actually change anything?"

Terry instructed: "Squonk, display current projections of enemy activity and the progress of the conflict, factoring all of the latest advancements."

On the wall, the map of Europe withdrew to display the landmass of the entire continent, with the areas the Caliphate already controlled coloured red. As Squonk spoke, the redness expanded to cover greater and greater area: "The most likely course of events suggests that enemy forces will overwhelm the main European landmass sometime between mid-April and mid-May. Thus far, the enemy has deployed almost unlimited volumes of munitions, while NATO remains materially outgunned in all theatres. Outlying European territories such as the British Isles can expect to be subdued within a maximum of two weeks thereafter."

Napier sipped at the last few drops of her white wine and took a long look around the room. Except for Terry, who dealt with these issues on an hourly basis, the others' faces were suitably ashen. Monica gulped down a large mouthful of wine and blinked eyes that glistened when she swallowed it.

Napier told Webb: "Deactivate it now, Crispin, thank you."

The view on the wall was replaced with the portcullis placeholder image of the English government. Blackwood said: "I find it incredible that they might continue across the entire continent without pause."

Terry said: "The computers give us extrapolations from all of the available data, and then allow a certain weighting for

239

unknown variables. What we have just seen is its most accurate forecast, but there is a chance it might not be right."

Blackwood scoffed and said: "Let us hope that is indeed the case."

Napier allowed a few seconds of silence to pervade the room before announcing: "Very well. Thank you, everyone, for coming along. If no one has any other questions, I'm sure we'd all like to spend some time with our families now, don't you agree?"

There came a few murmurs of assent. Monica rose, walked to the door and opened it as an indication the unorthodox meeting was over. The men finished their drinks and filed out of the room. As they left, Napier allowed herself a small metaphorical pat on the back. None of them had fully realised the real reason for breaking quite so many conventions. She knew Perkins at MI5 and Terry had difficulties with each other; she knew that Blackwood thought he would make a better PM than she, as though a woman could not fight; she knew that Aiden Hicks resented Blackwood with a vast but petty jealousy; and she knew that Gough wanted to quit his ministerial role but worried it might be seen as a cowardly act.

However, this evening she had shown them the true extent of the unfolding disaster. Tens of thousands of people just like them were suffering death and the most brutal injuries every day, hour by hour. She heaved a sigh and said to the empty room: "Let's hope these powerless men have the wit now to put their petty vanities aside."

Chapter 35

Turkish engineering student Berat Kartal awoke feeling the same way he felt every morning: as though this would be the last day of his life. The slats of the barn had gaps though which cold drafts blew. The straw in which he lay smelled of animal urine and rotting faeces, but he now regarded such accommodation as a luxury. Each day began with the same routine: he traced his fingers, numb with the cold, around the edge of his shrivelled abdomen. Berat had never been notably overweight but had always carried a few extra kilos. Now, he could feel each rib bone, he could push the skin up and under his ribcage, and he could prod almost all around each of his hips.

Once awake and with feeling having returned to his numb fingers and face, he got up and relieved himself in the corner of the barn, a pathetic trickle which emphasised how little fluid his body had and how reluctant it was to let it go. He collected his things and checked the seams on his boots as they became more frayed with each day's walking. He left the abandoned farm. Despite the cold, swarms of flies buzzed and darted around the dead, rotting cattle carcasses. He passed the pile of rubble that a few days earlier must have been a farmhouse. The previous day, he'd managed to get some withered carrots from it, but the smell stopped him searching for more or better food. However, far from sating his hunger, the carrots had merely served to reawaken it. Today, he felt a new feeling of aggressive deprivation—for the first time, he absolutely had to eat more food.

He set off on the dirt track in a north-easterly direction. Fatalism pervaded his spirit, caused not only by thirst and hunger, but by the destruction and victims. He struggled to recall what had happened. Somehow, Caliphate forces seemed to have overtaken him. For at least ten days, he had avoided all main roads and towns, knowing from bitter experience that the Caliphate destroyed them first. But now, without slowing or varying direction, he came across more and more evidence of the Caliphate's work. The farms he passed by were nearly always destroyed, he assumed by a Spider, while in daylight palls of smoke dotted the horizon.

On this day the sun rose with a brightness that stung his eyes. After an hour, the farmland ended and he entered a forest. For a while, he was able to follow vehicle tracks, but those ended and he had to push on through dense trees and bushes. He came to a stream and collapsed in overwhelming relief. When he had filled his container and could fit no more water into his stomach, he pushed on through the energy-sapping greenery.

Two hours later, he broke through the forest to see a village down a slight incline and across two fields. He hurried towards it and saw it consisted of two rows of small houses and a church, surrounded by farms and fields. As he got closer, he noticed a barrier across the only road into the village. He hurried towards it as fast as he could in his dilapidated boots, legs aching with familiar pain. Two masculine figures stood and regarded him. Abruptly, they raised what appeared to be rifles and pointed them at him.

He slowed in caution and shouted in English: "Do not shoot!" He repeated this as he got closer, his fear of them tempered by his burning hunger. They were both male, one young and the other middle-aged, so Berat took them for father and son. To Berat's relief, as he got closer they lowered their weapons.

The older man gestured and shouted words Berat did not recognise.

"Food," Berat said when he reached the barrier across the road, constructed from old farming equipment. "Can I have some food, please? I am sorry but I cannot pay."

The younger man murmured in the older one's ear. The older one shook his head and said a negative that left Berat in no doubt that he was not welcome. Despite the vast, angry hunger gnawing inside him, he felt no animosity towards them for their rejection. Perhaps they guarded their village from other people whom they distrusted; perhaps they harboured an illusion that their pathetic old rifles would somehow protect them from the Caliphate's machines. Whatever the reason, Berat said nothing and turned to leave. As he walked away, emotions clashed with common sense. Above all, he asked himself, would he not behave the same or a similar way if this were Turkey?

The forest curved around the village so he skirted it. The day wore on. He found another broad stream and drank. The late winter sun warmed him and he dozed by this stream until the first distant explosion woke him with a start.

He saw more plumes of smoke close to the horizon. He followed an overgrown walking path by the stream until he re-entered the forest. Towards dusk, with the sky littered with orange and red contrails, Berat heard a thump from nearby, the sound he knew all too well to be a Spider exploding. He hurried through the trees and saw smoke rising from the village he'd approached earlier that day.

He spent a fitful night in the cold forest that dragged interminably. But at the first light of the next day, he hurried across the field and easily passed the now unmanned barricade. Among the smoking rubble, he stumbled over bodies in the masonry. He found a number of sources of food. He ate. He sorted and packed more food with care into his rucksack.

When he left the village ninety minutes later, the pain had relocated inside him. From his shrunken stomach, which gargled and bubbled in expanding satisfaction, the pain had now moved to his head, which ached with a sense of unjustified—and unjustifiable—good fortune. Berat Kartal felt as though he were nothing more than some kind of rogue parasite, feeding off the decaying corpse of humanity.

Chapter 36

As time passed, Geoff Morrow's luck worsened. After they had dug the dead Spanish teen out of the wreckage at the monorail station, more senior rescue workers had tagged him and sent him north out of the danger zone and the country. While on the way, he had managed to contact Alan in London and sent him everything he had. Alan had promised to write some decent copy before using the material, and then insisted Geoff return south and get as close to the fleeing refugees and defending forces as possible.

Geoff arrived back in Toulouse in the dead of night, and throughout Monday, he battled his way through the endless, crushing crowds to hitch himself on a NATO supply transport going over ground to Montpellier and then to Avignon. But on Tuesday night, a Spider blew the front three units to smithereens and Geoff once again found himself assisting the search for and recovery of victims. On Wednesday afternoon, a fleet of Boeing 828 NATO air transports landed troops outside Montpellier and a French colour sergeant insisted Geoff had to return on the transports to northern France. Geoff got through to Alan, and his editor managed to have the instruction blocked.

Geoff had known when he took the assignment that freelancers like him had more problems than the embeds who went with the troops and who were, in truth, only mouthpieces for the military. Thus, every soldier with whom he came into contact gave him just enough courtesy and no more. Geoff did not mind: embeds seldom got the good stories.

With Alan using every contact his outlet had, Geoff managed to join a company of French troops and get on one of a fleet of air transports going across the Italian border to Turin. Reports from northern Italy painted a desperate picture with a high risk of extremely heavy casualties if the Swiss kept their borders closed. The Alps presented a barrier far more challenging to the hoards of starving, unarmed civilians than to the Caliphate's machines intent on hunting them down and eliminating them.

As the transport crossed the border with Italy, flying at lower than five hundred metres to minimise the chances of detection, an abrupt connection opened and Geoff could talk to Lisa in London, putting one hand over his mouth to give him a modicum of privacy as the troops in the fuselage stared at him. The thirty-three-second duration of the communication allowed Geoff to find out that the pregnancy was proceeding without complications, and allowed Lisa to tell him she missed him, and that he was still a bastard. The balance of eighteen seconds were filled with the awkward silence usual when he was on a job.

The transport landed at dawn on Thursday in a hastily constructed NATO airbase in a park in the southern suburbs of Turin. The company of troops disembarked and then Geoff alighted, his senses alive to his new surroundings. When his feet landed on the soft grass, he felt a horrible, bitter anticipation hanging in the air, like an early morning mist that the weak winter sun would not be strong enough to burn off. The tree branches hung bare and low, as though agreeing with the pervading sense of resignation.

More transports arrived. They emptied their military cargo of troops and equipment, and then lifted off to remove civilian evacuees. Geoff located the quartermaster and requested to go with the troops, closer to the action, despite his common sense suggesting that he was already quite close enough. He fought the urge simply to return to one of the transports and go with it to the evacuees. A voice inside impelled him to get closer to the action, for there he would find the best stories. An argument ensued because the quartermaster insisted that Geoff would have to embed or he wouldn't go a step further. Geoff tried to decline; the quartermaster made it clear there could be no alternative. Geoff thanked the man for NATO's assistance thus far and walked out of the airbase.

Three hours later, his mood had lifted: Turin remained unscathed, its historical and cultural treasures unmolested. Geoff's nerves tingled and he felt close to an alternate reality where he was merely one of a million tourists trying to visit as many of the city's attractions as he could. He pictured Lisa staring in wonder at the baroque architecture; arched frontages along roads that seemed to stretch to the horizon even though they were in the centre of the city. The absence of any crowds, however, acted as an anchor pulling him back to this reality—

A sudden flashing icon in his lens caught his attention: a civilian evacuation transport would shortly arrive from Genoa. It would unload its cargo of human suffering and return to the port city for more refugees. At once, Geoff broke into a sprint. His lens overlaid a map in his field of view to show him where to go. His breath left him before he was halfway and, gasping for air, he made a mental note to visit the gym when he got back. Then, the ludicrousness of that thought struck him like a hammer blow: all Europe was in the midst of being consumed in fire and violence, and the entire continent likely had a few weeks before it was all over. He felt certain he would not see the inside of a gym ever again.

He turned into the destination street, slowed to a trot, and reached the monorail station. Hundreds of people filed out of the exits, defeated, dishevelled, dismayed. The fear and pain he saw in their eyes concerned him more than their appearance. He tried to engage a few in conversation, but obtained only fractured responses in the most heavily accented, broken English. After easing his way through the throng and into the station, he intimidated a frightened-looking young guard into letting him on the return journey to Genoa.

The monorail did not leave for another four hours, after the sun had set and a latent fear evolved and thickened with the darkness. Without comms, Geoff was left to pass the time in the empty monorail, wondering what the holdup could be. At one point, a middle-aged woman wearing the uniform of Italy's intercity public transport operator came down the aisle. He tried to find out what the delay could be, but her irritation and lack of English only allowed him to establish that he still had a wait of several hours. He began to think it would be more beneficial to alight now and seek interviews with those who had arrived earlier.

Five minutes after the woman left, the monorail moved with an uncharacteristic jolt. It accelerated out of Turin South and reached its maximum speed in seconds. Geoff's lens told him how fast he was travelling, and his concern rose as the monorail's speed crept over the approved maximum and kept going up. His mind sought out the potential reasons. Outside, the dark night gave scant clues to his velocity, only the occasional trees flashed past close to the window in an instant.

Suddenly, the super AI controlling the monorail applied the brakes, throwing Geoff into the cushioned seats opposite him. The deceleration pushed him with greater force into the seats. In shock, he found he could not breathe. He clenched his eyes shut and tensed his jaw, praying for the incredible force to yield. Time dragged. His chest began to ache with the need for air. He fought to concentrate so as not to pass out. After interminable seconds, the brakes released and the immense pressure pinning him to the seats vanished. He gulped in a lungful of air, anger flaring at the monorail's dangerous behaviour. He saw nothing outside in the darkness, but his lens told him the monorail had stopped moving.

He elected to move forward and find out what had happened. Despite a furious twitching of his eye muscles, his lens offered no assistance. The lights in the carriages dimmed and flickered, and then shone normally again. Geoff trod along the central aisle noting the few other passengers as they stood awkwardly out of their seats, concerned expressions on their faces.

An urgent voice erupted from the sound system: "*Evacure la monorotaia!*"

"Shit," Geoff said, not requiring a translation given the panicked reactions he saw on the other faces.

"*Evacure ora la monorotaia!*" the sound system urged. "*Esci ora!*"

The double doors on both sides of the carriages slid apart and Geoff froze. The few other figures hurled themselves out and into the darkness. Geoff looked ahead to the front of the monorail and a sudden flash stabbed his eyes, as bright as the sun. It vanished at once and the front carriage, around a hundred metres in front of him, lifted into the air.

His instinct for self-preservation took over and guided his limbs to the open doors. He flung himself out of the carriage hoping for the best but fearing the worst. He landed badly at the top of a steep escarpment. The sound wave from the explosion whooshed behind him as he tumbled headlong over chilly, damp grass, a new pain cutting through the adrenalin in his blood to inform him he had incurred another injury that would require professional medical attention. The angle of the escarpment lessened and he managed to stop rolling, assured his clothes were now as battered and damaged as the rest of him.

He lay on his back and stared at the sky. A deep and painful throbbing rose up from his left leg. His breathing slowed and he noticed lines of white light zipping overhead, from south to north. The ground shook under the impact of another explosion. He tried to lift his head. When he did so, the pain in his leg became somehow electrified and shot through the rest of his body, touching the tips of each finger and tingling each hair on his head. In its wake, he felt nothing below his neck, as though he had been decapitated. More Caliphate Spiders, which must have been dispatched from the vast fleet passing overhead, proceeded to destroy the rest of the monorail, while Geoffrey Kenneth Morrow lay immobile at the bottom of the escarpment, paralysed from the neck down.

Chapter 37

"With respect, General, I think you should retire to your home now."

Sir Terry Tidbury looked up at his adjutant, John Simms, smiled and said: "You're being too polite, Simms. 'Should' instead of 'can'? I'm not the only one working hard in this place."

Terry watched the adjutant's angular face freeze in a moment's consideration before his bushy eyebrows came together and he observed: "Quite. Sir Terry, the retreat across the European mainland is being managed as effectively as possible, this week has been, shall we say, a little trying, and as you have had to make over five hundred deployment decisions since Mon—"

Terry raised a hand and broke in: "I haven't made any decisions, merely okayed what Squonk suggested and SACEUR approved in the vast majority of cases. Let's be honest, Simms, we have been reduced to the role of machine operators now. It's our computers versus their computers, and we're desperately trying to stave off what appears to be inevitable."

There came a rare pause between the two men. Terry was the superior officer and more experienced soldier; Simms was the better educated of the two. Terry occasionally wondered if his adjutant might harbour resentments that this entire fiasco could have been avoided if only those remnants of the British upper classes had been allowed a greater decision-making role over the preceding decades.

Simms said: "Nevertheless, a good commander still requires rest, Sir Terry. If I am speaking out of turn, please—"

"Don't be ridiculous, Simms," Terry dismissed. The General stood and paced around the War Rooms, looking at the screens as they relayed the current dispersals of NATO forces and the range of enemy formations facing them, both actual and estimated. To Terry, the analogy of the liquid egg yolk as blood came back to him. The enemy had been relentlessly gaining territory, spreading over the European landmass with an inevitability that—

"General?" asked a young female operator from the station responsible for Home Countries comms.

"What is it?" Terry asked as he strode over, Simms following.

"Air Chief Marshall Thomas requesting, Sir," she answered without looking up.

"Very well," Terry said.

The small, round face of the head of the RAF appeared on the screen above the station. "Thank you, Sir Terry," Thomas said at once. "I appreciate the hour is late, but I believe we have made a small breakthrough up here."

Terry let out a short chuckle and replied: "Good news is welcome at any hour. What is it, Ray?"

The Air Chief Marshall's face frowned as he asked: "TT, can we be completely sure our comms are still secure? The way things are going…"

"Squonk?" Terry called. "Potential for compromise?"

252

The super AI replied: "The enemy has made no apparent effort to break NATO's quantum encryption. The probability of it having been breached remains at less than three thousandths of one percent."

Terry looked up at Thomas and asked: "What's happened?"

"Very well," Thomas replied. "I have a young captain here, by the name of Evans. He's mucked about with a PeaceMaker training ACA and has brought the Pulsar cannon on it up to almost the same power as its fully-armed battlefield counterpart."

Terry frowned and said: "No, that's not possible. The training PeaceMakers are fitted with an inferior power unit which shouldn't—"

"The power unit is essentially the same, TT," Thomas interrupted with an edgy voice. "Captain Evans recalibrated the junctures, adding almost zero weight but ramping up its destructive ability. It's rather good, when you think about it," he concluded, beaming with pride.

Terry nodded in consideration and said: "Good work. Thank you, Air Chief Marshall. Oversee deployment plans for them. Oh, and pass on my thanks to your Captain."

Thomas's face smiled and then vanished from the screen, to be replaced with a map of the Home Countries and their available forces.

Terry barked: "Squonk?"

"Yes, Sir Terry?" came the instant response.

"Why didn't you think of that?"

"Think of what, Sir Terry?"

Terry quelled his rising anger and said: "Why did you not consider upgrading the training PeaceMakers to battlefield capability as an option in the defence of the European mainland?"

"I did, Sir Terry, although I did not flag it as having the potential to effect a material change on the course of the invasion. It will not substantially hinder the speed of the enemy's advance. Even with the most effective battlefield deployment of the upgraded two-hundred-and-seventy-three serviceable training PeaceMaker ACAs, in the most probable scenario, the enemy's advance will be delayed by three hours and twenty-one minutes. In the second most probable scenario, the enemy's advance will be delayed by four hours and—"

"Enough," Terry snapped. "Deploy the upgraded PeaceMakers to their maximum effectiveness." He turned to Simms and ordered: "Instruct all corps commanders to review this bloody computer's suggestions and other advice to see what else might have a bearing."

Simms nodded and left the War Room.

Terry turned back to the screens and analysed the latest NATO losses. He folded his arms and wondered when and how many times in history a weaker force had been so expertly crushed by its enemy. The Mongol Hordes? Attila the Hun? Alexander the Great? As he stared at the screens watching the enemy's inexorable advance continue over the maps of Europe increment by tiny, relentless increment, his imagination wandered to those innumerable wars in human history when the victors had written the vanquished out of the record altogether. He silently asked himself if there could come a time, millennia hence, when everything around him had turned to dust, forgotten and lost, trodden into un-knowledge by the victor, by this new caliphate that might well go on to even greater things, to a point where today's swift and untroubled destruction of Europe warranted not a single mention in its history books.

Simms appeared at Terry's side and said with a note of apology: "Sir Terry, I took the liberty of fetching you a cup of tea. Your order has been carried out."

Terry took the proffered mug and clamped both of his hands around it as steam wafted up from the brown liquid. It was too hot, but Terry preferred to absorb the pain through his hands. "Thank you, Simms. You can go now."

Simms returned the thanks and left. Terry glanced once more at the range of data displayed for his dismay. He retired to his personal office close to the entrance of the War Room. Once inside, he put the tea down on the desk, sat down, and said: "Squonk, open comms to Lieutenant General Studs Stevens, USAF."

His friend's clean-shaven face appeared on the screen in his desk and he responded: "Hey, Earl. I saw the situation report this morning. How you doing?"

Terry said: "If you saw the report, I'm sure an intelligent lieutenant general like you can tell how I'm doing. What news on the convoy, Suds?"

Stevens took a pull on a bottle of clear liquid and then said: "All looking good so far, but they're ready and expecting that the enemy won't just allow them free passage."

"We appreciate the effort, although it likely won't make much difference to the outcome. Are things as bad between Napier and Coll as I've heard?"

"Depends on what you've heard. The US government is doing all it can diplomatically, but those squares don't really get how difficult the situation is. You read any of Preston Grant's books?"

"The diplomat? No," Terry answered, somehow grateful and yet irritated by this irrelevant distraction.

"Most level-headed guy we had. I wish he were still here to tell these knuckleheads what they don't wanna know."

255

Terry said: "Napier mentioned the other day about the emergency evacuation Coll has offered VIPs here if we want to take it."

"How did that go down?"

Terry let out a mirthless chuckle and said: "Damn politicians looking for a way they could jump at it without looking like bloody cowards."

Silence settled between the two men. Terry could guess how Suds felt, safe as he was deep in the Nevada desert. The American airman offered: "Maybe it still won't come to that."

"Not very likely, but in the meantime, we can't get too many supplies from you guys, Suds. You think Coll will block any more aid to Europe?"

Studs shook his head. "I don't think so," he said. "She argues about our commitments but she usually signs off when she's through bitching."

"I hope it stays that way for as long as possible."

"It will. Take care, Earl."

The screen went blank and Terry's mind drifted to Napier's unorthodox briefing the previous week. He drank deeply from the hot mug and concluded that the war may well move too quickly even for such emergency evacuations; after all, few of the leaders in southern Europe had managed to escape, and Terry suspected the same fate awaited most of them in northern Europe.

Chapter 38

06.57 Monday 13 March 2062

The Englishman paced around his apartment in the English embassy, part of the diplomatic compound in Beijing. He unscrewed the cap of the twelve-year-old single malt and poured himself another large measure. He slammed the bottle down on the table, lifted the glass, and announced to the empty apartment: "And the toast is... Fuck you, China." He swallowed a gulp and pressed his tongue to the roof of his mouth, thereby stopping any air reaching his throat to prevent the spirit from burning.

The warmth spread from his stomach, across his chest, and up his spine to his head. His training back in London—more than two years ago, now—reasserted itself, reminding him that his apartment was not a secure place, that his hosts would know instantly of any indiscretion he should reveal. As he tried to focus on his reflection in the mirror above the ornate fireplace, he quietened the mischievous voice inside him which urged him to blurt out that he had been intimate with one of the Chinese military's key commanders for months; that he could describe the extremely modest size of the man's penis when erect and could list the recreational drugs Marshall Zhou preferred.

Marshall Zhou, the clever little bastard who, the Englishman wondered as the whiskey took control of his faculties, might have bested him in ways the Englishman had not considered. Marshall Zhou, who would now not even talk to him. Marshall Zhou, whom the Englishman had held in the palm of his hand for months. Because of the Marshall, the Englishman had been able to send warnings to London, he had been able to help protect his home and therefore his family and friends.

He had to report to London. He threw on a leather jacket as the temperature outside was only a few degrees above freezing. He left the block via the stairs and exited the compound into the cloudy morning. Ten minutes later, he strode quickly around one of the numerous small, landscaped parks in this part of the city, trying to compose his report. He came to a large pond enclosed by an ornate, Western-style wrought-iron fence. Two pairs of ducks hopped and fussed around the edge.

He took a hip flask from his jacket pocket and swallowed a nip. Putting it back, he turned around full circle but did not see the figure watching him from a copse of mature oaks some distance away. The Englishman's sixth sense tingled and he considered that perhaps he should ease up on the whiskey. He strode off, his long legs carrying him at speed. Several moments later, he came to an ornate bridge over a stream that joined two small lakes.

He selected the appropriate options in his lens and spoke: "The Englishman reporting from Beijing. Time of report: 07.41, Monday 12 March 2062. Report begins: the Chinese government continues to keep the Caliphate's invasion of Europe as much out of the country's most popular media as possible. This extends to failing to report UN resolutions condemning the Caliphate's brutality. The UN in any case carries nowhere near the weight that the Pan-Asian Confederation does, which of course has China as its most powerful member. For example, over the last fortnight, the most consistently reported and followed media event is the new trade pact between China and Japan. All Chinese media outlets and platforms are following every detail, including down to the size of the fucking rice cakes on the table at each negotiation meeting, if you'll excuse the profanity.

"At a more populist level, the actor Ying Yue Chu continues to be given publicity that far exceeds her talents. Over the last few days, the media has been speculating that she has undergone certain genital enhancements for a forthcoming film by one of China's better known directors. The next most popular story is the on-going voting in a country-wide poll to find the most influential man or woman in Chinese history. After that, the last few days have seen a political storm growing over alleged bribes paid by construction firms to mid-level government officials to secure lucrative contracts. Finally, and also reported ahead of the violence in Europe, a young, newly married Chinese couple were reported to be delighted because, while on honeymoon in Fiji, the wife lost her wedding ring, which a local miraculously found on a coral reef and returned to them. Such trivia is the mainstay of the bulk of China's population.

"The only support Europe's cause has had inside the country recently was a coordinated protest by several thousand Chinese students from a number of the most well-known universities, including all of the top universities in each region. The government suppressed the reporting of it, including using targeted *Abscondam* bots, and I only found out about it by chance. There may have been some greater—or perhaps I should say, less worse—progress in diplomatic circles of which the ambassador himself is better placed to inform you."

The Englishman stopped walking along the tarmac path and looked up at the bare branches that surrounded him. He concluded: "Finally, my primary contact has cooled recently and is not the source they used to be. It may take time for me to find someone in a similar position with similar appetites, so I will not report again unless and until something of some potential use comes up. Report ends."

With twitches of his eye muscle, the Englishman sent the message, all the while walking towards the exit, and all the time failing to see the figure that followed him.

Chapter 39

05.58 Wednesday 15 March 2062

In the eighteen days since Polish Major Kate Fus nearly lost her legs when the mid-range autonomous air transport evacuating her crashed in northern Serbia, she had grown used to the speed of the enemy's inexorable advance. Her freshly healed limbs tingled in anticipation as she observed the readouts in her mobile command post. She drew her index finger across the top of her cleft palate and recalled the previous evening with her lover, General Pakla, and how alive he had made her feel.

"Major," the Polish Army's super AI began, "all units are ready. I have detected a potential malfunction on Battlefield Support Laser GDR0776 in Sector West, as shown on the central panel."

Kate glanced at the data displayed and gave a wry smile when she saw a malfunction-probability figure of less than two percent. "Bolek," she said, "all BSL crews have been relieved and those units will operate autonomously, yes?"

"Yes, Major."

"Overlay the retreat routes for today's engagement, please." Lines appeared on the screen indicating how NATO troops would pull back when their meagre defences were overwhelmed, as they had during every engagement of this invasion. Kate sat in her mobile command vehicle in relative comfort. She felt a twinge of remorse at having run away from the refugees. All along the roads around Zagreb, tens of thousands of dishevelled people walked, trudged, shuffled and staggered onwards, desperate to avoid the approaching storm. Many fell, begged and gave up. Some died. The local emergency services had long since been unable to cope with more than a lucky fraction of the total casualties, and resentment was building between the civilians and NATO Forces because the latter could not spare the resources to aid the local populations. She'd instructed Bolek to take her vehicle into concealment in a managed forest close to the city but away from the roads and tracks the fleeing refugees used.

She said: "Are there any changes to the estimated enemy deployments?"

"Not at this time, Major."

"Bolek, when did the enemy's Warrior Group East and the Turkish spearhead join together?"

"Approximately fourteen hours and three minutes ago, at an estimated—"

"I have told you before: do not use 'approximately' with precise periods of time, okay?"

"Very well," Bolek replied. "Just over fourteen hours ago. Forecasts give higher probabilities that the next attack will advance more rapidly than any before it."

"I think we all expect that." She dabbed a green oblong on the central screen in front of her and announced: "Attention, all troops. We can expect the enemy to start misbehaving very soon. Do what you can to frustrate them, but no heroics. Remember your briefings: this is a fighting retreat, not a battle to hold ground. We can all see the civilians but we cannot help them any more than we have. Try to remember all of those who have already got out ahead of the enemy. Any questions?"

She saw a request from a Czech unit under the command of a Captain Fiala. A young man's reedy voice filled her mobile command vehicle: "Major, I am expecting my flank to be turned in less than five minutes. I put in a request for at least one more BSL but did not get it."

"I know," Kate answered. "We are quite stretched, Captain Fiala. Please use your common sense and follow the advice of your super AI."

"And what about the civilians? To retreat, my unit cannot avoid having to cross a major evac route."

Kate's brow furrowed as she asked: "Is this your first action, Captain?"

"Yes, it is, Major. Why do you ask?" came the defiant reply.

She smiled and said: "What do you think the civilians will do when the enemy begins raining death and destruction from the sky?"

"Panic, I expect," the Captain said.

"No, Captain," Kate replied, her patience straining. "They will seek shelter and hide. By the time your unit needs to evacuate, civilians will be the least of your worries."

"I see," came the suspicious reply.

"Any other questions?" This was greeted with silence so she said: "It's coming up to eleven minutes past the hour, which is sunrise. We have low, broken cloud with a surface air temp of plus eight degrees Celsius. If the enemy maintain their pattern of attacks to date, then—" she broke off as the array of screens flashed with red icons. The overviews withdrew, increasing the amount of territory represented, and numerous lines of light appeared, all approaching the NATO positions.

"And here they are," Kate said, "right on time. Good luck, everyone."

Kate sat back and refastened her belts for the inevitable retreat. Anger and frustration tinged the anticipation of battle. Kate had learned to loathe this enemy for its brazen predictability: it attacked NATO positions when it pleased because it knew it would meet only minimal resistance. This enemy could discard old, out-dated tactical considerations, such as ensuring the element of surprise, due to its overwhelming numerical advantage. She tried to recall any war games or training where an opponent had bested NATO so comprehensively and could not.

She put her attention back on the screens as the data changed. From high above them, a mere ten SkyWatchers led the charge of sixty-four PeaceMakers, most of which were armed with Pulsar lasers. On the ground, four Battlefield Support Lasers waited in autonomous patience, one pair to the east of Zagreb, the other pair to the west.

Kate felt her heart sink for the umpteenth time as, facing them, she watched lines of light converge on the NATO positions. A familiar pattern on the screen evolved as the number of enemy ACAs entering the battlespace crept up to dwarf the NATO forces ranged against them. She stared at the digits that changed so quickly: the swarm of approaching enemy ACAs grew at a similar rate as their distance to the engagement closed.

Kate muttered under her breath: "Captain Fiala will get his flank turned sooner than he thought."

Bolek announced: "Major, I have already instructed the forward units to retreat. The probability of a more greatly concentrated attack than before appears to be coming to pass."

"Is it because of the new inducer fitted to the PeaceMakers and BSLs? Do you think the enemy is deploying more ACAs to counter that development? Or is it that now two of their spearheads have joined up and can combine forces?"

"It is highly probable that the enemy's own super artificial intelligence would have anticipated the development of the inducer—"

"But did the humans in charge take any notice?" Kate interrupted.

"Insufficient data," Bolek replied.

Kate said nothing as the battle began in earnest, hundreds of Caliphate machines flying geometric circles around the defenders, swamping, smothering and eliminating them. She saw with depressing familiarity the inevitable beating NATO forces took, but she also saw novelty in the way the enemy dealt its blows. The ACAs from both combatants flew the most extreme contortions, seeking any sliver of advantage. She watched some enemy ACAs drop straight down from thousands of metres in the sky; their targets dipped, spun and dived to evade; the attackers matched these manoeuvres until exchanges of fire took place; fire was exchanged until destruction. Other ACAs came screaming in to attack as low as fifty metres from the ground. Squadrons undulated through the sky in the most graceful formations before opening fire. She tried to imagine how fast each super AI calculated its tactical decisions against its opponent.

"You should retreat now, Major," Bolek advised.

"Very well," Kate replied. "Give me clear sky in the roof; maintain other current displays."

Bolek carried out her instructions and among the patchy cloud, vapour trails and smudges of black smoke showed her how the battle progressed outside in the cold air, the reality of a confrontation she watched unfold on screens. She glanced back at her readouts to see Captain Fiala's flank had been turned after less than three minutes. Her concern grew as the units of which she was in charge retreated. She ignored the bumping and shaking of her own mobile command vehicle as it made its way through the forest southwest of Zagreb.

"Any signs of reinforcements?" she asked the super AI with more hope than expectation.

"No," Bolek replied. "Our remaining resources in this theatre are being managed to maximise a successful retreat of all NATO personnel."

"A successful retreat is an oxymoron," Kate replied testily. She pointed to one of the displays and said: "The eastern flank held out the longest. Why?"

"A combination of factors—"

"Just give me a summary."

"One: unanticipated increases in humidity at various, highly localised altitudes. Two: the pattern of coherence-length variation in the Pulsars of two wings of PeaceMakers. Three: a variation of two centimetres in the attack vectors of twelve Blackswans."

"Hmm," Kate mused, "if our other improvements have got us to a point where atmospheric variations can play a role, that would help."

"Major, you have a comms request from General Pakla," Bolek said.

"Accept," she said at once.

The General's low, gravelly voice filled the inside of the mobile command vehicle: "Major? I need to inform you of a diversion to your retreat."

Kate caught her breath at this unexpected news. "Go on," she said.

"We have VIPs struggling in the north of the city. As you can appreciate, AATs are out of the question now, so I have instructed the super AI to assign you and your units to pick the VIPs up and evac them. This is important and I need people on whom I can rely. Any questions?"

Shock froze Kate's jaw and disbelief paralysed her mind. She stammered an affirmative, which Pakla acknowledged, and then the comms ended.

The vehicle lurched and altered direction. On her screens, Kate saw its course change from travelling north-westwards on the straightest route away from the enemy, to a north-easterly direction towards the centre of Zagreb.

Bolek announced: "Route to new destination implemented. Major, the route is littered with debris; ETA is thirteen minutes."

Kate fought to regain her composure. Questions swirled through her mind: why her? The risk of the enemy's advance overtaking them would be high—had her General assigned her to this for an ulterior motive? She refocused and identified the most important issues. "Bolek," she said as she analysed the new objective on one of the screens, "who are the VIPs?"

"We have a number of Croat politicians and some family members who have made the request."

"But Zagreb is finished. And we have known that for some days now. What are they still doing there?" she asked, although she could guess.

"Several populist members of parliament decided to stay to offer moral support to the general population, whereas now they—"

"That's enough. What is the upper limit on our risk?"

"Sixty-two percent," Bolek replied.

Kate swore under her breath. She watched their progress to the VIPs as the mobile command vehicle made its way with painful slowness towards the north of the city. Trailing in her wake came two personnel carriers, one of which contained Captain Fiala. Combined, these three vehicles might accommodate ten VIPs if they squeezed in.

The risk limit—the forecast probability of the destruction of Kate's vehicle—crept up as time passed. She did not feel concern to begin with. She could recall many exercises with this kind of situation. However, on exercises the upper limit was never more than fifty percent, and that was when they were only pretending.

They entered the outskirts of the city and Kate asked: "Show me outside, all-round view."

The screens that provided her with all of the data she needed to monitor the troops under her command vanished to reveal a panorama of suffering. Her vehicle made cautious but certain progress along the arterial route into the centre of Zagreb, past refugees both living and dead, or possibly injured, Kate reflected, which in this environment constituted the same thing as dead. Palls of black smoke marked the results of attacks or the resting places of shot-down ACAs. Kate noted with curiosity that although to the south fires raged as they had over so many European cities in the last few weeks, north of the river Zagreb seemed unscathed. Overhead, the battle continued its inevitable pattern. As NATO resources dwindled, the enemy's Spiders busied themselves coming to ground to dismantle the capital city of Croatia.

"That's enough. Put the screens back up."

Bolek said: "You are still within acceptable risk parameters."

"You are including the potential for ambushes, yes?" she asked, recalling only too well the previous confrontation which had led to the deaths of several of her troops. "You remember your mistake last time, yes?"

"The total sum of the enemy's tactics and operations are always factored into the forecasts."

Kate didn't reply; she knew Bolek was just super-artificial intelligence, but irrationally hated it for the deaths she ascribed to its failure during the engagement in Serbia eighteen days earlier; deaths that had been required to allow her to survive.

Bolek spoke again: "We are within one kilometre of the VIPs. However, they are part of a larger mass of refugees and there is an increasing potential that their extraction may become complicated."

Kate shook her head in mounting frustration. "Look, the river is just to our north. Hold me back here," she instructed. She then dabbed an icon on the screen in front of her and spoke: "Captain Fiala?"

"Yes, Major?" came the response.

"Allow the super AI to manage the situation. If you feel it is unreliable, I will authorise you to override it. Be ready in case you need to clear your vehicle on short notice."

"Understood. Thank you, Major."

"Bolek, get me over the river before enemy ACAs target me, please."

"Only two bridges remain intact and will certainly be destroyed shortly."

"That is not helpful, Bolek," Kate said as her mobile command vehicle lurched again, turned, and bumped as it accelerated over the debris-strewn road. "So do your job," she hissed in frustration. "Either get me across the bridge or do not."

"Please specify your requirement."

"What? Can you get me across the river before the remaining bridges are destroyed?"

"Yes."

"Do it, then," she said in exasperation. At once, she saw the two personnel carriers stop and withdraw. "What is happening?"

"To ensure your safety, Major, the personnel carriers are being repositioned to draw enemy fire—"

"No!" Kate shouted. "Do not give me priority."

"That is against current NATO tactical poli—"

"I override that policy."

"You do not have the authorisation, Major."

Kate slumped back in the seat, suddenly realising that General Pakla had assigned her to this VIP pickup mission because he had known the super AI would protect her as the superior officer. She looked at the screens and demanded: "There, get me over that bridge now."

"There is a high prob—"

"Do it now, or give me manual control of this vehicle. That is an order based on protocol thirty-two," she said, using an override that officers were only permitted to use in extreme circumstances. And, later, she would be obliged at a court martial to justify her invocation of it. The vehicle swayed to the left and accelerated rapidly. It hit debris on the road with jarring thumps. "Bolek, what are you doing?" she shouted.

"In accordance with your instructions, the speed of this MCV must increase to lessen the probability of its destruction."

Kate caught her breath as the vehicle rattled and rocked. She managed to order: "Update on the VIP extraction."

"The personnel carriers are taking individuals on board now."

"I hope Fiala can extract the right people. How are the probabilities looking now?" she asked through clenched teeth as the vehicle careered along the road.

"Enemy targeting of the personnel carriers will become a certainty in forty seconds; of this vehicle, in forty-five seconds."

Kate knew it would not be enough to get them to safety. She asked forlornly: "Any hope of reinforcements?"

"The NATO forces remaining in the battlespace will be destroyed in... have been destroyed. The nearest support is too far away to affect the outcome."

"Rear-view window, now," Kate instructed, not wanting to die without seeing the real world a final time. On noting that her vehicle was the only one negotiating the wrecked vehicles and other debris on the bridge, she asked: "Where are the two personnel carriers?"

"In transit north over bridge zero-three."

"Will they make it, at least?"

"Highly improbable as there is now nothing to hinder the enemy's advance through the north of the city and beyond."

Kate wished she could speak to the General, *her* General, a last time, to say goodbye, but she preferred to compose herself. A blanket of black, dirty smoke shrouded the south of the city as her vehicle sped away from the chaos. Kate considered that the smoke might as well be shrouding the whole world. Against a puff of white cloud higher in the sky, she noted a procession of black dots descending in a spiral, as though performing a corkscrew pirouette for her entertainment. All too soon, the Spiders came down at the southern end of the bridge, smashed into the road, the debris, the stragglers, and detonated. Puffs of masonry dust billowed out from around the bridge and it began to collapse into the river.

Kate gasped as the vehicle lurched and swung to the right, and the disintegrating bridge was hidden from her view by the buildings on the north bank. "What are you doing?" she asked in frustration.

"Attempting to preserve your life, Major," the super AI replied with, as Kate imagined it, the faint tone of answering a rhetorical question.

"There's no point," she said, growing more amazed by the second that her vehicle had not been hit. Her vivid imagination threw up all kinds of suggestions of the last thing she would feel when a Spider clasped itself around her vehicle and blew itself up. She closed her eyes, wanting it to be over, wishing the shaking and twisting and turning of the vehicle would stop, wishing time would stop.

She felt she was slowing down. She wondered if the vehicle had been destroyed and her journey to the next world had begun with a pleasant deceleration. The vehicle stopped and the curt thump on the outside could not have been divine. She remained in this realm.

Bolek spoke: "Major, the enemy has broken off its attack."

For a moment, the words did not register in her brain. She instructed: "Repeat that."

"The enemy has broken off its attack."

"Explain."

"There may be a number of reasons, but the most probable is that the enemy is pausing to consolidate its gains."

"But why now? Why here, in Zagreb?"

"The River Sava makes a natural boundary. The enemy is proceeding with consolidating its position on the south side of the riv—"

"Did the personnel carriers get across the bridge successfully?"

"Affirmative."

"Good. But how can there be any need for natural boundaries?"

Bolek answered as the mobile command vehicle jolted and resumed moving. "There is no tactical or strategic need. However, the enemy has complete control over the territory it has gained in the twenty-four days since it began the invasion, and it correctly estimates there is little NATO can do to interfere. It is therefore at liberty to pause and build up in-theatre arms' supplies before proceeding to subdue the rest of the continent."

Numbness had overtaken Kate's limbs, a strange kind of apathy she ascribed to temporary safety having been secured. She found it difficult to concentrate on the super AI's dry commentary that disguised the millions of lives being torn apart and eradicated. "Where are we going now?" she asked.

"A forward HQ has been established at Ljubljana. Major, you are showing a drop in a number of physiological indicators. Do you feel all right?"

Through shallow breaths, Kate replied: "Fine, I just need some rest."

Chapter 40

15.00 Thursday 16 March 2062

In the War Rooms under Downing Street in London, Terry Tidbury sensed the expectation in everyone around him, as though they needed reassurance; or if not reassurance, then at least some answers. The staff had gathered in front of the NATO comms station. The broad, African-American face of the Supreme Allied Commander for Europe—SACEUR—stared back at them, emotionless, as he addressed them and numerous other NATO bases, stations and posts around the continent which NATO still held.

"Thank you for attending, everyone. We have just passed thirty-two consecutive hours with no offensive action taken by the enemy. I think we can all agree with our computers on one thing: that we have entered a phase of the enemy consolidating his gains. As we know, since the invasion began nearly a month ago, he has taken control of over one million square kilometres of our territory."

Terry nodded in appreciation of SACEUR's use of the personal pronoun, given that his audience included many Spaniards, Italians, Greeks, Romanians and others who had lost families and homes, and whose countries now suffered grievously under Caliphate domination.

Jones's face withdrew to a thumbnail to show a map of Europe that, with the use of shaded areas, described the territory now controlled by the Caliphate: almost all of Spain, with Portugal still free; Italy, up to a line from Genoa through Bologna and on to the Adriatic; most of Croatia, with a line from Zagreb straddling Hungary's southern border, which continued on across Romania until it reached the Black Sea east of Medgidia.

"According to forecasts," Jones went on, "this pause by the enemy to strengthen its forces and its control of newly acquired territory may last for anything between three weeks to three months. It's important to note that while our computers can extrapolate from every war and every battle ever fought, this war is new; it's the first war using this kind of tech. Now, given that not a single one of our computers saw this invasion coming to begin with, I feel that we ought to treat their advice with an element of circumspection."

Jones stopped, sipped from a glass of water, and continued: "We have a number of significant problems to overcome. Right now, the enemy can control all comms over the territory he has gained. On the plus side, this control is not absolute. As it has been throughout the history of telecommunications, atmospheric fluctuations and unexpected localised weather events can let us have some peeks into what's going on. The better news is, people, we got developments on the way which should negate this advantage altogether."

Terry glanced at the others inside the War Room and wondered what must be going through their minds. He knew SACEUR had precious little to offer them, and the multiple images of the death and destruction wrought in the invaded countries had been so widely disseminated across all media and platforms that everyone present must have felt the greatest sympathy for those involved, while at the same time being under no illusions at what awaited the countries yet to be subdued.

Jones went on: "In addition, material support will soon be on its way from the US. In northern Europe, as you might imagine, a vast organisation is in hand to retool manufacturing to produce as much ordnance as possible. Now, I know what you're all thinking, that our current equipment, our SkyWatchers and PeaceMakers and Battlefield Support Lasers, aren't up to the job. But for now, they're all we got. If we can manufacture enough—and I think we can—then we'll definitely be able to slow the enemy down, maybe even stop him. In the meantime, I want all of you to know that we have the best minds working on new solutions, on new weapons which will be able to really change the balance of power. But, and this is the most important thing I have to say to all of you today, we're going to need time to get those weapons ready. In the meantime, we all have to keep giving this managed defence the best each of us has to offer.

"Just a few days ago, I don't think any of us expected the enemy to cease offensive operations in this fashion. I think we all believed we were facing the abyss. Well, we still are, but now the enemy has given us an opportunity to reinforce our positions, and we need to take advantage of that. We can't know how much time we have. But I think we can all guess that there might be a political dimension to this pause in addition to the military one. Only time will tell.

"Finally, I want to end this briefing by stressing that this unexpected break is as much an advantage for us as it is for our enemy. While we can be certain that when he resumes, he will do so with great strength, now, today, we have a chance to build up our defences to absorb that blow. I also want to acknowledge the sacrifices member armies have already made.

For all of us, this is just about the toughest imaginable confrontation that we find ourselves in now, but I believe—"

"What about *Italia*?" a new voice shouted. Terry saw an Italian colonel who had escaped his country's predicament. Jones stopped and said nothing, apparently letting silence encourage the colonel. The Italian took the American General's muteness as an invitation to continue. In thickly accented English, he said: "Intel from the Mediterranean prove that the country to the south of Rome is being raped, is being just one big concentration camp—we must send help!"

Jones breathed in and said in a measured voice: "Colonel, the issue was covered at the situation meeting this morning. If we could do someth—"

"But we can," the Italian colonel enthused, "and we must! We have submarines, we must use them."

"Colonel, we can discuss this at greater length at your specific-theatre conference this evening." The General's polite rebuke had the desired effect, mollifying the Italian, and Jones concluded: "Okay, everyone, we've all got a ton of work to do, and I'm glad I've had a chance to speak with you and let you know that we are working very hard to get the odds coming a little bit back in our favour. But remember this: operation Defensive Arc is not done yet. If you have any questions, please raise them at your next specific-theatre conference. Thank you."

Terry realised that Jones wanted to do what he could to help morale, which was why he'd called the brief conference. Terry would like to have been able to have a private conversation with Jones, but he knew both of them needed to spend important time with their subordinates. With Europe still on the brink of total destruction, moments for private conversations were very rare.

Chapter 41

Crispin Webb could not help shaking his head in contempt. Anger bristled inside him, but he knew his job was to assist and only opine when he was specifically requested to do so. He stared at the back of Dahra Napier's head and thought it trembled slightly. She reached for the glass of white wine that seemed to be with her permanently when she was inside Number Ten. A voice in his head chided him for his hypocrisy, and reminded him that he also had his share of problems: falling down in the Houses of Parliament from a heart attack had elicited the usual predictable jokes about how surprised people were to find out the PM's top aide did in fact have a heart.

In the room with his boss sat the Home, Foreign and Defence Secretaries, and Crispin wondered what proclivities they depended on as they played their mostly passive roles witnessing the final destruction of Europe, and which they kept hidden from everyone else. Recent digging into Home Secretary Aiden Hicks' history had thrown up an interesting little titbit, as it transpired Hicks had fathered an illegitimate child.   Such scandals did not carry the political-career-destroying weight they used to, but with proper media management, they could be highly embarrassing.   Crispin glanced at Hicks, watching his chins wobble as the man shook his head, and wondered if Hicks thought he would make a better PM than Napier.

On the screen in the wall, the US President, Madelyn Coll, whined on about the Third Caliph's latest announcement from Tehran.   Crispin closed down the media lists in the view from his lens to focus on what the woman said, in the unlikely event it was important: "…should take it as a demand to surrender."

Napier replied in a determined voice: "I will take it as nothing of the sort.   That madman has made an obtuse claim which does not even deserve validation with a reply."

Coll appeared to concentrate, her face creasing into a frown.   She said: "Dahra, the situation is only going to get worse—"

"But 'annex'?" Napier broke in.   "He says he's 'annexed' the whole of Europe, prior to its assimilation into the Caliphate, as though it were a district or a province or some little backwater about which no one with real power really cared.   And you think I should take such a ridiculous thing seriously?"

"Dahra," Coll said with a faint trace of patronisation, "you need to appreciate how bad your situation is—"

"How bad?" Napier spat.   "Did you just imply that I do not know how fucking bad the situation is?"

Crispin nearly choked when he heard his boss swear. He saw the other cabinet members' mouths also fall open. The boss had been under enormous stress the last few weeks, but she'd always held her nerve in public. On the rare occasions Crispin had seen Napier's husband, Crispin could see the man had his work cut out, but who could blame him? His wife was likely to be the last PM of England after more than three hundred years.

From the screen, Coll seemed to be unfazed: "Of course I'm not saying that, Dahra," she said with, to Crispin's ears, increasing patronisation. "We will table another emergency resolution at the UN—"

"What for?" Napier asked in apparent exasperation. The PM put her wineglass on the ornate coffee table and stood. "The Caliphate is not a member of the UN," she said, holding her arms out. "How many resolutions has that toothless, redundant dinosaur of a forum already passed? And each and every single one of them has been ignored in the real world. The UN is neutered, rendered irrelevant by the Pan-Asian Confederation."

Coll shook her head and said: "We need to keep up the diplomatic pressure, especially now that the fighting has stopped. Whether we regard this announcement as a demand to surrender or not, we need to get our allies to put some real pressure on the Chinese to get the Caliph to reconsider."

Silence pervaded the room. Crispin glanced from the boss to the other ministers and waited for one of them to speak. Napier let out an impatient sigh, scooped up her wineglass and fell back into the comfortable beige couch. She sniffed and said: "I don't see the point of having the same conversation again, Madelyn. Constantly repeating that we need to increase diplomatic pressure when it hasn't made, and doesn't make, a jot of difference, is a waste of everybody's time—"

"But that's not true," the US President said in the nasal, Midwestern half-whine Crispin had come to loathe. "We're working very hard here to get historical allies to help us bring pressure to bear on Beijing."

Napier replied in exasperation: "So are we, but we both know all we are going to get is platitudes. The big global players, the countries that could and should help us, rely too much on trade with China. They're not going to risk losing that, and we can't offer anything comparable in return."

"Er, if I may, PM?" Foreign Secretary Charles Blackwood interrupted, eyebrows raised in a business-like attitude. Crispin immediately wondered if his interjection had been scripted. Blackwood said: "Madam President, while His Majesty's government is of course extremely grateful for any and all assistance our old ally can afford us, however we now believe that diplomatic efforts have become a secondary consideration next to material assistance in the form of arms and munitions."

"Sure," Coll said, nodding, "I totally get that."

"Good," Blackwood said. "So, could you confirm that you have approved the commencement of convoy shipments of materiel to your NATO allies here in Europe?"

Crispin thought Blackwood sounded like a smooth bastard, but didn't mind if it helped to make things happen. Coll's procrastination irritated the boss no end, although everyone knew that other, better informed, Americans were at work behind the scenes. But the President still had to sign the authorisation.

A slim male who Crispin recognised as a member of the National Security Council came into the shot of Coll sitting behind the Resolute desk in the Oval Office. The man leaned forward and whispered in the President's ear. He withdrew, she looked at the screen and said: "Yeah, sure, it's authorised. Jon will work with your people to work out the details, although from what I hear I don't think it will be anything like enough."

Blackwood enthused: "Thank you very much indeed, Madam President."

"Okay," Coll replied. "So we'll stop there for today."

"Thank you, Madelyn," Napier said in a more sombre echo of Blackwood.

The standard portcullis logo replaced Coll's image on the screen and Crispin smiled at all of the audible exhalations in the room which followed.

"At least she's signed the bloody authorisation, finally," Defence Secretary Phillip Gough said, stroking his trimmed beard.

"Let's hope she doesn't change her mind," Blackwood said.

"Thank you for helping out, Charles," Napier said. "She's getting very difficult to handle."

"Might have something to do with her domestic problems, PM," Home Secretary Aiden Hicks said with a shrug of his ample shoulders. "She's deeply unpopular outside the cities, so however she feels about what's happening now, here, I believe she's reluctant to commit to her NATO obligations."

Napier sighed, sipped her wine, and said: "And all this aggravation to get some thousands of tonnes of materiel that can't be replicated, assuming of course the Caliphate's ACAs don't send all of the ships to the bottom of the Atlantic first."

Crispin glanced at the other faces in the room and understood they'd had the same thought. He allowed himself the luxury of sharing the boss's despair at the atrocious way the Caliphate's invasion was going.

Chapter 42

10.00 Saturday 25 March 2062

Corporal Rory Moore of the Royal Engineers felt ready to explode. Three weeks inside a cramped steel tube under the Mediterranean Sea had confirmed to him that a career in His Majesty's Royal Navy was about the worst choice any young person could make. The claustrophobia addled his brain; the appalling 'hot-bunking', where he even had to share the place where he slept, removed any element of privacy and compounded his discomfort. The news, which had only arrived in the *Spiteful* a few days earlier, that the Caliphate had paused its advance to consolidate its gains, also increased the urgency inside him: now, after all, he might have a home to return to, at least for a little while longer.

The submariners transpired to be a friendly enough bunch if Rory overlooked the occasional weird second glance he caught from some of them, especially the chefs in the galley, who, Rory surmised, must lead lives of uniquely intense tediousness. Even the Chief Petty Officer who had grilled him and Pip after their arrival from the Caliphate-infested Spanish coast mellowed to a distant friendliness as the days passed. At one of the mealtimes on the first day, a planesman called David had struck up a conversation with Rory. With a dull monotone voice in a thick Yorkshire accent, David told Rory about 'super-cavitation', how the *Spiteful* could travel through the ocean depths at over three hundred miles an hour by projecting a thin envelope of a specific gas around the hull, thus removing the drag of liquid. Rory munched on his fresh salad, enjoying the luxury of such good food, while David enthused that *Spiteful* was the fastest sub in NATO, before conceding that the Chinese subs were faster still.

On the second day, a quartermaster had given Rory and Pip a tour of most of the vessel. This had made Rory feel more claustrophobic. He found it particularly difficult to function with no indication of daylight and night time. Worse, he'd had no time alone with his beloved Pip, as the male and female parts of the crew were kept mostly separate. In addition, Rory latched on quickly to the power of gossip among such a group of people spending months trapped together in a confined space. After Rory witnessed an altercation in the mess hall that involved much mockery, he resolved to keep his feelings for Pip an absolute secret until they got back to England.

All this combined so that after three weeks, he struggled to contain himself. He tried to find out when, finally, they would return home but each enquiry, either oblique or direct, was met with a shrug or a partially hostile 'when the Captain says so'. Rory eventually gave up asking as he sensed that most of the submariners actually rather enjoyed being inside their giant steel coffin.

Then, on this Saturday morning, although to Rory it could have been any period of the day or night on any day of the week, the submarine's tannoy crackled into life. "Attention, all hands. This is the Captain. Finally I can tell you that we have been ordered to return to base."

Rory couldn't believe his ears—after all this time, they would go home. And with super-cavitation, they would be there in just a couple of days. He clenched his fists and let out a whispered: "Yes," in delight.

But his relief was short-lived when the Captain added: "However, we will take the scenic route as we have a short diversion of a few days. We have to escort some ladies to a dance. In addition, due to the current risk of detection by hostile forces, we shall be making way under traditional propulsion only. Altogether, we should return before the end of next month."

Crestfallen by the news and confused by the message, Rory tapped a passing able seaman and asked: "Hey, what did the Captain mean about ladies and a dance?"

The young man looked back at Rory with a mix of incredulity and contempt. He scoffed and said with irony: "Ladies? I dunno, maybe, oh, surface ships? A dance? Maybe escorting surface ships to safe harbour?"

Rory replied, "Oh, right. Thanks."

The seaman said in mock sympathy: "They really don't teach you brown-jobs a bloody thing in the army, do they?" He strode off down the metal corridor, tutting and shaking his head as he went.

Rory leaned back against the bulkhead and spoke to himself: "Seriously, I am trapped in a giant steel coffin with five hundred missiles and one hundred complete wankers."

Chapter 43

From his private office in the War Room, Terry Tidbury addressed his friend in the screen on his desk. "I don't understand, Suds. Why does the enemy wait? Why doesn't he continue the invasion? He must have had enough time now, surely?"

Lieutenant General Studs Stevens of the USAF shook his narrow head and answered: "I don't think the issue is military, Earl, at least not wholly."

Terry's bald head rocked back and he said: "You think the enemy wants to put the frighteners on us? Given that he's already conquered half of the European landmass, I rather think that is no longer necessary. Our computers here are saying the enemy has probably amassed enough materiel by now to easily complete the invasion and dominate—"

"Yeah, but c'mon, Earl. He thinks he's holding all the cards."

"He is," Terry pointed out.

Stevens said: "We're just soldiers, Earl, not politicians, and I—"

"So let's pretend," Terry broke in with a sterner voice. "I'm not kidding, Suds. He could have hundreds of thousands of ACAs and warriors in the conquered territories; he certainly has at least tens of thousands. So why wait? In that first month, he lost no more than a handful of warriors, so his armies are still intact. It doesn't make any sense."

The American Lieutenant General drew in a deep breath and said: "In front of the cameras, I'd say he's trying to show some kind of moderation, maybe letting rich Chinese, Brazilians and Africans get the hell outta northern Europe. Behind the scenes, I'd say his warriors are satisfying their appetites on the local populations, but I try not to think about that too much. Publicly he can claim those people are being treated well, but we know that's a pile of shit."

"He can take as long as he likes, I suppose," Terry said. "By the way, I wanted to thank you for pushing the Atlantic Convoys despite your truculent president."

Studs' face creased in confusion and he asked: "What are you talking about, Earl? I was only a small part of the organisation behind that."

Terry chuckled: "So please pass on my sincerest thanks to all—" but broke off when a red-level comms notification flashed in the top-right corner of the screen. "I wonder what this can be?" he said without enthusiasm.

"Let's find out," Studs added unnecessarily.

A new image covered the screen, and Terry's heartbeat crept up when he recognised the same dark-skinned young man sitting at the same news desk with the official crest of the Third Caliph of the New Persian Caliphate. Terry knew that the young man would now speak in modern standard Arabic, and the English translation would scroll along the bottom of the screen. Terry calmed himself, slowed his breathing, and concentrated.

The young man spoke: "Today, the illustrious Third Caliph, leader and protector of the Persian Caliphate, calls on the remaining NATO Forces to surrender."

Terry swore under his breath when the words scrolled past; the moment he'd known would come sooner or later had finally arrived.

The dark-skinned announcer continued making the liquid sounds of that other language: "The illustrious Third Caliph calls on the whole world to encourage the remaining European countries to take this generous offer to avoid much unnecessary bloodshed and destruction. The illustrious Third Caliph has made his munificence plain in the last twenty-five days, pausing his great and powerful warrior armies to allow the infidels to consider their bleak future if they choose to resist."

"Christ on a bike, this is worse than I thought," Terry muttered.

"Those Europeans in the conquered lands have willingly agreed to be assimilated into the Persian Caliphate, and are even now beginning to enjoy improved, fulfilling lives. After blindness and ignorance, the infidels have been shown the Truth and now their eyes are open. However, the annexation of Europe has so far cost many innocent lives. The illustrious Third Caliph now calls on the governments of Europe and the world to ensure no more innocents have to be sacrificed to the petty vanity of Europe's leaders, who are too blind to understand how the world has changed in the decades since they passed their apogee, who would rather condemn to painful deaths those civilians they falsely claim to represent.

"As proof of his mercy, the illustrious Third Caliph announces that he will graciously allow the infidels time to consider his instruction. He urges them to acknowledge his generosity and thus act wisely. He gives the leaders of Europe the power to prevent the needless deaths of millions of their citizens, and allow their societies a peaceful assimilation into the welcoming arms of the New Persian Caliphate. God is great."

A placement image of the Third Caliph's crest replaced the view of the young man and Terry heaved a sigh. The face of his friend Studs Stevens then enlarged and he said: "Now I think we can guess the way the political storm is blowing."

"I don't think there's any doubt what our political masters will do, but that bastard really wants to bring the heat down on them from the rest of the world."

"Like you said, Suds, we're the soldiers and we do what we're told. But on the plus side, at least that means the Atlantic Convoys should be safe."

Studs' face creased in uncertainty. "You think?"

His friend's reaction made Terry stop and consider. He batted the question back: "You believe they won't be?"

The Lieutenant General shook his head and said: "I dunno, Earl, but we should remember this guy's word ain't worth shit. He could attack our ships, resume the attack on the mainland, tell the world it's not happening, that's it's all NATO lies, and if China backed him up, at least half the world would believe him."

Terry nodded his understanding. "Good point," he said. "Let's be in touch when our political masters have had a chance to cluck over this."

Chapter 44

Operations Specialist Andrew Powell stroked his trimmed, white beard and paced around the large central command station in the tactical management area of the bridge on the USS *George Washington*. The hologram projected by the central command station described his ship at the centre, flanked by four destroyers, and trailing in their wake the seventy merchant ships laden with power units for SkyWatchers, PeaceMakers, and Battlefield Support Lasers, as well as thousands of other parts whose construction was too complex for replicators to reproduce. Twelve more destroyers flanked them further out.

Although the green hologram displayed one of the most modern groupings of naval power, Powell couldn't help being reminded of a brood of lean, lithe hens shepherding their clutch of fat, lumpy chicks to safety. The US Navy was there to defend the merchantmen. The fierce pride he took in this ship and its crew shone more brightly now a real war had broken out. And as luck would have it, it had erupted only a few months before he was due to retire from the service, too.

His legs detected the slight movement in the massive battleship as it cut through the moderate Atlantic swell. He went over to a junior rating on monitoring duty at a station at the edge of the bridge. He looked at the display's light-graphs and asked: "What does Chester have to say about it?"

The young man answered: "The probabilities have been stable for awhile, Sir. Here and here," he said, indicating part of the image, "have shown the greatest variation over the last twelve hours, but that has not affected the overall numbers a whole lot."

"And we've still got seventeen hours to go."

The junior rating gave out a nervous laugh and said: "Hell, Sir, if it stays this quiet for the rest of the voyage, that'll suit me just fine."

Powell was about to give the rating a gentle reprimand not to tempt fate when one of the graphs changed from green to orange, and then to red. "What is it?" he asked.

The rating cleared his throat, all humour gone, and replied: "SkyWatcher zero-one-seven reports that it has detected—Ah, no, it is in fact under attack. Chester is already calling it as the beginning of an attack on the convoy, Sir."

Powell announced: "General quarters." He put a hand on the rating's shoulder and spoke over the sound of the klaxon: "Give full tactical command over to Chester and link to the main display."

"Aye, Sir."

Powell returned to the central console and tapped a lit panel. "Sorry to wake you, Captain—"

He stopped speaking as another crew member at a different station called out, in a determined female voice: "SkyWatcher zero-one-seven confirmed destroyed. Multiple contacts now emerging from south/southeast. Distance one thousand kilometres and closing in a straight line."

Powell resumed: "But an attack on this convoy seems to be developing rapidly, Sir."

The somnolent response came back: "Andy, take care of it till I get up there. I need ninety seconds."

"Yes, Sir," Powell replied. He pointed at one of the bridge crew he knew had a non-combat responsibility and barked: "You, rating. Strong, hot coffee, NATO-standard, on this command station within ninety seconds."

"Aye, Sir!" came the emphatic response as a young man on the bridge hurried away.

The crew member at another station called out: "Over three hundred confirmed contacts."

"Battle stations," Powell called out. He took in a deep breath and addressed the *George Washington*'s super artificial intelligence: "Chester, all known data to the central command station. What is the current status?"

The green shapes in the hologram that denoted the convoy shrivelled down to almost microscopic size, and then moved off to the far left of the central command station. At the other extreme, there appeared red dots that grew into straight lines as the gender-neutral voice of the ship's super AI spoke: "Tracking three hundred and twenty hostile ACAs approaching at a unified Mach nine-point-two at all altitudes."

Powell whistled through his teeth at the range of altitudes the attacking machines were spread over, from as low as one hundred metres above the ocean waves to the highest wing of thirty-two ACAs at fifteen thousand metres. He instructed: "Calculate their most likely point and shape of dispersal, and talk to the other ships to arrange optimum defence. Your priority is to protect the merchant vessels, got that?"

"Acknowledged," the super AI replied.

The rating returned grasping a cup from which wisps of steam wafted, and at the same time Captain Mitch Taylor entered the bridge in silence.

Powell knew all of the crew were aware that the Captain disdained fuss, so unlike some other ships, no one announced Taylor's arrival.

The Captain took the cup from the rating, drew in a deep breath that expanded his broad chest, and barked: "Chester? Three hundred and twenty what are inbound? And that number is too small—where are the other waves of attackers? A month ago, the Med and Arabian fleets were destroyed by thousands of them." He took a gulp of coffee and sighed in satisfaction.

The super AI replied: "All incoming targets identified as Blackswans—"

Powell spoke over the computer: "That's a total of one thousand, six hundred Spiders where just one will be enough to sink any of those merchantmen."

Chester continued: "Targets will be in weapons' range in seven minutes and in the immediate battlespace in eight minutes."

Captain Taylor stared at the central command station, watching the three hundred lines of red light as they proceeded inexorably towards the convoy. He took another gulp of coffee and rubbed the stubble on his face with a palm. He glanced at Powell and said: "You really believe that they think three hundred and twenty of those things will be enough?"

"Sorry, Sir," Powell replied over the noise, "but that is not our first concern."

The Captain chuckled and drained the coffee. He stuck the empty cup out in his hand and barked: "Another," and suppressed a belch.

The same junior rating hurried over, took the cup, and disappeared.

Taylor spoke to Powell, raising his voice above the klaxon and nodding at the display: "What do you think, soften the heading?"

Powell agreed with his Captain, thinking that this attack shared many similarities with a training exercise, apart from beginning when the Captain was at rest.

Taylor said: "Chester? Adjust our heading a few degrees to what you calculate is optimum. It's obvious we should present portside weapons to begin with. And shut the klaxon off now."

The noise stopped at once and the super AI said: "All weapons will be available to counter the expected multiple-axes attacks."

Taylor raised an eyebrow and then instructed: "Open comms to all ships in the convoy."

"Acknowledged. The request will be fulfilled in twenty to thirty seconds."

A weapons officer from a monitoring station called out: "Captain, request permission to raise the PeaceMakers."

"Granted," Taylor replied at once. "Put 'em up top and wait for my command."

"Yes, Sir."

Taylor lowered his voice and said to his colleague: "Andy, I still don't believe this is the whole attack."

Another voice called out: "Port-side Pulsars open and charged."

Powell's eyes did not waver from the holographic display over the central command station as the digits in the countdown continued marking time to the instant when the attack would begin. He said: "I think we're gonna know real soon... Assuming we survive the next seven minutes."

Chester announced: "Captain, comms to all ships in the convoy are established. Proceed when ready."

Powell looked at the Captain and saw him steel himself before beginning: "Attention, all ships. As you can see, in a few moments we will engage the enemy. Last week, the first relief convoy crossed the Atlantic without interference. I think we should consider ourselves flattered that the Mad Mullah in Tehran has decided we are worthy of his attentions. To all of you merchantmen, know that the Navy will do everything to protect you. Most of you have onboard Pulsars controlled by my ship's super AI. This will give you the best chance of making it through this contact unscathed. However, be advised that, should the situation require it, I will release control to individual vessels, as the US Department of Defense agreed prior to this convoy sailing.

"To all of my fellow captains and their crews: this is what we have been trained for, it is what we joined the United States Navy for, and, unlike the events of a month ago, now we have many new advantages to work in our favour. I believe these advantages will make the difference. Taylor out." The Captain tapped a small square on the station in front of him.

Powell eyed the Captain as Taylor took a step back and folded his arms. Powell said: "All PeaceMaker wings on deck, Sir."

Taylor nodded, "Get them airborne."

"Sir." Powell felt the tension on the ship build. All of them knew what had happened in the Mediterranean Sea and the Arabian Gulf, but the crew also knew of the hard-won developments NATO had made since then. Powell felt certain each man and woman on the *George Washington* asked him or herself if these developments would make any difference, some difference, or all the difference.

Chester's voice filled the bridge: "Captain, all weapons' systems are standing by. PeaceMakers are gaining altitude and have been placed under SkyWatcher direction. Hostiles will be in range in thirty-one seconds. Do you require an audible countdown?"

"Christ, Andy," Taylor muttered in a low voice, "sometimes I wonder why we're even on this ship." He lifted his head and announced: "Weapons free. Fire to automatic. No audible countdown."

"Here we go," Powell said, more to himself.

The holographic image of the fleet, now including white lines tracing the increasing height of the PeaceMakers that had recently left the *George Washington*'s upper deck, drifted back to the centre of the command station as the red traces denoting the approaching hostile ACAs closed in. The rating returned with a refilled cup of coffee for the Captain.

The 'In Range' countdown reached zero and the red lines bloomed out for their attack. Powell's confidence increased that these three-hundred-and-twenty Blackswans constituted the entire attack. He'd studied the destruction of the Mediterranean and Arabian fleets, and had realised that the enemy ACAs went at those ships in a straight line because thousands were following behind them, and they had no need to do anything tactical.

"Pretty," Taylor observed as the enemy forces attacked. The Blackswans at sea level split up, the outer ACAs flanking around to pincer the entire convoy. Those at higher altitudes changed to similar headings, diving as they did so, while the highest Blackswans abruptly dived straight down. Powell had to concede that from a geometric point of view, the image of the convoy being enveloped in the cloud of attacking enemy ACAs was indeed beautiful. The *George Washington*'s PeaceMakers accelerated to engage the enemy's machines at the higher altitudes, while the ship-bound Pulsar lasers opened fire on the ACAs approaching at lower levels.

Chester spoke: "All US Navy ships now engaged; merchant vessel weapons providing support."

Powell reflected how all of the people on the bridge might as well be thousands of miles from the battle for all the impact their presence had on the ship's ability to defend itself. He struggled to imagine that just a few feet away, on the other side of the hull, Pulsar laser cannons clicked out their shots, RIM surface-to-air missiles streaked from the ship into the grey, overcast sky, and NATO PeaceMakers took on the vastly better-protected Blackswans. Over the central command station, the white lines of light denoting NATO ordnance drew swiftly together to meet the enemy, and in each individual conflict, the white line vanished and the red continued towards the ships.

Powell glanced at the data and a flash of hope sparked inside him. Among the lists of figures that fluctuated as the battle wore on and Chester made its recalculations, a percentage figure denoted the anticipated proportion of the convoy they could expect to be destroyed. In the moments since the size of the attacking force had been known, this number had hovered around fifty percent. Now, despite the enemy burning up defending NATO munitions at a frightening rate, the number crept lower.

Captain Taylor said to him: "I see it as well, Andy. Some of us might actually survive this."

Powell acknowledged his Captain's observation, and then Taylor asked the super AI: "How well is the coherence-length variation working?"

Chester replied: "It has reduced the effectiveness of the enemy's shielding by between sixty and seventy-one percent."

"Captain," Powell said, "why can't the enemy's super AI just counteract the coherence length variation?"

"Because it's random," Taylor replied without taking his eyes off the display. "The enemy is reduced to guessing; of course super AI never just guesses, it makes billions of calculations every instant to try and estimate the right frequency to adjust the shielding on its ACAs, but the real pisser is that it just can't."

"Simple but effective," Powell observed.

"No matter the tech, Andy, the best advances in warfare always are—Chester, what's up with the *Mustin* and *Ross*?"

The ship's super AI replied: "The available margins to prevent those destroyers from damage or destruction are narrowing."

Taylor raised an eyebrow, "Due to?"

"The on-going conflict is too dynamic to sustain a response."

Powell felt his heartrate increase as the number of enemy ACAs in the battlespace kept dropping; more than half of them had been destroyed. Even though the *Mustin* and *Ross* were fighting off Blackswans that had reached to within two thousand yards, still after several minutes no Caliphate ACA had breached any ship's defences.

"Damn, look," Taylor said.

"Novel," Powell replied as the holographic image showed that some Blackswans had dispatched their Spiders directly into the sea to attack the convoy from underneath the waves. To compensate, the NATO super AI reassigned hundreds of missiles from the US Navy ships and PeaceMakers to intercept them. Incredulity increased inside Powell as Chester coordinated all of these missiles to hit the underwater Spiders repeatedly, often at distances of mere feet, to ensure they were destroyed before they could reach a ship.

The percentage figure denoting the anticipated proportion of the convoy they could expect to be destroyed dropped to less than five percent. All of the ACAs and missiles in the sky around the convoy flew ever-more complex and G-force-defying courses as the super artificial intelligences on both sides of the battle fought to outsmart each other, considering trillions of options in millionths of seconds. Chunks of red-hot scrap metal rained down from above, some clattering on the ships' hulls, and disappeared under the waves.

After two more minutes, fewer than ten Blackswans remained to threaten the convoy. Powell reined in his hope lest the patience of the maritime gods be tested too far. All of the *George Washington*'s PeaceMakers were gone, but the US Navy ships' Pulsar lasers continued firing shots that burned through the enemy's shielding fast enough to prevent it gaining an advantage.

Chester spoke: "Captain, we have insufficient missiles. If the enemy sends more Spiders to attack under the water, the Pulsar cannons will not be able to—"

"Oh no," Powell said. On the display, the image of the *USS Ross* shuddered when a single Spider reached her keel and detonated. She wallowed in the moderate swell before rolling under the waves, portside first.

"How soon can you divert other ships to pick up survivors, Chester?" Taylor asked.

"The on-going conflict is too dynamic to sustain a response."

"Damn you," Taylor muttered.

"Captain," Powell said, "it's almost over."

Seconds later, the ship's super AI announced: "All enemy ACAs have been destroyed. The battlespace is now secure."

"What about survivors from the *Ross*?" Taylor demanded.

Chester replied: "The *Mustin* is on site picking them up; the *Stockdale* and *Carney* will be on site in less than two minutes."

Powell asked: "Any sign of further enemy ACAs?"

"Negative."

"Assess the probability of further attacks. If we've used all of our missiles and they send more Spiders under the water, we could be in big trouble."

The ship's super AI answered: "Another attack is highly unlikely. Based on the enemy's tactics to date in all theatres, it has most probably decided that the tactical cost is not worth the strategic gain."

Taylor scoffed and said to Powell: "So, he thinks we're not worth so much effort after all, huh?"

Powell realised a flaw in his own considerations. He said: "After this skirmish, we have priority missile coverage from Europe, so I guess maybe we're not really that exposed?"

Taylor responded: "Unless the enemy is planning some kind of strategic multi-axes offensive?"

"That ain't what he said in public. It's been real quiet on the mainland for a while now," Powell said as he watched the Captain drain his coffee.

Taylor said: "Chester?"

"Yes, Captain Taylor?"

"Tell us again: what is the current condition of the battlespace?"

Chester answered: "The battlespace is now secure. There is no risk to the convoy."

The Captain smiled and said to Powell: "Hell, I didn't expect to hear that, to be honest."

Powell smiled and nodded his agreement.

Taylor ordered: "Stand down battle stations. Well done, everyone."

Powell sensed relief wash through the bridge like a summer breeze of fresh air. His eye alighted on the junior rating at the monitoring station, who now sat with his head in his hands. Powell strolled over to him and asked: "You okay, sailor?"

The young man looked up and responded: "Aye, Sir, absolutely."

Powell saw the relief and terror and shock in the rating's eyes. It reminded Powell of similar emotions he himself had felt twenty years earlier, when Chinese ACAs had attacked his ship on a pirate-clearing patrol in the Pacific. Powell nodded in understanding and said to the young man: "This is an important day. For the first time since this damn war began, we now know it's possible to get attacked by the Caliphate... and survive."

Chapter 45

Delirium threatened to overwhelm the Englishman as he staggered through the diplomatic compound in Beijing, certain only that his apartment in the English Section was about five hundred metres ahead, in the building on his left. Through his drug-addled drunkenness, he knew why the Third Caliph had paused, he knew how long that pause would last, and he knew, he finally *knew*, that the Chinese had lost control of the Third Caliph and in result the New Persian Caliphate.

"God, I need a piss," he said to himself, feeling the urge as he looked around at the lawns and mature trees on either side of the gravel path. He did not notice the figure trailing him. He burped and muttered: "Better not. If one those slit-eyed bastards catches me, I'll be in the shit."

He stumbled on, concentrating on making sure one leg kept going in front of the other, remembering times past, when he was a student at Cambridge University, out with his friends. He didn't have to worry then, he could piss whenever and wherever he felt like it. He recalled he and his friends stumbling along Cambridge high street and shouting into the night that it was the inalienable right of every free-born Englishman to be able to piss with absolute freedom. "And not have to be on the lookout for slitty-eyed bastards, even if they were the centre of the fucking universe."

He stopped and his body wavered for a moment. He felt movement in his stomach but could not be sure from which end any contents might be ejected. The chill of a certain wetness in his underwear made him recall the previous hour inside Marshall Zhou's suite and inside his body. "Shit," he said aloud, remembering, "did I do that bastard again?"

He hiccoughed and then tried to force the trapped air out from his diaphragm, but broke wind instead. He found this funny. He giggled. The giggle turned into a laugh. The exertion of laughing caused him to break wind again, a loud, ripping noise that echoed off the trees in the still night air. His laughter increased and he fell over at the base of a tree. He looked up at the starless black sky, still laughing, and noted how shadows seemed to move from right to left for a second, then revert to where they had been and move right-to-left again.

At length, the pain in his ribs made his laughter subside and he heaved for breath. He decided that the tree trunk against which he sat was in fact quite comfortable, and the night was not cold. As his breathing came back under control, he recalled the evening: an opulent party at the refurbished Galaxy building celebrating the five-hundredth-and-something anniversary of the final defeat of one of those great dynasties—Ding? Ming? Ping?—where the world's diplomats and dignitaries took care to pay homage to the leaders of the most powerful country on Earth.

But the Marshall. Oh, how Marshall Zhou had missed his Englishman. Memories of what had happened after the party surged through the Englishman's drunkenness. How many pills had he given Zhou? Too many. And the booze? There had been at least three different flavours of *baijiu*, and the Chinese alcohol did not mix well with single malt whiskey.

Ah, but the information Zhou revealed after they'd had sex; that was worth the worst hangover in the world. At first, the Englishman had thought Zhou mocked or teased him, but he knew from his youth that certain tears cannot be summoned at will.

Zhou admitted that his wife had confronted him about his indiscretions, which fact the Englishman found tedious beyond toleration. But suddenly, Zhou had drawn the comparison between him losing face in front of his wife, and China losing face in front of the Third Caliph.

The Englishman's head lolled on the hard, rough bark of the tree behind him. He said aloud: "Oh yeah, face. That's everything to these guys. No fucking compromise—you can't take a Chinaman's *face*." A familiar warning bell tinkled in the furthest recess of his alcohol-submersed sobriety, reminding him that he must not be indiscreet. He began giggling again, wondering if Zhou's anus could also be accused of indiscretion.

"Not if he gets a portion up it in private," he said aloud, wiping his hand across his forehead. "No," he went on, warming to the thought, "in private, everyone does what they fucking well like... In private, the Chinese President can threaten the Third Caliph that if he doesn't stop bombing the shit out of Europe, China will stop all exports." The Englishman giggled again but then reverted to sullen anger as he said: "But, in private, the Third Caliph can tell the Chinese President to go fuck himself." He mused: "Ah, the mad little fucker in Tehran stole the Chinaman's face, in front of the whole Politburo—" he dissolved in a fit of uncontrolled laughter.

Presently, the throaty guffawing transformed into sobs of utter despair as memories of the desperate images of Europe's suffering cut through the Englishman's drunkenness. He sobbed from depths of his stomach; loud, echoing yelps of crushing desolation. He stopped only when mucus ran out of his nose and he had to wipe his sleeve across his mouth and inhale the remainder back into his sinuses.

"Fucking bastards," he spat in a mix of anguish and hate, tears running down his face. "Fucking bloody bastards, playing Europe like it's a fucking pawn." He became aware of the approach of another person. He looked along the path to see someone coming towards him, but he found it difficult to focus.

"Hullo there!" called a cheerful English voice. "I am so sorry to disturb you, Sir, but I do think you need to come with me now."

The Englishman fought to get his breathing under control and to focus his eyes. A young man stood in front of him, slim and dressed in formal attire.

"What?" was all the Englishman could say as he looked into the unsmiling, Mongolian face.

The man offered a hand, but his eyes showed no trace of friendship. His polite voice dropped a tone, and the request became a demand: "I am dreadfully sorry, Sir, but you really do have to come with me now."

Chapter 46

The girl of Senegalese descent with porcelain skin leaned over to Maria Phillips and said with infectious enthusiasm: "Finally, we're going to get our hands on the serious stuff—I can't wait."

Maria smiled and said: "Come on, Nabou, it's already been intense. I swear I've never been this fit in my life."

Nabou grinned back, her brilliant white teeth completing her cheeky expression. "I think they want to stop us thinking about the future, you know?"

"Yes," Maria said, "stop us worrying about the war by keeping us worrying about locker inspections."

"That sergeant has it in for our squad, I tell you, Maz. Look at poor Ronnie, having the whole company laugh at him because he dribbled saliva down his front during PT. Only because the sergeant told the other squads."

Maria marvelled at Nabou's flawless, obsidian skin when the door to the classroom suddenly opened and the training sergeant strode in. The twenty-four recruits stood up as one and saluted.

"As you were, you Muppets," she said, a large-boned woman with narrow hips, who looked powerful and intimidating in her fatigues. She scanned the assorted recruits as they settled, and Maria noted the way the sergeant used just enough makeup to intensify the glare from her eyes. She stood at the front of the room on a raised platform, put her fists on her hips, and huffed in what, Maria had come to know, was certainly dissatisfaction.

"Miller," she said with a nod of her head, "you're still as ugly this morning as you were yesterday afternoon. Why?"

A male voice from the back of the room replied: "Sorry, ma'am. I have not been able to get compassionate leave yet to visit the beauty salon."

The sergeant said: "You'd be any beauty salon's worst nightmare."

"Yes, ma'am. Sorry ma'am," Miller repeated.

The sergeant paused and allowed the smiles to die down.

Maria looked on in admiration; she had never encountered people like those she had met during her basic training.

The Sergeant turned and touched the side of the large screen on the wall. As it came to life with an image, she spoke: "We have reached the stage of your Phase One training where, against my better judgement, we are going to let you touch some weapons. But before we do, we begin with this," she stepped to the side to reveal the enlarged, three-dimensional image of a quantum matrix. "This is your SQCH–77B Battlefield Management Support System, colloquially known as the Squitch. I won't bore you with the technical operational parameters…" she paused, then: "And besides which, most of you look too stupid to understand them anyway."

Maria felt everyone else in the room smile with her.

The training sergeant went on: "This piece of kit is the one thing that can keep you alive in a battle. We can fit it in your own lens if you use one. We can implant it below your ear, or, if you prefer neither of those options, we can put it into your standard-issue goggles, although that does mean you have to wear them permanently while on duty." As she described the options, images appeared showing example devices.

"The Squitch is merged with all of the Army's support systems. It allows your CO to know where you are and how you are doing, and it allows his CO to see how a firefight or battle is developing. The controller is this coin-shaped device that you keep in a special pocket.. Do not deactivate your Squitch. Ever. Without it, you are blind, totally defenceless, and completely disconnected from support."

The images of the types of device faded and were replaced with the outline of a rifle. The training sergeant went on: "Now, from among all of the small arms you will learn to use during your Phase One training, this is the most important: the NATO-standard issue PKU–48 smart assault rifle, called the Pickup. This weapon allows you to aim to within a few metres of a target, and still hit it. It fires smart bullets that adjust their explosive mix depending on the target. For example, if you are aiming at a building, your Squitch will adjust the compounds to maximise explosive damage, whereas if you fire at a physical enemy, the mix will be adjusted to do as much harm to human tissue as possible."

While describing this, the images in the screen displayed an enlarged smart bullet with simplified labels and other indicators of how it worked. A shiver ran through Maria when the sergeant mentioned human tissue, and despite wanting to contribute and do her duty, a small part of her hoped she would never have to fire the rifle at a real person.

"In addition, the smart bullet, while not an actual guided missile, can nevertheless have its trajectory tweaked in flight. This might save your life if, for example, you come upon an enemy unexpectedly and have only an instant to get the first shot off. The Squitch will then direct the bullet, during its flight, onto the target. Any questions so far?"

Silence greeted the sergeant's enquiry. She scanned the class and said: "I'm trying to decide if you have no questions because you all understand everything I've told you up to now, or if it's because none of you Muppets has a clue what I'm talking about."

A ripple of nervous laughter ran around the room.

The sergeant continued: "Of course, your Battlefield Management Support System links directly to—and should not be confused with—Squonk, the Ministry of Defence's, and therefore the British Army's, super artificial intelligence. Although they're part of the same super-AI operating system, the Squitch is your Squitch, just for you. It is your assistant on the battlefield. Squonk, on the other hand, is for everyone. Now, I expect all of you know and have worked with super AI in your miserable little lives. Is that right?"

The look on the training sergeant's face changed and Maria realised that someone had a question. The sergeant nodded to the person behind Maria.

A female voice behind Maria asked: "Excuse me, ma'am, but what is a squonk?"

The sergeant gave the questioner an incredulous look. She said: "I know I shouldn't be surprised by any of you Muppets, but really, you don't know what a squonk is? Okay, does any of you know?"

Again, silence greeted her question.

She let out a lengthy sigh and explained: "A squonk is an imaginary creature that, when captured, dissolves in a puddle of tears and bubbles. The British Army's super artificial intelligence was given that name by a general who, many years ago, had the misfortune to have to deal with the only group of recruits in the entire history of the British Army who were stupider than you lot, clear?"

Maria analysed the large image of the Pickup on the screen and shivered at the suggestion of lethality it presented. She questioned her decision to join up yet again.

"Right, that's enough of the jokes," the training sergeant said, a stern look on her face. "You must all remember that your Squitch is your best friend. The Squitch can and will do everything to save your life in a battle. The Squitch will warn you of approaching threats. It will tell you what to shoot and where. It will tell you where to find cover. It will tell you how to get back to your unit. It will tell you where your nearest support is. Most importantly, your Squitch makes you part of a single, seamless military operation. In effect, you become an integrated element of one of the most advanced fighting platforms the world has ever seen."

Maria exhaled in the silence. The training sergeant put her fists on her hips again and concluded: "Now I would like to invite all of you Muppets to come with me to the armoury, where you will be fitted with a Squitch and issued with a Pickup." She paused for a moment before smiling and saying: "And a few magazines of blank ammunition." The screen behind her deactivated and she strode for the door.

Maria stood with all of the other recruits. Over the noise of twenty-four chairs scrapping on the floor, Maria heard Nabou squeal in excitement: "This is going to be brilliant!"

Maria glanced back at her new friend and smiled, feeling warmed by Nabou's infectious enthusiasm.

Chapter 47

Napier's flesh crawled at the way the Brazilian Vice-President leered at her, and anger crackled inside as his words patronised her. In normal times, she would have put up with it because of Brazil's importance in global affairs. As it was the fifth largest country in the world with the fourth largest economy, English prime ministers had for years been obliged to be accommodating of the country's dignitaries in the hope of gaining a few crumbs of investment from Brazilian conglomerates.

Luiz Melo's perfect white teeth shone when he flashed his smile after telling Napier that she looked like an English rose. Perhaps in better times she might have felt a twinge of appreciation, but the weight of problems smothered such considerations, and in any case, she knew better than anyone how much she'd aged in the last three months. "Mr Melo," she answered, determined to apply whatever English aloofness she could muster, "my advisors tell me the Brazilian delegation will abstain on all of the resolutions which the European countries have put forward to condemn the Persian Caliphate. Is that true?"

Melo's smile softened when he replied: "Madame Napier, all of these resolutions are superficial. The Persian Caliphate is not a member of the United Nations, so those resolutions cannot carry any significance outside this chamber."

Napier sipped her water, glanced around at all of the other delegates about to enter the main chamber, and asked: "If they are not significant, why will Brazil abstain? Why don't you support them and give them added legitimacy instead? And thus show the world that the Brazilian government opposes the death and destruction in Europe?"

Melo's face dropped and Napier wondered if he were mature enough to take the point. He said: "You should remember that the UN is a lame-duck forum, especially compared to the Pan-Asian Confederation. You English, Americans, French, Germans and all the others, you are no longer as important as you think you are. Stop living in yesterday, stop think—"

"Millions of Europeans have died," Napier hissed, provoked by his smarmy indifference. "This is about genocide, genocide permitted by the world's richest and most powerful countries, because China allows it."

His black eyebrows rose in interest more than concern. He said: "But—how do you say it in English?—the shoe is on the other foot, yes? It was not so long ago that you sat back and allowed the most atrocious genocides to take place, and even supported them if Western companies could increase their profits. For example, what happened in Rwanda seventy years ago? Or the Holocaust? All the way back to the slave trade. Why do you smart and complain now because countries which are so much more powerful than you show little interest in your suffering or merely offer empty platitudes?"

"It is not the same thing," Napier averred, despite a kernel of doubt germinating in her mind.

"Oh, but it is, very much so," the Brazilian maintained. "You English and Americans do not understand. You are like an Italian who demands more today because Rome used to govern the greatest empire on Earth two millennia ago. You are living in a past glory that your ancestors lost many years ago. You would do well to understand that."

Napier did not need a lecture on history. She said: "Millions of people are dying, have died, and will die. Europe did nothing to provoke the Third Caliph—" she broke off when Melo scoffed. "What?" she demanded.

"Really?" he said. "Stationing those two groups of battleships in the seas around Caliphate territory? Making constant probing attacks on his satellites? Even sending Special Forces into his territory only to have the embarrassment of their dead bodies being put on display?"

A headache began with a piercing jab of pain above Napier's left temple. She wanted to blame it on the time lag after flying from London and arriving in New York a couple of hours earlier. She said: "Such actions were in no way deserving of the current invasion. You must give us your support. You must add your weight to the calls for the Third Caliph to withdraw his forces back to Caliphate territory immediately." As the pain in her head worsened, she thought the look on Melo's face showed some understanding if not actual sympathy.

"My dear Madame Napier," he said in a level voice, "we should go into the chamber as the debate regarding the wording of your resolutions is about to begin." He paused and then added in a quieter tone: "Perhaps you should look at this from a broader perspective? For example, what if the Third Caliph has grander ambitions? What if the invasion of Europe has another purpose? Europe is poorer and less populated than many other parts of the world, for example India, which the Caliphate borders and which the Third Caliph might covet. Perhaps even the mighty China herself? What if the invasion of Europe were merely a test, a kind of training exercise?"

"You can't possibly be serious," Napier heard herself bluster while realising that what the Brazilian said made perfect sense.

His black eyebrows rose again and he said: "The only thing the European countries can do to avoid more bloodshed is surrender—"

"Never," Napier choked out at the affront.

"The Third Caliph made another appeal this morning, did he not?"

"Yes, not that it's going to make the slightest diff—"

"He continues to hold his forces back in a show of mercy, does he not?"

"Merely so his 'warriors' can rape and steal everything they—"

"Perhaps," Melo broke in with apparently strained patience. "But again, Madame Napier, I would urge you to look at the broader picture. To the rest of the world, however violent his conduct to date, he has now paused and offered the remaining European countries an opportunity to surrender and avoid a great deal of unnecessary bloodshed—"

"What you are saying is preposterous," Napier said, her words laced with disgust.

"My point is only this: please understand that history may come to judge you and Coll and the other European presidents and prime ministers for actively choosing quite the most brutal—and completely unnecessary—annihilation for your peoples."

Melo strode off for the main chamber, leaving Napier staring after him in a new kind of shock—a shock of perspective—as the other delegates and representatives filed through the doors. The pain in her head felt like she'd been hit by an arrow, compounded by the shock and fear that the rest of the world would indeed blame the European countries' intransigence for prolonging the war as much as the Third Caliph, while conveniently overlooking his initial belligerence.

"Is everything all right, Prime Minister?" inquired a new voice.

"Yes, of course," Napier replied automatically, glancing down into the lined face of Dame Sally Rent, the English Permanent Representative to the UN.

"Hmm, if you say so," Rent replied in concern. "I didn't want to interrupt your chat with Melo. I assume he declined to support us?"

Napier looked into the woman's clear blue eyes, oddly noticing that she had the kind of lashes which reflected the light as though they were damp. Napier sensed the woman's concern and felt an abrupt, deeper connection. The Prime Minister said: "No, he gave me a lecture about history—as if I'd ever need such a thing—but we can forget about Brazil's support. Really, such arrogance. And from a man who comes from a country where the police force kill sixty thousand of their citizens every year. Disgusting."

"I think we had better get into the chamber, PM."

The two women's shoes clicked on the marble floor as they walked towards the entrance.

Napier asked: "India will still back the resolutions, yes?"

"Deshpande told me he would, but he qualified that it might not be possible in the future. If the Third Caliph offers surrender terms and keeps his warriors where they are, he says public opinion in India will harden against us. He said he's already hearing whispers in Delhi that trade with China is more important than supporting their previous overseers."

"Really," Napier muttered, the pain in her head acting as a permanent distraction. Both women stopped at the doors and allowed their lenses to be scanned before entering the main chamber. Napier glanced at the floor and noted how pieces of the tiled skirting had cracked and broken off.

Once inside, Rent took her place at the main table while Napier climbed the few steps up to the guests' gallery. Napier struggled to put on a smile and nod hellos to the other attendees. When she sat to watch the proceedings, the Brazilian's words came back to her. She looked around the chamber and tried to recall how many countries had left the United Nations in the preceding years, but the pain in her head ached too intensely. The Council passed the resolutions condemning the Caliphate's aggression, calling for its forces to leave the European mainland, and to open negotiations to pay reparations. But Napier knew Melo had been right. The Persian Caliphate was not a member of the UN. Neither was China, or any of the Asian nations that bordered China, and neither was any South American country except Brazil, nor any African country except Angola and South Africa.

The feeling of impotence overwhelmed her. The world had changed, and rules that she believed should not apply to Europe suddenly did. Or perhaps they had for some time, but she had not noticed? Somewhere deep in her mind, away from the pain in her temple and away from this crumbling, ineffectual edifice, she felt certain of future events: that the Third Caliph would make more demands for NATO and Europe's surrender already knowing it would never be forthcoming. He would continue building up his forces in the conquered lands. Then, on some future date, his warriors would sweep across the rest of Europe and destroy it. And by then, a fair portion of the rest of the world would blame her and Coll and the others for the disaster. The course of history would change, and life would go on for those that remained.

She fought to consider what she might do to stop or at least change this course of events. The approach of Dame Sally Rent brought her back to her surroundings.

"Hello, PM. Well, we got what we needed to get," she said with apparently feigned enthusiasm.

Napier nodded and said: "Thank you for your hard work here, Sally. I appreciate it."

"Thank you for coming all the way over here, PM."

"It gives me a chance to meet Madelyn and have a person-to-person chat with her for the first time since this debacle began. When do we leave?"

Rent's face dropped. "Ah, I'm afraid, PM, that Coll has cancelled your meeting with her."

"What? Why?"

"She claimed urgent business on the west coast, something to do with sea defences. Secretary of State Warren Baker is waiting in Washington to meet you."

Napier sighed and shook her head. She considered for a moment and then said: "No, he's an absolute letch and I have a rotten headache. I can talk to him on the AAT. I need to talk to people who might actually be able to help."

"Very well, PM. So, back to London at once, yes?"

"Yes."

Chapter 48

"You're a lucky one and no mistake," the slim doctor told Geoff Morrow.

"What happened?" Geoff croaked through a haze of exhaustion, wishing the hospital light in the ceiling above his bed did not shine so brightly.

The young man, whose pointed nose bent to the right, peered into Geoff's eyes and said: "You don't remember?"

"No, it's a bit hazy."

"You were blown up. On a monorail." His face flashed a half-smile. "You were hit by over a hundred pieces of shrapnel. One particular piece entered between vertebra C5 and C6 and severed your spinal cord."

"Jesus," Geoff breathed.

The doctor quipped: "He's not here, so talk to me instead. My name is Doctor Raymond."

"Er, right," Geoff mumbled, wondering if the man standing by his bed were a doctor or a wannabe stand-up comedian.

"Now," he said, placing open hands on the sheets covering Geoff. "You are going to have to take it easy for the first week—"

"Week?" Geoff repeated in horror.

"Yes, you've been lying in bed for the last few weeks in an induced coma—"

"Why? I thought the GenoFluid bots were supposed to be quick—"

"My, we are a curious one, aren't we? Well, the spinal cord was obviously no problem, but the bone tissue needed some days to knit back. However, the shrapnel also shredded your liver—you know how important your liver is, don't you?—and for good measure punctured your left lung. Thus, we decided it would be better to hold you in an induced coma while replacement organs were grown."

Geoff's spirits lifted as he said: "A brand new, cloned liver? That's fantastic news, thanks."

Doctor Raymond sniffed in dismissiveness and said: "If you're a heavy drinker, then yes, I imagine it would be fantastic."

Geoff felt his senses coming back rapidly. He blinked and blinked again, and then asked: "My lens isn't working."

Doctor Raymond said: "We'll let you have it back soon."

"So, where am I?"

"In an Italian military hospital a few clicks north of Milan."

"What? What's the date?"

"20 April."

Again, Geoff blinked his eye to try to get more detailed data from his lens, as he disliked having to rely on this strange doctor.

Doctor Raymond chuckled and said: "Nope, your lens still isn't there, sorry."

"That can't be right," Geoff insisted as recent memories flooded his mind. "The Caliphate was steamrollering right over the whole of Europe. We'd be finished in just a few weeks. If it's late April now, then those bastard ragheads should already be in London. Lisa, Lisa will be—"

All eccentricity vanished from Raymond's demeanour and he said: "Hold on a minute. The invasion paused on the night you were injured. For the last four weeks, there has been a break in the fighting. The Third Caliph has demanded that NATO and rest of the European countries surrender—"

"No shit?" Geoff said.

"So that he can look like the good guy when he's finally stockpiled enough ACAs to roll over the rest of Europe in all of five minutes."

"That's mad. We can't surr—"

"We won't, sweetie-pie," Doctor Raymond said. "Our nutcase in Tehran is not the only one who has been building up forces."

Geoff exhaled and closed his eyes. He waited for the shock in his mind to settle. Doctor Raymond told him to rest and that he should not try to do too much. Even though he was young and fit, spending so much time immobile necessitated a period of physiotherapy to get his muscles working properly again.

When he was alone, Geoff tried to get out of the bed and only then understood the importance of the Doctor's instruction. He wisely lay back down. The details of the monorail exploding came back to him and he realised how lucky he'd been. He had more questions about who had found him and how. These queries faded to leave a new and alien feeling: a desire to return to Lisa. A voice in his head kept telling him that he should be dead now, dead like so many other people the Caliphate's machines had slaughtered since February.

His breathing accelerated and dampness spread over his chest and arms. As he lay sweating, he realised his luck must have run out. At any other time in history, any combination of his injuries would have killed him. And for what? His name on a by-line? Where exactly would he find his Big Scoop that would make Alan in London give him a proper contract, that would see him pick up a gong at the next Press Awards? Not that there would ever be another Press Awards.

Of greater significance, if he had died on that monorail, what would have happened? Alan would have found another desperate stringer and paid them even less than Geoff. Lisa would have given birth, and their child would have grown up with a different father, for Geoff had no doubt Lisa would move on eventually, and he'd want her to be happy in any case.

More than any other, the thought of his child growing up without him gripped Geoff. In an instant, he realised he had to do everything to stop that happening. And going to the frontline of a war NATO was bound to lose, no matter how long the enemy prevaricated before delivering the final blow, was about the stupidest thing he could do. His imagination roamed the possibilities: he and Lisa could escape with the child to somewhere remote like Scotland. Then he chided himself for such ludicrous fantasies, as though there'd be any escape. Perhaps it did not really matter. Europe and England were finished. But that did not mean Geoff had to accept the fact.

He wiped the sweat from his forearms on the coarse hospital sheet and spoke aloud: "One thing at a time. First get better. Then get out of here. Then get back to Lisa. Then make sure she gives birth okay. Then think about safety."

Chapter 49

Crispin Webb stared at his boss with renewed respect. As the days turned into weeks and still the Caliphate made no move beyond the territory it had gained up until 15 March, she seemed to regain more of her composure, her old grace. He followed her along the corridor to the COBRA meeting room, noting her improved posture, how she carried her head higher and kept her shoulders back, like she used to before the war.

She walked alongside General Sir Terry Tidbury, in conversation with him. As they were of equal height, she looked the soldier straight in the eye as they spoke, and a flame of pride flickered more brightly inside Webb. Part of his cynicism wondered if she were taking illegal substances, but he believed he would be the first to know if she were. His own intake of all drugs bar those that actually helped him medically had fallen to almost zero since his heart attack nearly two months earlier. In an ironic turn of events, he had begun regular, vigorous physical exercise and found the high from swimming sixty lengths in forty-five minutes was almost comparable to the artificial highs he used to get before his heart let him down.

The boss had benefitted as well, in many ways. He smiled when he recalled her description that they were sitting on a bomb that could go off any second, or maybe not for months, so therefore the concern had to be managed. She'd taken more time to be with her family and more obligations had been delegated.

Terry and Napier reached the entrance to Cabinet Briefing Room A and Napier's PA, Monica, opened the door for them. Crispin heard Terry insist that a young lady should not be obliged to hold doors open for men, and he saw Monica's pasty white face redden under the General's gaze. He knew the soldier was a family man—both of his sons had followed their father into the British Army—but he still wondered if he could detect an element of lust behind the General's chivalry, for Monica, while not having the natural elegance that real feminine beauty required, did have in abundance that certain quality of handsomeness which made some women highly attractive.

None of that mattered to Crispin, despite his habit of analysing what made heterosexual women attract heterosexual men in the event he could find some titbit that might help him obtain a better quality of homosexual man. He let out a sigh of melancholy for a time in the past when the stress of his job—which he now realised was no stress at all—led him to the seedier clubs in London for some hot and dirty escapism, escapism which in fact he now understood was merely a physical balm for a confusion inside him that the present conflict did little to assuage.

He followed the others into the meeting, already knowing that his group was the last to arrive. He scanned the faces of the attendees and sat at his designated seat next to the handsome, bald general whose politeness carried an erotic undertow of constrained violence.

The boss started: "Okay, everyone. Thank you for coming this morning. Most of today's agenda is not dissimilar to what we cover most mornings, so in the absence of a sudden and unforeseen eruption from Southern Europe, I don't anticipate we'll be here very long. Before we begin, however, I'd like to introduce you to the new Defence Secretary, Mr Liam Burton."

A lean man with narrow limbs rose from the seat next to Napier, nodded his head and gave the room a confident-sounding, "Hi," before sitting again,

"As you will have anticipated, I thought it wise not to delay appointing a replacement after Phillip resigned on Tuesday. While I was sorry he decided to go, I think he was aware of his shortcomings in handling his portfolio."

Crispin glanced around the room to see eyebrows rise at the boss's polite understatement of Gough's deficiencies; after all, he'd been a career politician, and England's immediate future did not offer the job of politician as a viable career choice anymore.

Napier went on: "However, I am delighted Liam has agreed to take the portfolio on. Some of you might know he spent twelve years in the army before embarking on a career in politics, and had held a number of Parliamentary Secretaryships before being appointed to the role of Chief Whip, from which position he has been promoted."

Crispin stared at Burton while Napier made the introduction and noted a plainness in his mannerisms; he did not preen with arrogance nor look awkward with self-consciousness.

Napier sat and Burton rose. He said: "Thanks very much, PM. I actually went into politics because I wanted to help ordinary squaddies get kit that actually works for a change," he paused and then looked in abrupt surprise at Sir Terry Tidbury and blustered: "Oh, no offence intended, General Sir Terry."

Terry laughed and replied: "None taken."

Crispin nodded in appreciation at Burton's smooth execution of the joke.

Burton assumed an affability and said: "Anyway, as this is my first COBRA I'll probably just observe and get the hang of things before I start sticking my oar in."

"Thank you, Liam," the boss said. "We'll begin as usual with the daily threat level. Terry?"

"No change, PM. The computers' predictions still have the same margins for error which they've had for a couple of weeks now. As we all know, every day there are incremental probability increases as we assume the enemy continues to build up his stockpiles of munitions to execute the next stage of the invasion as efficiently as possible. Yet again, today our computers estimate he has not yet reached a position where he is more likely than not to recommence his advance."

"Thank you," the boss said, as though she were talking to a food delivery service as they confirmed her order. She addressed the rest of the room: "One item I want to deal with quickly is opening England's borders to European refugees. I will put it to Cabinet at our regular meeting this afternoon, but I just want to ask all of you if you'd like to make any comments or suggestions. Anyone?"

Foreign Secretary Charles Blackwood cleared his throat and said: "Frankly speaking, PM, I'd imagine only the most racist of people would consider refusing our fellow Europeans help in this time of extreme crisis."

Opposite Blackwood, Home Secretary Aiden Hicks shrugged his ample shoulders and said: "If the roles were reversed, we'd hope—even expect—them to do the same for us. I have instructed local authorities to reactivate their emergency shelters, to take them out of mothballing and provide estimates of the numbers they can accommodate."

Next to him, the Head of MI5, David Perkins, sniffed like a rat that scented food and cautioned: "I would urge certain restrictions, PM. We won't know if the Persian Caliphate has placed advance agents among those refugees—"

Napier broke in: "Even if they had, what information or other advantage could such individuals gain and pass on to the enemy?"

Perkins stammered and gave a half-smile that appeared to Crispin to be a sneer. Perkins said: "With the greatest respect, Prime Minister, my business is to minimise and if possible neutralise threats to the security of England. If we throw open our borders, we could allow in all kinds of undesirable—"

"So what?" Napier interrupted.

"Excuse me?" Perkins said.

She answered with care: "Do please explain to the COBRA committee, Mr Perkins, precisely how a citizen of a European country can represent a threat greater than the threat we currently face? I do not for a moment believe that a single, or even a few, of the enemy's forces would trouble themselves to hide among refugees because any miniscule gain would not be worth the effort. If I understand the military situation properly, then our foe has us completely where it wants us."

Perkins considered this and then said: "As you wish, PM, but I would only like to note that every society has its, shall we say, undesirable elements? And with unrestricted access, we could be leaving ourselves open to unscrupulous members of those societies who will use the current chaos to sow a nihilistic discord in our own society."

Napier shook her head and said: "I don't regard that as a convincing argument. We have enough 'nihilistic discord' running rampant as it is." She glanced at the Police

Commissioner for England, a rustic brute of a man with thinning hair. She asked him: "Are the numbers of suicides still increasing at the same rates?"

"Yes, ma'am," the brute answered with deference. "But my colleagues and I are looking forward to the new laws restricting alcohol and other drugs," he added with shrewdness, Webb thought.

The boss reached for her water and answered: "The House will vote on that tomorrow; the legislation will face no hurdles." She sipped then turned back to Perkins and said: "Anyway, your objection is noted."

Perkins nodded.

"The next item is civil defence. Tom?"

The brutish Police Commissioner gave a short cough and spoke with greater precision than Crispin would have thought possible: "No significant changes to the plan, ma'am, and its implementation continues as scheduled. While I think we will come in for some criticism for a few of the suggestions, it is better than telling the population that there is no choice and they have no chance of survival."

"We don't know that for certain, Tom," the boss said.

"Sorry to sound fatalistic, ma'am."

"Never mind," she said, shaking her head. "We all know there are hard choices to make."

"And that's the real problem, ma'am. All of our construction replicators are needed on the flood defences. Many people are complaining that shelters could be built if it weren't for the constant need to keep the water out."

"But we have more than mere shelters, yes?" Napier asked.

"Of course," the Police Commissioner said, puffing his chest out. "Practical defences are set up all around London, although under military control."

"Thank you, Tom," Napier said. "Terry, can you update us on the military side?"

"Yes, PM," Terry said at once. "Despite the increasing enemy attacks on the Atlantic Convoys, he is not making a serious effort to stop them, which might be connected to his public position to be seen to be allowing us time to consider our surrender. We are all quite sure he has enough ACAs to destroy those ships if he really wanted to. However, this means that we can now put up a much better defence than we were able to offer in February or March. If I may, PM?"

Napier nodded her assent and Crispin had to smother a laugh as Terry took out a slate, opened it, and placed it on the table. For the hundredth time, he asked himself why those things hadn't been banned and wrinklies like the General obliged to have a lens.

The walls around the conference room lit up with a map of England with indicators in different colours and shapes. Terry said: "The computers are allocating Battlefield Support Lasers to match the most probable attack scenarios. Despite the current political stand-off, we can be certain that in any resumption of hostilities, an air attack on the Home Countries is a certainty, so BSLs and missiles are being brought over, produced and deployed with the utmost urgency."

On the other side of the table, Home Secretary Aiden Hicks cleared his throat. His chins wobbled and he asked: "Looking at those images, we don't seem to have half of what we need to protect everything. How are the priorities set? Are we protecting homes, hospitals, schools, architecture, historical monuments, what?"

Terry said: "The computers work on the assumption that the protection of human life has primacy, although priorities do need some flexibility. For example, if a hospital is close to a bridge over a river, it's debatable what better deserves defending: without the bridge, no one can get to the hospital, but if the defences only defend the bridge, the hospital will be destroyed. The computers are allocating the defences as prudently as possible, but there is some room for local authorities to make their own decisions."

"Thank you," Hicks said.

Terry continued: "However, that analogy also extends to the defence of the rest of Europe itself. Difficult questions need to be answered regarding how many Battlefield Support Lasers and missiles should be assigned to civil defence, and how many should be given to the military to actually battle the assault when it comes. If too much goes to civil defence, then the military—"

"Yes, thank you, Terry. We'll move on now," Napier said.

Webb caught the underlying tension from the boss. He looked at the General but did not see the slightest flicker of emotion on that round face. If the General had problems with getting things done his way, he hid it very well indeed.

Terry's head tilted and he murmured: "As you wish, PM."

Foreign Secretary Charles Blackwood said: "Er, PM, what's the situation with our neighbours? Are they also preparing?"

Napier said: "Yes, I spoke to both the presidents of Scotland and Wales last night and, given the geography of any attack on the British Isles by Caliphate forces, it is clear they will know well in advance. In any case, they have their own allocations of these weapons and are facing identical problems as we are."

Blackwood scoffed and said: "Hardly worth breaking up the Union thirty years ago."

Napier shrugged in dismissiveness: "Just another anniversary no one will mark on Monday." She looked around the table and asked: "Any questions before we wrap this up for today?"

Silence greeted her question. She said: "Very well. Thank you all for coming along. In the absence of any surprises, nasty or otherwise, we shall reconvene at the same time tomorrow."

Chairs scraped on the floor as the attendees rose. People filed out of the meeting room. Napier shook her head and whispered to Crispin: "Every day nothing happens and we don't surrender, it's another day closer to the war picking up again. It can't go on forever."

Crispin caught a glimpse in her eye that raised his concern. She hissed: "You realise we're wasting our time over nothing while waiting for the inevitable."

Crispin had no answer, so he just nodded in agreement. A voice somewhere in the back of his mind asked him, not for the first time, why he stayed in London doing a job that would almost certainly see him killed when the invasion reached the British Isles.

Chapter 50

Maria Phillips emerged from East Grinstead station, and with her free hand shielded her eyes from the glaring spring sunshine. She looked among the other people thronging the platform for her older brother.

"Maz, over here!" she heard a voice shout.

"Martin," she called, pushing her way through the crowd to him. She reached him and they embraced. Maria felt the passing of time: a little over two months and not only had she changed, she knew her older brother had also grown.

His round eyes shone with affection as he asked: "We have transport in seven minutes, or shall we walk home?"

She said: "Let's walk, I could do with the exercise."

"Just what I thought you'd say. Need a hand?" he asked indicating her canvas holdall.

"No, thanks," she replied with a sardonic frown.

"Sorry we weren't at your passing-out; that was bad form for Brass to stop families from attending."

Maria shook her head and answered: "The invasion has changed a lot of things. Passing out now only means we're barely ready to face the threat; it doesn't carry the significance it used to before the war."

"The short hair suits you, Maz. Makes you look like you won't take any shit," Martin said with a chuckle.

"I could say the same thing about you, dear brother. I don't think I'm the only one who has a different outlook now."

The crowd thinned as they navigated through the backstreets towards their familial home. Maria enjoyed the warm breeze that rustled the shrubs in the front gardens and lifted the new leaves on the trees lining the pavements. Suddenly free after her basic training, she felt as though the British Army had given her an entirely new perspective on the future, however long or short it might be.

She glanced at her brother and said: "I have a question for you."

"Oh yeah?"

"What exactly does a 'Forward Observer' observe these days? I heard your job was to go and wave at the raghead's ACAs so they would blow you up first. Is that right?"

"Ah, now, you see, Maz? You're just giving away your intense jealousy that I made it into the best regiment in the Army while you flunked everything you tried till they dumped you in the Medical Corps. I mean, seriously? Your idea of a military career is picking up the bits and pieces of the unlucky squaddies? How much fun do you think that's going to be, Maz?"

Maria laughed and answered: "About as much fun as you're going to have counting the thousands of ACAs coming at you just before they blow you up."

The banter continued as the siblings wended their way through residential streets and past parks and open spaces Maria had known since childhood, some areas now sporting mounds of fresh earth that hid air attack shelters.

When the jokes subsided, she confided in him just how stressful the previous weeks had been. She said: "The fact that the Army has doubled the length of its Phase One training for new recruits gives you an idea of the blasted uncertainty the generals must have concerning what we'll have to face. And you know what? In Harrogate we even drilled what we'd have to do if our Squitches packed up altogether, something we all thought was as close to impossible as it was possible to get."

She listened as Martin told her of his own shock at the Phase One training he completed in Warwick, which included battle tactics reintroduced years or even decades after the development—and then the supremacy—of the ACA on the battlefield was thought to have rendered them permanently redundant.

"Seriously, me and my squad had to practise doing covering fire for advance and retreat," he said.

"We did, too," Maria said.

"But what's the point? Either you're in the advance, in which case your ACAs are burning and blasting the shit out of the enemy, or you're in retreat, in which case you're fried, or running for your life about to get fried."

Maria said: "I remember years ago, when I was at school and our history teacher used to say that the old style of war was over, that from now on wars would be fought only by those machines. Soldiers wouldn't have anything to do."

Martin let out a mirthless chuckle and said: "I think they think they're going to throw nobodies like us straight at the raghead's ACAs if they have to, not that it would change the result."

"If it won't make a difference, then they won't do it, dear brother. Dad was not right when he claimed we would just be used as cannon fodder," Maria said with assuredness. "But yes, all of my squad also debated why they were training us like that."

They turned into their street and Maria looked for Billy, the faded wooden rabbit that sat on the chimneystack. He came into view from behind another roof as they walked. They reached the front gate and Maria thought it seemed to have shrunk a little since the last time she'd walked through it.

"After you, Maz, and I'll take your bag now," Martin said. "I got back yesterday, so it's you they're waiting for."

Maria let her brother take her bag. Their parents appeared at the door and Maria hugged them. Twenty minutes later, Maria answered her parents' questions over steaming mugs of tea.

"So is a medical orderly the same as a doctor?" her father Anthony asked.

"No, Dad," Maria replied, "but I will be helping people who get hurt."

"Must be that kind heart you inherited from me," her mother said with a smile.

"Do you think you'll get posted to Europe?" her father asked with concern.

"It depends on what regiment my unit is assigned to, but I don't think so."

Martin said: "The rumours in my crew are that Brass wants to keep as many British soldiers back as possible for home defence—"

"You know," Maria broke in, "to a large extent it's not our choice."

"Yeah," Anthony grumbled, "all our futures are being decided in Tehran."

Martin sipped his tea and said: "The super artificial intelligence says that every day the enemy does nothing, it becomes gradually more likely that he will resume his attack."

"Yes, dear," Jane said, "but all of our computers never saw this war coming to begin with, did they? So why should we believe them now?"

"Because that's the best we've got," Martin said.

"I was talking to Mrs Withers at number thirty-five and she says we should surrender—"

"She's over a hundred, she must be losing her marbles," Martin said.

"She remembered what her mother told her about the Second World War, and how it should never be repeated—"

"Too late, Mum, it already has," Maria said, sounding a little more direct than she'd intended.

Martin said: "And no one can be in any doubt what that would really entail. It's enough to see how they're behaving in the areas under their control. The little info that's leaked out has been terrifying. Surrender is not an option and never has been. And for a change even those callous, idiot politicians have been able to see that."

"Where's Mark?" Maria asked suddenly.

"Immersed, like he usually is," her father replied in indifference. "He appears maybe once, twice a week, just to… you know."

"Yes, we know," Maria said, her mood darkening. She took a gulp of tea, put the mug on the table, stood up, and said: "So I will go and let him know that his younger sister is back home." She strode for the door.

"Leave him, Maz," Martin called after her.

Maria left the living room and strode along the short corridor to the old utility room that Mark used as his gaming base. For the first time, she felt different emotions, or perhaps they were same emotions but were now easier to control. Her frustration no longer led to impotence; instead, it allowed her to focus with greater clarity.

She entered the room without knocking. Her brother, Mark, lay in a couch that curved like a hammock. A black suit with large pockets and other features covered his entire body, and an oval helmet surrounded his head. Maria's nose

341

wrinkled at the smell of urine in the room. She watched her brother in fascination as his limbs jerked sporadically up and down, and then left and right. With little concern, she walked to the nearest wall, bent down, and yanked the power transmitter from the socket. She held it up to the light and deactivated the reserve supply provider, thus depriving her brother of all power.

Mark reacted at once. His whole body shuddered. He ripped off the oval helmet and stood, shouting: "Who the fuck just did th—"

"Hello, dear brother," Maria said, feeling only a slight satisfaction among the disappointment that she'd had to take drastic action to get her brother's attention.

She saw the fury on Mark's face as he spluttered: "You idiot, you stupid, stupid little girl. You absolute fucking idiot. You have no idea where I was and what I was doing."

Maria said nothing as Mark expelled his rage at her, placing the power transmitter on the table among half-empty cups and food containers.

He went on: "If you were anyone other than my little sister, I'd cave your skull in—"

Maria laughed, even though a voice in her head cautioned her to be more careful. However, she could see that Mark's ridiculous outfit prevented him from moving quickly or exerting any significant strength, and the hours of self-defence and unarmed combat training leant an assuredness that even in his fury, her older brother would be containable from a military viewpoint.

She said: "Oh, sorry, dear brother. I am home from my Phase One training and might be posted away at any moment. I wanted to see you before I go."

Her brother peered at her and said: "Do you mock me, little sister?"

Maria replied at once: "I do not mock you or anyone else because it is not in my character, but the situation out here in the real world needs all of us to pay attention, not hide away in pretend—"

"Don't!" Mark shrieked. "Don't ever lecture me about the real world, or about 'hiding'. You have no idea what I and the people I associate with in there are planni—"

"Plan away, little boy," Maria said, pleased that her voice remained flat and emotionless. "Just let me tell you that the storm of violence—real, unstoppable violence—draws closer every single day. Out here, we have a word for people like you."

"Oh yeah?" Mark sneered.

"We call you 'heroes', because you are all so heroic, hiding away—"

"Piss off, little sister. You are a fool; a fool for thinking your pointless real-world efforts will make any kind of difference, a fool for giving in to your desire to 'do your bit' by agreeing to be NATO's cannon fodder—"

"There is a name for it, dear brother. The reality that will overtake you, me, and all of us. Its name is 'the battle for Europe', and it will be here soon. See you at the party?"

"Piss off," Mark snarled, awkwardly moving to get the power transmitter and plug it back into the socket.

Chapter 51

Corporal Rory Moore stepped out of the autonomous transport vehicle, turned to Pip and said: "It's been twenty-four hours since we got off that submarine, and I still don't feel sure when I put my foot down that what it lands on won't move."

Pip walked around from the other side of the vehicle and said: "I thought the *Spiteful* was a lovely boat, not as cramped as you made out."

"It was horrible, Pip. No privacy at all."

The ATV moved off and left them standing in the parade square of their home barracks at Catterick Garrison in Yorkshire. Rory looked in front of them as, in the bright blue sky, small puffs of cloud floated over the large, rectangular Victorian redbrick building and sunlight glinted off its slate-grey roof. His spirit lifted; this was where he had become a Royal Engineer.

He heard Pip say: "So, here we are again. I never expected us to come back via submarine, Corp."

Rory answered: "After what happened in Spain when the invasion began, I never expected to see this place again at all." Images of recent events surged up from his memory, and he saw once more the Caliphate Spider racing towards him as fast as it could over the Spanish scrub. He felt the light recoil from his Pickup as he held his nerve, wondering whether he would be able to destroy the Spider before it killed him. He shivered.

"You all right, Corp.?" Pip asked.

"What? Yeah, of course," Rory said. "Just strange to be back. Just the two of us, you know?"

"Oh yeah, I know," Pip said.

"Come on," Rory said, "better not keep the Colonel waiting."

They strode across the parade ground and entered the building. Although he knew the layout well, the lens in Rory's eye navigated the route to the Colonel's office for him, up the broad, elegant staircase and four doors along the left wing.

They reached the office. Rory glanced at Pip and said: "Ready?"

She nodded.

Rory rapped his knuckles on the panelled door.

"Come," said a voice at once from the other side.

Rory and Pip entered the expansive office. Colonel Doyle was already striding towards them, steely eyes shining out from a friendly face. He looked smaller than he had at the airbase in February, when he had addressed the whole regiment before their deployment.

Rory closed the door and he and Pip stood to attention and saluted. The Colonel stopped, returned their salute, and said: "At ease." He first shook Pip's hand and then Rory's. "Now we've got the formalities out of the way, come over here and sit down."

Rory and Pip followed their commanding officer over to his desk. Rory felt like declining the offer to sit in one of the chairs opposite the Colonel as it did not seem appropriate, but then considered after all that had happened in the last four months, he didn't want to come across as churlish. He sat and saw, by the look on her face, that Pip had entertained similar thoughts.

The Colonel sat on the other side, stroked his full moustache with a thumb and forefinger, and said: "First things first: welcome home. How are you feeling after a couple of months on a submarine?"

Rory said: "The captain and crew of the *Spiteful* looked after us well, but Colonel, Sir, I think Private Clarke and I would really like to know about the rest of the regiment."

"Of course you would," the Colonel said, and clamped his hands together on his desk.

The door opened and a young orderly came in carrying a tray. He sat the tray on the table and served the Colonel, Corporal and Private either tea or coffee. Rory felt the tension increase as time passed while the orderly did this and then left the room.

When the door closed, the Colonel said: "You two are the only ones to have made it out of Spain from the regiment deployed in February. Now, I want to stress that we expect other troops have survived in theatre, but obviously we can't get to them now."

"My god," Rory breathed. He'd expected that might have been the case, but confirmation from the Colonel still shocked him. He glanced at Pip and saw the news have a similar effect on her.

The Colonel sipped his tea and paused before continuing: "You should also bear in mind that the pair of you have become somewhat special."

Neither Rory nor Pip spoke.

"You are two of a privileged handful of NATO troops who have engaged the enemy in battle and lived to tell the tale. Now, I've read the reports from your debriefs on board *Spiteful*, and my instant reaction was to ensure you both play a role in training in the future. We have thousands of new recruits—"

"Thousands?" Rory interrupted, too shocked to stop himself.

The Colonel said: "Yes, thousands. Since the invasion began, every week from five to ten thousand people have applied to join the British Army. Thankfully, Squonk has been more than up to the task of organising everything. And, by the way, your regiment is already back up to full strength. Anyway, I discussed your case with General Sir Terry Tidbury himself, and we reached an optional conclusion."

The Colonel stopped, stared from Rory to Pip and back, and said: "Really, do please close your mouths; you look like my pet fish when I drop pellets of food into their pond."

"Sorry, Sir," Rory mumbled through his shock.

"Hmm," the Colonel said, stroking his moustache with his thumb and forefinger again. "The General and I concluded that your futures will be subject to events. For as long as the current impasse lasts, you will be assigned to training. If, however, the enemy recommences his attack—which we believe to be a probability rather than a possibility—you will both return to combat duties. But before then, we have some other business to attend to." The Colonel stood and cleared his throat.

In response, Rory and Pip stood at once and came to attention. Rory heard the door behind him open and at least three pairs of feet shuffled into the office. He daren't risk snatching a glance behind him and kept his eyes firmly on the windows behind his CO.

The Colonel announced: "Corporal Rory Moore, you are hereby promoted to the rank of sergeant. As a non-commissioned officer, you will be expected to obey the orders of your superior officers, while at the same time, you can expect to be obeyed by those holding ranks lower than your own." The Colonel waved a hand and the same man who had served the tea now approached and handed the Colonel a leather folder. The Colonel opened it, took out a single sheet of A4 paper, and handed it smartly to Rory. "To accept your promotion, please acknowledge and confirm the notification in your lens."

Through his shock, Rory stared at the sheet of paper he held in his hand, used purely for ceremonial purposes. The notification in his lens flashed patiently. With a twitch of an eye muscle, he accepted the promotion.

"Thank you," the Colonel said.

Rory saluted the Colonel, who returned the salute.

Then the Colonel turned to Pip. "Private Philippa Clarke, you are hereby promoted to the rank of corporal. As a non-commissioned officer, you will be expected to obey the orders of your superior officers, while at the same time, you can expect to be obeyed by those holding ranks lower than your own." Another leather folder appeared in his hands and he repeated the same order to Pip.

But Pip did not take the offered sheet of paper. Rory sensed Pip take in a breath—what she was waiting for?

Pip said: "With gratitude for this promotion and the greatest respect, Colonel, I would like to apply for a commission."

The Colonel's eyebrows rose. "Really?"

"Yes, Sir," Pip confirmed.

Rory's spirit sank in despair. If Pip accepted her promotion to corporal and they were both assigned training duties, they would be together, either here in Catterick or down

349

the motorway in Harrogate. But if she got a commission, she would be off somewhere far away, at least Warwick, and he might never see her again.

Pip spoke, "Yes, Sir. It's the direction I really want my career in the army to go."

The Colonel withdrew the sheet of paper and said: "Very well. Given your performance in the field to date, I am inclined to approve your request. How does your CO feel about it?" the Colonel asked, looking at Rory.

Emotions clashed inside Rory. He thought of asking for his own commission, but even then, there would be no guarantee he and Pip would be assigned to the same officer training base. He could refuse her request, but what reason could he give? And in any case, who was he to clip her or anyone else's wings? Rory looked at the Colonel and said: "I approve Private Clarke's request, Sir."

"Excellent," the Colonel said, "that's settled then. Squonk? Organise officer training for Private Clarke and Advanced Sergeant Training for Sergeant Moore, giving appropriate notifications to the concerned parties. Also, factor in twenty-four hours' unplanned leave to commence now."

"Acknowledged," Squonk's disembodied voice replied.

The Colonel smiled at his subordinates and said: "I can imagine you'd both like to get home and see your families after what you've come through. We will organise transport for you both."

"Thank you, Sir," Rory said.

Pip echoed Rory's thanks.

The Colonel came around to the other side of the desk and guided the two junior ranks to the door. He lowered his voice and said: "You've both brought a great deal of credit on the regiment, and I'd like to extend my personal thanks. Well done, the pair of you."

Rory wondered if he might turn this imaginary debt to his advantage. They reached the door and Rory opened it. He said to the Colonel: "Thank you, Sir. Request permission to speak freely."

"Granted," Doyle replied with an expression of curiosity on his face.

"For most of the time I spent on board *Spiteful,* I never really expected there to be an England to return to. I see why the enemy stopped in March to consolidate his rapid gains, but the tactics he's now using do not seem to make any sense to me. What are your feelings, Sir? Is consolidation the only reason for this length of delay in finishing the job off, or is there something else?"

The Colonel appeared to consider Rory's question. He said: "Well, Sergeant Moore, there may be an element of politics involved, it is difficult to say. Off the record, one thing I think we can all be certain of is that we cannot reinforce with anything like the munitions we have to stop his continued advance. No matter how many BSLs, PeaceMakers and tanks we can muster, we can be sure the enemy will have mustered the means to obliterate them, probably quite quickly. I think we can be clear on this: if and when the battle for Europe starts, it will be very brutal and over very quickly. And NATO will not be the victors."

"Thank you, Sir."

Chapter 52

Geoff Morrow put his hand to his ear to keep the surrounding noise down as Lisa complained: "I worry and the bots know it. I'm producing too many stress hormones and the bots are struggling to manage them all."

"Lisa, I'll be home in a few days, okay?" Confusion reigned inside Geoff. If he had to pick one word to describe Lisa, it would be 'feisty'; but now, as the Tense Spring wore on, her approaching motherhood seemed to have blunted her sharp edges.

"How long exactly? The baby is almost ready. The date for the birth is fixed for 2 June. I want you here with me. Will you be here?"

"I should be," Geoff said, trying to sound positive.

"But you're only in central France. What's the delay?"

"Try to stay calm, Lisa," Geoff said at the increasing tone of complaint in Lisa's voice. "It's not like it used to be."

"God, from there, you could walk back to England between now and 2 June."

"You don't know, Lisa. It's really bad over here."

"I've seen it, but I thought your press clearance counted for someth—"

"No, it doesn't count for much when people are dying. It doesn't entitle me to jump queues of starving and injured refugees. They've got bodies lying out on the streets here because the super AI is prioritising the needs of the living. It only sends an autonomous meat truck when it can assign one, and sometimes the bodies are really festering by then."

There came a pause and Geoff hoped his words had made an impact. He went on: "I don't want to stress you any further, but I can't lie either. Before Alan gave me this assignment, I'd only seen a handful of dead bodies. I've seen hundreds in just the last few days. I hope that mad bastard in Tehran watches the European media, although I expect he'll keep using it to say Europe is bringing this on itself."

Heart-breaking scenes he'd witnessed in recent weeks suddenly came back to him in the sharpest clarity: a bar drenched in the blood of the victims of a local feud; the young female suicide draped over the smashed roof of an autonomous vehicle; the crowd of fifty or more apparently uninjured bodies that spilled out of emergency doors that had remained locked during a panicked stampede at a monorail station; the unexplained hundreds of bodies that collected together at a bend in the River Saêne just outside Chalon-sur-Saêne.

Geoff's spirit raged not only against the injustice, but also against the concept that history was being made and the details instantly forgotten. The hack reporter inside him reacted in fury to the knowledge that the people of Europe were enduring the most brutal punishment, many incidences of which—as he had witnessed—were going unrecorded. On the other hand, did it really matter? He asked himself silently how many other empires in history had been consumed in a whirlwind of violence, yet almost nothing had been handed down of the lives destroyed, of the appalling injustices never righted.

"Geoff, just get back here as soon as you can, please," Lisa pleaded.

"Of course. That's what I'm trying to do."

"Please, Geoff. You understand, don't you?"

Geoff felt his eyes well with frustration, futility, and longing. He whispered: "Yes, I understand. And I promise you that when we are together—all three of us—I will do everything I can do to protect you and our child."

Chapter 53

Major Kate Fus relaxed back into the soft couch and watched the General—*her* General—pour two glasses of wine. His quarters were small but well furnished. The candlelight cast long shadows from the pictures on the wall opposite her, shadows that flickered and juddered when the slightest movement of air disturbed one of the small flames.

She ran her index finger along the lip over her cleft palate and then smiled when he returned, handed her a glass, and sat next to her. "Tell me your schedule?" she asked.

He sat next to her and said: "From tomorrow, I will go to the troops on each front and inspect their readiness. I have agreed with Gunther and Lars that each of us will continue on rotation to keep the armies sharp. The problem is with the interminable delay."

"What about the English General and SACEUR?"

"Tidbury and Jones?" Pakla shook his head and said: "Both of them have too much else to deal with. Jones will

357

need a new HQ and the British Isles will be quickly overrun with refugees if the attack resumes."

"But yes, I have noticed similar feelings among my own troops. I have to explain to some of the keener ones why we cannot attempt to drive the enemy back."

"I find many of them are quite stoic about the deficiencies in our weapons compared to the enemy's," he said with an ironic chuckle.

"What will you say?"

"For our troops, the Poles, it will be easy. I will of course invoke past glories: Vienna in 1683, the Miracle on the Vistula in 1920, the Battle of Britain, the Uprising in 1944. Europe is in the greatest peril today and it has fallen to Poland—yet again—to save it. For the other NATO Forces, I need to be more circumspect. You know, my sweet Katy, the Germans, French and British have never had their countries wiped from the map like Poland, and I think the prospect scares them far more that it would frighten any Pole."

"I know you will say the right thing, my General."

"Perhaps, but it is also a question of repetition. The troops see us, and hopefully we can inspire them a little, but the stress of waiting is an evil in itself. The enemy's delay has a great deal to be said for it as a tactic. All of us remain trapped in a kind of limbo. From one week to the next, nothing changes. We build up our munitions, the enemy builds up his—"

"Do you think there might be a way to any kind of peaceful resolution?"

Candlelight reflected in Pakla's thoughtful eyes. He sipped his wine and said: "Never. Everyone knows it is the enemy's ruse to keep as much of global public opinion on his side as possible."

"So he will resume his attack, sooner or later?"

The General nodded his head and answered: "Doubtlessly. It is only a question of when; perhaps the next moment, next week, next month. Only he knows."

"Then you and I need to keep treating every opportunity we can steal as though it might be our last time together." She saw his gaze change and sensed his care for her come to the fore.

He said: "You know, it is still not too late for me to transf—"

"Do not say it," she said, putting her hand on his arm to stop him. "We agreed, remember?"

"But when the attack comes, you will be in the greatest danger. Look what happened in Zagreb. I had no choice but to approve your selection to try to evacuate those VIPs; all I could do was insist you had support. In this coming battle for Europe, my sweet Katy, the odds are the worst for us Poles and all Europeans than they have ever been, worse even than Vienna in 1683."

"I told you I would never use our relationship to protect myself if war ever came. But three months ago, a computer decided to allow my subordinates to be killed so that I would live, and I still have nightmares about that injustice. Besides, I suppose there remains a slim chance the attack might never come."

"You do not really think that, do you?"

She looked into his narrow eyes, so full of self-assuredness, and warmth spread downwards from her chest to make the rest of her body tingle. She sipped her wine, her thoughts moving ahead to how complete he would make her feel in a few moments. "Perhaps not, but what are we without hope, my General?"

He took her glass from her and placed both on the occasional table next to the couch. He turned, stroked her smooth hair, and kissed her deformed mouth with a lover's desire.

Chapter 54

20.52 Thursday 1 June 2062

"It is nicer now the evenings are getting longer again, don't you think, Terry?" Maureen Tidbury said as she put a steaming mug of tea on the bench in her husband's garden shed.

"Thank you," he said. He put down the mallet and fine-edged sculptor's chisel, and sighed. He picked up the tea and blew on the steam rising from it.

Maureen peered at the fat wooden Buddha, its base clamped in the vice on the bench, and said: "Do you think his head is a bit lopsided?"

Terry sipped his tea and replied: "It won't be when I've finished taking a bit more off his shoulders, here and here."

"I expect so."

"How were the 'knit and natter' ladies today?" he asked, referring to Maureen's group of friends who met for tea, cake and gossip every Thursday morning.

"Oh, they have their concerns."

"Do they expect that you know more than they do?"

Maureen chuckled and said: "Of course, but what can I offer them, Terry?" she said with a shrug of her slender shoulders. "And anyway, 'knit and natter' usually becomes 'stitch and bitch' after the first few minutes." She smiled.

"Yes," Terry said, still feeling uneasy. "I've been concerned recently that it could, perhaps, be a small burden on you."

Maureen giggled as though she were a schoolgirl again.

Terry said: "What?" as he put his tea down and brushed some wood-dust from his partially carved Buddha.

Maureen replied: "We've been married for over thirty years, Terry, and we've never been a 'burden' on each other yet."

"Well, these are... tricky days," he said with caution, knowing well that the woman he'd decided so many years ago to share his life with could still wrong-foot him with the occasional surprise.

She shook her head and said: "I—and I am sure the rest of the ladies—do not think they are 'tricky' days at all."

"That's good then," he answered, smiling.

Maureen's face softened in warmth. "Terry, we know what is happening. The worst thing about being your wife is that the ladies might feel some sympathy for me, and that would make me feel... uncomfortable."

"They would never make you feel like that, would they?"

"I don't think so; it would embarrass them too much to know that they had. But apart from that little thing, if you really think about it, it doesn't matter so much. *Tempora mutantur et nos mutamur in illis.*"

Terry said: "I'm going to be stubborn, you know. However much times change, I happen to think we should not always change with them, dear."

Maureen smiled at her husband. "The point is that we don't realise we change, as we change with the times."

Terry left the Buddha in the vice on the bench, picked up his tea, and said: "Let's go outside."

Maureen followed him into the warm spring breeze. The high cloud glowed with fiery streaks of red and orange as the sun approached the distant sea on the horizon.

"I think it's important we don't change, Maureen; not now, not when things look as they do."

She put a hand on his shoulder and said: "So come home and have a brandy and cigar in the viewing room upstairs, before it gets completely dark. You know it won't be long before they will want you for one thing or another."

They walked back to the house together, and Terry decided not to say anything more. He knew the final darkness could arrive tonight, tomorrow, or not for weeks or months. In the meantime, he resolved not to change with the times any more than he had to. His slate vibrated in his pocket.

"Unfortunately, they already do want me."

Maureen frowned.

He took his slate out and opened it. He said: "SACEUR would like to have a chat."

"Then your brandy will be waiting for you afterwards."

"Thank you, Maureen."

Five minutes later, Terry sat in his home office looking at the latest deployments. He felt relieved to see a further twenty Abrahams N4–1A autonomous main battle tanks had arrived to reinforce the line at Tarbes in France, bringing the total there to fifty. Battlefield Support Lasers and many batteries of missiles had also arrived at the mostly German positions to the north of Milan. In the east around the Hungarian town of Pécs, the build-up of troops and munitions impressed Terry the most, as the mainly Polish formations there were expected to bear the strongest attack.

A thumbnail image of General Joseph E. Jones appeared in the corner of the screen. Terry raised it and said: "Good evening, General. How are things there?"

"Not good," Jones said without preamble. "Some high-level SkyWatchers are picking up increased activity from behind enemy lines."

"Anything concrete?"

Jones shook his head and frowned: "Nope, and that's the nervy part. The enemy's blanket jamming is leaking more than usual, but not that much more."

"Are we getting anything comprehensible?"

"Negative, just tiny fragments," Jones said. Then he added with heavy sarcasm: "I know how much you trust our super artificial intelligence, and that's saying the risk of assault has gone up by fifteen percent in the last two hours."

"That doesn't mean a thing, General. All of our forces are stood to on maximum readiness around the clock anyway."

"Yup, but I think it would be good to know when he's decided he's stockpiled enough kit to wipe us out."

"It's been three months," Terry pointed out, "and he might wait another three if he thinks it will help him keep global public opinion on his side. In any case, our progress has not been too shabby of late. If he attacks, I think we can really hold him up. At least for a while."

"Let's hope it can make some kind of difference." SACEUR paused, and then finished with: "I just wanted you to know about the increased probability, General Tidbury."

The image of Jones vanished, replaced by the map of deployments. Terry stared at it for a moment, looking at the vast, estimated armaments the Caliphate was assumed to have amassed since March, and the defences NATO could deploy in response.

A sixth sense began inside Terry. He reasoned: there had to be a tipping point, there had to come one single moment when the benefit of attack finally outweighed the benefit of delay. Throughout history, any army that had been massed invariably went on to launch its attack; seldom were men and weapons deployed in threat only to be withdrawn. At a certain point in the massing of arms, events gained their own momentum, and the inevitable attack commenced. The sense of premonition inside him gained strength. Terry kept his breathing even, staring at the map of deployments. He nodded and asked himself aloud: "Maybe he's waited long enough?"

There came a gentle tap at the door. He stood and opened it. Maureen held his snifter of brandy and stared at him with an inquisitive look.

"Thank you, Maureen," he said, "but I have a feeling. It may be nothing."

His wife tilted her head, eyebrows raised.

Terry said: "The brandy will wait."

"Of course," she replied.

"Squonk?"

"Yes, Sir Terry?" came the disembodied reply from the super AI.

"I need to get to Whitehall as soon as possible."

"Understood. Your vehicle is ready. Journey time will be sixteen minutes. Please proceed to your vehicle at your earliest convenience."

Terry said to his wife: "I expect nothing will change, but I want to go there just in case."

Chapter 55

23.03 Thursday 1 June 2062

"What is it, Aiden?" Napier asked, squinting at the image of her Home Secretary in the screen on the far wall.

"Only the same old thing I'm afraid, PM, but I thought I'd let you know anyway. The Leader of the Opposition was in the Members' Bar this evening bleating on about how you had 'rejected' him again and how, in the past, we used to have cross-party governments in times of crises."

Napier smiled and shook her head: "And was he very drunk?"

"Oh, yes, but I thought you should know just in case the media tomorrow gives his self-serving wittering more coverage than it deserves."

"Thanks, Aiden."

The screen went blank and Napier relaxed back into the comfortable chair in her private offices inside Ten Downing Street. She closed her eyes and controlled her breathing, counting the seconds between inhalation, pause, exhalation, and pause.

In the darkness of her closed eyes, her lens flashed up another communication, this time from a more trusted ally. "On the screen," she instructed.

"Hello, my dear Dahra," said Peter Mitsch, the Chancellor of Germany. "Am I contacting you too late this evening?"

Napier smiled on seeing Peter's kind face. The heavy bags under his eyes seemed to have deepened again since the last time she'd spoken to him. "Not at all, it's always a pleasure to talk with you," she answered. "How are you coping over there?"

His large head tilted in consideration and his wispy white hair curled away from the wrinkles on his face. He said: "I leave a great deal to my cabinet and the soldiers, Dahra. I do not wish to complain, but my dear wife is having some problems with the... situation."

"I'm sorry," Napier replied.

"I am contacting you to thank you for the open borders policy."

"You're welcome. If the roles were reversed... Well, Germany and England have been allies for well over a century."

"Yes. How are your preparations?"

"As far as I know, everything is in hand as much as it can be. I had another difficult conversation with President Coll earlier today."

Mitsch didn't say anything but his eyebrows rose in inquiry.

Napier felt suddenly glad she was able to share her concern with a fellow leader. "Madelyn tried to imply that it still wasn't too late to surrender. She thought it might be the path of least death and disaster."

"Ha! I expected as much," Mitsch said with a Teutonic slap of his hand on his desk. He wagged a finger at Napier and urged: "You should not listen to her. She has that idiot—what is his name, Bradly?—whispering in her ear that the American companies will lose business to the Chinese if the US supports the European countries. If he could, he would convince her to stop the Atlantic convoys."

Napier nodded and said: "My chief military general specifically told me not to mention the convoys in conversation with her."

"But she must know about them. That Bradly fool must have told her, yes?"

"I think she knows they happen, but NATO has strong supporters in the United States military and body politic. These people are as loyal to the founding principles of NATO as they are to their own flag."

"Good," Mitsch said in resolve. "We will need such people yet."

There came a pause between them before Napier said: "My concern increases with each passing day, Peter. Our super AI keeps telling us that the invasion could resume at any minute, or perhaps not for days or weeks or months. The stress is relentless. After so long, it can be difficult to think clearly sometimes."

She saw sympathy on the German Chancellor's face. He said: "I know. Our computers say the same thing. But every day our defences get stronger, better. Me, I think he already leaves it too long. Over two months. Far too long."

Napier smiled at Mitsch's imperfect English that added so much to his character. "It's funny," she mused, "but the lack of any change seems to me to be the strangest thing of all. He has called on us to surrender, what, ten times in the last ten weeks? And all through that time, all of our diplomatic efforts have fallen on deaf ears. The Chinese have dodged their responsibility, and I've lost count of the number of other leaders who have told us that we brought this on ourselves."

369

"It is all about business, Dahra. Those other countries, in Asia, Africa, South America, they are owing too much of their prosperity to China. And perhaps the intelligence reports we had recently are true? Perhaps the Chinese president really did tell the Third Caliph to stop, but now he is too powerful, yes?"

"Perhaps."

"And also, perhaps the others are more worried? I think they are fear for their own countries—"

"Then why don't they help us defeat him now?" Napier asked in frustration.

Mitsch tutted and shook his head. He said: "I think two main reasons, Dahra. One, they not want to upset China. And two, they think once Europe is finished, he will either stop and be satisfied, or he will attack India, and everyone is thinking India can stop him. This, I think, is their concern since he stopped his attack in the middle of March."

"But that doesn't help us at all, Peter."

"Of course," he agreed. "But he makes a very big mistake waiting so long. We get stronger every day. Who knows, perhaps it might be enough when he finally does try to destroy the rest of us?"

"Perhaps," Napier replied without conviction.

Chapter 56

Terry blew the steam from his fourth cup of tea and thanked the orderly who had provided it. He felt relieved he had been incorrect, that his premonition had not come to pass. He glanced at the four operators manning the consoles around the main War Room, as they observed the constantly updated information supplied by computers that never needed to sleep.

He half-smiled to himself when he recalled the looks of nervous shock on the faces of the operators when he'd arrived unexpectedly. He had done his best to calm them with words of reassurance. Terry understood that each member of the War Rooms' personnel had concerns for the future, for their families and loved ones, and for themselves. Then he reviewed current deployments again and put himself in the enemy's sandals. At that point, he concluded that the time was not yet right.

"Squonk?"

"Yes, Sir Terry?"

"Get my vehicle ready. I think I will return home for a few hours."

"Yes, Sir. I will instruct your vehicle to—"

Terry looked at the screens, knowing there could only be one reason Squonk had stopped in mid-sentence. Red icons appeared and flashed across the maps of Europe as thousands of lines of red light, each indicating a hostile ACA, emerged like a swarm of locusts from enemy-controlled territory in northern Spain, Italy, and the Balkans, and converged on the NATO defensive formations. A shrill klaxon sounded in the War Room, rebounding off the surfaces in half-second surges. The breath stopped in Terry's throat. He frowned as he looked at the current threat probability level. It had increased to one hundred percent.

The suddenness of the assault made him pause while his heart pounded in his chest. All of the flimsiest hopes he'd harboured over the preceding weeks withered like shards of ice in glaring sunshine as the number of enemy ACAs approaching NATO positions increased to the tens of thousands. His premonition had been correct, after all.

An unknown voice abruptly became audible over the klaxon. Terry saw on the screen that it belonged to a comms officer at Air Command HQ at RAF High Wycombe. "Urgent contact to all locations: multiple incoming hostile ACAs are about to swamp our defences. The battle for Europe has begun. I repeat: the battle for Europe has begun."

In the awful backwash of shock after the announcement, General Sir Terry Tidbury sipped his mug of tea and uttered: "So, now the end finally begins."

THE END

Coming from Chris James in 2020

The Repulse Chronicles
Book Three

The Battle for Europe

For the latest news and releases, follow Chris James on
Amazon

In the US, at:
https://www.amazon.com/Chris-James/e/B005ATW34C/

In the UK, at:
https://www.amazon.co.uk/Chris-James/e/B005ATW34C/

You can also follow his blog, at:
https://chrisjamesauthor.wordpress.com/

.

Printed in Great Britain
by Amazon

55462595R00229

The Last Call

DEEP REFLECTIONS ON DEATH

Aishah Adams